FOX

The Elmnas Chronicles

Kaylena Radcliff

Science Fiction and Fantasy Publications

FOX
KAYLENA RADCLIFF

Science Fiction and Fantasy Publications

HTTPS://SCIFIFANTASYPUBLICATIONS.CA
A division of DAOwen Publications

Fox/ Kaylena Radcliff

Edited by Douglas Owen

ISBN 978-1-928094-42-5
EISBN 978-1-928094-41-8

Jacket Art created by MMT Productions

10 9 8 7 6 5 4 3 2 1

For my Family

Prologue

Blade had no time. The woman pounced upon him, savagely jabbing her swords at his chest.

They walked right into her trap. This woman, this ruthless bounty hunter, waited for them. With patience, so much patience, she had hidden in the clefts of the pass. How she must have slunk along its walls for hours, in the way only true hunters could, preparing for the moment they arrived. And far too late did Blade, the last Guardian of Elmnas, realize it. As the sheer faces of rock shuddered and buckled, as they crashed down and the avalanche of rubble careened toward them, he knew. And he should have known better.

Blade took a sharp breath. Excruciating pain emanated from his cracked rib. Had it not been for the strength his Cardanthium swords gave him, he would not stand now. Had he been any other man, his companions would even now fall into the bounty hunter's merciless grasp. But Blade was not any other man. He had been someone once, someone he himself was remembering. And this imposter would not best him. Never would he spare this blasphemy of blasphemies, this abomination who presumed to carry the ancient blades of his people. With renewed ferocity, his twin swords smashed against hers, the flashes like green flames against the dark sky.

The Guardian's terror-stricken companions looked on as the battle raged. Young Toma of Maiendellclung to his energy pistol, frozen with desperate hopelessness. Mouse stood beside him, clenching her jaw. Anger colored her face. No longer the starved, frightened child Blade found at Pilgrim's Pass, she reached for Theana's dagger. Blade's gift, this blade, had sensed her and sought her in the way only Guardian-forged Cardanthium could. The dagger glowed a bright shade of blue-green as Mouse charged. Toma's fearful trance snapped, and he pulled her back.

Blade pushed hard against the bounty hunter, chancing a quick glance at the two as she twirled around him. They were shouting at each other now, unaware that Dane, their wounded and unconscious guide, slipped slowly off his stamping horse.

"Get to the river, now!" Blade commanded between violent clashes. "Wake Dane! Go!"

He heard them scramble in the debris, the horse's terrified whinnies echoing in the narrow corridor. The bounty hunter advanced again in fiendish fury. Hooves stamped. Shouts echoed in the corridor. Blade glimpsed the two teenagers, clutching Dane, as they sped past on horseback.

Relief flooded him. *If I can only slay her here, they might yet make it.* The thought gave him strength, and Blade swung his swords with furious force. They came down hard upon the bounty hunter's own swords, crushing the wicked blow she had planned for him. Still, she persisted. Their blades and gazes locked. A wild and delighted fire filled her eyes. Unnatural, unexplainable power flowed through her as she shoved back. She grinned. Blade knew the look, had felt it himself from the close battles of a lifetime long past: the face of a warrior, besting his opponent. He pushed down harder. For a moment, she faltered under the weight, but with another wicked smile, she slipped out of the fatal lock. In one nimble hop, she avoided the sweep of his swords. But Blade, just as nimble, sped toward her, poised to rain down blows.

Metal clashed against metal. She met his onslaught with terrible precision, executing assaults of her own with flawless agility. The deadly dance continued. They battled on, each watching for the misstep that would surely come. It may have gone on like this forever, but the woman was growing impatient. She leaped toward him. Blade braced for the impact.

She diverted course at the last moment, spinning out of the path of his counterattack. Her right sword stung his upper thigh as she flitted by. A mean sneer curved her lips.

"My, my, must be quicker than that!"

She sprinted toward the river. Blade grimaced as hot blood seeped through his clothes. He looked down, finding the wound shallow. With a defiant roar, he surged after her. Blade closed the gap between them in a few bounding steps. She turned to face him. Blade threw his swords against hers and shoved with all his might. The blow flung her into the dust, her weapons falling out of the reach of her searching hands. Triumphant, he raised a blade to her throat.

"Who are you?" he demanded.

The woman sat up slowly and dusted herself off, ignoring him. Her raven hair had slipped out from beneath her cowl and whipped roughly around her face in the gathering wind. She met his steely gaze with her own, impudent and rebellious despite the razor point against her neck. Angry and ragged as he was, Blade's eyebrow twitched in surprise. It did not last. Another infuriating little smirk played on her lips.

"I have killed for less," he said, applying a little more pressure to prove it. "Especially for those who have desecrated the Way. Now, what does the Coalition want?"

She relented, raising her hands. "I will tell you."

Blade pulled the sword back slightly, allowing her to stand and face him. He wished he hadn't. A weary numbness coursed through his muscles as the adrenaline wore off.

"Tell me what they know," Blade demanded, panting. "Or there will be consequences."

She crossed her arms, the smirk widening into an arrogant grin.

"Are you so sure of that?" she asked haughtily.

Blade growled and made to lift his sword again. His arm quivered, and suddenly strength fled from his shoulder joint and escaped out his fingertips. The sword slipped from his grasp with a hollow thud. Blade swayed, each limb now succumbing to uselessness.

"You look tired, friend. Why don't you rest awhile?" The woman chuckled and snatched up her fallen weapons. Through narrowing eyes, he watched her take off toward the river, swords in tow.

Blade staggered and collapsed to his knees. Numbness trickled through the gash in his thigh until it drained into nothingness.

"Sleeper's poison," he mumbled, and his world went black.

1

Year 113 *of the Glorious New Era*
45th of Sun's Wane
Northeastern Wilds, Gormlaen

Fox wasted no time watching the Guardian fall, but smirked as she heard the heavy thud behind her. She sprinted toward the embankment, her swords whistling as she pumped her arms. The old Guardian might be wise enough to stay out of the river, but she could not anticipate what those young ones would do in their desperation. Fox rounded the bend and crested the slope above the embankment. Sure enough, the boy and girl had climbed into the tied-off boat, which bumped and eddied in the ripping current.

Their guide lay awkwardly in the middle of the skiff, his chest depressing slowly as he breathed. *So I haven't killed him,* she thought. *He certainly isn't going anywhere fast, though.* Fox turned her eye to the boy, who held an oar with a clueless expression. Scratching his head, he peered down the roaring river. The girl wrung her hands, too worried, it seemed, to even bother with the oar sticking up out of the boat's other end and bouncing precariously in the vicious current. Fox sniggered. *How sad they look without their precious Guardian.*

The girl looked up the slope and caught sight of her coming down toward them, and the color drained from her face. She opened her mouth wordlessly, meeting Fox's gaze with wide, terror-stricken eyes. They darted to Fox's blades, still streaked with Blade's blood and flashing dangerously as Fox closed in.

With a grotesque twist of her face and, to Fox's surprise, she pulled a glowing dagger from her waistband. Waving it menacingly, the girl roared, her cry merging with the voice of the raging river. The Cardanthium dagger glowed hotly. It burned a piercing sea green, wild and untrammeled. Fox knew that glow.It had blazed many times through her own swords, full of wrath, primal fear, and desperate survival instinct. *There is fight in her after all. Let her come. Let her try.*

Fox's blood quickened, the anticipation of finally seizing her prey urging her on. And as valiant as that prey might be, no mere baring of teeth and claws would dissuade or even slow a gaining hunter.

Let her try.

The girl lurched forward, but the boy was quicker. He grabbed her arm and yanked her back into the boat. Still, Fox approached fast. She was almost there. Already she saw her victory. With one sword, she would slay the boy; with the other, disarm the girl. One blow with the pommel would quiet her. The child was already Coalition property; the bounty already tingling in the hunter's hands.

The dagger gleamed as the girl raised it above her head. Hesitation, and suddenly, she swung down hard against the taut rope. Splitting beneath the humming blade, the rope snapped away, and the boat sped into the roiling river.

Fox skid to a halt in the sandy pebbles of the shore. Icy water frothed against the toes of her boots. Muttering a curse, she watched impotently as they escaped. The boat was shrinking as it tore away, but Fox could see the girl staring with cold gray eyes from the boat's stern.

She blinked in disbelief as white jets pierced the air. Instinct took control, shattering the blasts from the girl's pistol into licks of sizzling flames as they exploded against her swords. Heat grazed her face like a scorching Heibeiathan desert wind.

The small figure grew smaller, but Fox could not yet look away. She saw something there, etched in the girl's steely countenance; something Fox had nearly forgotten. The boat rocked around a bend and was gone.

Fox dipped her swords into the water to get rid of the blood, but most of it had bubbled off where the shots had struck. She replaced them on her back and sighed. *What to do now?* It was possible they did not all die in the river, but she imagined it unlikely. Perhaps she could find the bodies farther up the river in Thunder Run's calmer waters. *What good would it do you to turn in the dead?* Fox grimaced at the thought. The Coalition wanted the girl alive; they made that clear enough and never had she known them to take kindly to failure. Indeed, they would find some creative way to punish her for it. *Sniff out the vermin first,* she decided. *And then we shall see what comes of it.*

Still, if the girl survived, Fox had no idea where she was going. If they made it to Elmnas' shores, the wilderness would be treacherous. Mists and their horrors infested the land beyond the mountains, and where the mists receded, the Coats teemed like lice. *Even if they survive,* Fox mused, *they won't last for long. They'll be in the bellies of a pack of Mistwolves or in the clutches of the Coalition before I even come close.*

Odds were she lost the little fugitive for good.

But there is the Guardian. The thought did little to cheer her, though, as she trudged slowly up the rocky slope. After all the waiting, the sudden heat of battle and the thrill of the chase, she was tired. In this respect, she preferred kill jobs. Assassinations were quick, requiring little more than a token to prove the deed was done.

But capturing her quarry and returning it alive – this was an undertaking. One must secure the target, appropriate transportation, and plan the rendezvous. She abhorred the tight timeframes, the risk of failure, the maintaining of the hostage. Having to keep someone alive and relatively healthy for gods knew what awaited him was always far more demanding, even if it paid better and the person probably deserved it. *All work and no blood. What's the fun in that?* Fox dragged herself over the slope's edge, sapped of desire to do anything but drink. That is until she recalled who else had hired her.

If she thought the Coalition vindictive, she knew Myergo's wrath would be far worse. Perhaps the crime lord of Lilien's slums offered great rewards, but his punishment for a job even poorly done? It would be a cruelty that knew no bounds. Her last meeting with Myergo confirmed that. The image of his yellowed, sharpened teeth came quickly to mind, drawing close to her in a hungry, hollow parody of a smile. She remembered the empty animal eyes and the heat of his whispered threats. *You know what Myergo promises for your failure.* Fox shuddered and picked up her pace.

The Guardian lay crumpled where she had left him, the dark stain of blood coagulating on his trousers. Fox placed a boot on his leg and prodded him, cautiously at first and then with some force, but only his chest moved with the heavy breaths of deep, unnatural sleep. She crouched over him. It ought to have been a superficial wound – the man moved so fast Fox wasn't even certain her blade bit flesh until he stumbled – but she ripped back the fabric to check, anyway.

"Can't have you dying too, can I?" she said. "Huh, I barely touched you."

The gash ran for several inches, almost surgically even, at a downward angle along his outer thigh.

"It won't even leave much of a scar. Pity." With an unconscious movement, Fox reached up and brushed the three jagged lines of puckered skin marring her own face. She withdrew her fingers quickly, refusing the thoughts such actions invariably brought from entering her mind. Instead, she found her field kit hidden in a crevice on the rock face with her other necessary items, and dressed the Guardian's wound.

"Now... What did they say you were called? Blade, was it?" Fox stood. "I think it's time to get moving. Someone special is waiting for you."

Rummaging among her things, Fox produced a long, thin, silver board. She slid it beneath Blade's inert body, and pulling back her sleeve, awakened the board with a few touches of the obsidian device around her wrist. The board lengthened beneath him, and with a few more touches, it whirred and levitated. The pulsing circles of light on its underside illuminated both the ground below and the canyon wall beside it, casting bright, strange shadows in the reddish haze of day.

"Best coin I ever spent," she muttered.

After strapping the unconscious man atop the hovering stretcher, she gathered her things and scrambled up the wall of crumbled rock. The board followed behind, vibrating and disturbing the loosely lodged piles of dust and stone. She bounded from damaged boulder to boulder, springing up and over the trap she had set with impressive agility and speed. Fox breathed lightly despite the exertion. Indeed, this was nothing, considering. Years of discipline, seasons of subjecting herself to a harsher rule than any wretched desert ascetic could even dream up, had resulted in a body and mind that was as strong and unyielding as the Cardanthium blades she carried. Yes, she had known far worse trials, and she had survived them all. For the bounty huntress, the impossible was paltry.

She alighted on the far side, the levitating gurney in tow. Ahead of her and above the fallow valley that stood in the shade of the Jagged Jaw Mountains spread the Swaying Forest. True to its name, the forest's tall, thin pines creaked and waved as the cold northern wind whistled through them. The vermilion hues of the constant cloud cover were dulling into the rusty tones of dusk. Nightfall and its utter darkness would come soon.

Fox trudged at something like a trot toward the minimal shelter of the pines. She moved along the ridge for some miles, the stretcher now situated ahead of her to light the way. Just as the sky darkened into the color of a sultry wine, Fox arrived at her encampment hidden in a jagged crevice.

"Yes, I've been gone too long, and I'm sorry," Fox said to her mare, which greeted her with an indignant whinny. The horse stilled at the offering of a fresh bag of feed and a sugar cube.

She staved off her own hunger with the rationed remains of her last catch, a fat, sort of stoat-like creature with razor-sharp fangs the size of a viper's, and warmed what she didn't devour immediately over her now roaring fire. This night brought with it an incomparable chill. Fox was not looking forward to spending it out of doors in northern Gormlaen's desolate wilderness. Though the mists hardly touched this country's lands, she knew they crept up the Elmnas side of these very mountains, spreading their ghastly tendrils among the low peaks and trickling over forgotten foot trails like dark streams of poisoned water. Yes, she knew the mountains stood tall and vast, an impassible barrier for everything both in and out of Elmnas, but in the cold, silent dark, it was hard not to imagine the mists flooding up and over the summits to rush down the Gormlaen side and envelop her. It was hard not to imagine the nightmares that dwelled within those mists hurtling toward her; hunting and devouring all that stood in their way.

Mistwolves. Fox drew her cloak tighter about her and sat as close to the fire as she could stand. *Where had they come from?* No one could say for sure. Some said the creatures were evil spirits or demons, taking the form of corrupted wolves. Others looked to more natural theories. Perhaps these monsters were the offspring of common bears and wolves, forced together during the chaos and distress of the Great War, one more unholy creation of war's making. Fox rejected these from a purely scientific standpoint, and though she could draw no certain conclusion, she had well-founded suspicions the Coalition was involved. If she knew the Coats as well as she thought, and she did, the horrors belonged to them.

Fox avoided the known paths of the mists: the southwestern

corner of Maiendell, the far northeastern reaches of Gormlaen's wastelands, and practically all of Elmnas. She had heard and seen enough to convince her that an encounter with a pack of Mistwolves was not worth any amount of gold. Give her rock drakes, lions, serpents, trolls, or whatever else Reidara contained, but she drew the line at Mistwolf. *How ironic it is that the country I've long avoided is the one I'll need to scour now. So much for drawn lines.*

As she pondered her entry into Elmnas, the image of the feral, caged creature in Myergo's lair came back to her. Sad as it was, its misshapen snout and glazed eyes still searched for prey, tasting the air of the subterranean cave with devouring hunger. She imagined it loosed, as Myergo had planned, upon the Guardian bound and unconscious beside her. Fox almost felt bad. Almost. The cruel tyrant of the underground would take her as a plaything just as readily as anyone else to satisfy his whims and lusts. They would not snare her.

Fox stood and paced away from the fire, lifting her sleeve to fidget with the wristband. The smooth, dark device on her wrist served several functions, but right now its most important one was to maneuver the silver board serving as a gurney for her hostage and to serve as a communicator. It mimicked a holograstone, although the technology for the wristband was refined to perfection; able to function over long distances and shedding the thin spindles that held the orbed holographs of its stationary counterparts. Fox activated the communicator, watching as a spherical, glassy surface projected from the band. Presently, a smoky image of a gaunt face swam into the holographic bubble.

"Who's there, then?" the grainy voice asked.

"Who else, Dervish?" Fox asked. "Were you expecting a suitor to call on your holograstone?"

"That's Fox alright," the man chuckled. "So what news, huntress?"

"I have the Guardian, but there is other business I need to attend to. Myergo must send someone to claim him immediately."

"Alive, even? I don' believe it!"

"Believe," Fox said flatly, thrusting the communicator close to the Guardian's face. "I trust this is the one Myergo was looking for."

"Why look at that," Dervish whistled. "King of the Shadows, in the flesh. You'll have made Myergo's day."

"I'm not far from the Jackal Syndicate's old smuggling outpost by Thunder Run. Your people ought to know the place. I'll expect a rendezvous within two days."

"It's taken you weeks to get there. How d'you figure we'll be able to manage that?"

"Don't be obtuse, Dervish. I know you and your ilk have your grimy fingers everywhere. Two days, or I'm selling the Guardian to the Coalition. Gods know they'll pay better."

"That would be foolish, even for you," he answered darkly. "But I'll see what I can do."

"Yes, you will. Two days."

Fox switched off the communicator and sighed. Relief at seeing Dervish flooded her; she'd always prefer Myergo's right hand man to the man himself.

Now, she thought. *When will my other employer get curious?*

She darkened as she imagined it. Fox had been in infrequent contact with the Coalition page who had found her in the Borderlands Brighouse those weeks ago. She had promised silence as she drew close to her targets, warning him that any interruption would endanger her chances. Still, he'd be expecting contact any day now. He'd grow impatient. And then what?

Fox needed a plan. And a good one.

Taking a deep breath, she lifted her communicator once more. Before the face even resolved on its surface, a sharp voice spoke.

"Have you done it?" it said.

Fox sighed, sensing the restrained excitement.

"Not yet," she answered. "But very soon."

Fox hoped the tone exuded confidence and not arrogance; as much as she despised the little sycophant, she needed to be on his good side.

"You said you would have them by now," the page grated. "I wrongly assumed you could catch a little girl. Have they escaped you?"

A little girl who escaped from prison, survived the Mistlands, and picked up a Guardian along the way. A little girl who has eluded your agents twice already.

Fox gritted her teeth, willing herself not to bite back. Instead, she imagined cutting off his hands and feet, watching him wail and writhe in puddles of blood until he passed out from shock. A polite smile formed on her lips.

"I did battle with the Guardian. It is true the girl managed to flee into Thunder Run before I got to her, but she will not get far. At least not alive."

"And what of the Guardian?"

Fox did not hesitate. "He's dead."

"Hm," the page mused. "I suppose you did not fail entirely. Still, there will be no bounty without the girl. Our deal remains, if she lives. Expect much less otherwise... and consider yourself fortunate that I won't count her death as a breach of contract."

That seems... gracious. Fox thought. She hid her surprise but continued to wonder at it. *What exactly am I dealing with here?*

"I need to cross the river," she continued. "Can you grant me access to transport?"

"There is a security outpost some miles south along the mountains. You can obtain a hovercraft there. I'll let them know to expect you."

"Thank you."

"Have I been graced with your gratitude?" The page snorted. "You do grow wise, don't you? I don't think you'd be thanking me if you knew what punishments I have devised if you fail. Two weeks, Arctura. That is the limit of my patience. And no amount of humility will help you then."

The image disappeared. Fox cursed loudly, tore off the obsidian band, and hurled it at the ground. She jumped when a voice spoke out of the darkness.

"I'm dead, am I?" it asked. "I do not mean to offend, but I had hoped to meet different faces in the afterlife."

Fox whirled around. Staring back at her were the alert, pale eyes of the Guardian.

2

Her swords flew out of their sheaths, casting a cold, green glow across the Guardian's pallid face. He shifted against his bonds and groaned. Fox replaced her weapons and approached, scowling.

"How are you awake? This is no normal sedative. It's one of my own making. I've had men twice your size unconscious for two days with it."

"I'm no normal man," Blade replied. His face contorted with pain as he tried to loosen the restraint against his side.

"I suppose," Fox said. "Or maybe it's hard to sleep with fractured ribs."

Fox rummaged through her bag, producing her field kit once again.

"You'll find that I am no ordinary woman, either," she said. "Try anything stupid, and you'll regret it."

Blade nodded, wincing and closing his eyes. Fox got to work. Without moving the restraints much, she lifted his shirt and inspected his side. Blade grunted as she pressed on the tender area.

"It could be worse, which is lucky for you," she said. Fox

produced a tonic from the bag and lifted it to his lips. "Drink this. It'll speed up the healing process and grant you true sleep."

"Why?" Blade asked suspiciously. "Though it is a puzzle, I know you aren't trying to kill me. You have had ample opportunity for that. And if you've told the Coats I am dead, why keep me alive? Why heal me?"

"Because I'll end up killing you out of annoyance if I have to listen to you grouse all night long," she replied. "Don't be a fool. Drink it."

"You have another buyer," Blade said quietly. He turned his head, refusing the bottle.

Fox sighed. "Congratulations, you are not as thick as you look. I am tiring of your puerility. It is not a matter of if you will take the tonic, but how. I keep a stock of injectable forms. Would you rather I stab it into you instead?"

Blade glared, but accepted the tonic.

"Good Guardian," she said. "Now relax."

"I don't need my swords to kill the swine, or you, for that matter."

"I would not be so sure." Fox returned to her place by the fire. She perched herself opposite the Guardian, keeping her eyes on him through the flickering orange glow of the flames. Within forty-five minutes, he would be unconscious, but she wasn't quite sure what he would be capable of until then. He had surprised her once already. *Unacceptable,* she thought. *It cannot happen again.*

Blade leveled an emotionless stare back, studying her in an objective, hawkish manner. She could see the years in those eyes: experienced, cunning, hardened. The dossier she received from the Coalition certainly did little justice to the man it supposedly described. A beast hunter, she recalled, with some other sparse information and a sketched-in shadow where his face ought to have been. Obviously, it missed everything about him, like the straight nose and penetrating gaze, the rugged cut of his jaw and impressive litheness of his tall frame. Tangles of gray hair in his unkempt beard and lines at the corners of his keen eyes suggested the sneaking frailty of age, but his physique and strength told a different story. No doubt he was a warrior. Were things different, she would have respected him, maybe even found him appealing. Of course, attraction and loathing were two sides of one coin. Flip, spin, or drop the coin, and everything could change.

Very little justice, she decided.

They continued their staring contest in silence. The fire flickered, and Fox caught glimpses of the Guardian's weariness in each spout of flame. *Such weariness.* In any other quarry, she would have attributed it to the tonic, but she could see he still bore no intention of sleeping. At least not yet. His muscles remained coiled, his jaw set, his fists clenched, as if preparing to strike as soon as she dozed off. There was only one other weariness she could imagine, one that she knew well enough herself. He wore the heaviness of his true age. Indeed, if he *were* a real Guardian once, an original forger of his own Cardanthium weapons with their own secret names, he had to be over one hundred years old.

Here we are, she thought. *The last of the Ageless, each bound to those never uttered runes forever enshrined on the flats of our blades.*

Fox's gaze flitted to where she had bundled the Guardian's swords, imagining what someone like him might call them. Even wrapped in cloth, they still exuded their ghostly, mystical glow. The runes, of course, did not make them do that, no matter what they meant to the owner. It was, she believed, truly the Cardanthium alone. An element unlike any other, its deposits had once hid deep in the mountains of Elmnas, glowing with untapped energy in both crystalline and metallic forms. For the forger in the old ways, for the wielder of the emerald blades, the hallowed ore bestowed seemingly magical qualities: vigor and longevity to the blades' owner. Not immortality, but lives so long that empires could rise and fall in a Guardian's reign.

How the Elmlings had kept its secret for so long she could not fathom. In the early days, the blind fools of the Coalition had no comprehension of Cardanthium's true power. They continued to burn it, waste it as fuel as their predecessors had. When they finally took control of the Cardanthium-rich hills of Elmnas, they mined it out of existence. And then it was too late to harness the precious element. Most of it, at least. A few had, she well knew. But even then, the ore seemed a living thing, offering its power to one while withholding it from another. It had chosen her, after all. To this day, she did not know why.

Her thoughts turned to the beginning of the Great War, when Gormlaen conquered the last threat to the sprawling Coalition Empire. Her people subdued Elmnas and eradicated the rulers in the Guardian Purge. With them died the vast history and ancient secrets of its people. She had long believed no Guardian had escaped it; the Supreme Chancellor had seen to that. But at least one had managed to survive.

And what had he been doing all these years?

Here she filled in the gaps. A beast hunter, yes, but so much more. He had that wild look of a predator himself. At times, more animal than man as he haunted desolate places, hungering for the climax of the hunt. She looked into his stormy eyes, considering what sort of monsters and men he had slain in his lonely wanderings.

He'd kill me without a second thought, given the right opportunity, she thought with a small smile. *How strange to find him here, tending to that little helpless brood.*

"Tell me, Guardian," she said, the smile broadening into a wicked sneer. "What exactly did you plan to do with those children? What is waiting for them in Elmnas? I am quite curious."

Blade returned the mirthless grin, his teeth flashing in the firelight. "I am certain you are. The dog must catch the scent for her master."

"The 'master,' as you say, pays enough to put me on the trail. Besides, if I'm the hound, that makes you the hog," she cocked her head, smirking. "I sniffed you out and trussed you up, after all. So please, by all means, smile at your little jibe. Who is on the spit? Hm?"

Fox threw a log onto the fire, watching Blade's composed, controlled expression through the shower of sparks. He held her gaze, but the slight droop of his eyelids betrayed a creeping drowsiness. The tonic was working.

Finally.

She pulled a steel-plated flask from within her tunic and unscrewed the top.

"Get off your high horse, anyway," Fox said, taking a drink. "We aren't so different, really. You hunt beasts to turn a profit. I do much of the same, except the creatures I capture or kill almost always deserve it. Like you, Blade. You've crossed a lot of the wrong people. Why is your head in such high demand?"

The Guardian said nothing. He stared through the fire, past her head, gaze lingering just over her shoulder. Fox turned slightly, catching the faint glow emanating from the swords slung onto her back.

"You'd like to see these better, wouldn't you?" She removed her weapons, flourishing a little so that they hummed through the air. Even after all these years, their beauty and perfection still entranced her. Fox held them aloft, staring up at the blades' intricate runic designs as they burned with jade light. They responded to her touch, the radiant hues shifting slightly, calming, it would seem, to match Fox's own pensive mood.

"They are yours," he drawled. "You have named them. I can see it in the workmanship. They were crafted for you. *By you.* And yet, you are a foreigner, a stranger to our ways. How?"

Images flooded Fox's mind. Depths of darkness, reaching down, always down, into the roots of the ancient mountains. The red light of fire, the virgin green and blue phosphorescence twinkling in the bottomless black. A thin face in the glow crinkled and creased like old paper. Eyes as green as the waves of Cardanthium ore deep in the earth. The heat of the forge, sweltering and bubbling up at her, the hiss of cooling metal. A voice from the past cracked with age.

They are yours. You must name them.

Fox looked past the green glow of her twin swords into the face of the Guardian. She looked into the face of the only other person on Reidara who knew how to wield them. Whether it was the effect of the tonic or the weight of his own words, Blade seemed to soften. In those hawkish eyes, she saw something she would have never imagined finding there. Understanding.

For the first time, she considered their odd kinship; two warriors trained in the same dead customs and yet ordained to meet as enemies. Perhaps in another life, another world, they would have fought side by side instead of sword to sword. Or perhaps even this was the purest kind of kinship; the respect that exists only in battle between great contenders. Indeed, it was an understanding of one another, a seeing of their likeness even as they strove with the primal hatred of survival. It was the kinship of war. And in that realization, Fox found herself saying words never spoken to any living soul.

"I was a stranger," she said. "Until an old man took pity on me and taught me everything I could stomach about your old ways."

Blade lifted his drooping head at her words. Fox wondered how much of it he even comprehended. He seemed to understand its importance as he peered hard at her, as if willing away the bleariness clouding his vision and mind. Instead, he yawned.

"Why did he pity you, bounty hunter? Was it the wound on your face?"

Fox reached up and touched the scars. Blade could barely keep his eyes open, but she answered anyway.

"No, I don't think so. He pitied wounds much deeper."

Fox stared into the fire. Engrossed in the glow, she traced the marred skin on her face lightly, lost in the memories of a life as dead and numb as the flesh beneath her fingers.

3

Year 13 of the Glorious New Era
     23rd of Sun's Reign
Southeastern Province, Gormlaen
100 Years Ago

The city of Pardaetha sparkled like a gilded diamond as it overlooked miles of turquoise waves below. It sloped up and away from the white sanded shores of the Mican Sea, its alabaster buildings hemmed in by semi-circular, glimmering tiers of ancient sandstone. Red rooftops glinted in the bright afternoon sun, and figures moved along the streets lazily in the heat of the day. The sea breeze ruffled the leaves of the city's old cypresses, growing between tiers and buildings, and moved ever upward to grace Pardaetha's crowning jewel, the great domed palace of Kyma. Here lush gardens of fragrant blooms and verdant greens, shining pools, and delicately crafted fountains adorned the grounds, a paradise itself among the riches of Gormlaen's southeastern shores.

Pardaetha. The pride of the Coalition. Not that the Coalition could truly claim credit for her magnificence; Pardaetha stood long before the Coalition's rise, once inhabited by the ancient kings and queens of Gormlaen, in days long past, when she stood as an ode to the old gods, a bastion of light, the very heart of Gormlaean culture.

These days, the city yearned for more. In these days, revolution had swept over Gormlaen like a wave, and in cities like Pardaetha, it rushed at tsunami strength. It washed the people clean of her dark ages, of superstition and of folk mythologies that muddied the mind and strangled science. A new age had come to Gormlaen, and now Pardaetha housed impossible dreams, whispers of change, the spark of the conflagration of progress.

Put away were the old hierarchies, the ancient kings, and gods who enforced them. Gone were the useless traditions that divided Gormlaen instead of uniting the common cause of her people. They were now a coalition, a great Assembly, a force of equality. From Pardaetha came the cry – One Gormlaen, One Reidara – Hail the Coalition, the Great Uniter!

Arctura Vipsanius draped herself over a lounging chair atop the outermost balustrade of Kyma, above the sounds of the city and the excitement of sweeping change. Curls of shimmering auburn-black hair fluttered in the breeze and tickled her face, rousing her from a lazy session of sunbathing. Arctura looked about and sighed.

The opulence of Kyma bored her. Its constant state of control and perfection mirrored the state of her own life. For fifteen years, she had grown up in the confines of this palace, learning the arts of perfection and control. Of course, she was mastering them, as she mastered everything, but her excellence did not make the cloistering any less dull. And here in Kyma, she had everything she required for comfort; truly, almost anything she desired to the point of excess. A life of luxury. Of opulence. It was a life that anyone outside of Kyma's walls would ache for.

Ugh, she thought. *Can this day be any duller?*

She peered down into Pardaetha, watching the crawl of city traffic as the small figures of people streamed into the outer gate. In a few hours, the massive gate would close, and in the dusk the city would come alive with lanterns and merrymakers, hungry and thirsty patrons, merchants of carousing and hedonistic deeds. After the day of work, Pardaetha awakened in the night to play.

"I thought I'd find you here, Rah."

Arctura looked down from her elevated position, locating the owner of the voice hanging from the large Ficus in the garden below. The boy, a near mirror image of her except for his short, straight hair and nut-brown eyes, gazed back. He grinned as he dangled from the tree's branches.

"Have you nothing better to do than pester me?" she asked lightly.

"Of course I don't," the boy replied. He clambered up a fat tree limb, settling at eye-level. "My other choices were arithmetic or Coalition international policy. And then I thought, 'Why, forget academia! When has learning helped the cause of the Coalition?' It all became clear then. There is but one way to unite Reidara. I must ruin this fantastic day for my one and only sister."

"A necessary task, indeed, Turo," she smirked. "You were simply compelled to burden me for the good of the Assembly."

"It is a pity," Turo continued gravely. "Father does not understand my serious undertakings. One day, all his light-heartedness and merriment will catch up to him! An empire cannot endure under such frivolity."

Arctura stifled a giggle. "Shush you! He'd throttle you if he heard you say that!"

"Nah, he'd just lecture for me *hours*. He'd say" –Turo sat up straight and set his face into a tight grimace– "you are a disgrace to the family name, Arcturo Vipsanius."

He mimicked his father's deep, gravelly tone with perfect sobriety and disappointment. "Where is your dignity? Where is your drive to rule? Why can't you be more like your sister?"

Her twin stood on the tree branch, drawing himself to his full height. He thrust out his chest, crossed his arms, and put on an exaggerated scowl. "Think this world runs itself, do you, boy? We must have order! We must have discipline! We must have–"

Arctura gasped as Arcturo slipped and tottered backward. She leaped up from her chair to catch him, but Arcturo grabbed hold of a leafy branch and struggled clumsily until he righted himself.

"That is what you get for disrespecting your blood," she snorted.

"Is it?" Arcturo replied. "And here I thought I'd get the curses of my ancestors and spirit hauntings instead. I have to say I'm a bit disappointed."

Arctura shook her head and chuckled. "You are a mess, Turo. Stop being a fool and join me up here."

"I can do at least one of those things." He grinned. "Here, catch!"

Arcturo tossed some ripe figs he had pulled from the uppermost branches to his sister before making the short jump to the balustrade. He stole back a fig and sat, allowing his long legs to dangle over the wall as he bit into the fruit.

"Mother says the Malatesta family will be dining with us tonight," Arctura said. "She may have also mentioned something about being on your best behavior."

"Hm. You know, I'm suddenly feeling quite ill."

"Turo! Tyranna's not that bad."

"Her name means 'tyrant,' Rah."

"*Ruler.*" Arctura corrected. "It means *ruler.*"

Her brother raised an eyebrow. "Tell me I'm wrong, then."

"Alright, she can be... a bit of a brute," Arctura admitted. "But at least she's pretty. And I suppose she can be charming in her own way."

"Then you marry her," Turo said, bitterness edging into his voice.

Arctura snapped her head toward him as he stared out blankly at the city. "You can't possibly mean..."

"Think about it, Rah. We've been having these 'dinners' for months. Somehow, I always end up taking Tyranna for a walk in the garden. Father and Senator Malatesta have gone off and reposed together over Father's finest black leaf and liquor. What do you think they're talking about?"

"Strategic alliances, naturally," Arctura answered. She tried to mask the shock in her tone. "We all know Father needs ties to the western province if he's to be elected Chancellor-Advisor one day."

"And how are those ties made?"

Arcturo wound up and chucked his half-eaten fig high and hard into the air, watching in silence as it grew smaller and bounced off a distant roof. Arctura said nothing. She knew the answer, of course, but she had no desire to voice it. It would become real then; irreversible, irretractable, an inevitability. And she would lose her only brother for the sake of power. *And if they're already looking for Turo... what about me?*

The thought did not frighten her as much as it did for her brother. Maybe it was because she knew Tyranna well enough; indeed, she did not want to be in Turo's shoes. *You know it's more than that. Turo jests, but you both know who father favors. You know his designs for you.*

She glanced covertly at Arcturo, imagining his fears for the future, his grief over lost secret dreams. There might be complaints, there might even be tears, but he would accept his fate and comply in the end. That's what Turo always did. And Father would have his western province.

Politics, she thought. *Basic politics.*

"I better ready myself," Arcturo sighed. With a knowing look, he added, "I'll just have to decide what to stuff my ears with. What do you think? Cotton or wax?"

"I don't see the point of either," Arctura replied with a small smile. "There's no substance on Reidara that could muffle the sound of Tyranna's cackle."

Arcturo nodded appreciatively. "Not bad, not bad at all. It seems I have had some influence over you. Father will be most displeased."

"Shut up," she said, punching him in the arm.

"Speak of the devil..." Arcturo mumbled.

A tall, lean figure strode toward them on the catwalk, wearing the black and red of a Coalition Party Representative. He carried himself with the imposing pride a man of his stature always wore. Wisps of gray streaked through the black of his temple, but his full head of hair and dark mustache displayed no other signs of age.

He stopped short of the pair, drawing his arms behind his back as he looked down his aquiline nose at them with shrewd, piercing eyes. Arctura noticed the additional white bar on his right breast above the silhouetted twin lions, the standard Coalition insignia and indicator of rank among the Party. *So, the Assembly has favored him over Silen Onesti.* If she remembered correctly, that made Father not only the ruler of Pardaetha, but in control of the entire eastern province as well.

As custom demanded, Arctura and Arcturo stood and faced him, Lucan Vipsanius, Senator of Pardaetha and now Steward of the eastern province. They bowed their heads in the formal and salutary gesture, balling their fists and crossing their straightened arms in front of their waists.

"Look upon me," he said.

For the citizens of Gormlaen, such a greeting from a Party Representative served as an invitation to engage, but Father's cold tone suggested otherwise. The twins gazed at him meekly, and Arctura found her suspicions confirmed.

"Arcturo," he said, his eyes narrowed and lips set in a tight line. "You have not attended to your duties, yet you remain in my home, idly eating my bread. Like a common beggar. Do you know where beggars belong, boy? If you continue to squander my resources, you will learn it for yourself."

Arcturo hung his head in shame.

"Prepare for our guests," Father scowled. "Do not make a fool of yourself if you can manage it."

Arctura watched her brother slink off along the wall's narrow walkway, not even daring to share a parting look with her. Father motioned to her impatiently as he headed toward the ancient stone stairs carved into the fortress wall's interior side.

"Walk with me."

She obeyed, falling in step with his long strides. Now at her tallest, she stood nearly as high as Lucan Vipsanius and shared his build. Arcturo, still growing, would likely outstrip them both, but when the two stood side by side, her brother seemed to shrink, dwarfed by the immensity of Father's presence alone. Indeed, she felt the immensity keenly now. It seemed no matter how much she had grown, she would always be a child beside him.

They passed into the garden, weaving between the vine-covered trellises bursting with dark grapes and shallow pools of glassy water, golden with the rays of the sinking sun.

"I have news," Father said.

"Is it to do with your promotion to Steward, Father?" Arctura ventured slyly. "You are to be congratulated on your victory."

He nodded with perfect composure, and as always, hid any trace of emotion behind his hard eyes. It was as Father preferred it. If neither enemies nor friends could unravel him, it would not concern him if one became the other, as they so often did. But Arctura, being at the moment neither, could detect the pleasure beneath his stolid demeanor. And by the slight turning at the corner of his lip, she knew it pleased him most that she understood the gravity of his victory.

"It will not come without retribution. Silen will try to wrest that honor from my hands. Not by sanctions from Andalan, I expect. Our seaport is far too valuable. He will find other means to challenge my success. But it is no matter. I have eyes and ears everywhere. If even the least of his house moves against me, I will know."

"Yes, Father."

They arrived on the other side of the garden, where Kyma reared up on their right and the whole of Pardaetha tumbled down the mountainside to their left. Far below, amidst the brilliant sheen of the ocean waves, the dark hulls of the fishing ships moved slowly toward shore. Father lingered, staring out over the vastness that, for all intents and purposes, belonged to him.

"You are progressing well in your studies," Father said after some time. "The tutors have sung your praises to me. They say you have the innate subtleties, the cunning, the makings of a true ruler."

Arctura forced each muscle on her face to remain perfectly still. Father meted out punishment, not praise, and she had seconds to discern his purposes and act appropriately. *He tests your pride as well as your drive. Give him no cause to find fault.*

"My life is to serve the Coalition," she said. "I seek excellence for her glory."

She felt Father's penetrating stare as she gazed out to sea with placid indifference.

"It is spoken well," he finally decided. "We shall see where such excellence leads. Perhaps, if you watch and learn closely, you will find the Coalition serves you."

The surprise Arctura felt manifested in the involuntary rise of her eyebrow, but Father did not wait to see her response this time. He strode away briskly and disappeared into the shade of Kyma's vaulted archway. Arctura remained working her jaw. Greedy anticipation and troubled doubt competed inside her.

"You will find the Coalition serves you," she whispered, and marveled.

4

rctura stepped into the magnificent dining hall of Kyma, glancing at the entwined golden figures of gryphons, unicorns, serpents and nymphs as they danced along the tops of the colonnades and over the vaulted ceiling. Over the years she could only steal glances — it was a grave offense to appear disinterested in those who dined with her — but even if she could study the ancient filigree, she wondered if she could manage to digest every majestic detail. Or maybe, like everything else familiar to her in Kyma, she'd soon find it common and its beauty lost forever. *Maybe only the forbidden things, all that is out of reach, appear wonderful*, she mused.

She gazed at the immense amboyna wood dining table as it stretched out before her, the excessive number of hand-carved chairs remaining empty. Senator Begato Malatesta waited next to his wife, Lucia, and Tyranna stood on the opposite side, crossing her delicate hands in deferential greeting. Though, like her mother, Tyranna had perfectly straight raven hair, tonight she wore it in glossy curls, held in place and crowned by a thin braid. As was custom she wore signifiers of Coalition Party status, an obsidian twin lion pendant about her neck and an insignia on the cloak now in the hands of a servant, but the corseted black dress with flairs of crimson took certain liberties by accentuating her petite, curving figure and the sun-kissed olive skin of her chest.

Tyranna quickly scanned Arctura's own outfit choice: a conservative but elegant dark gown terminating in a flowing skirt and flaring sleeves stitched with a rubicund fabric on its underside. Arctura thought she caught a flash of hideous contempt, but soon Tyranna's gaze rested on Arcturo. She quickly averted it, but the hazel irises gleamed below her long lashes, an eager hunger glinting in her eyes. Arctura did her best not to roll hers.

"Welcome, once again, honored guests of Pardaetha," Mother said warmly. "How much we enjoy the favor and friendship of the house of Malatesta."

"Oh, Eufemia, *we* are the favored ones!" Lucia gushed. "Look how wonderfully stunning you are!"

Mother clasped hands with Lucia. "No, no, my dear, I am but a candle to your harvest fire. Just look at you! You are simply glowing this night! What magic do they work there in Qynesa? Is it those glorious salt springs? You *must* tell me your secrets!"

Arctura wanted to smirk. *That's not quite how you described her this afternoon.*

The women prattled inanely as the party found their places at the great table, moving from current fashions to imported delicacies to coalition gossip at a rapidity that was impressive even to Arctura. An untrained listener might have missed the subtle shift and tuned them out by now. Arctura, of course, was no untrained listener. Methodically, slowly, she unfolded the silk napkin and rearranged it in her lap as Mother corralled Lucia and circled around to the desired topic. Arctura listened with convincingly feigned incomprehension as the women spoke.

"And did you see what Laenil *wore* to the Assembly Ball? I daresay Gebaln was supposed to be a prosperous city! As soon as I saw her I thought to myself: your husband is aiming for Steward and you arrive dressed like *that*? Well, well, it didn't inspire confidence in his abilities, if I do say so myself! Truly, dear, Lucan already deserved it, but I'm certain your absolute radiance just sealed the deal. Steward could not have been borne by a better name than Vipsanius."

Mother smiled in her disarmingly humble way. "Oh, Lu, you are too sweet to me. Laenil, for her part, did her best to put a brave face on their struggles. She should be commended for trying."

"Well, she might think about trying harder," Lucia said with a nasty giggle. "Anyway, enough about the Onestis and that dreadful city. Gebaln is such a *bore*. Have you heard what they're working on in Lilien?"

"Oh, no I haven't. Interesting fashions?"

"More interesting than even that, I should say. According to Daeli Borgias– you know, Daeli, don't you? Wife of the Senator in Kanah? Anyway, she says that Senator Orsin has been trading them those rare ores, the ones they've gotten from that pathetic little king in Maiendell. Loads of them. And do you know what Lilien wants?"

"I simply could not say. What does Kanah have that Lilien does not?"

"That is exactly what I said. Well, Daeli tells me they want *people*. Their best healers, polymaths, philosophers, savants. I said to Daeli, 'what on Reidara could they be doing with them?' and she has no idea. But *then*, I remembered Begato saying that Senator Orsin requisitioned research funds at the last Assembly."

"How fascinating."

"Fascinating, indeed. I shall eagerly await what will come of it. For the good of Gormlaen, of course."

A sly grin played on Mother's full, sanguine lips. "Of course. Any progress benefits us all."

Arctura gave a sidelong glance to Arcturo, hoping to gauge his reaction, but found him rather occupied instead. Tyranna, who sat beside her and across from Arcturo, cackled loudly.

"You are far too witty," Tyranna said. She bit her lip suggestively. "Tell me another one of your stories."

She placed her hands in her lap and leaned forward, aiding her corset's best efforts with a squeeze of her arms. The pink flush in Arcturo's cheeks and his bouncing gaze gave Arctura the impression he had noticed; an impression confirmed when Arctura's glance met his and his face reddened further. *Oh, please,* Arctura thought, and this time she could not help but roll her eyes.

Her attention turned to the farther end of the table, where Father and Senator Malatesta reposed. They spoke little, and when they spoke, it was of matters of little consequence. That did not surprise her. Father had no need for veiled business at the table when he could do it plainly in private. Even so, Arctura burned to know what plans Father, and the Senator devised, and how they shaped Gormlaen and even Reidara itself over their drinks and pipes.

As the conversations carried on, Kyma's servants had filed into the dining hall, the refilling of goblets and setting of courses well underway. Arctura ate sparingly, as she had been taught, though she felt she could have eaten the entire spread herself. Seasoned greens and pine nuts to start, figs, pomegranates, and grapes heaped in bowls, sea urchin bisque presented in the creature itself, braised eel, swordfish, root vegetables of the north and summer squash of the south. The servants brought strong drinks to sample, bold and sweet reds, fiery and honeyed meads, dry and fizzy whites. The sound of laughter and conversation rose and echoed about the hall as all indulged. *Or at least, they pretend to,* Arctura thought, barely sipping at the many glasses passing before her. *I wonder if Lady Malatesta really is quite as besotted as she looks.*

After eavesdropping on the conversations on either side of her and politely adding to them when appropriate, she still found it hard to say. Arctura turned her attention to the group of musicians playing through their fourth instrumental ballad since they sat to dine. The band played in the staged area between the hall's massive hearth and yawning stone windows. As the last glowing embers of sunlight faded outside, the dimmed row of wall sconces brightened the room and illuminated the strange people beneath them.

Arctura looked on with interest. Their attire exploded with color, each scarf and tunic some bright shade of pink or blue or yellow. The women wore pantaloons like the men, a scandal within the Coalition Party circles, but a fascinating oddity to Arctura. Their almond eyes smiled as they swayed in rhythm to the drummer's beat; one woman beatifically dancing with her tambourine as the other trilled the melody on her aulos. Arctura's gaze passed over each of them, coming to rest on the boy plucking the oud. His dexterous fingers flew over the strings, playing each note of the haunting tune with complete mastery. Eyes closed and shaggy head of black hair tilted upward, the boy seemed to meld with the drifting sound. It as much a part of him as he of it. He plucked out the last notes of the ballad. His dark eyes opened, meeting Arctura's gaze with an intense, brazen stare. Her breath caught in her chest.

"Arcturo," she whispered, interrupting one of Tyranna's tedious tales. "Who are those musicians? I've never seen them before... I've never seen anyone like them. Where are they from?"

"They're not *from* anywhere," Tyranna interjected, snorting. "They're of those steppe wanderers, those city-less, primitive horse riders who roam all over. The misborn of the Heibeiathan nomads and those barbarians of old Gor, I expect."

"The Samras," Arctura said, shooting a covert glare of disgust at Arcturo. Her brother shrugged and sighed, taking a pull of his recently filled goblet.

"Ah, so you have been tutored in the inferior peoples of the Four Dominions." Tyranna picked delicately at the remains of her meal. "I've learned much myself. Many such peoples pass through our borders, and I've studied them all. Samras, old Gor, Elmling, Heibeiathan, Dell people, even those remotest islanders in the far east. My father says it's very important to know your neighbors. You ought to know *everything* you can. Knowledge, he says, is the scythe of submission."

Arctura held Tyranna's gaze, a snide smile playing on her lips.

"That knowledge can go both ways. One ought to be careful, lest the scythe sweep across your own neck."

Tyranna hardly blinked. "Well spoken, my dearest friend. It seems the houses of Vipsanius and Malatesta have much in common, indeed. I'm so glad to get to know you better."

Dessert was set before them, and the aulos quavered gently to begin the next song. The rhythm of the drum joined, steadily beating on. Arctura glanced again at the oud player. This time, his eyes did not close. They gazed into hers, curiously, invitingly. She never wanted to stop looking.

"Tell me your name."

The oud player balanced precariously on the outside of the old balistarium beside Arctura's bedroom window. How he had gotten there or even known which room's long, narrow window belonged to her baffled her completely. She inspected the garden below and the outer wall. He had inexplicably avoided Kyma's security force, though they might make their rounds either in the garden or on the wall any minute. Arctura noticed an offshoot of thick, climbing ivy up the corner of one of the towers. An old, sturdy olive tree inhabited that part of the garden, its branches butting against the stone of Kyma.

He must have climbed the tree and pulled himself up the ivy!

"Who let you in here? Who told you where I slept?" she hissed. "I ought to have them flogged."

His dark eyes glittered in the shadow. A flash of white indicated a broad and mischievous grin.

"You ought to thank them," he replied. "I've come to rescue you, pretty princess."

"Shut up, you idiot." Arctura whispered. "If the guards find you, you'll be executed!"

"Then we better not let them find me. Got anything up there to help me up? This ledge is not as comfortable as it looks."

Arctura huffed, but raced around her room in search of something that could serve as rope. Her eyes fell upon the heavy cord drawing back her curtains; she liberated it from its place on the wall, anchored one end to a heavy bureau and threw the other down to the oudist.

He sprang catlike up the cord, climbing with such astonishing speed that the furniture hardly strained from the sudden weight. Arctura flew around the room, dimming all the lamps except the one by her bedside. The boy, on the other hand, lounged beneath the window with an easy smile. He ran a hand through his hair, chuckling.

"You think this is funny?" Arctura whispered indignantly.

"A little," he admitted. "I'm always a little giddy after some exciting sneaking about. You should try it sometime. It's terribly fun. And I've never climbed a palace before. Boy, those guards! Yikes! I think their muscles had muscles."

"What are you doing here?" She punctuated each word through gritted teeth.

"I wanted to know your name," he grinned in reply.

"You and I both know you didn't have to climb up my window to find that out."

"Maybe," he agreed. "But I count the risk well worth it to look upon your beautiful face again, even if just for a moment."

Arctura sighed and crossed her arms. "How often do you use that one?"

"Not ever, that I can remember!" he laughed. "Now, would you like me to leave, or will you *please* tell me your name?"

She could not help but smirk at that. "I haven't decided yet. You first."

"They call me Fox," he said, rising to his feet and offering a grandiose bow. "Reylas Fox. Traveling troubadour and infamous oudist, at your service."

"Infamous, hmm? I supposed all that fun sneaking about has its consequences."

"There are no consequences if you don't get caught," Reylas winked.

"I think," said Arctura, her tone light and playful. "You are trying too hard to impress me."

Reylas shrugged apologetically. "You're very impressive. A Samrasine vagrant can't simply call on an esteemed Senator's daughter, can he?"

"So, you *do* know who I am," she said.

"I only knew Senator Vipsanius had a family," Reylas corrected. "Your house steward hired us two days after we came to Pardaetha. We weren't told much. Certainly no one told me that behind the walls of Kyma, I'd find Reidara's most enchanting woman."

Arctura eyed Reylas suspiciously. From anyone else, she would disbelieve the flattery. Not that what he said did not have the ring of truth to it. With her pristine skin, blossoming figure, and waves of silken hair, she knew she carried a unique appeal. Men often turned their heads when she passed by. But for a Senator's daughter, for a Coalition Party member of any rank, compliments came with an intended price. Never was there flattery without a hope for favors. *How could I possibly believe this boy is any different?*

Reylas smiled with his eyes and his lips, genuine joy etched into his countenance in a way she had never witnessed in anyone else. Not even Arcturo. It pleased her to look at him; like turning her face toward the sun on a crisp morning and drinking in its light and warmth. *Can I dare to feel so?*

"How long will you stay in the city?" she asked.

"I'd stay my whole life if you asked me to," he said.

"You couldn't."

"I would."

She faced him, this boy sitting beneath her window, quiet in the low light of her dimmed chamber. Strange ideas raced through her head, dreams that had never once crossed her mind exploded into being and shouted blissful possibilities. It was as if the world was all winter before now. Finally, at long last, she found her summer.

"My name," she said. "It's Arctura."

"Arctura," he repeated softly. Reylas took her hand in his and gazed deeply into her eyes. "It is just as lovely as you are."

He leaned in, but Arctura turned her face away and looked down at the floor.

"You better go," she replied.

Demurely, she peered at him. Reylas gazed at her as if she were a goddess, and Arctura wished she had never suggested he ever go anywhere. There were many things she wished, things that had no words but inflamed every longing that she never knew she held inside.

"Okay." He lifted her hand to his lips and kissed it gently. "Not forever, I hope?"

Arctura shook her head with a smirk. "Not forever."

His eyes glittered, and a rakish grin spread broadly over his face. With one last squeeze of her hand, Reylas dashed out the window and disappeared into the night.

Arctura waited as long as she could stand before clambering up on the window ledge herself. She stared down at the twinkling city lights. Outside the walls of Kyma, somewhere in the lonely streets below, the faint whistle of a merry tune echoed triumphantly and faded into the night.

The fire crackled, sending up a spout of sparks into the black night. Fox stirred from her reverie as it did so, startled by how easily she had slipped back into those days. She refocused with some trepidation at the Guardian, but the soporific effects of the medicine had already taken place. He slumbered deeply despite bonds and broken ribs. Fox calculated how much sleep she might safely get; the elixir's effect differed from man to man, but still she could usually count on eight hours of unconsciousness from even her hardiest catches. She scrutinized Blade. *Better to only give him five.*

The bounty huntress arranged her belongings and stretched back onto her bedroll, hands behind her head as she stared into the enigmatic black. The picking of an oud, the haunting beauty of her favorite tenor's voice, and a familiar melody filled the void of northern Gormlaen's sightless and soundless night. She drifted to sleep, dreaming of beloved eyes and rough hands and soft words that even one hundred years of absence had not dulled the ache for.

5

Year 113 of Glorious New Era
45th of Sun's Wane
The Wolf Barrens, Elmnas Territory

White-capped waves frothed into the spinning boat. Mouse gasped, both from Thunder Run's startlingly cold waters and her most terrible realization: the boat was going down. It rocked violently. Toma dug his oars in to no avail. Dane sputtered and choked as water lapped into the bottom and over his inert frame.

Rage. Blind rage. Mouse succumbed to it as hope sunk with their overwhelmed craft.

It's all my fault. They will die – just like Red, just like Blade – because of me.

Her final moments with them spun through her mind. She saw Red, dropping the crowbar and the will to fight, to save her. There was Blade, locked in deadly combat as they raced by him, the bounty hunter's twin swords eager for the kill. For her. All for her. As she felt the waters rush over her, she realized no sacrifice had been more meaningless than the ones they made... for her. Darkness swallowed Mouse as tears blurred her vision.

Meaningless.

Light and sudden calm surrounded her. Mouse looked drawn to the light now blazing ahead. The smooth feathers of a fiery wing rose out of the light and stretched before her. Transfixed, ashamed, emptied, Mouse watched.

And then–

The small craft creaked as it bottomed out in the black-pebbled shallows. Thunder Run had slowed to a relative gurgle now, the wild rush of white-tipped waves far behind the boat and the three stunned travelers it carried. Ahead, it tapered and snaked through the mountain range, disappearing altogether behind walls of unscalable shale. Mouse gaped.

She scanned her surroundings in disbelief as the forested hills and expansive solitude of Elmnas spread out before her, its beauty marred only by the blackened trench stretching into the woods. Mists seethed in the massive scar, striking apprehension into her already racing heart. But it was a fleeting feeling, overwhelmed quickly by the wonder of a foreign but familiar land. She had no recollection of this country, but somehow, her arrival on its shores felt like returning home.

"Elmnas."

We made it, she thought, tears of relief stinging her eyes. Confusion followed in relief's wake. *But how? How did we get here?*

The brilliant, undulating light, a fiery wing, dipping into the turbulent river's surface, peace passing out of understanding, seared her memory.

"Mouse? Mouse! Hey! What are you doing?"

Toma's agitated voice shook her from her thoughts.

"What?" She turned, unable to shake the annoyance at the interruption.

Toma stared, wide-eyed and mouth gaping, his usually ruddy face pale and sickly. At the bottom of the boat, Dane giggled faintly.

The smuggler, forgetting his brusqueness, chortled. "That was some ride, youngins."

Pieces of the perilous journey on the river returned to Mouse now. They were about to capsize, the river poised to drag them down to its black depths forever. But that didn't happen. She recalled Toma's words now, the troubled exclamation at her sudden ability to navigate the fraught waters. Her own eyes grew wide. Mouse gripped Toma's arm so hard her knuckles whitened.

"The phoenix," she whispered. "I saw it. I think... I think it saved us."

"That bird you dreamed about?" Toma looked around skeptically. "I don't know about that, but something amazing did happen. You did the impossible. We got here without him."

He nodded toward Dane with a raised eyebrow. Their guide stared skyward, babbling and laughing at some private joke. Toma sighed. "Well, we won't find any answers right now. We've got bigger problems. Do you still have your things?"

Mouse patted around, finding that the pillowcase full of Red's belongings remained secure. She felt around her jacket and sighed in relief. The strange electronic chip, the last thing Red gave her, was still snug in her pocket. Like the wage card once embedded in her hand, it was a technology far beyond the machines she once tinkered with at Misty Summit's Manufacturing Facility. She knew the prison camp she had long called home kept most of its secrets from her still. Not all, but many.

Mouse recalled with a shudder the terrible moment she and Toma discovered the subcutaneous chip's other capability: a tracking device that gave the Coalition her exact location. She flexed her hand, remembering the sharp knife, the pool of crimson, and the blood-spattered rectangle in the basin. The chip she carried now looked very similar, but even she could see its design was more nuanced, better suited for some higher and probably more nefarious purpose. And Red's life, as she knew it anyway, ended soon after he handed it to her. She did not yet understand why, but Mouse knew life and death hung on that little device. And she needed to find the Elmlings, who would know what to do with it.

"I've got what I need," she said, gazing empathetically at Toma's empty lap. "Sorry about your stuff."

"Hey, I'm alive, right?"

He attempted a laugh, but it came out as a breathless wheeze. Shakily, Toma climbed out of the boat, offering a hand to Mouse when he splashed onto the sandbar. She clambered out after him, stepping ankle-deep in the icy water. The two heaved the dinghy out of the shallows and onto the slippery bank. Now it was Toma's turn to look around, his eyes coming to rest on the misty gash ahead.

"So... what now?" he asked. "That bird pointing you anywhere in particular? Not that direction, I hope."

Mouse followed his gaze toward the swirling mists. Her skin crawled to look at it. She did not know when night would fall, but she knew she didn't want to be here when it did.

"Not there. That's just asking for trouble."

"Definitely," Toma shivered. "But where are we going? And how are we going to get there? And what are we going to do with you know who?"

Toma pointed back at Dane and added in a whisper, "He's out of his mind."

"My mind's just fine," Dane growled from the boat's bottom.

A perturbed and muffled scrabbling followed, and two hands grasped and white-knuckled at the boat's side. Dane groaned. His hands slipped back down as he unleashed a string of vile curses. Mouse and Toma hurried over to help, but she jumped back as she looked down at his glaring, contorted face. Dane clutched the seared wound on his shoulder, puffing and screwing up eyes as he tried to move. Toma was braver, and tentatively, he reached into the boat, fingers outstretched as if he were grabbing hold of a viper. Dane struck out like one as he slapped at his hands with an angry hiss. Toma drew back hastily, his mouth opening and closing as he stuttered a reply.

"How are you feel–"

"How d'ya think I'm feelin', you moron?" Dane roared. He winced and exhaled painfully through his teeth. "My arm is useless, and everything else has gone to the pits, but I've still got more brains than the two of you combined. The nerve of that whelp, sayin' I'm outta my mind."

Toma scowled as Dane continued to mutter curses and threats at them, his mouth now open to shout in protest. With a sharp look and shake of her head, Mouse silenced him. Toma huffed and crossed his arms, but said nothing. Mouse took a deep breath.

"Dane, I know it must feel awful, but we've got to get you out of the boat. We've got to get you somewhere safe. I've seen the monsters that live in the fog before... I don't want to see them again. You've got to let us help you. Where should we go?"

Dane eyed her, his jaw rigid with either anger or pain. Or both. Mouse could not tell. Dane's face was inscrutable; he might burst out in another laughing fit or explode once again in rage. Neither would be overly helpful. She gazed back with what she hoped was a neutral expression.

"Fine, fine," he muttered. "Where are we, anyway?"

"Have a look," Mouse said, and with Toma's help, she heaved the smuggler upright.

Dane surveyed the scene, gripping the side of the boat with his good arm. He exhaled heavily.

"Well, girl, your gut is right about this place," he said. "We weren't to land here. You ain't likely to find something that won't shoot or eat you before you could tell it your name."

"Where were we headed?" Toma asked.

"Smuggler route," Dane grunted. He nodded downstream of their position, where the mountain chain continued northwest along the Gormlaen border.

"There's an outpost some ways down the river where I do most of my trading. No offense to you two, but you're useless on the water, and that's the only way to get to it... at least in my current condition.

Anyway, I'm not so sure we'd want to try. There were only two outfits that knew of my usual route, but if that woman figured it out, we're in some trouble. There ain't no way the outpost isn't crawling with Coats now... or worse."

Dane hawked and spit into the reeds.

"Nope," he decided. "Can't risk it. Out of the question."

Toma sighed, placing his hands on his sides as he gazed in the same direction as Dane.

"Alright," he said. "So, what do we do? What *can* we do?"

Mouse and Toma stood around the boat in silence as their guide maintained his inscrutable stare. With a sudden and loud obscenity, Dane broke it. Mouse flinched, looking to Toma in perplexity. He simply shrugged. For some time, Dane continued, mumbling out scattered protests interspersed with angry curses. By all appearances, he was arguing with himself, and he was losing. Dane kicked a boot against the side of the boat and swore again.

"Well, there ain't nothin' fer it," he grumbled, throwing up his good hand. "We'll have to go to *them*."

"Who?" Toma exclaimed.

"Are they dangerous?" Mouse added.

"The sisters? Ha! They're a danger to my coin purse and my sanity," Dane muttered. "But... no. Their old fortress is solid and safe. The only safe place for miles. I don't see how you'll suffer 'em long, what with their draconian rules about drink and showin' ankles, but at least they got grub and beds in the Priory. As much as I'll regret it, I'm desperate. We'll have to go to the Ameliorites."

Toma scoffed. "The what-erites?"

Dane rolled his eyes and shrugged. "Ask them. Strange, dusty ol' bats."

"Sisters?" Mouse probed. "What is a family doing out here on their own?"

"Penance," Dane snorted. "It ain't the kind of family you're thinking of. You'll see when we get there."

"I don't care what they're doing. Sleeping indoors and eating something other than gamey gopher sounds like paradise," Toma said.

"But do you really mean safe? We're not exactly *allowed* in Elmnas." Mouse grimaced, recalling the Breythorns' conflicted decision to turn her over to the Coalition. "To be honest... I'm not allowed anywhere. I'm sure you figured it out, but people are looking for me. What will these sisters do with a fugitive?"

Dane shook his head. "You needn't worry about that. They take in all kinds of strays, and they're no friends of the Coats, neither. I may not like 'em, but you can trust 'em."

Mouse was still wondering if she could trust Dane, let alone more strangers. *With that woman after us, he's in it now as much as I am.* Mouse thought. *Would betraying me stop her from hunting him down? And do I have any other choice?*

Her gaze strayed to the undulating blanket of mist in the dark rift.

"Okay," she said.

Toma scratched his head. "So... how do we get there? And how do we get *you* there?"

A sly grin broke out on Dane's tired, pain-etched face.

"I'm still alive and smuggling for a reason, farm boy." Dane pointed upstream. "Head south along the big boulders here. You'll find a little copse of stubby trees with a narrow mud path leading in. If I'm not mistaken, you'll find my pushcart inside."

"I'm on it," Toma said.

Mouse watched as he took off at a brisk run along the bank, veering around the rising piles of rock. The small strip of riverbank where they landed seemed to be the only break in the mountain chain for miles. Northwest and southeast, peak upon peak, it reared up as far as she could see. If what Dane said was true, they really did not have other options. They would need to take refuge with these Ameliorites, these strange sisters that so rankled their smuggler. Despite brimming with questions, Mouse decided it best not to press the injured man. She flopped down on the bank beside the boat and tossed black rocks into the water.

"You're that girl the Coats want, aren't you?" Dane said, peering down at her.

Mouse snorted as the last rock she threw plunked into the meandering shallows. "I guess I made that obvious, didn't I?"

"Eh, don't give yourself too much credit. I figured it out. Oh, don't look surprised, I've ferried enough fugitives for Woldyff to know what to look for. And in my line of work, I hear things, too. Things like a bounty out for a dangerous little lady. Seems to me they pegged the wrong gal. You don't look the mean and murderous type."

"I never killed anyone," Mouse said quietly. "I just watch them all die."

Dane grunted and pursed his lips. "Blade didn't make it."

Mouse shook her head. Dane paused for a long moment as he stared over the water.

"I always liked him, you know. He was one of the good ones. I don't know how well you knew him, but I'm sorry all the same. It ain't no life for a young lady. I hope you get where you're going. If not for you, for him."

Mouse's eyes burned with tears as she nodded. In the weeks she had spent with Blade, trudging through Gormlaen's wilderness and out of the Coalition's grasp, he'd become something like a brother. Despite the journey's difficulty – the heat, the cold, the exhaustion, the hunger – Mouse felt it the best days of her life as she now remembered it. It was the first time she had anything like a family; lessening even the sharp sting of losing Red. Blade taught her and Toma all he knew about survival, and she drank it in, learning all that he would teach her.

As they grew closer, she knew the bond was not superficial. Their shared people, shared suffering, shared desire to set things right in Elmnas sealed them in a way Mouse still could not describe. More than that, Blade knew of things long ago, things that could explain her dreams and visions. The bird that had appeared to her three times now, this phoenix, Blade called it the bringer of change. And he had given her hope that her purpose in this journey was more than what she originally could fathom. Something far bigger was unfolding, and Mouse teetered on its cusp. With Blade to guide them, they might even see what the harbinger would bring.

And just like that, he was gone.

The loss sat like a stone in her stomach. Another crushing weight added to the burden of grief she carried wherever she went. Red, Blade, 135... and who would follow? She looked up at Dane, her gaze wandering to his mangled shoulder. Her thoughts strayed to Toma, his laughing, golden eyes and playful, easy grin, the endearing wildness of his hair and the way he ran his fingers through trying to tame the locks. *Why did you come?* she thought. *Why did you risk everything for a stranger? For me?*

A hollow rattling shook her out of her dark musings, and she peered down the bank to find its source. Toma trundled up with the cart, grinning as he made his way to them.

"Here it is, just as Dane promised," Toma said. "I guess he's not out of his mind just yet."

Dane needled Toma with a sharp glare.

"Oh, stop it," Mouse laughed, amused despite the circumstances. "You *were* acting very strangely not too long ago. Come on, let's get you to the... what did you call them? Ameliorites? Hopefully, they have some healers among them. You really need one."

Mouse and Toma arranged the belongings they had left in the handcart, using some of the softer material as bedding for their injured guide. With help and only a few curses from Dane, they managed to get him on the platform.

"Alright," Dane said breathlessly. He raised his good arm and signaled away from the mists, along the northwesterly edge of the mountains. "Take us that-a-way."

"How long until we get there?" Toma asked.

"Couldn't say with *you* pushing. It's some miles down. I could make the trip in two hours."

Mouse suppressed a smile as Toma dramatically rolled his eyes. Though there wasn't really room for the both of them, they wedged in between the long handle and the two spoked wheels. Pushing together, they drove the cart along the grassy meadow between the unyielding mountains and dark forests of Elmnas.

"Now I know how the oxen feel," Toma panted.

"The what?" Mouse said.

"Get yerselves moving!" Dane hollered. "Hyah!"

6

Sweat dripped into Mouse's eyes as they labored along the valley. What had looked like the pleasant rising and falling of gently rolling hills felt like barbaric, steep slopes now. A light drizzle fell upon them, and they staggered up the slick grass on one side of a hill and slipped and slid down the other. Ruts, rocks, and roots snagged the wheels, forcing them to slow or stop more than once as they maneuvered out of each annoying obstacle. Dane swore under his breath at each jostle, which happened to be every several minutes. Over the course of the long trek, Mouse could no longer distinguish the grumbling and cursing from the heaving of the wind or the humming of insects.

"How much farther?" Toma gasped as they trod up another swell in the rolling landscape.

"Not too much," Dane said.

The roughness was gone from his tone, now replaced by the even, tense timbre of a man forcing himself to remain calm for the sake of others. Mouse looked up at the sky, trying to judge the time until nightfall. The strange orange brightness of day bathed them beneath the unbroken clouds, promising a few hours more of relative safety.

Her gaze darted to the shadowy forests far off to their right. The barren trench filled with low-lying mist was far behind them, but she spied tendrils of gray slithering through the dark trees, stalking beside them. She did not need the edging of anxiety in Dane's voice to reveal the danger. Mouse sensed it herself.

We'll die if we don't get there before dark.

She glanced over at Toma, who had not spoken much since they began their laborious march. He was gritting his teeth, shaking the sweat from his thick, black eyebrows and windswept hair. Since their adventure on the river, Mouse thought he seemed withdrawn and uncharacteristically brooding. She longed to know what he was thinking. *At least, I'd like to know what he's thinking about me,* she admitted. *Toma hasn't looked at me the same since the river.*

Mouse felt she could not blame him. Even as she struggled to put a finger on it, she felt sure something new was happening to her. It was as if escaping Misty Summit had done more than free her body; in the depths of her a barred door broke; a passageway opened that allowed her to breathe in real air and see real things. Whatever they had done to her at the prison, its hold over her senses dissipated with every step toward Elmnas. This was what she had wanted, of course. She had yearned to break past the door that the healers of Misty Summit had imprisoned her behind. Mouse could almost relive the memories feeding her dreams, the answers to the strange riddles of what she believed to be her past as each night's sleep brought renewed clarity to them. But the thing that complicated it all, the thing that seemed to have no place and make no sense in it, was the phoenix.

The image of the flaming bird filled her imagination, and though it frightened her to dwell on it, Mouse found she could not tear even her mind's eye away from its fiery wings. *What does it mean?* she wondered. *And how could a vision be so... real? How could it save us?*

Uneasiness filled her as she relived the events on Thunder Run. The thing saved them. Mouse knew that never in her own strength and ability would she have been able to navigate the treacherous waters. And she knew what she saw and what she felt. It was something wholly *other*. After her first vision of the phoenix, Blade, who had been there to explain it, suggested it had meant something monumental, something that spoke good omens of renewal to a land torn asunder. She found the mystical, supernatural quality of the idea intriguing, even comforting, but never did she think it was an actual... being. *Isn't that what it is?* she thought. *Is there any other possibility?*

The thought filled her with both dread and excitement, and she could not decide which feeling made her more uncomfortable. *Who am I? And what in the world am I doing here?* Mouse stole another glance at Toma. No wonder he was brooding.

As they crested the hill, Mouse strained to look ahead. In the distance loomed a dark shape, jutting out from the side of the mountains. At first, she only thought it an extension of the chain as it infiltrated the hilly land, but as she peered harder, the rigid geometric shapes of ramparts and towers rose out in stark contrast to the eroded, wild slopes beside them. White flags emblazoned with purple symbols she still could not quite make out fluttered above the towers, offering a welcome touch of life and color to the otherwise lifeless, gray fortress walls.

"Is that it?" Mouse called back to Dane excitedly. "Is that the place?"

Dane sighed. "Yep. But it still ain't all that close. We gotta keep moving."

"What happens if we can't get there before dusk?" Toma asked darkly.

"I couldn't tell you," Dane said. "I've never been in these parts at night."

"Is it because of that great empty thing we saw? That deep trench in the land where nothing grew? What is that, anyway?" Mouse asked.

Dane scratched his chin. "A remnant of the war, or so I've been told. That was long before me, you see. My contacts in the area say they're used to be quite a number of settlements along this side of the mountains. One of the bigger Elmling tribes controlled the area, you see. When the Coats invaded, they killed, captured, or drove out most everyone and torched everything. Well, everything except the Priory, which was an Elmling fort they took early on. I couldn't tell you all the details, but that big gash was cleared and dug as a supply line for the Coats' army. Wanna know what the locals call it now?"

"I have a few guesses," Toma muttered.

"The Wolf Barrens," Dane said. "The mists don't ever go away. If you ask me, that's where those things are breeding. There's more than one reason I don't come this way. That's a big one. The sooner we're out of the open, the better."

"How do the sisters fit into all this?" Mouse asked. "You said the Coats took the Priory."

"Yep," Dane sniffed. "But they gave it up pretty quickly once the Mistwolves started picking off their men. The place is a wasteland, anyway. Coats had other things to do, as always, and no one wants to guard a border only idiots or the suicidal would cross, anyway."

"What does that make us?" Toma whispered to Mouse. She grimaced.

"Now here's the real funny part," Dane continued. "The Ameliorites are *Gormlaean*. Coalition citizens. They asked the Coats– *asked them*– for a charter to inhabit the fortress. They up and left civilization to live in this forsaken wilderness with man-eating monsters roaming outside their walls! Can you believe it?"

"They must be very brave," Mouse said. "But why? Aren't they afraid?"

"Didn't I tell ya they were insane already?" Dane scoffed. "The sisters told me they're *called* here. That they're not concerned about the outside because they're *divinely protected*. You know what I said? I said, maybe you ought to give your big ol' walls that credit instead."

By this time, their weary steps had brought them much closer to the Priory. It loomed ahead, growing larger with each passing minute. The vermillion sky seemed to darken with each passing minute as well, and Mouse could not help glancing nervously behind them. At the very least, their imagined hunters and eagerness to arrive brought renewed strength. Toma snorted like a draft horse as he pushed the cart with all his might, driving them down the next hill with increasing speed. Mouse jogged to keep up.

She almost cheered as they stepped onto level ground, the final stretch before the doors of the fortress flattening out into a broad valley. Before them, a packed dirt path sprung up and widened. Toma maneuvered the cart toward it, and the two hurried along. Her feet ached and her arms trembled, but thoughts of food, drink, and a bed kept her going. Now Dane watched behind and around them, scanning their route for insidious mists in the gathering dusk. Though she saw no signs of mist ahead of them, Mouse felt its presence at her back, slinking down the gentle slopes in stealthy pursuit.

They stopped just short of the heavy iron bars that guarded the great wooden doors of the Priory. Mouse peered up in awe of the colossal wall of mortar and stone. Misty Summit had its own wall, an ugly metal thing that contained its captives and oppressed them with its arrogant impermeability, but this was something else. Mouse noticed craftmanship and purpose in its shapes, as if it stood proudly to defend those inside. And it had endured. Time had hardly left a mark on the impressive facade. The only evidence of its age was the wornness around the edges of each huge block that built up the fortress.

Mouse searched for faces on the battlements, but nothing stirred above. Toma set down the cart, gazing around in confusion as he caught his breath. A wind kicked up behind them and whistled through the forlorn valley.

"I guess we can't just knock, huh?" Toma asked.

"The rope, you moron," Dane replied. "Pull that rope."

Toma opened his mouth and closed it again, sighed, and reached for the rope dangling against the iron gate. Clanging issued from within as he pulled it and echoed against the wall of stone. Mouse fidgeted in the long silence that followed, unable to stop herself from casting wary glances all around her. The sky was definitely darkening now, and she thought she heard a spectral howl carried along in the wind. She started in surprise when a weak voice croaked above them.

"Dane? Dane the Debaucher?" it wheezed. "And what business brings you here, eh? If I remember rightly, the Prioress condemned your depravity and made it clear enough that it had no place among women of virtue. But for the youths with you, we would have no other words between us."

The speaker peered over the battlement at them with beady eyes, the rest of her stern face obscured by the wall below, and the curious white head covering that jutted above it. Mouse could see the deep creases of age around those eyes, telling of a life years longer than Mouse had thought possible.

"Well, well, sister Krelah, that is some welcome for a waylaid wanderer, *debaucher* though I am. Aren't you supposed to be the forgiving type? And b'the way, what a surprise to see you," Dane answered. He added in a mutter, "Alive, that is."

"I'm not deaf, you knave. I can still hear you," the sister scolded. "Why are those poor children dragging you about? What ill tidings has your wickedness brought this time, eh?"

"Excuse me, ma'am— uh, sister— but he's injured," Mouse said, cutting off Dane mid-holler. "We were attacked, and we really need your help."

"It wasn't his fault," Toma added.

"I find that hard to believe," the elderly woman sniffed, scrutinizing the trio. "But it isn't for me to judge. Stand back, I'll have the novices open the portcullis."

Sister Krelah disappeared from the battlement.

"What happened last time you were here?" Mouse whispered, turning toward Dane with a serious look.

Dane attempted a shrug, wincing and gritting his teeth as he remembered his wound. Even so, his mouth twitched into a roguish smile.

"I did nuthin'," Dane said. "Well, except help m'self to their consecrated wine... and perhaps pay too much attention to one of the sisters. And since they're ascetics, all into self-denial and constant sorrow, flirting and fun are off the table."

Toma gave an amused snort. "No wonder she's so mad."

Soon, with a heavy thud and the clanking of rolling chains, the iron bars lifted and ascended into the stone archway above them. More sounds came from behind the great wooden doors, and after a few more dull thuds, they groaned outward. Toma and Mouse cautiously pulled the cart into the opening.

Mouse gawked as they entered. An enormous courtyard stretched before them. She imagined that only moments before, it must have been bustling with activity; leafy plants stirred gently in the gardens that dominated the open space as hens strutted among them. Sudsy wash basins swirled beneath strings of fluttering laundry. A goat lazily crunched on scraggly weeds growing up around the massive broken stones buried intermittently in the courtyard. Now there stood about around a dozen women, gazing back at the sweating travelers in stone-still silence.

They were unlike any group of women Mouse had ever seen. All wore the peculiar white head covering, which draped around their necks and fell down the backs of their long, well-worn robes that matched the deep purple of the Priory's standard. Some seemed as old as Sister Krelah, but many of them were far less so; Mouse noticed one girl who could not have been more than twelve.

More faces appeared from the dark recesses of the fortress beyond the courtyard, all watching the three with curious, quiet stares. Mouse felt sheepish, only moving her feet when Sister Krelah harangued them for lingering in the gateway.

"Want to let in that nasty wind and all the monsters of Elmnas, too, eh? Come on then, hurry on inside. Now someone shut this gate up. Go on and set the cart there. Well then, Dane, you sure are worse off than last time you came, eh? You'll be wanting the healer, I expect. Oh my, I do feel a terrible fog follows you. We oughtn't open up until next morning. O'course the Prioress will decide, but I know well that sickly vapor. They'll be about tonight, I say. And what's all this standing around, eh? Back to your chores, little sisters, off with you!"

The bent old woman shooed away the younger women, who hurriedly returned to their duties. Only one looked back, her sympathetic and concerned gaze lingering on Dane. He grinned back stupidly.

"Sister Ilidette, I'll have you peeling potatoes for the rest of the day if you aren't gone *at once*," Sister Krelah admonished.

Sister Ilidette sighed but disappeared into the Priory. Dane continued to grin, even as Sister Krelah threw up her gnarled hands and puttered away in exasperation. His impish smile quickly faded as another Ameliorite approached them. Though nothing in her dress or stature set her apart from the other sisters, the austere expression and stately poise attested to her authority. Mouse tensed as the Prioress converged on the three, her purposeful gait like a bear charging on the unlucky creature between her and her cubs.

"Uh oh," Dane mumbled. Mouse thought she saw him cringe.

The woman drew up short, sizing up the group down the bridge of her thin, pointed nose as she folded her arms behind her. Except for the howling gale outside the fortress walls, nothing made a sound. She turned a penetrating eye on each, her last scrutinizing gaze falling with something like anger and pity on the injured smuggler. The Prioress looked upward as she placed a hand in her pocket, her mouth moving wordlessly as she thumbed the beaded cord Mouse saw hanging there. A green glow illuminated the woman's fingertips. *Is that... Cardanthium?* Mouse wondered.

The Prioress looked once again upon the travelers; this time the sternness all but melted away.

"Welcome," she said in a strong but gentle voice, and she held out her hands to them. "Welcome, weary ones. There is rest for your sleeplessness, balm for your tender wounds. The Unseen Sees, the Unknowable Knows. Welcome to the Priory, the Wolf Barrens Refuge, the home of the Ameliorite daughters. Something tells me you still have so very far to go."

7

A strange shiver overcame Mouse at the Prioress's greeting. Was it excitement? Recognition? Or something more? She stared in wonder as the Prioress continued her introduction.

"Though I am the leader of this humble commune, you may simply call me Sister Alba. It has been some time since we have received visitors. For whom do I have the pleasure of offering hospitality?"

"Pleasure's all mine," Dane answered flatly. "This one's Toma and the other's Mouse. I've been shot through by a bounty hunter thanks to them, and I'd rather stop jawing and get something done about it before it kills me."

Sister Alba turned sharply and leveled a searing glare. "Do you dare think I have forgotten any important detail? You have no right to demand *a thing*, so still your tongue. I tolerate your presence for the sake of these little ones. Even if I am bound by my order to have compassion for your misfortune, which will be allayed in moments, I have no qualms against casting you out as soon as you are tended."

"Some compassion that is," Dane muttered. "Decent folk shouldn't need no order or invisible deity tellin' them to be kind and not throw someone out to the Mistwolves just because you don't like 'im."

"I think you grievously overestimate the natural kindness of the children of Reidara," Alba said, her lips tight and grim. "Even the 'decent' ones. But let the debates of the mundane and the divine wait; at least until we can spar at our best."

The Prioress sighed and thumbed the beads in her pocket again. A conflicted gloominess came over the Ameliorite's face. Mouse wondered if there was more to the sourness between Alba and Dane than he had originally let on.

"Much weighs on my mind these days," Sister Alba continued. "I'm afraid we've caught each other at difficult times. Still, the Unseen sees. I didn't expect to find you at our walls again, but you have been brought here for a reason. Here comes our healer now. I will pray for a full mending and that we may talk in good faith again."

Dane grunted incomprehensively and nodded; a far more respectful gesture than Mouse thought he could muster. Soon, the healer and a few other sisters joined them, bringing medical implements and a stretcher with them. With impressive speed, the Ameliorites got Dane out of the cart, onto the stretcher, and into their capable care. Toma and Mouse offered brief goodbyes and best wishes to the hapless smuggler as they carried him into the Priory. She could hear his gruff voice carrying across the courtyard as they brought him indoors.

"You'll need your stiffest tonics, ladies. I ain't no lightweight, and this pain would've killed one of you by now."

Sister Alba rolled her eyes; Mouse thought she saw a smile as well.

"Well," she said, turning her attention back to Mouse and Toma. "You two don't seem like the ruffians I'd expect in Dane's company. Indeed, you aren't what I would expect at all. I'm very curious about you and what brings you here."

Toma ran his fingers through his hair and let out a nervous chuckle. "It's a long story."

"I'm sure," the Prioress smiled, her eyes resting on Mouse. "In good time. But now we must be your ready servants and helpful hosts. To rooms, baths, bed– whatever we can offer as we prepare a meal in your honor. Though I warn you, our way of life may be much more meager than to what you may be accustomed. We want for little, but we do subsist humbly in the Priory."

"Thank you. I can't remember the last time I've seen a bed," Toma said. "I'm sure they'll be great! Well, as long as they're not stuffed with rocks and roots."

"Indeed," Sister Alba laughed. "We reserve those types of beds for the flagellants."

"What?" Mouse asked.

"Never mind," Sister Alba said with a chuckle. "Come with me."

The Prioress showed Toma to an old barracks of the original fortress, now repurposed to house male visitors. Though the outside of the little building seemed gloomy and maybe too reminiscent of the barracks Mouse once called home, it was cheery and welcoming on the inside. Mouse got a quick look before Sister Alba lectured both of them on the rule of separation of the male quarters from the sisters' rooms and shooed her out. She was sure Toma was already snoring by the time they got outside.

Soon Mouse was following close behind Sister Alba into the Priory, through softly lit corridors, and up several flights of wide, smooth steps that twisted oddly as they went. Walls of masoned stone and laid brick suddenly gave way to rough, striated slabs of rock.

"It is incomprehensible, given what we know of technological advances of the time, but the ancient Elmlings who built this fortress burrowed much of it into the mountain itself. The sisters sleep in the first rooms embedded in the rock here, but we have not ventured much farther than that for safety reasons. It may go deeper, much deeper, in fact, but many of those old passages have caved over the long years. As you will see, the sisters' rooms are quite close to the surface. It may be rather silly, but even with what prowls outside the walls of the Priory, I prefer to have my exits outward instead of within."

Mouse walked behind her in the dimness of the mountain tunnel, wishing the Prioress hadn't said anything about the unsettling depths the Elmlings may have plumbed. They rounded the corner, coming to an open hall. Rows of lit sconces brightened the wide space, illuminating the carved open doorways of the sisters' plain bedrooms. Many of the rooms were empty, but Mouse also saw women kneeling beside their beds, reading tomes by lamplight in their bedrooms' corners, or scratching quills on yellowed parchment as they leaned over simple wooden desks. The crushing and unsettling feeling of entering the mountainside left her, and Mouse breathed a sigh of relief.

"Here we are," the Prioress said, showing Mouse inside one of the small, vacant rooms. "More sisters will return here to their quarters before supper as they finish up the day's duties, but they shall be quiet and will not disturb you. Here is a clean bed and an extra lamp should you require it. A chest here – I apologize, we have no locks here for the sisters share all in common – but I hope you shall find us trustworthy and honorable; no one shall enter your cell without your permission. There is also a bath pool at the far end to use as you need. Another ingenuity of the Elmlings. It is fed by heated springs within the mountain."

"Thank you, really. You've been very kind," Mouse said, already imagining how luxurious a warm bath would be.

The Prioress dipped her head in acknowledgment. "Is there anything else I can offer, child?"

Mouse rubbed her arms, sighing as she surveyed the room. Ever since she arrived at the Priory, Mouse felt the emptiness of her lost memory more acutely than before. Elmnas as of yet brought no flashes of the past, despite Toma's optimism that it should. Instead, her mind seemed drowned in shadow, and the roiling red skies and sinister mists only added to her sense of foreboding. *What if Blade was wrong? What if I find I don't belong here at all?*

"I do have a question," Mouse said. She looked away, biting her lip. *How much can I say?* "Do I look like an Elmling to you?"

Sister Alba cocked her head. "Do you not know?"

"I don't," Mouse said. "The truth is, I don't remember anything before a few years ago. Before..."

She trailed off, fidgeting and scratching the scar on the back of her hand. Even so, the Prioress nodded knowingly, her face stony. "It was the Coalition, wasn't it? Holding you in a prison, somewhere, far from home."

Mouse's eyes grew wide. "How did you—"

Sister Alba held up her hand, peeked out the door, and lowered her voice. "It is unwise of me to say, child. It is not safe to talk of what's happened in Elmnas – and out of Elmnas – not even for those of Gormlaean blood. But I must say it. You see, I have lived here long, and have seen and heard many things. Terrible things. Too many horrors I cannot bear to repeat. But I can say this: no Elmling is human in the eyes of the Coalition. I'm so sorry, but I am not surprised they have taken your past from you."

"So, you think I really am from here?"

"Well, you seem to have Elmling blood, but you are not quite... You seem a bit..."

"Different?" Mouse supplied.

"Yes, child. You might pass for Gormlaean in some ways. I am curious about your past."

"Me too," Mouse said. "But I'm not so sure things would be better if I knew. I don't know what else they took from me, but I have some ideas."

The Prioress smiled sadly. "I wish I had words. But the Unseen sees. May it be that he restores all things in your days."

"You keep talking about the Unseen," Mouse said. "I had a friend who mentioned it, too. I gathered it was a deity of Elmnas. But why do you follow it?"

"That is a good question. It has a long answer. Please–" She lowered herself into the wooden chair by the desk and motioned for Mouse to take a seat. Mouse obliged, plopping onto the springy, quilted blanket of the surprisingly comfortable bed. If she had laid down, Mouse might have fallen asleep. But as the Prioress spoke, sleepiness fled, and Mouse listened.

"Long ago, in the days before the birthing of the Coalition's revolution, when my people still worshipped spirits, Gormlaen was a much different place. The cities of Gormlaen each had kings of their own. We were becoming something of a real nation then. The Gormlaean Civil War had ended and there was peace. My people looked to the future with hope. We were becoming a great and strong empire. It was then a stranger of the far north passed into the land. He was beggarly, entering cities and shouting in the streets, but it was known to all who heard that this was no ordinary man. He was called a seer, a knowing one, for he spoke of things no foreigner could know. And yet he did not speak his name. He called himself only Eneshkin. That is, as we Ameliorites later came to learn, a Guardian of Elmnas. Specifically, a Keeper."

"This Eneshkin had come with an oracle. And everywhere he went, he spoke these words:

Hear, old Gor! Raise your heads, ancient Mlan! Listen, cities of Gormlaen, to the voice of the Unseen.

You whose hands still drip with the blood of your brothers,
Who still hunger for war,
Who devour the weak,
You who wrest power from all–
Your hour of glory comes.
Only remember:
The Unseen Sees, the Unseen Knows.
Every deed done in darkness shall be excoriated in light;
Though you blot out the sun and smile in shadow.
The lion prowls proudly in the night,
But Dawn comes with Fire; new life with death.

And from a child's hand shall your ruin hasten.

"As you might imagine, this wasn't exactly a popular message. The Eneshkin was driven from every city; many sought to put him to death. Eventually, they would succeed. The Keeper perished in the last city; Pardaetha. But not before he bestowed his last gift. You see, there were a small number of Gormlaeans who truly heard, who believed and desired to avert our people's doom. Before he died, the Eneshkin entrusted them with a collection of oracles, scrolls of the Guardians. His last words called them to make amends.

"This was the beginning of the Ameliorites. For years, this small sect of men and women alike copied and studied the scrolls in secret, fearing the same fate as the Eneshkin. Some sought pilgrimages to Elmnas, but none succeeded. But as with all things, the strange seer of Elmnas passed from Gormlaen's collective memory. Only the Ameliorites kept him alive and sought his Unseen; only we trembled when the city states revolted and the Coalition rose to its power; only we wept during the Last War and when the sun was veiled in the rolling curtain of red cloud. After the war it was finally possible for the brothers and sisters to come to Elmnas. Too late, I fear. Far too late. For Gormlaen and Elmnas alike. But we are here, seeking after the Unseen and making our feeble amends."

Mouse eyed Sister Alba thoughtfully, brimming with questions as she absorbed the tale. She tried to focus on her most pressing ones.

"So... what's become of the Elmlings?"

Sister Alba sighed. "The Guardians are gone, but the people are still here. They are sorely oppressed by the Coalition, though there are those who work willingly with them and have profited at the expense of their neighbors. Other tribes have retreated to the far north, where the Coalition has not yet conquered or stamped out the remnant's will. You see, some years ago, as we Ameliorites spread and established our communes throughout the country, there was a rebellion, but it failed."

"The Elmling raids."

"Yes," Sister Alba nodded. "They might have succeeded, too, had their own kin not betrayed them. The Coalition crushed many mercilessly after that."

"Did you know the rebels? Did you know Grigus Gildar?" Mouse asked hopefully.

"I did not. It was before I was Prioress here, though it is rumored that Grigus visited the Priory once. It is said he believed us Coalition spies, and came to kill the Ameliorites as traitors, but was persuaded with the sisters' humility. And vats of wine." The Prioress smiled. "It may be misremembered, though. Our oldest sister was here then, but she is prone to embellishment."

"I see," Mouse said with some disappointment. "I had a friend who I think fought beside him. There is someone I need to find for him... because he can't."

"Your loss is great, child." The Prioress placed a gentle hand on Mouse's. "Much has passed from the world's memory, but what is lost may yet be found."

"I hope I can believe that like you do," Mouse said. "Although I don't get it. Even you said you think it's too late. How do you trust this 'Unseen' when nothing good has come of all your efforts so far?"

"I do fear it, yes, but I would not say nothing good has come of it. We are here, yes? Even with much evil, great kindness has been brought to Elmnas as the Ameliorites follow the Unseen's guidance. Indeed, we still have the Guardian scrolls, and in them there is hope. I believe 'Dawn comes with Fire.' We await the revealing of the Unseen. Though it is long coming, we will live and die with that hope, working tirelessly to make this world brighter. We seek to make it ready for the Phoenix to come, when all will be reborn. It's what the oracles have foretold."

Mouse eyed the Prioress warily. "And what if someone saw visions of this Phoenix? What would you say to that?"

Sister Alba scrutinized Mouse in return. "I would say that someone should heed it closely. Such a vision is a gift and a warning.

The Phoenix will come in the power of the Unseen. We do not bid or control its arrival. One will either be purified by its fire or consumed entirely."

Mouse let out a long sigh.

"Thank you for sharing your story. It's helped me understand a lot. I think, anyway."

"I am glad," Sister Alba smiled. "Now, off to washing up and a rest. I look forward to speaking with you and your companion more at dinner."

Mouse nodded in return, watching as the Prioress rose and left with graceful, quiet steps. Sister Alba shot stern glances at the other sisters close by, five of them who Mouse now realized were lingering by her doorway. They dispersed quickly at the Prioress's shooing, except for one. A pale, freckled face gazed into the room, sea-blue eyes wide in wonder. Mouse smiled and offered a little wave.

"I'm Mouse. What's your name?"

The girl hurried off without a word. Puzzled, Mouse sighed and laid back on her bed.

Dane was right, she thought. *These people are strange.*

8

Mouse followed a group of sisters through the winding corridor to the dining hall, wonder-struck as she touched her hair and skin. The naturally warm and mineral-fed waters of the underground spring rejuvenated both her body and spirit, and for the first time since she could remember, Mouse was smooth all over. She didn't even have grit in her hair, which had grown long and unruly outside of Misty Summit's walls. There she had taken a pair of stolen scissors to it weekly – long hair was a liability there – but on their long journey it had fallen down past her shoulders. And now, when it was clean, combed, and left to dry without tying it back or stuffing under a cowl, it shimmered in the lamplight and curled delicately at its ends.

As much as she liked that new style, Mouse was less enthusiastic about the other new thing: a loose-fitting burgundy gown the sisters insisted on her wearing. She had refused, of course. Her traveling garb would suffice. But as she tried to grab for her mud-splattered boots and sweat-drenched trousers, the knot of women snatched them away with motherly horror and proffered the clean clothing instead. There were no mirrors in the sisters' quarters ("Vanity leads only to idleness and pride" one sister explained), so Mouse had no idea what she *actually* looked like, but she felt stupid. She wriggled under the heavy fabric, tripped on the too-long hem, and tugged at the knotted cord around her waist. Mouse sighed. *Well, at least these little slippers are comfortable*, she thought, wiggling her toes.

The group emerged from the mountain caverns and into an upper corridor of the old fortress. No light came in through the thin arrow slits in the wall's recesses; only the sconces between illuminated their way. Outside, a spectral howl keened in the distance. Mouse shuddered, and it seemed the quiet group of Ameliorites ahead picked up their pace.

But as they twisted along, descended stairs, and followed the inviting glow of the lit halls to the mouth of the dining room, Mouse forgot the ghostly wail and its monstrous owner. She beheld instead the cheerful sight of food-laden tables, a blazing hearth, and smiling faces as she and the sisters filed in through the door. Mouse quickly found Toma at the other side of the hall, conspicuous among the purple-clad sisters. Also newly washed and wearing what appeared to be an oversized brown woolen dress of his own, he grinned and waved.

Despite the movement and busyness that normally accompanied a mealtime, Mouse thought the room unusually quiet. The sisters did not speak, but shuffled silently to their places and stood in front of the benches that served as seats. She tentatively followed, standing awkwardly beside one sister at the end of the table. The swishing of dresses and the soft padding of slippered feet ceased, and the hall became still. All eyes faced the far end, where, from a low, dark doorway, the graceful figure of Sister Alba entered. She glanced around for a moment, and, seemingly satisfied, closed her eyes and stretched her arms up and out. In one hand she raised aloft the beaded cord, holding the iridescent green stone between her thumb and forefinger. Mouse noticed the sisters also holding beaded cords and little green stones of their own in the cupped palms of their hands. She peered intently at the one in the hand of the sister beside her. *Definitely Cardanthium*, she thought, and marveled.

Sister Alba's voice boomed over the motionless congregation. "From the oracle of Keeper Beatana, a song and a blessing."

Who among you desires joy and plenty?
Ask your Maker, who gives all good things.
Flower in spring, fruit in harvest.
The Unseen sees, the Unknown knows,
And those who seek well shall be well in soul.
At his table alone does the cup overflow;
Joy and plenty is in his words.

"May it be so?"

Mouse peered about with curiosity as the women answered in chorus.

"May it be so."

Benches scraped as the Ameliorites sat down, and with relish they passed around the heaping bowls and filled goblets. Mouse began to sit, but the Prioress caught her eye and beckoned to her.

"Mouse, good to see you refreshed!" She said as she met her, clasping her hand warmly. "I thought you might like to sit with Toma, me, and some of our other esteemed sisters. Is that alright?"

"Yes, thanks," Mouse answered, sitting down beside Toma.

"Here we are," Sister Alba said. "Dane is too unwell to join us tonight, but I assure you, he is in good care. Isn't that right, Raelin?"

The sister beside the Prioress, a younger woman that reminded Mouse much of her first friend at Misty Summit, nodded. "Yes, indeed. He should recover quickly, thank the Maker, although I don't think that shoulder will ever be quite the same. Your friend should feel blessed, though. If that blast had been any closer to his chest, I don't think he'd have survived. I've done what I can, and I pray it will be satisfactory."

"Oh Raelin, you are far too humble." Sister Alba smiled. "Your skills as a healer are beyond any I've seen in all my years here."

"I heal only through the great healer himself," Raelin said.

"Yes, of course. But your training in the greatest healing school of Reidara may have helped. Raelin comes to us from Irala, a city in Heibeiath," Sister Alba explained. "Irala's knowledge of the workings of the body is legendary."

"Don't healers make a lot of money? What brought you here?" Toma asked incredulously.

"I was called here," Raelin smiled gently. "Even the lure of wealth is not as lovely as the song of the Unseen."

"I'll take your word for it," Toma shrugged.

As they spoke, the sisters passed along the dishes, all of which made Mouse's eyes bulge. Roasted pheasant swimming in gravy, cooked cabbage, heaps of mashed potatoes, honeyed carrots, and flaky biscuits came across her plate. The meal, as Sister Alba implied, may have been simple to Gormlaean tastes, but Mouse had not seen such a spread since breakfast at the Breythorn family farm ages ago. She tucked in eagerly, remembering with delight that seasoning existed, and not everything needs to be cooked unevenly over a fickle campfire.

The Prioress continued to make introductions between the pageantry of plate passing. "This is Sister Astri, a wise and honest woman indeed, and Sister Lael, our very gifted gardener, and Sister Tanys, who has just graduated from novice to full initiate. She takes a vow of silence now, so please do not think her rude if she does not answer. And this–"

Sister Alba motioned to the freckled girl sitting farthest from Mouse, whom she recognized from earlier. The young sister joined them and silently waited beside the Prioress, her cheeks pink with embarrassment. Her eyes flitted from Sister Alba to the strangers before her. Sister Alba placed a hand gently on her shoulder, looking directly at the girl as she spoke.

"This is Sister Fraeda. She is our second youngest novice. Oh, I suppose I should explain that to you. A novice is someone who comes to the Ameliorites as a sort of... an apprentice. She works beside us, memorizes the teachings of the Guardians, and learns the disciplines of the way of the Unseen. The time is fast approaching for her initiate interview."

At this, the Prioress grinned, turned to Mouse and Toma, and covered her mouth. "Between the three of us, I can think of no reason to refuse her should she choose us. Her gentleness, work ethic, and compassion put even me to shame."

Sister Fraeda waited nervously as the Prioress turned back toward her. "This is Mouse and Toma."

"Hey, how's it going?" Toma said between bites.

"Nice to meet you," Mouse added, smiling. "I hope I didn't scare you earlier."

Fraeda watched Mouse intently as she spoke, then turned and made motions to Sister Alba. The Prioress watched closely and then turned back to Mouse.

"She says she hopes she did not frighten you! She was just very curious."

"Have you taken a vow of silence, too?" Mouse asked.

The girl shook her head sadly and looked down at the floor.

"Fraeda has been deaf from a young age," the Prioress explained. "She does not speak because of it. This was a challenge when she first came to us, but our little sister is bright and resourceful. Fraeda can read lips flawlessly, in both Gormlaean and Elmling, and we have developed a system of hand signs to help her communicate."

Sister Alba squeezed Fraeda's shoulder lovingly. "It's nice to meet some people your age, isn't it?"

Fraeda looked at Toma and Mouse thoughtfully. She smiled more with her large blue eyes than her mouth as she allowed a timid nod and then hurried back to her place.

"Give her time," Sister Alba chuckled. "She's very shy."

Mouse glanced down the table at the Ameliorite novice, trying not to appear nosy. Fraeda sunk back onto the bench meekly, reaching with unobtrusive hands for the last biscuit in the basket in front of her. The girl's eyes continued to flick about the room observantly, resting occasionally on Mouse and Toma. Mouse sensed not much escaped Fraeda's comprehension, as unassuming and inconspicuous as she seemed. *And a true Elmling!* Mouse thought, itching to know more of her story. Their eyes met, and Mouse offered a reassuring nod and wave. This time, Fraeda smiled easily.

The meal continued for some time, though after the initial introductions, it became a far quieter affair, and no one spoke much as they finished their dinners. Sister Alba asked about their journey, and Mouse and Toma told the story as vaguely as they could. Mouse left out the ominous charge from Red to deliver the odd piece of Coalition technology to who knows where in Elmnas, as well as the strange visions of the Phoenix and the trio's miraculous river crossing. It was impossible to avoid their troubles, however, and Mouse's search for her home and family in the forbidden country. The Prioress did not press for details. Mostly, she listened sympathetically. *Maybe,* Mouse thought, *the story I bring now is not so different from the many she's heard before. Who else have the Ameliorites sheltered from stalking death?*

All too soon, the hall filled with the sounds of clinking cups, of scraping against plates, and the movement of the sisters as they cleared away the meal's remains. Toma stood to help, but Sister Alba insisted they enjoy being guests for the evening.

Toma sighed and plopped back down, deciding instead to nurse the mug of steaming tea Sister Raelin urged both of them to drink before bed.

"I'll tell you something," Toma said, staring into the muddy liquid. "I've never been anywhere as strange as this place. I can't make sense of half the things they do or say."

"Glad it's not just me," Mouse whispered in agreement. "By the way, what's with the dress? Does no one here wear pants?"

"It's not a dress!" Toma said indignantly. "They call it a *robe*. But I guess not. It's what the male Ameliorites, the brothers, they call them, wear. It's actually kinda... roomy. Of course, as soon as my pants are clean, I'm ditching it."

"Yeah, me too," Mouse scoffed, examining the skirt of her own dress. "I feel so weird."

Toma shrugged. "Well, it's not so bad. You look really... uh, really nice. Not that you didn't before! It's just, um, different. Good different? Uh..."

He puffed his reddening cheeks, swirling the tea vigorously. Mouse also gazed into her tea, wondering what in the world she was supposed to do with that. And why did she feel so warm all of a sudden?

"Well, thanks. You, um, look nice too," Mouse said, and she immediately regretted it. She quickly added, "I mean, look how clean we are! I can see the actual color of my fingernails for maybe the first time ever."

Toma chuckled gratefully. "Yeah, it's good to have all that Gormlaean dirt off my face. Really, I still can't believe we got here."

"About that," Mouse said, fishing out the loose tea leaves in the bottom of her cup. "What do we do now? We're here, and I had an interesting talk with the Prioress earlier, but I don't think I learned anything... immediately helpful. In fact, I think I'm even more confused about my visions now."

"What did you talk about?"

Mouse recounted the conversation. Toma let out a low whistle. "And you didn't tell her what you saw?"

Mouse shook her head. "She seems like a kind person, but it still didn't feel like a good idea. What if the Coats *do* come here looking for us? Maybe I'm selling her short, but she doesn't look like a great liar. Not to mention this whole Phoenix thing... these sisters have come from all over, waiting here for something big to happen, for the fulfillment of these old writings. How do you think they'd act if I told them what I'd saw? And what if nothing came of it? How can I know what's real when I can't even remember who I am?"

"Hm, I see your point," Toma said. "It was probably the right thing to do... although I'd love to hear her thoughts on our little boat ride of certain death."

"I wonder if someone else could help with that," Mouse mused, watching the freckled novice busily clearing dishes.

"Sister Fraeda?" Toma asked. "Don't you think it might be hard to, um, get anything out of her?"

"If she can read, she can probably write. We both know Elmling, right? We could talk that way."

Toma gave a noncommittal shrug and half-stifled a yawn. "Worth a try, I guess. As for me, that bed is calling my name. You should get some rest, too. It's been... a hard day. We can talk about an exit strategy in the morning?"

"Sure." Mouse stared into the bottom of her empty mug.

"Hey," Toma said softly, touching her arm. Mouse looked up into his amber eyes, seeing weariness and concern. "It's not your fault, okay? Blade would want us to go on. And I think... I think maybe he'd have a little more hope himself if he could've seen what you did today."

Mouse mustered a weak smile. "Okay."

With a parting nod, Toma bade Mouse and the sisters a good night. As she watched him leave, she wondered at his words. Toma could say it wasn't her fault as much as he wanted. Maybe he believed it himself. That didn't make it true.

One thing's certain, she thought. *There's no way I sleep as well as him tonight.* Losing Blade had not hit her full force, not yet – not when there was work to do and people to navigate. But in the deep, black quiet, in the empty night when survival and subterfuge no longer pressed hard and occupied her every thought, Mouse would be alone with herself. She'd be left to drown in her compounding grief, every loss she had witnessed chain-linked to her weakness, her utter dependency, her failure. Why couldn't she fight, or save, or shake off the death that trailed her everywhere? And where would it end? What was the point?

Suddenly, the clear voice of the Prioress rang out across the hall, echoing off the ancient stone in a haunting melody.

When deepest dark o'er take thee

All joys forsake and hopes flee
When wells of grief are too deep
Where does thou find true peace?

Mouse's gaze snapped up to Sister Alba. Had she somehow... known Mouse's thoughts? She relaxed as she saw the Prioress in a posture of prayer, her arms outstretched as it was at the beginning of the meal. The Ameliorites responded in kind, dropping their cleaning accessories and kneeling wherever they stood. With palms up and outstretched, the sisters held their glistening green gems above them. Sister Alba continued:

Courage, dear heart, must thou seek
In fear, distress, calamity
One day the Light shall bind these
And cause every sorrow cease.

As the soft glow imbued the hall, the sisters added their voices to the song:

So we are made for times as these
As starlight speaks of Dawn's decrees
Night must yield, and we shall see
The undying Fire, Sun and Key
All made right, all made free
May it ever be.

Even as the reverberation died away, and the soft sound of slippered feet shuffled off to finish chores or to bed, Mouse stared up where the green glow seemed to linger. A tickle against her cheek broke the trance, and she wiped at it, amazed to find a shiny streak of a tear on her fingertip. Before that moment, it had never occurred to her that she could not remember the last time she let herself cry.

9

Go back to sleep.

Mouse gazed up at the familiar dark brows, knit together with concern. She stared at the corners of the frightened eyes, creased with the hints of age and care. Strong arms, safe arms, arms she longed to hold her forever, tightened, shielding Mouse from the raging wall of flames, the screams of terror, the thuds of falling silhouettes that spasmed briefly and exhaled into silence.

Overhead, a pop, and the crimson sky exploded. Mouse hurtled forward, tumbling into the conflagration of white and orange light. It dissipated into darkness, and she tumbled on, rolling down, down, down. Her body came to rest. Long blades of grass brushed against her arms and legs. She smelled the must of Reidara's soil, felt its rocks and roots beneath her. *I'm dreaming,* she thought. *But where am I?*

Mouse stood up, brushed herself off, and gazed around. A valley, shrouded in shadow, stretched to her right and left, its tall grasses and wildflowers whispering softly as the breeze breathed through it. Behind her, the slope of a great hill loomed, and before her rose a tangle of dark, tall limbs and trunks. And among them, she sensed a familiar presence.

Light weaved among the trees, disappearing and reappearing as it passed slowly beyond them. Mouse waited, breathless, but it did not emerge. It came to rest at the edge of the forest, just behind the first row of foliage. The effervescent form of the phoenix rustled its gilded wings and cocked its head. She perceived an eye fixed upon her, emerald green and as bright as the bird itself. And there they stood, staring at one another, Mouse transfixed and unsure of its intent.

"Well, little one, what do yeh think it wants?"

Mouse squeaked at the voice, turning sharply to its owner. Standing beside her, as if he had been with her all along, was none other than Red. He, too, looked out at the forest, his massive arms crossed over his barrel chest.

"Wh-what are you– how–" Mouse sputtered. "Are you– are you actually here? Are you... a ghost?"

Red chuckled, smacking Misty Summit's soot from his coveralls before shrugging. "It's your dream, little one. How should I know?"

Mouse stared back in confounded silence.

"Anyway," Red continued, nodding toward the trees. "Maybe it's not that important. Tell me what yeh think of that, and I'm sure it'll all come aright then."

"I–" She stopped herself, turning and straining to comprehend. Red was becoming hazy and muddled, his voice like a distant memory. But the bird; the bird remained clear. Its eye, it's emanating heat, its shimmering form now seemed to enlarge before her.

"Focus, little one," Red said quietly. "What do yeh need to do?"

"I think..." she drawled. "I think it wants me to follow it."

Red nodded approvingly. "And what then?"

"I don't know." Mouse answered. "How can I know?"

Red grinned and ruffled her hair. "Yeh'll know soon enough. Look again."

Ahead, dark figures streamed into the trees. She recognized some of them. Toma turned and gave a thumbs up. Sister Alba strode in wonder. The woman... dark brows relaxed as she gathered her skirts and ran with abandon. Many appeared that she didn't, or couldn't, recognize. Tall, cloaked figures, hints of a greenish glow hazing about their waists, stalked along the tree line with a stream of people, all kinds of people, in their wake; following came warriors armed with broadswords and battleaxes all silhouetted against the phoenix's unburning fire. They approached it, brightened gloriously in its glow before becoming light themselves as they huddled under its outstretched wings. There was singing, she was sure of it, a wordless song rising from the rocks and trees themselves. Flashes like lightning illuminated the forest, and Mouse saw strange and changing things, things she could hardly begin to understand let alone describe. Two things remained comprehensible; the image of a man, the feathers of the phoenix extending beyond his raised arms and coalescing into the distinct glow of sharp, Cardanthium blades; and a freckled girl, clothed in the habit of the Ameliorites, standing at the gate of Priory.

Even now, will you follow?

A tempestuous roar now swelled in the valley, and Mouse looked around wildly. The clouds above swirled with an increasing wind, and the forest bowed to its growing power. Black, seething mists poured out from the tree line, funneling toward her, and in it, nightmarish shapes and blood-curdling howls. She cried out as the shape of Mistwolves loped toward her at breakneck pace. And still there were other things, monsters without names, whose very forms tore the breath to scream from her lungs.

Will you follow?

And just as intensely as it had come, it was gone.

Mouse and Red stood alone in the quiet field, the smell of dewy wildflowers, grass, and earth heavy in the still air. Red let out a low whistle.

"My dreams never did that, I tell yeh!" Red laughed.

"What's happening to me, Red? It still doesn't make sense. What does it want from me?"

"Follow," he said.

She turned to her old friend, her heart dropping as even now he became translucent, wisping like smoke beneath the starless sky. Tears filled her eyes. "I wish... I wish you could come with me."

Red smiled tenderly, sadly. His face hovered in the consuming tendrils of smoke and shadow. With one final breath of the twilight breeze, he was gone.

Mouse opened her eyes. Dim lanterns passed by her doorway, disturbing the darkness of the Ameliorite chamber. She pushed off the heavy quilt, the chill of the cavern's early morning air a welcome respite for her sweat-drenched limbs. Mouse wiped sweat from her forehead as well, aware that her pillow was unbearably hot. It puzzled her for only a moment as she remembered what she had placed beneath it the evening before.

Lifting the pillow, Mouse cradled the Cardanthium dagger Blade left with her only two days before. From beneath its leather covering, Mouse could see its blue-green glow, and cautiously she withdrew it from the case. She shielded her eyes at its sudden blaze and gasped when a wall of heat slammed into her face. Hastily returning the dagger to its place, Mouse hopped out of the bed and searched for her gown from the night before. Instead, she found another outfit, compliments of the sisters: a muted green frock with stockings and clogs. Mouse grimaced but pulled them on, anyway.

At least it has pockets, Mouse thought, jamming her hands into the pouch-like openings on the sides. She cast a glance toward the dagger resting on the bed. Its glow had dimmed now, and Mouse sensed the inexplicable heat had dissipated as well. This she grabbed, along with the wad of Red's journal and the chip that she could not bear to keep out of touch or sight. Looking out the door and finding herself alone, Mouse slipped into the adjoining cavern and through the halls of the Priory.

She emerged from the Priory and stepped out into a crisp, chilled morning. The light of dawn was just cresting the fortress walls, changing the deep shadows of night into a lightening gray across the Priory's grounds. Nothing stirred outside except for her, but the drone of chanting and snippets of song somewhere within the Priory told Mouse that the sisters had already started their day. Mouse wandered slowly along the grounds before pausing in a serene garden. She sat on the stone bench within it and closed her eyes, breathing in the scent of dewy flower, grass, and earth. *I can see why they live here now*, she thought.

The sound of a metallic scrape roused her. Mouse looked round to see an old sister raking the dirt bed a few yards off. To her surprise, the woman was already looking at her, a toothless grin on her face.

"Good morning," the Ameliorite said. "Have we met before?"

Mouse searched the woman's face, which was exceedingly pale and crinkled. She frowned. "I don't think so."

"Are you sure?" the old sister asked, her wrinkles deepening as she peered intently at Mouse. She set down her rake and shuffled toward her. "I think–"

At that moment, the woman's dull eyes lit up. "Niiri! Why, it must be Niiri. But then... again..." Her face scrunched together in thought. "No, no, that can't be it. Niiri would be quite a bit older, quite a bit indeed. Why, but you *must* be Niiri. Or something like her, I expect. Yes, yes, of course! What is your name, child?"

"Um, well, I don't know, to be honest. People call me Mouse."

"Is that so, hmm? I think I shall call you... daughter of Niiri." The old woman grinned again. "Yes, that is it. A lost one returned from the Succor of Samras."

Mouse leaned forward. "Who are you?"

At this, the sister cackled. "I'm certain I don't know. And who are you? Why, it's Niiri! Does your papa know you've run off again?"

"There you are, Sister Legathe! I thought I might find you here."

Mouse looked to see the gardener, Sister Lael, approaching. Relief and daughterly concern mingled in her features.

"Sister, we have been worried sick about you! Why have you left bed without telling anyone? It's a wonder you haven't fallen and broken anything!"

"I must tend the garden," Sister Legathe said vaguely, grasping weakly at the rake. "It has been my duty for... for..."

"For thirty years, of course," said Sister Lael gently. She placed the rake behind her. "But I care for the garden now, remember? Why don't you come rest? Sister Raelin is waiting with your tea."

"Who?" The old woman crinkled her brow. Her eyes lost focus as she stared at the dirt.

"Come, elder sister. We shall walk together," Sister Lael lifted her carefully. Mouse moved to assist, shocked at the feel of papery skin and light, brittle bone. Sister Lael mouthed her thanks and more or less carried Sister Legathe off the grounds.

Mouse watched the women go, dazed by the odd conversation. *Daughter of Niiri?* Mouse pondered the words of the aged sister. Were they the meaningless prattlings of a senile old woman, or was it more? Did Mouse resemble someone the sister knew in a past life, and was that someone...

She shook the thought away. Speculation would not do her any good; and that would be the best she could get from even Sister Alba on who she might be. Still, maybe some real answers would. With last night's strange dream resurfacing in her mind, Mouse hurried off into the Priory in search of a certain someone who might have them. Sisters smiled and nodded to Mouse as she passed inside, and Mouse searched their faces for Fraeda. She found the Prioress instead, who bowed serenely at her approach.

"Good morning, child. I see you are an early riser as well. Are you in search of your companion? I have not yet seen him emerge from his quarters, but the morning bell shall announce breakfast soon. I hope that is enough to rouse him! Would you like to accompany me to the dining hall?"

"Actually, I'm looking for someone else," Mouse cocked her head. "Do you know where Fraeda might be?"

"Ah, of course. Take this corridor. You ought to find her at her chores there."

"Thank you," Mouse said, hustling through the passage without another word.

The corridor remained dark despite the brightening of the morning, and Mouse descended some stairs into a dim, cool passage. The air changed, exhaling the musty scent of an underground world beyond the tunnels. Phosphorescent fungi pushed through the cracks of stone on the floor and walls, casting the passage in a muted blue glow. Even so, Mouse grabbed the walking lamp at the mouth of the passage and continued on.

Presently Mouse came upon stone doorways as she passed. She peeked inside the first, finding an unoccupied cellar filled with enormous wooden barrels. A dark sticky substance covered the floor in places, and spouts toward the bottoms of the barrels indicated the cellar's purpose. *Ah,* she thought. *This must be where Dane got himself in trouble.*

Shaking her head at his hubris, Mouse pressed on into the tunnel. It began to slope downward, the cobbled stones of the floor becoming slick with the growing damp. Ahead, the yellow glow of a lamp spilled out onto the passage's floor in a soft semicircle, revealing another doorway in the lonely tunnel. Mouse slipped inside and peered around. Though the lamp sat unattended on the floor, it illuminated the room; or rather, the piles of things filling it. Everywhere Mouse looked, she saw fantastic treasures. Shelves overflowed with rusting swords and battleaxes, large, empty portrait frames, worn pots and dust-choked glass jugs. The things that could not fit on the shelves were strewn about, piled against the shelving in no discernible order. Mouse wandered through the rows, holding her lamp up to get a better look.

"Hello?" Mouse called, then cringed as she remembered Fraeda wouldn't hear or answer. "Guess I'll just have to try not to sneak up on you."

Sweeping the lamp from side to side as conspicuously as possible,

Mouse walked slowly along a tight row of shelving. The narrow row grew even smaller as Mouse brushed past the junk spilling from the shelves. Lamplight glittered on their many surfaces, refracting and bouncing off the objects it touched, even as the layers of dust muted them. One such object, a peeling and dust-marred mounted canvas, jutted out from beneath piles of defunct machinery. Mouse tried to squeeze past it, but the fabric of her frock snagged on the splintered wood of the now exposed backing. The picture shifted, along with everything piled on top of it, and tumbled to the floor.

"No no no no!" Mouse cried, dropping to her knees and desperately gathering the gears, bolts, and washers rolling in every direction. After she had caught a handful in her skirt, she turned to attend to the canvas.

Mouse gasped, promptly dropping everything once again. Though on its side against the shelf and obscured in gray dust, the prominent portrait seemed to leap out of its frame and grab her by the sleeve. In it stood a man, broad and imposing, leaning against his massive battle-axe and staring back at her with brilliant green eyes. A shock of red, shaggy hair crowned his head, matching the round, rubicund cheeks beneath it. Gingerly Mouse wiped the dust away, her breathing shallow and labored as each gentle brushing revealed what she already knew.

"Red," she whispered. "Is it really you?"

10

As the years of grime came away on Mouse's frock, the image beneath resolved all the more clearly into a young, robust Red. The background behind him, a forested hill somewhere in Elmnas, revealed few other contextual clues, but his heroic pose exuded all the strength and confidence of a celebrated warrior. *But why?* Mouse thought. *Who could you possibly be?*

"That's Grigus Gildar."

Though as gentle as a soft breeze, the voice startled Mouse. She jumped up abruptly, turning to see Sister Fraeda. The freckled novice looked on bashfully, twisting and bunching the front of her purple robe in her small hands.

"What did you say?" Mouse said breathlessly.

Fraeda pointed. "That picture you're looking at. His name is Grigus Gildar. Leader of the Elmling Raids."

Mouse struggled to find words. "Are you– are you absolutely sure?"

Fraeda nodded. "Of course. If you've read any of the forbidden history, there is no one else he could be. It helps that I've lived through some of it, too."

"Forbidden?"

"Oh, not by the sisters. The Coalition. The true past of Elmnas isn't openly spoken of in our country, unless you want a one-way transport to the closest prison."

Amazement and disbelief stole Mouse's ability to speak. Red, *her* caring, compassionate, dedicated Red, was the fearless, terror-inducing, hardened rebellion leader Grigus Gildar? It seemed impossible, but the truth stared her in the face. Her world spun as she tried to comprehend it. Mouse turned back toward the portrait, studying the proud young man within its bounds. Memories of the first day she met him sprang into her mind. His immensity, the jagged, terrible scars running along his back and arms, the noble way he carried himself through the masses of Misty Summit as a beacon of charisma, hope, wisdom. She saw the same man staring out at her now, his bright eyes brimming with youthful ambition, daring hope, and the fierce yearning for freedom. *It's you*, she thought. *I can see it's you.* The disbelief melted away as Fraeda's words confirmed what she had always suspected. *Wait a minute. Fraeda's words?*

She eyed the novice in confusion. "You're talking. You talk. The Prioress said you couldn't."

Fraeda shifted, bouncing on her heels as she cast her eyes down to the floor. She answered haltingly, her voice soft and timid.

"That is true. I couldn't... I... didn't. I mean to say... when I came to the Priory..." Fraeda swallowed hard. "The Coats... they take people with... with defects away. People like me, you see. They come to the villages, the clans, what's left of us, and they take what they need for... for testing, they said. I was six when they came for me. My parents... you have to understand, no one dares put up a fight. Not against the Coats. I had to go... and then they did things. Things that made the words go away."

Mouse nodded vigorously as Fraeda sniffled and rubbed a hand across her eyes. Her head bobbed in the silence that followed, an attempt, she realized, to dispel her own threatening tears. Her vision blurred anyway, and Mouse wanted to run, to hide, to do anything that could shake away the nearness of the pain she had long since pushed down and convinced herself she had conquered. *Weakness,* she thought angrily. *It'll kill you if you don't get rid of it.*

Fraeda took a step closer, the light of Mouse's little lantern glinting off the shiny smear on Fraeda's round, freckled cheek. Tentatively, the girl reached out, finding Mouse's hand. Mouse went rigid. A feral part of her screamed, demanding Mouse throw off the touch with savage ferocity. But she paused as another part, small and quiet, whispered to let it be. *Does it make you stronger to pretend you don't need anyone?* She heard it say. Mouse bit back tears, and slowly, reluctantly, gave Fraeda's hand a squeeze in return. Fraeda smiled; a true, grateful grin, and Mouse realized she wasn't the only one who needed a friend.

"By the grace of the Unseen, I got away from that awful place," Fraeda continued. "I knew I couldn't go back home, so I wound up here. Like you. The sisters are good and caring, in their stern, serious sort of way. Still, I never spoke. I don't know that I could, even if I had tried."

Mouse looked at her thoughtfully. "What's changed?"

"I don't know for sure," Fraeda answered. "Like you lost your memory, I lost my words. But I think... I think when you came, I found them again. It's hard to explain. Maybe I sound crazy, but I knew it was time."

"I don't think it's crazy," Mouse said. "But it sure is convenient. I wasn't just exploring; I was looking for you. I was hoping you could help me."

"I'm not sure I can help much," Fraeda answered shyly. "The older sisters know a lot more than me about most things."

"But you're an Elmling," Mouse insisted. "And you've said yourself you've studied the forbidden history. You've lived it. Out of everyone here, I think you're my best shot. Please, does any of this mean anything to you?"

Plopping down and sitting cross-legged on the floor, Mouse pulled Red's journal from her pocket and carefully spread its contents within the ring of lamplight. Fraeda knelt beside her, her quick eyes darting from page to page. She squinted back at Mouse.

"What is this?"

Mouse pointed at the portrait behind them. "That man, the one you call Grigus Gildar, wasn't executed. The Coalition sent him to the Misty Summit Manufacturing Facility, miles away in Maiendell, where they took his memory as well as mine. I knew him as Red."

Fraeda's eyes widened as Mouse went on to share her own story; of the days in Misty Summit, the sinister administration of "physicals," and the dreaded fates of those taken by the prison's healers. Mouse's voice fell to a whisper as she recounted the events of that last day, from Red's ominous portent of his own fate to the harrowing flight into the mists. She also explained Red's findings and conclusions in these pages; what she and Toma had managed to figure out and what still needed deciphering.

"Like this," Mouse said, holding up the wild scrawl in the margins of Red's dream log.

"Take it where the light touches two giants..." Fraeda traced the words as she read them. "Hm."

"It's the thing I keep coming back to. I think I've got the 'it' worked out–" Mouse patted the place where she had safely stowed the chip. "But what's this place? Does it mean anything to you?"

"I don't want to get your hopes up." Fraeda thumbed the page as she frowned down at it. "But it's possible... No, it's more than that. There's only one place I can think of that fits that description."

Mouse restrained herself from exploding with questions as Fraeda squinted and mouthed the words on the page to herself a few times more.

"In the history I've read of a place where the Guardians of old would meet with the clan chieftains," Fraeda finally said. "It's a sacred place; a place for deciding important things for Elmnas. They call it 'Titans' Rest,' this little valley between two great big mountains on the northeastern shore of Elmnas. I can't say I *know* for sure, but if Grigus – well, Red, I guess – talks about 'two giants...' There's an old story about Titans' Rest in the history, you see. In it, Gairiel the Quick, a scribe to the Guardian Masters, so confused and exhausted two hungry giants with enigmatic riddles that they fell asleep right then and there. Being unable to dream up any answers, the giants remain that way to this day as the two mountains: Jatti and Merihr. Anyway, the point is that seems like the only place that it could be."

"Huh, I think Blade actually told us that story. But not about what Titans' Rest was for. He didn't like to talk about the Guardian stuff too much." Mouse bent over the page ponderously, cupping her chin as she rested her elbows on the floor. "But what about that light part? Red wouldn't remember the sun, would he? I thought that happened a hundred years ago."

Fraeda shrugged. "I don't know. But if you looked at Jatti and Merihr on a map, you'd see they're the country's farthest points east. When the sun rises, its first light would fall on them before anything else in Elmnas. Maybe that's important."

"Could be," Mouse nodded appreciatively. She gave Fraeda a sidelong glance. "Do you... know how to get there?"

"I don't think it's a matter of finding the way," Fraeda said softly. "That wouldn't be too difficult with a good map. But knowing *how* to get there. That's the hard part. And I can't say what you might find at Titans' Rest."

"Coalition?" Mouse asked grimly.

"Probably not, actually," Fraeda mused. "Titans' Rest happens to be one of the few places still outside of the Coalition's control. The forests are dense and confusing, impossible to navigate if you don't know it. It is said the free tribes live there still, and from the north Elmnas will find her strength again. I don't know about all that, but I do know the Coats don't like it much up there. There don't seem to be many people up there to bother with, and plenty of things you don't want to bother you. When I escaped, that's the direction I went. It's cold, even in the summer. I didn't see a soul. The wilds are dangerous, though I didn't realize just how much until I found our Brothers' monastery. They said it was a miracle I made it that far on my own. So, who knows what's at Titans' Rest now? Or what you'll meet along the way?"

I don't know, but a certain Guardian I just got killed could have gotten us there, Mouse thought. She sighed and began gathering the pages, lingering on the dream log page before she placed it within the folds of Red's cracked leather covering. Another trek through unforgiving wilderness, more creatures and Coats to avoid, all for the slim hope of finding the place Red *might* have been telling her to go. Maybe, thanks to Blade, she and Toma could hold their own in the wilds now. They might even be able to make it to Titans' Rest. But what then?

Don't forget all the impossibilities you overcame just to get here, Mouse chided herself. *What's one more? It's not like you could stay here for the rest of your life... or could you?*

That thought came with some surprise. Mouse tried to imagine herself as a novice, wrapped in a worn purple dress while scrubbing floors, reading dusty old scrolls, singing the Ameliorites' strangely beautiful songs and fully believing in the sisters' just as strange unseen. It seemed an impossible iteration of herself – trusting and faithful, gentle and communal, hopeful and content. But she could not shake away the appeal of that Mouse. Something had been stirring in her since she entered the Priory... was this it?

Mouse glanced up at Fraeda, who was now reading Red's "Accounts of the Taken." She grimaced at the revulsion in Fraeda's features, the comprehension that things Fraeda had seen herself were happening elsewhere; maybe all over the Four Dominions. Guilt bubbled up inside of Mouse as she remembered the people she knew who still lived in that nightmare. *What was the Coalition planning?* Mouse shuddered and released any pretension of staying. No, her path, wherever it led, would be haunted by the ghosts of the dead-eyed prisoners she left behind; ghosts whose ranks grew every day thanks to her delay. How many more were there now? Who else must be parted body from soul in the Coalition's unspeakable manipulations? And how could she afford to hesitate when help might be waiting for her to find it?

"Maybe there's nothing good at Titans' Rest, and maybe I'm an idiot for asking, but you said a good map could get me there," Mouse said, getting Fraeda's attention first. "Any chance you have one on hand?"

Fraeda screwed up her face and lowered her eyebrows in deep consideration. Her face softened, and Mouse thought she saw something like fear, but also something like resolve, knit her freckled forehead.

"I do," Fraeda said. She tapped on her temple and smiled back weakly. "But I keep the better one up here. You should take both."

11

A thin line of burnished orange gray crested the black mountain peaks on the Gormlaen-Elmnas border, hinting at the approach of morning. Fox's breath hung in the chilled air around her as she crouched over the remains of the fire and thwacked the charred stumps of wood. What remained split and spilled dull red embers, which writhed like fiery worms as the cold air cooled them to ash. Fox blew gently and threw sticks of increasing size into it, feeding and breathing life into the flames until they reared up again with a vengeance.

With a sidelong glance at her unconscious bounty, she set out a skillet and the five eggs she had pillaged from an unattended nest a little before dawn. She rapped them against the edge of the skillet one by one, their contents sizzling sumptuously as soon as they hit the hot pan. Leaving them to cook on the flames, Fox warmed her hands and face at a more comfortable distance away and resisted the urge to rub her eyes. She rummaged through her rucksack instead, finding a tin kettle and the last muslin bag of qava in the sack's bottom. Heibeiathans swore by the invigorating properties of the gritty powder, made from the Qavalar plant that grew abundantly in Heibeiath. The Coalition had imported it in earnest years ago, and now she wasn't so sure that most Gormlaeans could live without it. *Most Gormlaeans, including me*, Fox smirked.

Fox filled the kettle with water, set it on the fire, and watched impatiently. She hefted the muslin bag. One *could* eat qava, of course, if one was desperate enough, but it was best enjoyed brewed or, in her case now, steeped in hot water. Fox lifted the bag to her face, breathed in the qava's rich scent, and considered how desperate she was.

Rest had not come easy last night. In the shadow of these mountains, haunted by both her memories and the dangers of this wild land, she lay awake for much of the night. It came as a surprise that sleep had come at all when she jolted upright in the early hours before dawn. The Guardian had been as dead to the world as a common drunkard. Another surprise, considering his fight for consciousness yesterday. Fox peered at the Guardian again. His chest rose and fell in deep, slow breaths, but Fox marked the twitch of discomfort on his otherwise serene face with each inhale. *It's working faster than I'd expect*, Fox thought, both with concern and curiosity.

She rose from the fire and stood over Blade, arms crossed, and she wondered whether the healing tonic was the right move. Last night, it seemed the reasonable thing to do. She needed the Guardian *without* internal injuries, if Myergo wanted him alive upon arrival. In these healer-less and help-devoid wilds, the damage Blade sustained could easily spell the end of his days. The tonic also had the added benefit of relieving some of the worst effects of the sleeper's poison – splitting headaches, nausea, and fatigue – and she'd rather have the Guardian able to walk a few miles. Sure, Fox could have strapped him on the board for a while, but that would drain the power completely. She didn't have any backup crystals, so her only other option would be to coax Blade onto the horse. She scoffed. *Not much chance of that.*

Despite his current comatose state, Fox felt a flutter of nervousness in her gut. She'd had the upper hand in yesterday's fight, and still the Guardian fought with more skill and fury than any man she had encountered yet. It had taken every bit of her tactical mastery to get a sword tip near enough to even nick him. What was he like at full strength?

"Should've given you a full dose of sleeper's poison," she decided, jabbing him in the ribs.

Blade sucked in air sharply, opening his eyes as he groaned.

"Good morning, dear," she sneered. "How did you sleep? Hope the bed was comfy enough for you."

He flexed beneath the bonds on the stretcher, frowning. With a wiggle, he tested the healing of his side, and with a slight flinch signaled the tonic hadn't done its work entirely. Blade turned his stormy gray eyes upon her. "I've had worse nights."

"And worse ones to come, I'd imagine," she said. "Now, to business. I'm certain you're famished."

Blade raised an eyebrow. "How hospitable."

Fox rolled her eyes. "I have an appointment to keep, which means we will be doing a bit of walking today. If you behave, you can share my meal and have the strength to keep up, or I can drag you behind my horse."

The bounty hunter tapped her obsidian wristband. "Your choice."

He glared contemptuously, but remained silent.

"Good," Fox poked at the wristband, causing the board to whir to life and hover before her. She reached beneath the stretcher, pulling a black ring from the underside. With a few taps on her wristband and the ring itself, it separated into five, and Fox clapped one on each of Blade's feet, wrists, and his neck.

"Ah, that's better."

Fox lowered the stretcher and unfastened the straps. Blade jerked to his feet and coiled, ready to pounce in moments, but just as quickly, Fox tapped her wrist. The black rings gleamed, snapping together at Blade's feet and arms. He tottered and fell, writhing and groaning as the ring around his neck sent tiny sparks into his throat. *Too predictable.*

"I distinctly recall asking you to behave," she chided. "That was very impolite."

"*Du koul vil av minhan,*" Blade snarled.

Fox clicked her tongue and shook her head. "Such language."

She strode to the fire, pulling the sizzling skillet and the steaming kettle off the flames. "Alright then, curse me or threaten me all you want, but now you're not getting any eggs."

The Guardian convulsed. Fox ate her breakfast and enjoyed her qava.

The dark mare ambled through the sparse pines at the edge of the Swaying Forest, her footfalls deadened by the carpet of needles and moss. Fox glanced to her right, watching the Guardian through narrowed eyes as he strode alongside the horse's flank. Though the rings shackled his hands tightly to one another and a rope anchored him to the saddle, Fox's fingers still hovered close to the wristband. She didn't have to see his face to know he was watching, waiting for any opportunity to grab at her holsters, slam her from her mount with his own brute strength, or smash the wristband to pieces with the weight of his bonds. If he was hungry or fatigued or hurting, the Guardian showed no sign of it. Predatory calm masked any discomfort. He watched and waited.

How long will I have to endure this? Fox thought. She gazed up through the arms of the pines to the red-lined clouds above them. When Dervish contacted her this morning as the Guardian slept, offering coordinates to a rendezvous northwest along the mountain range, Fox immediately agreed to the compromise. Even with the extra travel to get back to the Coalition outpost, it would be quicker than waiting for Myergo's men to reach her. She could always make up the extra time. Even at a canter, her horse would cover the distance with little delay. And if she were honest with herself, the idea of spending idle time with the Guardian unsettled her. *Movement*, she decided. *Keep him moving, keep him distracted, and maybe he won't have a chance to kill you.*

Fox glanced at him again, and this time, his gaze locked on hers, unblinking, hawkish, and horrifically patient. A memory from her childhood flashed through her mind. Fox's nurse taking her and Turo to a traveling circus in Pardaetha – a glimpse of the mighty beast they called a gryphon behind rows of iron. Its eagle eyes unblinking and patient right before it pushed through the weakened bars to skewer its hapless trainer. Seconds; mere seconds. That's all it had needed.

A sharp exhale escaped her lips.

"Your buyer must be generous," Blade said, breaking the silence. "It isn't wise to hold on to merchandise for so long, I imagine."

"Generous?" Fox scoffed. "Compared to a crossroads demon, maybe, and that's stretching the definition."

"A paltry offer, then?"

"If you consider my life paltry, which I'm certain you do."

"Hmm," Blade grunted quietly, but he said no more.

Fox glanced at him discreetly, gauging his reaction, but as always, he remained impassive. She had said too much, of course. It was stupid to give the Guardian any information at all, especially information that softened her, made her vulnerable or comprehensible. Still, she couldn't help it. Her resentment of Myergo was starting to get to her. She'd gotten the information she needed to track the Guardian and his young charges down, but only in exchange for the Guardian himself; alive, no less. And the cost of her failure? Her own body for the Guardian's, in any way Myergo chose to dispense of it. If she were younger, and a lot dumber, she might have ignored the threat and killed Blade when she had the chance. But Fox had made the mistake of crossing Myergo once before; a mistake she had barely survived. He was generous alright: generous enough to allow her to keep breathing despite past missteps. So here she was. Transporting a dangerous warrior bent on killing her to a dangerous crime lord bent on violating her *or* killing her if she didn't deliver. Myergo had left that last part up to her. *So generous.*

"All your pay in exchane for the girl. Why, I wonder, do the *H'rot Afbern* want her alive?" Blade said.

H'rot Afbern. Fox knew that one. Loosely translated, it meant something like "born of wrath," or "children of wrath" in Elmling, which the natives spat out like the nastiest insult they could think of for the Coalition. In her few encounters with Elmlings, they flung it at her. Maybe, if she understood – or rather, cared to understand – why the curse was such a pejorative, it might arouse her own wrath. It might even hurt her feelings, if she had any left to spare. But she didn't. Fox laughed instead.

"Why do you think it matters to me? My business is gold, not my employer's banal purposes."

"It should," Blade growled. "If the Coats hate anything, it's loose threads. Free agents. Like you, bounty hunter. I despise you, but I know you're no fool. You have seen them mobilizing; you have sensed the shift in the winds. Whatever is coming, you aid them by retrieving this child. Do you truly believe that once that end is tied up, they won't snip any other unruly ones?"

Fox yanked on the reins and turned the mare sharply into Blade, kicking out at him as she did. Her boot caught him on the shoulder, knocking him off balance and into the trunk of a pine. She glared down at him, eyes blazing. They kindled all the more as he peered up and grinned.

"Do you know what your kind are like? Cockroaches," Fox hissed. "The Coalition crushed you Guardians underfoot like little pests. I'm assuming that if any survived, they hid in dark holes like you did all these years. That's the only way you could survive, isn't it? Once you crawl out into the light–"

Fox smashed her fist into her palm and flashed an ugly smile.

"If I'm a cockroach, you're a rat," Blade said, unruffled. "Grin all you want from your position on the food chain. You're still vermin to the *H'rot Afbern*."

With a grunt of disgust, Fox pulled the reins left and kicked the mare's side. She started off at a lazy trot, and Blade stumbled to keep his feet. To Fox's disappointment, he recovered easily and jogged beside the pommel. She ground her teeth as the horse's pace slackened to a walk once again, as if it sensed its master being cruel to the human tethered beside it. *Don't let him anger you*, Fox reminded herself. *Why be angry? You'll be rid of him in a few hours, and once he figures out where he's going, he won't be smirking anymore.*

With that in mind, Fox thought better of encouraging the mare to a gallop. As much as she'd like to watch the Guardian's face drag in the dirt, it wouldn't do to bring him to Myergo in pieces. *No,* she thought, grimacing, *Myergo likes to do that part himself.* Besides, there was gold and Cardanthium waiting for her. She simply had to endure and catch up with the girl wherever she ended up. Soon enough, she'd be rid of Myergo, the Guardian, and the Coalition, and everything would go back to the way it was. *Just a little longer.*

Fox fought the urge to glare at Blade. Despite her self-soothing, the fury was still there, seething in her tense grip on the reins and burning like fire behind her irises. Try as she might, she could not brush off his words. They burrowed beneath her skin, worming into her brain as they echoed around her head. *Infuriating*, Fox wanted to shout. *Absolutely, infernally infuriating.*

Infuriating, because he knew the Coalition. Infuriating, because he was right.

12

Year 14 of the Glorious New Era
1st of Sun's Wane
Southeastern Province, Gormlaen

Arctura Vipsanius drummed the slender fingers of one hand nervously on her wooden desk, poising the ivory bone-handled pen over a sheet of parchment with the other. She stared at her open arithmetic book, trying to make sense of the equations she was supposed to be solving. Ink dripped from the pen's tip, spattering in tiny droplets as her fingers trembled. Across the room, her math tutor gazed languidly out the study's open window, occasionally flicking his eyes to the sundial visible in the garden below.

"A few more minutes now, Miss Vipsanius," he said with boredom.

Arctura's stomach churned. The hard chair squeaked beneath her as she readjusted and moved her face closer to the book. Arithmetic wasn't actually hard for Arctura. To be blunt, none of her studies were all that difficult. Father did not exaggerate her tutors' words: she indeed excelled at everything. To be sure, it was not her strongest subject, not in the least; but it was no small secret that she far outstripped Turo even in her areas of relative weakness. And by the gods, she ought to be able to spit out a memory-work sheet of simple equations!

This isn't hard, Arctura told herself. *Just focus!* But the numbers and symbols seemed as indecipherable as ancient Mlan runes. The Senator's daughter sighed, feeling a twinge of sympathy for her brother's struggle. Only a twinge though, because the clock was running and Arctura had yet to make a cogitable mark on the page. The churning in her stomach sloshed into a wave of nausea. She threw down the pen to cover her mouth.

"Time," the tutor sighed, smoothing his long, gray beard as he approached Arctura's corner. His bushy brows shot up at the sight of the ink-speckled parchment. He adjusted his spectacles, frowned, looked up at Arctura, and frowned again. "Hmm, not what I was expecting. Are you well, Miss Vipsanius?"

Arctura swallowed down bile. "I–I'm fine, Master Corazan. I'm–I just need a few more minutes. That's all. I apologize for my inattention."

"Why don't we try this later, hmm?" Master Corazan pulled the parchment from beneath Arctura's shaking hand and gently closed the book. "I understand Senator Vipsanius has requested your presence in some administerial matters today, yes?"

Arctura passed a hand over her perspiring forehead and nodded. Master Corazan pulled a face; the kind that old men make when they'd like to speak their mind, but know they shouldn't. She knew why, of course. Father had started to make a habit of interrupting her studies, and to Master Corazan's displeasure, he had been fairly unconcerned about the impact such interruptions were having on them. Admittedly, Arctura sided with Father; her future wasn't in the theoretical mathematics Master Corazan loved so much, but rather in the duties of the state. It was a kind of learning in itself, and Father was, indeed, the best tutor she could possibly have on the subject.

Master Corazan pulled off his spectacles, frowning as he polished them. "Let us return at a time when there is not so much else on the mind, hmm? You are dismissed for today. I expect this page turned in at our next appointment."

A flash of resentment burned in Arctura's cheeks. *He thinks I can't handle my workload alongside duties to Father. Does he truly think I'm so feeble-minded?* She wanted to shout at the doddering fool that she, Arctura Vipsanius, was not so weak as to crack under a little pressure, but what else would explain her failure today? The truth? *Not the truth. That is far worse.*

"Yes, Master Corazan," Arctura finally answered, biting her lip.

Master Corazan nodded and turned to gaze out the window. Gathering up her supplies and leaving the old man to brood, Arctura hurried down the hall. With a covert glance, she stopped in an alcove, slipped a hand into her satchel, and pulled a slice of yesterday's bread from the bottom. A few tentative nibbles determined it was stale. Exactly the way she wanted it. Arctura devoured the slice and shook the crumbs on the floor, feeling the queasiness ebb away as it hit her stomach.

Feeling more herself again, Arctura strode on. A few of Kyma's servants crossed their arms downward and bowed their heads low as she passed by, but Arctura hardly glanced in their directions. Not that such behavior was unusual from Coalition Party members and their families, but she did like to ingrain her position in their minds. Ever since Father took an interest in Arctura's political involvement, she pointedly gave up the feminine demure typical of Coalition men's wives and daughters. Instead, she stood tall and proud before anyone equal or lower to her, gracing them with her gaze and an occasional "Look upon me," as if the moment was suitable.

Mother hated it, of course. It was unbecoming of a high-status woman, at least according to her. Mother showed her displeasure best in her flamboyant displays of appropriate femininity; embracing friends with saccharine affection; curtsying and batting her eyelashes at men of standing, and offering a welcome smile to the palace servants. It worked for her, Arctura supposed. Mother got what she wanted out of it. Her incomparable beauty and calculated warmth had earned her the title she cherished most: the "Lily of Kyma."

More like the Narcissus of Kyma, Arctura scoffed.

Love, adoration, worship. That's what Mother wanted from the people, and that's what Mother got. And she was content with that power. But what did worship matter, what did love matter, if there was no force of authority behind it? One could not run an empire on something so inconstant as the populace's adoration. Such was the tactic of Gormlaen's kings and queens of the past. In the end, the mob's affection descended into loathing, turning as quickly as the tide on Pardaetha's shores. Love, for all its noble esteem, could not placate the people. Father knew that. Father had already planned for that. Fear, Father had told her. Fear ruled the hearts of the weak and strong alike. It struck deeper than love ever could, touching the primeval part of a person that will do anything to survive. Father liked to say it was the great equalizer, the greater impetus and, in the right hands, the greatest tool.

Mother could keep her adoration, her delicate moniker, her position of swaying the mob but never ruling them. For her part, Arctura intended to be feared. Respected. She'd sooner be the Tiger of Kyma than its Lily.

Rounding another corner, Arctura slowed as she came to Kyma's Great Room, only paces ahead. She paused, collecting her thoughts and examining herself in one of the passage's extravagant mirrors. The girl who stared back was not much of a girl at all – well, not anymore. Her dark hair, plaited professionally but tastefully, rolled back off her scalp and down her shoulders. Its unmistakable wine colored undertones gleamed in the corridor's chandelier light. She tugged at the crimson collar of the black dress, noting with pleasure that its embroidery and silver buttons brought it as close to a Coalition Party Representative's official uniform without being offensive to true members. Father had given it to her; and though it clung stiffly to her body and hugged too tightly to her abdomen, the dress matured Arctura beyond her almost seventeen years. She smiled, or sneered, rather, at the reflection, a glint of hunger in the yellow rings circling her brown irises. Father had taught her well. And on the heels of his unprecedented rise in the Party, Arctura could already see her own prestige growing behind him... maybe even beyond him.

If I can figure this out, she thought grimly, smoothing the hardly detectable puckering in the front of her dress.

With a deep, calming breath, she tucked a stray, curling lock behind her ear and knocked on the Great Room's heavy door. It creaked open, guided tentatively by the stout palace servant who ushered her in as soon as he recognized her. He pushed the door back into place with a soft thud before bowing his head deferentially in her presence.

Across the room, Father sat at the Great Room's round table. Its volcanic rock surface gleamed luxuriously beneath the chandelier's soft light, reflecting the dark images of Father's serious countenance and that of his guest.

Arctura cocked her head, taking in the visitor. He sat opposite of Father, pudgy hands folded over the enormous girth of his belly. Three white bars above his Coalition insignia indicated his position as Senator, the ruler and primary Coalition Party Representative of some city in Gormlaen. Of what city, Arctura could not guess. She had never seen this man before in Kyma's halls.

Strewn out before the two men lay files and stacks of parchment, fascinating contraptions, and an oval-shaped emerald stone held upright by a spindly, metallic stand. It pulsed softly with innate light, casting eerie green refractions on the obsidian table below. Arctura recognized it as Cardanthium, the rare metal sometimes found in the mountain mines that had powered their cities for years.

Father peered with unconcealed interest at the ore, addressing his guest with a question here and there. The Senator's two small, keen eyes darted toward Arctura and then back to Father. She caught the snatches of their conversation as it echoed across the room.

"This is quite a scientific breakthrough," Father was saying. "How did your men of learning discover these additional properties?"

"As with much progress, it was more or less an accident!" The Senator chuckled. "But I have paid them well for their efforts, and they inform me that all this Cardanthium they've been digging up in Maiendell is more promising than we initially realized. There is more to it than just raw power. So much more. And as I've shown you already, we're exploring the possibilities. Very interesting so far, but I believe we could go even farther. If only I could requisition more funds..."

Father waved his hand dismissively. "That is a non-issue."

"Thank you, Lucan," the Senator said, smiling broadly. "Had I known the support you would grant me, I'd have come to you much sooner. Much sooner, indeed!"

"It is my duty as Eastern Province Steward. What your people are doing... that is what the Coalition needs. Even if both provinces do not understand it yet," Father answered sagely. "I am confident that together, we can achieve what you have dreamed of and even more. And then... then we can make the western province understand."

Father reached out and grasped the fat man's hand firmly. The Senator's little eyes nearly popped out at its intensity, and Arctura thought she detected a slight squirming in Father's grip.

"Now, to other things," Father said, a hint of a smile on his lips. He turned toward Arctura. "Join us, Arctura."

Arctura obeyed, approaching and offering not a curtsy or smile, but strong crossed arms with eyes forward. Just as Father had taught. The Senator tilted his head, lips pursed and brows furrowed. A cloud of consternation masked his features for but a moment; hazarding a quick glance at Father, he quickly changed his tune.

"Look upon me," he said, an amused grin tugging on the corner of his jowls.

Arctura folded her hands behind her back and nodded.

Father waved toward her. "This is my daughter and the

Coalition's newest Junior Representative, Arctura Vipsanius. Arctura, meet Senator Kollo Orsin, of Lilien."

"A pleasure to meet you, Senator," Arctura smiled and extended a hand. She wondered if her smile was disarming like Mother's, or saturated with terrifying prowess, like Father's. Judging by the flash of skepticism in Senator Orsin's eyes, it was neither. Even so, he returned the smile and held her hand lightly.

"The pleasure is mine."

His fingers felt like sausages left uncooked too long on the kitchen counter. She let her hand fall away, controlling the impulse to grimace in disgust and putting on her usual stoic expression. Like Father, neither ally nor enemy could read her, and now she understood why Father liked it that way. Even over senior Coalition members, the inscrutability held a measure of power. Arctura reveled in it.

"I can see the lovely Eufemia in you, Miss Vipsanius," Senator Orsin appraised her slim form none too slyly. His shrewd eyes rested on her unreadable face. "Ah, and there is Lucan."

"Arctura has been assisting me with city administration and is now well-acquainted with the processes of Pardaetha's governance," Father said. He beckoned to the servant at the door, who unlocked the desk in the Great Room's corner and produced two piles of parchment. Father lowered his voice. "It is still a time of discretion. What do you think, Kollo? Shall she be a suitable witness to our contract today?"

The Senator answered quickly under Father's burning gaze. "Certainly, certainly. Let us proceed."

As she had done several times already these past few months, Arctura positioned herself behind the round table as Father and the Senator leaned over and scanned each signature page. They put pen to parchment, signing both Pardaetha's and Lilien's copies of the contract. Arctura noticed that the contract was not at all unlike the others Father had signed – one city's goods, research, and secrets in exchange for the other's – but the length of it suggested a more nuanced deal. Her eyes flitted over the agreement, picking out phrases like "extensive genetic manipulation," "behavior modification technology," and "longevity augmentation."

All Gebaln really had to offer was potatoes and prisoners. What in Reidara are they doing in Lilien?

They flipped through the agreement, now in the pages specifying Pardaetha's allotted funding for projects that encouraged "human flourishing." Arctura had seen these pages in each of the contracts Father had made with his other eastern province cities. Other than the strikingly high amount for Lilien, she didn't see anything out of the ordinary. The craftily written caveat here, of course, was support for Father's rise in Coalition ranks. She wondered if these senators knew how high Father aimed; his bid for Chancellor-Advisor, she was certain, but did they know he would not stop there?

Father swept his pen gracefully over each signature line, adding "EPS" for "Eastern Province Steward." Arctura wondered how long it would be before his abbreviated Coalition Assembly Chancellor after his name.

"Now for the witness," Father said, finishing his last signature.

Arctura leaned in between Senator Orsin and Father, inking the witness line with "Arctura Vipsanius, JR" on each contract. Father gathered up the copies, handing a stack of parchment to Senator Orsin. He gripped the Senator's hand in another crushing handshake.

"This is the first day of our future," Father said, leaning in furtively. "For the good of Gormlaen."

"For the good of Gormlaen," Senator Orsin repeated, pulling back as he did.

Father released him with something like a smile. "Remember Kollo, I'll be expecting results soon."

Senator Orsin dipped his head as much as his fat body would allow. His eyes darted to Arctura once more, a mote of fear lingering in his discriminating gaze. He turned swiftly, and Arctura held in a snigger as he squeezed past the servant and out the door.

Father watched the door thud to a close before turning his sharp eyes on Arctura. "Come."

Arctura followed Father and stepped out onto the Great Room's balcony. She blinked in the sunlight as she sidled up beside him. Though she could survey Pardaetha from any of Kyma's glorious balconies, the Great Room's view seemed more expansive; at least to Arctura. From here, as the city stretched out and down to the sea, the most prominent gathering places of its people remaining in direct sight. Every year, during the harvest celebration, Father addressed all of Pardaetha as its inhabitants gathered in the flat square just outside the palace walls below. No one, not even the most talented member of the Coalition Assembly, could out-orate Father. His voice dripped like honey and roared like a lion's; he hushed crowds and drew eyes from the moment he spoke. To both the simple-minded fishmonger and the brilliant academic, he was enthralling. No one fell outside the power of his spectacular rhetoric, the charm of his person, the spell of his presence. Maybe no one ever would.

Except for a few merchants and busy Patrons hurrying on their way, the square lay silent. Father and Arctura stared out together, breathing in the salt of sea and spice of pine on the breeze. It was Father who broke the silence.

"This contract with Senator Orsin is my greatest accomplishment yet." Father spoke with a deliberate calm that made Arctura nervous. "Do you know why?"

Arctura went over the contract again in her mind, latching on to the bizarre research jargon. "Other cities offer trade goods, labor, sometimes useful information. But Lilien offers... progress."

The corner of Father's lip arched in satisfaction. *He's positively giddy*, she thought.

"Lilien is by far Gormlaen's most technologically advanced city," Father continued. "Even now, they have achieved the impossible. By accepting our funding, Kollo has effectively given me... everything. Their research, their technology, their advancements... it is all in my hands."

Father turned toward her, a wild hunger burning in his eyes. Terror iced through Arctura's veins, the look freezing her solid with its implications. *Does this mean...*

For the first time in Arctura's life, Father grinned. "The Coalition Assembly does not know it yet, but they have elected their first Supreme Chancellor."

13

Year 113 of the Glorious New Era
46th of Sun's Wane
Northern Province, Gormlaen

Fox shielded her eyes against the icy autumn deluge crashing down from the pitch sky. Biting gusts howled through the pines, the Swaying Forest now in danger of becoming the Flying Forest as roots tore from the ground and trunks groaned in protest. Lightning flickered, illuminating the landscape for a split-second before it returned to night-black darkness. A cacophonous boom resounded and rolled. Fox's shivering horse whinnied and pranced in terror. Tugging sharply on the reins, Fox cursed, but it was lost in the roar of the storm. Pooling water sprayed against her boots as the frightened horse stamped. Fox cursed again.

"Shelter!" she shouted, turning her attention to the Guardian and pointing south, deeper into the trees.

Not too long before the sudden storm raged overhead, they had passed the beginning of a boulder field within the wood. It was their best shot for quick cover. Fox might have tried to shelter in the shadow of the Jagged Jaw range instead, but the open expanse between it and the forest deeply concerned her. A flash of lightning forked into the mud of the open valley, confirming her suspicions.

"In front!" she barked, pulling the rope to her mount's withers.

Blade nodded in comprehension, positioning himself slightly ahead of the mare's head. Fox scanned the shadows for the best path, blinking water out of her eyes, but nothing seemed to turn up. Small, rushing streams careened over the once-safe forest paths, quickly turning their situation desperate. They needed high ground and shelter, and fast. She hesitated. *Where in this gods forsaken wilderness are we going to find that?*

"This way!" Blade raised his shackled wrists, pointing to a passable route to their left. He turned toward her with a smile.

"Yes, yes, you're very clever," she muttered, but she nodded her assent.

They weaved their way farther into the Swaying Forest, wind and rain still pelting them with a vengeance. Despite the storm's wrath, Blade hurried on, moving nimbly along the invisible path and pointing out debris and obstacles that could easily turn her horse's hoof. His speed and expert navigation were surprising, even to Fox, who was no stranger to the wilderness herself.

Presently, Blade stopped and pointed, and Fox halted her mount beside him.

"There," he shouted, indicating a rise some paces ahead.

Fox squinted, the shape of a massive rocky mound looming in the darkness. The forest floor seemed to flow up over top of it, thin trees sprouting from the top of the boulder. From beneath the mossy carpet, the gaping mouth of a wide crevasse opened before them. Water cascaded down the ledge, but otherwise it seemed dry.

"Looks cozy," Fox said. "But is it occupied?"

Blade shrugged. "Probably."

Fox sighed and dismounted. Leading the horse carefully, they followed a slope up toward the cave. Fox unsheathed her blades, the green glow lighting their way. Their feet found slick stone. They continued to climb, and soon the drenching rain no longer beat on their heads. The mare's hoofs echoed loudly in the cave mouth's smooth entrance.

"Come on," Fox said, untying Blade's tether from the pommel.

They ventured in by the light of Fox's Cardanthium swords. Their green glow bounced off the walls.

"Ah, I believe we're alone," Blade said, his voice now much louder than the muted pounding of the rain outside. "It's more of a hollow than a cave, it would seem."

Sure enough, Fox saw the back wall of the cave herself. Even so, she paced up and down the breadth of it, keen on uncovering any surprises. Satisfied, she replaced her blades and, noticing a brush pile fortuitously kept dry in the cave, set quickly to making a small fire. As it crackled, she turned her sharp gaze on Blade.

"That was impressive," Fox admitted. "I shall have to watch you all the closer as we wait for the storm to pass."

Blade stretched out by the flames, steam rising from his sopping attire.

"What a compliment," he said. "Especially for one as hated and hunted as I seem to be."

"Did I hurt your feelings?" Fox snorted. "I don't have to like you to recognize your abilities. As for my affections, you are hardly special. I hate everyone."

"That explains much," Blade replied, and to her surprise, with a chuckle.

Fox crouched by the fire. Watching the Guardian warily, she removed her swords and her wet outer garments. Nothing would dry much, but at least she wouldn't freeze to death.

"Don't get any stupid ideas," she warned him, pulling her tunic into a knot and wringing it out.

He shrugged with disinterest, but his observant gaze fell on her bare stomach. Fox huffed in annoyance, but was certain he wasn't ogling. The raking scars dragging in macabre slashes all across her midsection usually ensured that.

She ignored him and any observations he made of her, focusing instead on shaking the water out of her boots. A peal of thunder resounded around the cave, and Fox sighed. Between the lightning strikes and the fury of the wind, she could hear the water rushing down the slope. Even when the rain stopped, they would have to travel cautiously amid the flash flood-prone paths. She fiddled with her wristband, debating on contacting Dervish to ascertain her contacts' whereabouts during the storm. *This better not delay us too long.*

Fox cast a sidelong glance at Blade. He remained stretched out on the rock, studying her by the flickering firelight with that cool detachment she'd come to know so well.

"What is it, beast hunter?" She shot derisively. "Are you a man still? If you're curious, I am not interested."

"There are other things to be curious about." His eyebrow arched slightly. He nodded toward her. "What gave you your distinctive markings?"

"That's forward of you," she scoffed. "Figure it out yourself."

"How about a wager, then?" he asked. "Three guesses as to the creature responsible, and you give me something to eat."

Fox considered the challenge, amusement tugging at the corner of her mouth. "Come now, I doubt that even you are that good."

"Doubtful enough to wager a morsel?"

She rolled her eyes. "Fine. But one guess, Guardian."

"Two."

"One."

Blade nodded. "One, then."

He peered at the scars that crossed her stomach in triplicate lines, tapping his steepled fingers against his lips.

"I know of no beast that attacks like that," he said. "Not without disemboweling its prey. Perhaps a drake could do it, but you'd have teeth in you as well. And you would also be dead."

A wry smile twisted his lips.

"One guess, yes?" she said. "I will not confirm or deny your speculations."

"A gryphon is unlikely. I might say the talons of a smaller terror bird, but the attack pattern is all wrong. They use their beaks for the assault."

"Is terror bird your guess, then?"

Blade shook his head. "It is not a terror bird."

"Now you are stalling." Fox bared her teeth in a grin. "Out with your answer."

All traces of amusement left his features, replaced by an impenetrable mask. Fox's own grin faded as she tried to read his stormy eyes. All at once they looked like fury and pain... and sadness. She wanted to avert her gaze, but she held it, hating how it made her insides churn.

"The monster who marked you," he said in a quiet, deliberate voice. "Was a man. One with a uniquely cruel weapon designed to inflict pain and fear rather than outright death."

Fox's eyes hardened. "Some monsters forge their own claws."

She tore open her rucksack and, producing a slice of venison jerky, tossed it into Blade's open hands.

"Well reasoned, beast hunter."

Blade did not reply. She felt his eyes on her as she replaced her swords on her shoulders and stood just behind the curtain of rain outside the cave. The storm showed no sign of slowing, and a pervasive gloom snaked through the pines and settled over the forest floor. Fox glowered and crossed her arms over her chest, her thoughts as dark as the storm. This reverie effect the Guardian seemed to stir in her was becoming tiringly irksome. It had been years since the memories had surfaced; years since she had recalled their unique sting. Absent-mindedly, she brushed the tips of her fingers against the scarred skin that began at the bottom of her ribcage. She looked down, remembering what once lay beneath the mangled flesh.

Rain fell and wind blew. Fox drummed the slender fingers of one hand against her arm, trying not to remember the day like this one. The day that so long ago changed everything.

14

Year 14 *of the Glorious New Era*
 1ₛₜ of Sun's Wane
Pardaetha, Gormlaen

Shadows stretched along the dusky streets of Pardaetha, extending
like spindly claws across the backs of the cloaked forms scurrying to
cover. Passersby cast wary glances toward the sea. A storm was
coming. Arctura gazed seaward as well, watching the black tumult fill
the sky, billow, and roll in roaring torrents of rain as it rushed to shore.
The wind struck her first, then the rain; relentless, driving,
unforgiving. She pulled the hood of her cloak low over her eyes and
shivered. Few would venture out in this slop; at least she could
breathe easily knowing that. Still, Arctura waited for the street to
clear, only stepping cautiously from beneath the dark facade that had
sheltered her when she found herself alone.

Water rushed down the street and squelched in her boots as she
splashed along. Arctura counted the buildings, shielding her eyes

from the stinging rain each time she had to lift her head. *Three, four, five... turn right.*

Leaving the howling wind and buffeting rain behind, Arctura sidled into an alley. The tall sides of the adjacent buildings rose on either side of her, so close and so narrow that she swore they were touching at the top. Down below, at ground level, only two people could walk abreast. To her relief, she still walked alone.

Arctura continued slowly, counting doors quietly. At the fourth, she stopped. *This has to be it,* she thought, studying the door. *Now, where is that symbol?*

A stone on the stoop caught her eye, and she snatched it up to examine it. She smiled, tracing the etching of a rooster holding a lute on the rock's slippery surface.

"It is indeed a house full of cheer that bears the sign of balladeer," she whispered, shaking her head and chuckling. She thought the rhyme absurd the first time she heard it, but its quaint charm had grown on her. Arctura replaced the rock and rapped her knuckles on the door. *Knock, knock, pause... knock, knock, knock.*

A slice of warmth and light bathed the alleyway as the door creaked open. Before Arctura could begin to enjoy it, though, a hulking figure stepped between her and the light. A wild eye appeared at the crack, and a terse voice croaked back at her.

"Whaddya want?"

Arctura licked her lips nervously. "I'm here to see Reylas. Reylas Fox, the musician."

The eye narrowed. "Never heard of 'em. Get off my stoop."

"You have the sign of the minstrel!" she protested.

"Yeah, and you have the sign of a nosy city official," the man growled. "And I don't see no entry dictum. Off with you!"

Arctura looked down at the elegant red stitching embroidering her cloak and sighed. She should have worn the green one, but she opted for her darker Coalition garb instead. She stood out less in that, or so she thought.

"I'm not here on city business," she insisted. "It's personal."

The door slammed shut. Arctura lifted her fist angrily, ready to beat on the door, when she heard something else from the other side.

"Ay, wait a minute, Jonz. Who was that?" A woman's muted indignation carried through the wood. "I know that voice! Get outta the way!"

Arctura listened, catching the muffled sound of a whispered argument and scuffling. Once more, the door cracked open, and half of a familiar face peeped out. White teeth shone in a wide grin. "Is that you, Princess?"

Arctura rolled her eyes but pushed the hood back.

"It IS Princess!" the voice squealed.

The door flew open, and out rushed a flurry of color and smiles.

"Hello, Erhi," Arctura managed as the Samrasine percussionist engulfed her in an exuberant embrace.

"Oh, this is so great! I was sick with the thought we wouldn't see you before we left the city!" Erhi drew back, shaking water from her magenta blouse. She pointed to Arctura's cloak, grinning. "Wet one out there, huh? Well, come on in, stranger!"

Arctura followed the bobbing Erhi inside, staying a few steps behind the swing of her long ponytail. Erhi stopped suddenly, turning toward Arctura and mouth splitting in yet another wide grin. She adjusted her yellow head wrap as she nodded to the towering man with his arms crossed behind the door.

"Don't worry about Jonz," Erhi said. "He's an alright guy. Just likes his job a lot."

"Which is?" Arctura muttered, avoiding Jonz's suspicious gaze.

Erhi shrugged. "Roughing up Coats? Scaring young ladies? Pretending to be tough?"

"Security," Jonz grunted.

"Sure, that's what we'll call it," Erhi winked. "Thanks a mil, Jonz. Well, what d'ya say, Princess? One last hurrah before you run off to rule the world? Can't send off sweet baby Rey without one more smoochie from Princess, can we?"

Arctura winced at the nickname. When Reylas first introduced her to his group of musicians, they recognized her as the "pretty princess" he had gone to rescue that night so many months ago; a story he had apparently relayed as soon as he left her window. At first Arctura had been quite rankled by it. No one had ever dared call her a diminutive before. It took her a while to understand all the friends gently mocked each other, and with their irreverent but affectionate moniker, they had accepted her into their circle. As much as she disliked it, she would endure any silly name they foisted on her, if only to feel friendship for the brief moments she escaped Kyma's walls.

"Yes, thank you," Arctura replied, shedding her outer cloak on the rack in the hall and spraying droplets of water everywhere. Jonz frowned.

Arctura rubbed her chilled hands together nervously as Erhi led her up the steep, narrow stairs. They plodded up the short steps, catching their breath as they reached a landing at the top. Arctura surveyed the old city house suspiciously. The troupe often chose unsavory places to sleep, but by the looks of it, this one was the worst. The old flooring groaned beneath Arctura's ginger steps. Spots of mold bloomed on the ceiling where water seeped in and plunked into strategically placed tin buckets on the floor. Plaster peeled away from the walls, exposing beams and dusty rat droppings. Arctura hissed as a dark shape skittered just out of her peripheral vision and disappeared into a hole between the baseboard and the floor.

Erhi took no notice as she pranced ahead, the bells on the tips of her turquoise slippers jangling cheerfully. It was always that way with Erhi; never walking but gliding, stepping, dancing to her next destination. Reylas had once said that the rhythm of the world was in her soles. Arctura had scoffed, but whenever she watched Erhi dance, she thought she might believe it. Focusing on Erhi's graceful steps instead of the vermin in the walls, Arctura followed. Erhi yanked open a door on her right and sashayed inside.

"Sweet baby Rey!" Erhi called in a sing-song voice. "Look who's dropped by!"

Arctura entered close behind, coughing at the swirling black leaf smoke hanging in the room. Reylas, inhaling from a hose attached to the odd, bubbling contraption, looked up in surprise. Delighted surprise, she noted, but filled with pining and... was that pain? Their last meeting rushed vividly into her mind, and her breath hitched. *How could I be so foolish?* She thought. *How can I crush him all over again?*

"Arctura!" he shouted, hurriedly handing the hose off to one of the other room's occupants. "I thought you weren't– I mean, I had hoped you would, but–"

He hopped off his cushion and bounded toward her, pushing past Erhi to gather her in his arms. Arctura breathed in the scent of honeyed black leaf and jasmine as he enfolded her, and at that moment she wanted more than anything to melt into his embrace forever. If she could only bury her face against the warmth of his neck, press her lips against his, cradle his head in her arms... maybe it would all go away. Maybe it would be okay.

No, it won't, she reminded herself, the thought steeling her resolve. *I can't, I shouldn't. Not today, and not ever again.*

"We must speak," she said, staving off his touch with a hand on his chest. Arctura lowered her voice, nodding past him at the curious faces peering out of the hazy room. "Alone."

Reylas looked down, his brow wrinkling in confusion. Gently, he brushed her arm and wrapped his fingers around her hand. He raised his gaze to meet hers, and Arctura felt her resolve bleed away into uselessness.

"Okay," he said, squeezing her fingers. "Um, to my room, I guess?"

"That will do."

He didn't let go as he guided her to his sleeping quarters, an almost closet-sized room with two sets of beds and a beat-up wardrobe. Over-stuffed travel packs bulged in one corner, while an oud rested in the other. Reylas shut the door behind them and gestured for her to sit next to him on his bed. Arctura did so with unease, her breath stuttering as he scooted close and stared into her eyes.

"I thought I would never see you again." His voice was as gentle as his fingertips as they traced the curve of her jaw. "I couldn't bear it. Every minute without you..."

He brushed her lips, caressed her neck, and ran his fingers down her shoulders to find her hands in his. Arctura shivered, lingering on his touch, feeling the familiar calluses on his instrument-worn skin as their fingers laced. It was easy, far too easy, to drift back into that blissful dream, to sink into sweet, brief oblivion and cast aside every responsibility piled on her shoulders. Arctura closed her eyes, and for a moment, only a moment, she hid in their dream. But even as she grasped at it, the sharp edge of reality pierced through, bled out their stolen time, screamed the consequences of their secret love. Her eyes fluttered open. They had stolen all the time they could.

"Reylas, I..." Arctura searched for words as her voice faltered. "I need to tell you something. It's not good."

The smile at her arrival faded. "What's going on? Are you okay?"

Her breath caught in her ribs. *It's time.*

"It's early still but... I'm carrying your child. Our child."

Reylas gulped, his nervous gaze darting from her face to her stomach. He let go of her fingers. His hands trembled as he stretched them toward her belly.

"Are... are you sure?"

Arctura tensed, ready to push his hands away if he tried to touch her. They dropped as she bit her lip and nodded.

"You know," he smiled weakly, running a hand through his hair. "I was going to climb your window again. Try to convince you to run away with me forever. I never thought..."

"What? That if you put a brat in me, we might actually have a chance?" Arctura answered. Her anger rose like a sea squall, sudden, whipping, reckless. "How wonderfully things have gone for you, Reylas Fox."

"Th-that's not fair!" Reylas sputtered. "I never imagined... I wasn't trying... For as much as I love you, I would never try to win you like that. To ask you to throw your life away for... for this."

He gestured to the stained walls, the grime-streaked window running with soot and rain. His voice became strained and small.

"I know it's impossible."

"For once, the dreamer has pulled his head out of the clouds," Arctura retorted, much harsher than she intended. She steadied herself with a deep breath. "Listen, you had a right to know. I owed you that. But I've made my decision."

Reylas narrowed his eyes. "What are you saying?"

"I know political things do not mean so much to you, but Father will soon become the most powerful man in the Coalition. There are... responsibilities expected of me. Responsibilities I will need to take, that I can only take if... if I do not shame my house. Please understand, Reylas."

"I don't understand," he said bluntly. "And since I am such a simpleton, you'll need to spell it out."

"Fine," she said, gritting her teeth. *Why did he always have to be so emotional?* "I cannot have this child. I will not."

"What?"

"I have decided I can't go to any healers in Pardaetha... not without someone seeing me and recognizing me. But there is an old temple to Derebor, a Gormlaean goddess of women from the ancient times. No one goes there, and there are only a few old priestesses there now. But they have knowledge of herbs to end..."

Arctura lowered her gaze, unable to watch the mixture of horror and repulsion twist and darken her lover's face.

"I will purchase a concoction from the priestesses. And then it will be over."

"Yeah, sure, then it will be over," Reylas cut back bitterly. "And everything will be just good as new, isn't that right? Just like it never happened."

Disgust pinched his lips. "I'm just a Samrasine vagrant, after all. What could I offer to you, oh daughter of the rich and powerful

Coalition Steward? I'm nothing. I'm a minor hitch in your daddy's grand plan. A mud pit you wallowed in for a while until it became a problem. Why should this little one, tainted and mixed as it is, be any different?"

Arctura stood abruptly and fixed Reylas with a sharp, seething glare. Her words hissed like steam from between her clenched teeth. "Don't you dare speak to me like that! Don't you dare make it sound like... like I never loved you. Like I don't love you– even if I am what I am, and you are what you are. Don't. If anyone is wallowing right now, it's *you*. Because this isn't just about you, as much as you'd like it to be. It's about what's right. For all of us. It is about what must be done."

Reylas dropped his cold stare in defeat. He never could argue with her, even when he tried. Even when it was important. *Just like the last time*, Arctura thought. *A dreamer and a lover, but not a fighter, not a rhetorician. Not like me.*

His body sagged, and he looked worse off than when she had said her last goodbye – what she thought would be their last goodbye – only a month ago. Her anger ebbed, replaced by the gnawing guilt of Reylas's fair accusation. He, a Samrasine. She, a Gormlaean. And not just any Gormlaean, but a rising star in a new world order. How could their love survive? Even then, Arctura shuddered at the consequences of being discovered, of what Father might do to him. And now?

She looked down at her belly, tight and distended, but hardly round at all. No one else could tell – she doubted even Reylas could – but it already felt so swollen, bursting, full of the life nestled there. Yet how could she bring it into this world? A world that would be far crueler to such a life than the swift, merciful end she offered? No, she couldn't. Not into this world, the one she was meant to rule, the one that maybe, just maybe, she could mold into a place where young women didn't have to make the choice she was making today.

"Don't you dare..." Arctura whispered. "Not for one moment,

don't you dare think I'm not falling to pieces about what I've created with you."

Reylas fell to his knees, clutching at her hands as he buried his face in them. Hot tears spilled onto her palms. Arctura's throat tightened as he wept. Despite herself, she collapsed into his arms, hugging him fiercely as his tear-stained cheek brushed against hers.

"Then please," he begged, his voice a hoarse whisper in her ear. "Don't do this."

"What else am I supposed to do?" she whispered back in despair.

Reylas pulled back, placed his hands firmly on her shoulders, and gazed resolutely into her eyes. "Marry me."

Arctura wanted to scoff, but the hard determination etched into his normally playful features stifled any of her usual flippancy.

"You're serious."

"Dead serious."

"How does this solve anything?" Arctura said with a shrill, disbelieving titter.

"Maybe it doesn't," he replied, his face softening. He brought a hand to her cheek and rubbed his thumb gently along its contour. "But it was the biggest mistake of my life to let you leave last time. I'll never make that mistake again. You, our baby, our life together. That's all I care about."

"But Reylas, my father, the Coalition—"

"What about them?" he said. "Do you really, honestly want that life? Say you get your shiny insignia, a position, all the power that you've ever dreamed of. Do you think your father still isn't going to marry you off to some strategic city's chump just so he can get what he wants? Do you think you could pretend to love someone else for the rest of your years?"

"I'm going to change things," Arctura replied, but even she didn't think she sounded convincing.

"Come with me," he implored. "And maybe you can change everything."

Arctura let out a slow sigh. What *did* she want? Her two futures spread before her, and she tried to imagine them. In one, she stood beside Father, proud and tall as he reached his ambitious post as Supreme Chancellor. Perhaps he'd hand her Pardaetha. And there she would rule in strength, her every comfort cared for, her every whim met, every demand answered with swift and complete loyalty. She imagined how it would feel; she imagined the thrill of power, the elation at her subjects' respect and fear. Even so, her mind drifted to Turo, arm in arm with Tyranna, holding a false smile as every secret desire he harbored shattered to pieces. She thought of Mother and her meaningless existence tucked in idle luxury. How she'd never even heard Father express affection for Mother, let alone show it. She saw a life bound to a strategic ally: a hard man like Father, or a boneless sap like Turo. Could she stomach either? Could she survive having *his* children, when all the while wondering if Reylas's child would have had his eyes, his wit, or his incorrigible smile? She dwelled on the curse of comfort and control at the expense of joy and love. Is *that* what she wanted?

In the other future, she had nothing. Only the necessities she could smuggle from Kyma on her arduous trek to... where? To the Samras? Some small Gormlaean village where no one would know her name? She thought of her growing belly, the incomprehensible pain and danger of birth, the incessant cries of a hungry infant. She imagined judging eyes and whispers, the shame of poverty and the sting of need. Even there, her mind drifted to the sun in her beloved's grin, the tender care of a new father cradling his baby in his arms, the honest goodness of a life free from the evils of power and the regret of its sacrifices. She thought of the troupe accepting her as family; Erhi as Reidara's best auntie, a home she and Reylas could build together. And then there was the child; smiling with Reylas's eyes.

It had been so clear only an hour ago. Now, Arctura was not so sure. She rubbed her temples wearily.

"You're asking the impossible."

A jaunty smile lightened his face. "I know."

"My dreamer," Arctura sighed, but affection filled the words now.

"Every possibility today was someone's impossible dream once," Reylas replied.

"Did you read that on a poster somewhere?" Arctura snorted, laughing.

"I'm surprised at you!" Reylas waggled his finger. "You know peasants can't read."

"Shut up," she grinned, drawing him close and brushing her mouth against his. "Now, this is the part where you kiss me."

Reylas exhaled shakily, his heart thumping wildly against her own as they pressed together, lips meeting, passion soaring. Arctura tasted jasmine and honey, sweetness and security, hope and love.

15

Year 14 of the Glorious New Era
*   14th of Sun's Wane*
The Palace Kyma
Pardaetha

"You're really doing this, aren't you?"

Turo leaned against Arctura's dresser, watching in defeat as she folded the last of her clothes and tucked them into the bulging travel bag. She leveled a stern look in his direction.

"I didn't change my answer the last four times you asked me."

He flapped his gangly limbs in exasperation, reminding her more of a struggling baby bird than of the man he was growing to be. A man, she noted, who increasingly resembled Father. Soon it would be hard to tell them apart, provided Turo managed to grow more hair on his face than the scraggly tuft now dominating his chin. But inside, the boy remained; goofy, timid, juvenile, dependent. Arctura sized up her brother, softening. *How is he going to survive here?*

"There's still time," she added, zipping up the bag. "Until the moment I walk through those doors, there is time. Come with me, Turo! It's the adventure you've always wanted. No Father, no Tyranna, no strategic alliances. Just... freedom. Real freedom. Don't you want to taste it? Don't you want to know what it's like to not have your whole future planned for you?"

Turo rubbed the back of his neck. "I mean, yeah, but..."

"But what?" Arctura sighed. "We've been over the pros and cons for the last month. We both concluded that this is the best course of action. What must I convince you of now?"

"I can't," he whispered. "I'm not like you, Rah. I'm not... brave. I never will be."

Going to her brother, Arctura wrapped his hand in hers. It trembled, betraying the terror she saw written all over his face. She tried, but she could not understand him. Despite all her persuading, much of which he had agreed with, it was Turo's fear of consequences that continued to paralyze him. His fear of Father.

For her, since the moment she decided she would leave Kyma, join Reylas and his troupe, and enter into motherhood and whatever else life had in store for her, all fear had simply vanished. She knew what the consequences would be. In her mind, she had already faced them. Why fear it? What could worry do except addle her senses and make her chosen path that much harder? Fear was not only pointless, it was a hindrance. Yes, there was Father. But there was also a world without Father. And for that world, Arctura began to ache past all the terror of his wrath. *Turo,* she wanted to cry. *How do you not ache for it, too?*

"You will always be afraid if you remain here. Put on courage for just one night, and I promise, you will wear it forever."

Turo considered her words. A wan smile crossed his lips.

"Does it have to be this night?"

"It can't wait much longer," Arctura replied, placing a hand on the growing bump beneath her loose dress. "The 'rich palace food' excuse isn't going to fool anyone anymore."

Turo stifled a sniffle. He looked away, but she could see his eyes growing wet and red, and her heart dropped into her stomach. *He isn't coming. He really isn't coming.*

A tear slipped out of her own eye as she hesitantly reached up to embrace him. Even as children, Arctura had never hugged her brother. Mother discouraged affection, despite their closeness. To be truthful, Arctura never was truly sure if Turo loved her as much as she loved him. Even as her twin, her only sibling, the friendship nearest and dearest to her heart. But as she felt him shudder with sobs, hugging her back with all his might for the first time, for the last time, Arctura finally knew.

"Please, Rah," he pleaded, pulling away to wipe his face with his arm. "Just stay. I know you love him... but what's going to happen to you out there?"

"I don't know," she answered honestly. "But I have chosen my way."

Turo nodded, but said nothing.

"I'll write you, somehow," Arctura said, gathering up her things. "So you know I am alright. And maybe... maybe then, you'll see Kyma too small for you, and you'll come find me."

"One can dream," he smiled sadly. "Don't go, Rah."

"I'll miss you, too, Turo."

With one last Coalition salute, Arctura shouldered her things, leaving her brother to cradle his head in his hands behind her dark bedroom door.

Arctura stood alone in the dark street, her head down as stars winked from above. A pale moon hovered over the horizon, rising out of the sea to take its silent watch in the late hours of the night. Somewhere, a sentry shouted out the time. She lifted her head, turning her ear to catch it, but she could not discern his words. Well past midnight, she knew that. But how long before dawn?

She held out the creased piece of parchment, placing her forefinger beneath the words she had read a hundred times. For the one hundredth and first time, Arctura scanned the directions and the tavern where she and Reylas were to meet:

The Lonely Siren

Dock Street and Fish Alley

Breathing heavily, Arctura set down her cumbersome bag to surmise her position. The shadowy sign some paces ahead offered no help, but she was close. She had to be, if her aching feet and the stale scent of briny water and spoiling fish were any indication. Coming down from Kyma to the harbor gate was no easy task on a normal day, but stealing down in the dead of night, laden with child and now her only worldly possessions, had been almost insurmountable. Despite the chill that portended the coming of the rainy winter season, Arctura wiped sweat from her forehead and fanned herself with the crinkled parchment. Her eyes swept up and down the street, alighting on the yellow glow of a large grimy window at the far end. Even from where she stood, she could hear the faint creaking of the sign that jutted out from the building and from within, the clinking of last rounds at the bar.

"Finally," she whispered with a tired smile.

Arctura grunted as she lifted her bag and shuffled toward The Lonely Siren. The next steps of their plan played through once again in her mind: inside the tavern, Arctura would gather some sustenance and strength for the journey with Reylas and the troupe. They would set out before dawn when the harbor gate opened, trundling out on the musicians' travel wagon with the throng of fisherman and dock workers. Nothing unusual there. Hiding beneath the wagon's festive cover, Arctura would rest and wait, but she was certain no one would be the wiser. Reylas, Arctura, and the troupe would be out of the city well before anyone at Kyma realized she was gone.

Her spirits cheered at the thought. A playful spring entered her graceful step. *Is this what happiness, true happiness, feels like?* She wondered. Arctura smiled, vivacious in her newfound freedom. Nothing, it seemed, could stop her now.

Out of the corner of her eye, movement caught her attention. Arctura paused, peering into the deeper shadows of the narrow alley on her right. Her heart thudded in her chest. Though she could not see anything, ice seeped into her belly. It seemed to crystalize around her ankles, freezing her in front of the open mouth of that impenetrable darkness.

"Who's there?" she said, with all the authority her previous position had granted her. Even so, Arctura could not stifle the frightened stammer as she added: "Sh-show yourself."

No one answered. With a deep breath, she adjusted her pack and turned to continue. A faint greenish gleam flashed briefly in the dark.

Run! A hysteric voice inside her screamed.

Arctura threw down her bag, stretching her legs to sprint away. Luminescent green flickered into her vision as something heavy smashed into her cheek. She had no breath to scream as it clawed into her skin and ripped the flesh from her face as it pulled away.

The blow sent her sprawling to the street. Blood poured into her eye, blinding her. She choked as it ran into her mouth. Arctura whimpered, raking the ground with her fingernails as she tried to crawl. A vice-like fist clamped down on her ankle. Again, Arctura opened her mouth to scream, but it filled with dirt as the iron grasp dragged her into the dark alley.

Her fingers tore as she clawed at the ground. The nightmare fiend dragged her deeper into the pit from where it came. She shrieked freely now, but the street seemed worlds away. With a deft twist, the monster tossed her like refuse against a wall.

All the breath left her as her body crumpled. Arctura wheezed. The thing approached. It resolved, only slightly, and she could see it was a man. A greenish glow, emanating from the place where his hand ought to have been, illuminated the three wicked curves of a metal claw. She touched the side of her face, throbbing and swollen from its impact.

"Who are you?" Arctura whispered hoarsely.

"A lesson," he croaked with a horrid chuckle.

Arctura recoiled as he passed the glowing claw before his pocked face, revealing a blackened grin and murderous dark eyes.

"Learn you well, Miss Vipsanius," he laughed, and the green talon launched from its place and lodged itself into her belly. The clinking crank of a chain yanked it back.

"No!" she wailed, weakly clutching at the gaping gash.

Blood. So much blood. He slashed again, the claw now an extension of his arm. With his other hand, he jerked her hands away, exposing his target. He ripped again, and again, so close that his acrid breath sheered through the excruciating pain. The green sheen dimmed with the sticky coating of dark blood. It splattered her face and her eyes, mingling with the gaping wound flowing down her cheek and onto her chest. Arctura sputtered, unable to even sob.

"No," she moaned.

The monster retreated. Silence. All the world went numb and black.

Year 14 of Glorious New Era (Year 1 of the Honored Reign)
   22nd of Sun's Wane

Sunlight dappled the quiet room in dancing rays as the ocean breeze ruffled the dark silk curtains above the window. A stream of light splashed across the bed and into Arctura's half-opened eye. She rubbed it, still bleary with the crust of heavy sleep, and winced as her hand brushed across the bandaged left side of her face. With her right eye, Arctura swept the room. A figure rocked in a chair in the room's corner, his knees tucked under his chin as he hugged his shins.

"Turo?" she asked, her mouth as dry and gritty as sand.

He stopped rocking. Arctura placed her hands on the bed to push herself up, but agony shrieked through her body and pulsed into her temples. She collapsed, gasping for air.

"You're awake," Turo's voice cracked.

He bolted out of the chair. Arctura reached out, expecting him to come to her bedside, but he loped toward the door.

"Father!" he shouted. "She's awake!"

"Turo," she repeated, groping for him. "Where am I?"

Her brother backed against the wall, gulping. She could see horror and weariness in his bloodshot eyes. How long had it been since he slept? How long had *she* slept? Where were her friends? Where was Reylas? Had that demon of a man done to him what he had done to her? More questions cascaded into her mind, terrible questions that she was afraid to answer. But even as the possibilities made her tremble, she needed to know the truth. Steeling herself, Arctura focused on her brother.

"Tell me where we are," she demanded. "Tell me what happened."

"You are home, Arctura," a stern voice said from the doorway. "Where you belong."

Father strode in, his hands behind his back. Mother glided in behind him, her lovely features contorted. To Arctura, she looked as if the room stunk of dock hobos. Turo bowed his head and crossed his arms subserviently as they entered. Father waved him off.

"Leave us, Arcturo."

With one last forlorn glance, Turo slunk through the door. Mother occupied the chair he left, glaring in contemptuous silence. Arctura wanted to shrink beneath the covers, to muffle sight and sound in their heavy folds. She tore her gaze from Mother instead, fixing her unhindered eye on her inscrutable father.

"You ask what happened," Father said, his boots thudding softly as he took slow steps toward her bed. Arctura detected no malice, no contempt, not even anger, but still she cringed at his approach. She rubbed her parched tongue over the inside of her lip, feeling chipped teeth and stinging cuts. Everything hurt, but the presence of her parents now felt like torture.

"What happened is you have shamed us," he continued. "Your disgraceful actions have displayed the inherent weakness of your sex. I am rarely wrong, Arctura, but I imagined you had the making of manly strength about you; that you might have carried the pride of our house in the dignity it deserves. I considered you worthier than that effeminate excuse for a man you call your brother. But you have made me a fool."

Arctura's eye burned, threatening tears as she looked into the cold, emotionless face of Father. She couldn't even bring herself to look at Mother, who snorted scornfully but said nothing.

"Women," Father scoffed. "No wonder that spy of Onesti house set his charms on you. It's in your nature to be ensnared."

"Reylas is not a spy," Arctura objected. Though fierce loyalty rose in her chest, her voice sounded small and unconvincing. "He loves me."

It was Mother who let out a cold, joyless laugh. "Love you? Dear, how could he *love* you? Samrasines are as capable of humanity as cave trolls. That primitive ape used you and discarded you. For coin."

"No," Arctura whispered, shaking her head so vigorously that it made her wounded head spin. "I won't believe it."

"Believe," Father said, thrusting a parchment below her nose.

A scrawling hand came into focus; Reylas's own writing style on the crumpled paper. Arctura read its smudged ink with sinking despair.

The Vipsanius girl can be intercepted tonight at The Lonely Siren. *Send the Drake. For the glory of Onesti house!*

In your service,

R.F.

"It can't be true," Arctura said quietly, blinking away tears. "Reylas would never... he couldn't..."

"Sic the Drake, one of Gormlaen's foulest cutthroats, upon the mother of his misbegotten?"

Father's reply cut deeper than any of her attacker's lacerations. The remaining shreds of self-control, confidence, and ferocity bled out of her faster than she could stymie the flow. Was it true? Did Reylas really send a madman to butcher his beloved and unborn child for the Onestis? Arctura searched her mind for any indication of treachery. She could not find it. *But the note was in his hand!* Its undeniability jarred her to the core. *The baby...* Arctura's lip quaked as she gingerly touched her bandaged torso.

"It did not survive," Father said.

"You ought to be grateful," Mother added. "Now only your family is burdened with your humiliation."

She'll make me atone for this for the rest of my days, Arctura thought, turning toward Mother listlessly. Mother eyed her with all the spite and hatred of a spurned lover, but Arctura felt nothing. She was too weak to muster scorn, pain, or sorrow. All that remained was one last burning question.

"What now?" Arctura said, looking back at Father. "What will you do with me?"

"I have yet to decide your place." Father put a hand to his mustache, considering the question. "It hinges on how useful you remain. And time will tell that. For now—"

Father stood and opened the curtains. Arctura shielded herself against the flood of light.

"Perhaps you have learned something invaluable," he said, facing the open window. "No one can be trusted. All who stand in the way of our house's rise are enemies and threats. But our enemies gravely miscalculated. And now they will learn a lesson of their own."

"What do you mean?" Arctura's heart thumped. *Does he have Reylas?*

Mother giggled with delight. "Have they brought out the condemned, Lucan?"

"Soon," Father replied.

The condemned. Dread filled Arctura as she imagined what was going on in the square below Kyma. Public executions were not a frequent spectacle, but if the city knew a criminal had tried to murder their own Senator's daughter... Was it Reylas down there? Erhi? The entire troupe? Despite the excruciating pain, Arctura forced herself up. Even if he was guilty, even if they were all guilty, could she bear to watch them die?

She craned her neck to look out the window, where a throng of people milled restlessly in the square. On a newly raised platform, a black-hooded man thumbed a massive axe. He shifted impatiently, and the crowd mirrored his excitement as they chattered and stirred. Suddenly, loud whoops and cheers went up, and the crowd ebbed like a wave as three figures, roped together and led on by a Pardaetha official, strode to the platform.

Arctura's breath caught in her chest, but as they lifted their faces to Kyma's walls, she cocked her head in confusion. The three, a man, a woman, and a young woman like herself, climbed the platform. Their party insignias blazed against their black and red uniforms.

"The Onestis?" Arctura gasped. "But how? By the laws of the Coalition, there ought to be a trial."

Mother smirked at Arctura, clucking her tongue mockingly. "Why, you little idiot, don't you know? Much has transpired this week, as our healers kept you alive. It seems your reckless foolishness has had at least one positive effect: all of Gormlaen rages for justice. Pardaetha's thorough investigation of the matter was all the Coalition Assembly required to confirm the Onestis' treachery. To harm the house of the Supreme Chancellor is treason, of course."

Supreme Chancellor? Already? How could it be? Arctura's eye widened as the house of Onesti waited bound upon the platform. Silen Onesti stood grimly beside his wife, gazing up at Kyma with hatred. The woman wept and leaned into her blanching daughter, who swayed on her feet. Arctura did not know their names. She knew nothing about them. But as she gazed into the terror-stricken face of the young Onesti, she knew at least one thing: ignorance and innocence meant nothing to Father.

The executioner forced Silen's head on the block. He raised the axe head, its sharpened edge winking in the sun. Silence. A thump. The crowd roared.

Father's eyes gleamed.

"Retribution."

16

*Year 113 of the Glorious New Era
46th of Sun's Wane
The Ameliorite Priory
Refuge of the Wolf Barrens*

Sister Alba tapped on the wooden table, her eyebrows drawn and lips pinched in thought. The dining hall had long since cleared as the rest of the sisters attended to their post-breakfast duties, but the Prioress remained with Mouse, Toma, and Fraeda. She and Fraeda sat on one side; Mouse and Toma waited on the other. On the table between them lay the rectangular electronic chip. Mouse stared down at it, her gaze following the strange, metallic patterns interconnecting on its hard surface. She chanced a sidelong glance at Toma, who also studied the peculiar Coalition technology with a troubled expression. She wondered if his thoughts were occupied with the last piece of technology they encountered that looked like that – the one the Coalition used to track Mouse outside of Misty Summit. Mouse rubbed the scar on her hand and shuddered.

The Prioress exhaled slowly as she turned her attention away from the chip. She looked hard at each of them. "Do you know its purpose?"

"Not exactly," Mouse replied. "I had something like it once before. At the Summit, they called it a wage card. I thought that one was just for identification, but the Coats used it to find me when I escaped. Now, this one..."

Mouse stared at the table.

"Whatever it is, it's important. Getting it out of Misty Summit was the last thing Red wanted me to do. I think they took him... because of it."

"And they sure have been hounding us ever since," Toma muttered.

"I will not mince words," Sister Alba said, steepling her fingers. "This revelation you shared with me bodes ill. It may be far worse and more urgent than you realize."

Mouse and Toma exchanged dark looks.

"Well, Ma'am," Mouse ventured hesitantly. "What is it?"

The Prioress looked past them as she spoke. "The Coalition would have all of Reidara believe that by and large, the great Elmnas of the past is extinct. They have convinced the lower Dominions to regard her as a cautionary tale. That only the shell of a subdued people remains."

Her gaze returned to Mouse. "That is not the whole truth. The crushing of the Elmling rebellions dealt a devastating blow, yes, but there is yet a remnant. Free Elmlings live in the far reaches of the wild north, and as much as the Coalition denies it, they are free of Coalition control. Rumor has it that their strength is returning."

"But that's good news," Toma said, his brows knit in confusion. "It means there's hope for Mouse. I mean, if the rumors are true."

"That is precisely the danger. If I have heard the whisperings, I am certain that the Coalition knows far more. And they will not be unprepared." Sister Alba sighed. "Mouse, and even my dear Fraeda, have seen such preparations firsthand."

"You mean the weapons, the experiments, the terrible things they're doing in the camps..." Mouse said slowly. "It's all to stamp out Elmnas for good, isn't it?"

The Prioress gave a curt nod. "The Coalition wearies of subjugating those who won't conform to their idea of a perfect Reidara. If they cannot have complete control..."

"Are you saying they'll just... just kill *everyone*?" Toma whispered, his eyes growing round.

"They have done so to others before," Sister Alba said quietly. "Perhaps now, with this?" She rested her finger beside the chip. "They now have the means to destroy their nuisance once and for all."

"But how?" Mouse asked.

"Mouse," Fraeda said in a whisper. "Remember what you said about the taken? Didn't Red write about them being controlled somehow? What if this... thing is the way they'd been doing it?"

Mouse grimaced. "Yes, and it's horrible. But I can't see how they'd be able to do that to everyone up here. It'd be less trouble to just burn everything to the ground."

"But they don't need to do that. They don't need the people here..." Toma trailed. "They've already got the people they need. Whole prisons full of them."

"An entire, expendable army," Sister Alba said in a low voice. "Unable to feel fear, sorrow, or pain. May the Unseen have mercy."

Mouse's mouth went dry. The horror of the realization washed over her like a tidal wave. How had she not seen it before? What use could the Coalition have for controlling people so completely other than for unprecedented destruction? And if these experiments were happening in prisons all over the world, what untold thousands were being prepared even now for an invasion that would result in the death of millions? Her breath caught in her throat as she slowly reached for the chip and held it between her thumb and forefinger. All watched in silence as she turned it in the light. Red may not have understood it, but he had given Mouse the ultimate weapon, the one that would lead to Elmnas' final demise. If she didn't act.

"We have to find the remnant," Mouse said. "Somehow. It's what Red was trying to do, even if he didn't remember why. Grigus was still alive in him. He was still trying to save his people. And he's shown us the way."

"I agree, the free clans must be warned." Sister Alba drew her fingers over her face and frowned. "But you must also know that any journey north is nothing short of suicide. Southern Elmnas belongs to the Coalition, and where they are not, the Mistwolves are. And even if you do come safely on the other side, you cannot be sure you'll find the clan chieftains there. Nothing is certain. Perhaps we ought to contact our brothers first. They might be able to give you a better idea of where the remaining clans have gathered."

Mouse shook her head. "I don't think there's time. And we can't risk the message getting out or getting lost. We will have to go, and as soon as possible."

Sister Alba gazed up at the ceiling, sighing, then to her pocket, where she produced the beads and Cardanthium stone. With a long gaze at it, she looked back at each of the three youths before her. "As Prioress, it is my purpose, my calling, to care for the well-being of all who pass into our sanctuary. I wonder, how can I send you children out alone, and say to myself that I have done my duty? I fear it is a fool's errand, and I will have your blood to atone for if I allow you to go."

"We aren't children," Toma snorted indignantly. "I'll be of age at the end of the season. Mouse, well, I guess we don't know about Mouse for sure, but she's definitely close!"

The Prioress leveled a stern, motherly glare, and Toma closed his mouth.

"You are children compared to my many seasons' reckonings. I must advise you according to my experience."

"Sister," Mouse said. "There's... something else you should know. Do you remember when we talked about the Phoenix?"

Sister Alba arched an eyebrow in surprise. "Why yes, child, certainly."

"I don't know if I believe or understand any of it," Mouse said, and took a shaky breath. "But I think I ought to be safe and 'heed the warning.' Don't you think?"

"You have seen it?" Sister Alba whispered. Her eyes fastened on Mouse as she raised a hand over her mouth.

"More than once," Toma muttered. "She's pretty sure it saved us on the river, too."

"Can it be?" Sister Alba gazed intently at the beads in her other hand and gently touched each one. "The final beacon to light the way?"

With a quick flick, the Prioress put the beads back in her frock. She exhaled slowly, but there was now a spark in her eyes as they rested again on Mouse.

"But then, what leads you to Titans' Rest? Why are you so certain you'll find the clans there?"

Mouse squirmed in her seat as the other sets of eyes rested on her as well. She had kept her last dream to herself, choosing instead to share the details of her encounter with Fraeda in the storage room and the revelation of Red's true name with Toma in their brief moments before breakfast. They didn't know what she saw; to be honest, she didn't want them to know. How could she explain the dark things she now believed were to come, the horrors yet to be unleashed despite all they had come against so far?

Even so, will you follow?

"The phoenix. It came to me again last night, in a dream. It wants me... to follow." Mouse pointed at Fraeda, and looks of surprise registered on everyone's faces.

"You saw... me?" Fraeda gasped. "It told you to follow me?"

"As much as dreams tell anyone anything," Mouse smiled sheepishly. "You were there. When I found you today, I just wanted to ask you a few questions. But then you offered to take me to Titans' Rest... and I just knew."

Toma let out a low whistle. "Boy, that's putting a lot of faith in dreams."

"Yeah," Mouse chuckled. "I thought that too when you came with me in the first place."

Toma grinned, his expression softening. "Yeah, I guess you're right. I'm past the point of no return, aren't I?"

He met Mouse's gaze, and her heart warmed at its tenderness. Gratitude did not describe what she felt now. What did she feel? *A little too warm*, she thought as her cheeks flushed.

Outside their moment, Sister Alba sighed.

"This goes against every practical bone in my body," she said. "I would wish to send you safely to our brothers, and from there, decide on a course of action. But practicality only goes so far, does it not? The Unseen sees and knows. It seems it is outside my authority to bind your consciences and ask you to remain under my care or delay any longer. I cannot interfere with a seer."

Mouse's mouth dropped open. "What do you mean?"

Sister Alba gave her a matronly smile. "Well, it seems so to me, anyway. Visions, dreams, and an overshadowing of the Unseen don't happen to everyone, child."

Toma looked at Mouse with wonder as Fraeda nodded in vigorous agreement.

"No way," Mouse said, shaking her head. "I'm no one. I don't even have a real name."

"Everyone is *someone*," The Prioress said. "Whether the memory of this world recalls them or not."

"All is known to One," Fraeda said softly. "Not even the least of us is forgotten."

Sister Alba turned her attention to Fraeda, warmth and sorrow evident in the way she clasped the novice's hands.

"And you, dear one. How can I doubt anything when the Unseen has returned your voice? It is joy upon joy. And yet, a sorrow, too, for I perceive there it bestows upon you a new purpose. Shall I consider your initiation interview canceled, little sister?"

"On hold, if you can wait for me. I think I must do other things," Fraeda replied, squeezing Sister Alba's hands in return.

A tear rolled down the elder's cheek as she drew Fraeda into a tight hug. "So you shall. Marvelous things you shall do, my sister Fraeda."

The Prioress released her and looked at each of them in turn. "Let us waste no more time. Your journey awaits you, dear ones."

Mouse, Toma, and Fraeda stood in the courtyard before the entire Ameliorite community, bidding goodbye with embraces, handshakes, and tearful words. Most of the embraces and tears were reserved for Fraeda. The sisters gathered around her as tight and as loud as a flock of birds.

"Remember to send a message with the brothers!"

"Take these remedies and teas. You never know when you will have need of them."

"That frolicking adventurer getup doesn't suit you nearly as well as your habit, little novice. You must return as soon as possible!"

Fraeda beamed from ear to ear, tucking the escaping frazzled wisps of bright ginger hair back into her long, low-tied ponytail. She indeed looked quite different from when Mouse first met her: With a traveler's tunic, cloak, and trousers, a pack, and a heavy, carved staff, Fraeda hardly resembled the timid novice peeking into Mouse's rooms. Fraeda looked over the heads of the crowding sisters at Mouse and, with a laugh, shrugged her shoulders. It was a sight to behold, and not just because of her new look. Mouse wondered if for the first time, she realized just how much the sisters loved her.

"So you're just gonna leave me with these old bats, is that it?"

Mouse turned toward the familiar voice, grinning as Dane shuffled slowly toward them.

"It'll do you good," she said.

"I'll say!" Toma added. "You look worlds better than when we showed up."

Dane rotated his shoulder with difficulty, wincing and grunting. "It ain't ever gonna move right again, I'm sure of it."

Mouse sighed. "Dane..."

"Alright, alright," he conceded. "That Raelin knows her stuff. I'll give her that."

"And you'll be back to your smuggling in no time," Toma reached out his hand. "I wish you the best. You've done something great here. I hope it wasn't too much trouble."

"Don't you worry," Dane grasped Toma's hand firmly, but with a fond smile. It quickly devolved into an impish grin. "I reckon Woldyff now owes *me*. I'll collect on it soon enough."

"Until then," Mouse added, offering her own hand. "Behave."

Dane leaned in instead, surprising Mouse with something between a thump on the back and a hug. He whispered as he came close to her ear.

"And you look out for yourself. Save this broken world, if you gotta, but stay safe."

Mouse stepped away, dumbfounded. She said nothing, but nodded.

Sister Alba approached with Fraeda, the group of sisters trailing behind.

"I'm afraid the time has come," the Prioress said. "With the Unseen's blessing, you ought to pass safely out of the Wolf Barrens before nightfall. Fraeda can show you the way. The Coalition's presence is not as pronounced around here as you might think, but proceed with caution. I do not know who or what may yet be searching for you."

"We'll be careful, Sister," Mouse replied. "Thank you."

The clank of the Priory's rising gate resounded throughout the courtyard. Mouse, Toma, and Fraeda gazed out over the widening awning of its now open doors, the hills and forests of Elmnas stretching out before them. Mouse suppressed a shudder, trying her best not to dwell on what else would be out there with them.

"Here's to new friends," Toma smiled, acknowledging Fraeda with a nod. "And the next part of our impossible journey."

"No kidding," Mouse muttered.

With a deep breath, she shouldered her pack and followed them beyond the safety of the Priory's walls. She glanced back as they crossed the gate's threshold. Some sisters peeked over the battlements and waved. They remained there, watching the group grow small as they crossed the great vale and crested a hill above it. Mouse stopped, looking back for the last time over the valley. The dark, strong fortress it stretched to meet had now disappeared from sight. She could no longer see the distinct purple frocks or the women who wore them, but she caught a glimpse of the Priory's flag as it fluttered proudly on the wind.

"The Priory has been my home for a number of years," Fraeda said, following Mouse's gaze. "The only home I can remember, really. I'm not sure I'm ready for this."

Mouse paused, looking between Fraeda and Toma. Both had now left the places they called home to help Mouse find hers. They were risking so much... for her. The guilt of the thought swept over Mouse, causing her knees to buckle. Her dream rushed back to her unbidden once more, and she shivered to think what terrors they approached so willingly. How could she allow them to continue with her on this foolish quest?

Another thought broke through Mouse's guilt and worry. *It's not just about you anymore.*

That was true. Mouse had a duty to Red to reach his people, his remaining rebellion, to warn them of the abominable plans the Coalition harbored for them. More than that, something else called to her – not just the woman of her disjointed dreams, but the Phoenix, the bringer of Elmnas's redemption itself. She had no idea what that really meant, if she were a seer as Sister Alba believed, or anything else so impossible. But she knew this was her path, her purpose, drawing her far from the walls of Misty Summit's prison, delivering her past the snapping jaws of the insatiable Mistwolf, over the waters of Thunder Run's certain death to find herself here. Whatever happened next, Mouse would see it through. Even to her last breath.

Mouse considered her friends, who looked back at her with the same determination she felt rising in her own chest. She knew, for whatever reason, they felt it too. Finally, she answered Fraeda.

"None of us are. But it looks like the time has come, anyway."

Fraeda let out a little laugh. "That was perfect. Just like something I might read in the scrolls of the Guardians."

"Definitely," Toma agreed. "Blade would've been proud."

"You must tell me more about him," Fraeda said as the two headed toward a worn game trail that disappeared into the ancient forest of thick pines and white birches.

"You'd have liked him," Toma replied.

The conversation continued, but Mouse did not hear it. She stared at the strange forest, a chill running up her spine as she remembered the closeness of the mists and its hungry inhabitants in the nearby Wolf Barrens. Her mind drifted to another strange forest, one where a vision and a warrior set her firmly on the path that led here.

"We could've really used you now, Blade. More than ever," she whispered.

"Hey!" Toma shouted from ahead. "Are you coming or what?"

"Yeah, coming!"

Shaking off the bite of the autumnal air, Mouse jogged to catch up to her friends. Her feet found the trail, overgrown but not lost, and she followed it as it wound up the hillside and disappeared beneath the trees. A shuddering breath escaped her lips as they walked into the shadowy canopy.

Okay, I'm following. What's next?

17

"So let me get this straight," Toma said between breaths. He pushed back the unruly hair dripping sweat into his eyes as the trio stomped along the lonely forest path. "You can really understand what people are saying just by reading their lips?"

"Not just by lip reading," Freda replied. "People tend to say more with their faces and bodies than their actual words. So even if I can't catch everything someone is actually *saying*, I can usually guess and fill in what I missed by watching *how* they say it."

"Wow, that's fascinating," Toma said. "I've also heard that deaf people have like, enhanced vision or other senses to take place of their hearing. Is that true?"

"That's a myth," Fraeda laughed. "I just have to rely on my other senses more, senses that others don't practice using as much as I have to. Now, stop trying to talk to me. It's hard enough to keep us going the right way without having to turn around and read your lips every 30 seconds."

Toma raised his hands in apology. "Sure, sorry!"

Mouse chuckled as they trundled single file through the dark and previously still forest. Now, as they forced their way into its confined and snarled undergrowth, the silence fled, filled with the sounds of brush swooshing, twigs cracking, and stones rolling under foot. More than once, Mouse worried they had lost the path entirely: a fatal mistake to make in the unforgiving woods when the Coalition and other monsters lurked close at hand. But Fraeda was an able pathfinder, moving with the ease and familiarity of one whose childhood had been marked by forest amblings. And despite the fear that came from the unknown, Mouse found Blade had successfully impressed at least some of his survival instincts upon her. Mouse recalled his lessons as she oriented herself by the moss growth on rocks and tree trunks.

The path turned, and Fraeda's head of red, frazzled hair bobbed out of view. Mouse hurried to catch up but scrambled to a halt at what lay ahead.

"Whoa."

Toma also stopped short as they stumbled into the sudden brightness of day. Roughly hewn stumps stretched for miles of what should have been forest. The clearing lay littered with the wreckage of rusting machinery and the skeletons of decaying trees. Mouse stepped gingerly out of the forest, feeling naked herself on the exposed earth.

"What happened here?" she wondered aloud.

"The Coalition's work," Fraeda supplied. "It's like this all over Elmnas. In my village, almost everyone worked in the Cardanthium mines when Elmnas fell. And when the Cardanthium was gone..."

Fraeda gestured to the wasteland. "There were the trees."

Toma shook his head in disbelief. "And I thought Maiendell had it bad."

"Is the village that did this close, then?" Mouse asked.

"Not too close," Fraeda said. She pointed beyond a rocky rise in the sea of stumps. "See that over there? That should be an old Cardanthium mine. And past that, maybe a mile or two, should be its village, Ervandas. Looks like the Coalition went to logging almost all the way up to the Wolf Barrens. But they stopped here, for some reason."

"Maybe for game," Toma guessed. "Not much to hunt, if there are no trees at all."

"I don't like it," Mouse said, rubbing her arms. "There's gotta be Coats close by if it looks like this around here. Toma and I stick out enough as it is. What are we going to do with no cover at all? We ought to steer clear of Ervandas. Maybe head along the tree line here."

"I don't think we have much of a choice," Fraeda said. "Look, if we travel that way, we're bound to run into the Coalition. Their presence gets heavier the farther along this forest we go. And in the other direction, we're way too close to the Wolf Barrens. The only way we can go is through Ervandas."

"We need to find somewhere to shelter," Toma agreed, shivering. "Seems likes it's gotta be the village. Nowhere to sleep out here. Ugh, I'm gonna miss the Priory a lot more than I thought. Weird robes and all."

"Walking right up to Ervandas doesn't seem wise to me," Mouse said, shaking her head. "Are you sure there's no other way?"

Fraeda rubbed her thumb against her lips, thinking. "How about this? When we get to the mines, you and Toma wait there while I go up to the village. I can check it out alone and come back with word one way or the other. If it's safe, we find somewhere to spend the night. If not, maybe we can pass through Ervandas at dusk."

"Why not just shelter at the mines, anyway?" Mouse asked.

"I wouldn't recommend it," Fraeda said with a sharp breath. "Abandoned dark holes tend to be home for some nasty things. Things that are more likely to come out at night when we're sleeping."

"Ah, more monsters. Of course," Toma said. "In that case, I like Fraeda's plan. What do you think, Mouse? Worth a try?"

"As long as it doesn't put her in any danger," Mouse said. She turned toward Fraeda. "How safe is it for you?"

"Safe enough," Fraeda replied. "No one will think anything of another Elmling girl hanging around. It shouldn't be much of a problem even if the Coalition is there. When I escaped them the first time, I got in and out of towns without being noticed."

"Okay," Mouse agreed. "But no need to take extra risks, alright? If you see anything that worries you, get out. We'll figure out what to do when you come back."

Fraeda smiled. "Of course. One step at a time, right?"

"Right."

"You'll be out of sight here, I think," Fraeda said as they stood before the abandoned Cardanthium mine.

Mouse nervously adjusted her jacket as she looked around. By all human measures, the mine was indeed abandoned. The paths leading into the hillside had long ago eroded, though the faint imprints of wheel ruts in the graveled dirt and the weedy overgrowth remained visible. Scraggly trees grew at odd angles out of the hillside; twisted sad things that had received pity from the cutters' axes after they felled their worthier companions. Nothing moved except the loose shale disturbed by the trio's trek over the rise.

The mineshaft itself was little more than a gaping hole. Rotting wooden supports framed the rectangular opening, leading down into an impenetrable abyss. Mouse could feel the cold, damp air seeping out of it. She leaned away from the current. *Abandoned by people, but not by everything*, Mouse thought, and shivered.

"It's no wonder if we are," Toma grimaced. "It doesn't seem like the sort of place sensible people hang out."

Fraeda offered an apologetic shrug. "I shouldn't be long. Maybe only an hour, if we're lucky."

"No, no, take your time. I'm sure nothing will eat us. Ow!"

Toma rubbed his side after Mouse jabbed it with her elbow.

Fraeda grinned. "Can't seers sense trouble before it comes?"

"Don't *call* me that," Mouse said, rolling her eyes. "Besides, it doesn't work that way."

"I guess we'll find out soon enough," Fraeda laughed. "Be safe, friends."

Mouse watched as Fraeda followed the ghost of the path flowing toward Ervandas. Her figure grew smaller, and soon she clambered over a little ridge and disappeared from sight.

What now? Mouse thought, sucking in her cheeks and rubbing her hands. There was, it seemed, nothing to do but wait. Selecting a boulder a comfortable distance from the mine's entrance, she sat down cross-legged and let out a long sigh. Shifting, she tried hard not to focus on the dark mineshaft and whatever lay within. Still, she could not abide ignoring it entirely, so Mouse settled on keeping it in her periphery. It did not seem like a good compromise, but it was the best she could come up with at the moment. With some effort, she turned her attention elsewhere.

Toma, who had been milling around anxiously for a few minutes, had now shed his pack and coat. Mouse observed him thoughtfully as he extracted his dagger and postured in the stances that Blade had taught them. With practiced fluidity, he rolled through the movements. The dagger flashed as he twisted and thrusted, the strength of his arms and chest visible beneath his thin tunic.

Mouse tilted her head as she considered him. In just the short time they had spent together, Toma had already seemed to change. His lean frame had become all sinew, and Mouse swore he had grown an inch or two during their journey through the Gormlaean wilds. And though it hadn't quite filled in on his cheeks, a thick, black scruff covered his neck and climbed under the chin. Indeed, the patchy facial hair was the only thing still boyish about him. More than when she had first met him, Toma looked like a man.

His amber eyes flashed toward her, and he grinned. "Wanna join in? I could use a sparring partner."

Mouse felt for her own dagger, its strange heat emanating into her open hand. She wrapped her fingers around the intricate hilt and tugged, observing as the exposed Cardanthium edge pulsed in anticipation. *Is it just me, or does that seem brighter now than before?*

"I don't think so," she said, replacing the dagger carefully. "It feels a little irreverent using an ancient dagger for play."

Toma shrugged and returned to his previous movements. He concentrated on his forms, sliding once again into the graceful dance of a swordsman. And once again, his glance flickered toward her, his steely concentration softening as their eyes met. Mouse frowned as her stomach seemed to flip on top of itself, and she clapped a hand over her heart to stifle its unbearably loud thumping. *Why's it doing that?*

She tore her gaze away, hopping down from the boulder with unsteady legs. There were a lot of things she didn't understand about the world she had stumbled into after escaping Misty Summit; the incomprehensible weirdness that had exploded in her the more time she spent with Toma continued to be the most confusing. Part of her knew it had to be normal; *good,* even, to feel so – not everyone interacted out here the way they did in Misty Summit – but the last thing she wanted was to sort through it and decide what it meant.

It's not like I don't have enough problems already, Mouse scoffed to herself. She jammed her hands into her pockets and crunched the old gravel of the abandoned path beneath her feet. Sighing, she walked along it, her gaze sweeping over the sad trees and carved canyon walls instead of lingering on the abyss of the mine. Even so, something stirred out of the corner of her eye.

She snapped her attention back to the mine opening, peering hard into the darkness and holding her breath. It seemed perfectly still and quiet, the only sound of Toma breathing and slashing air behind her. Mouse squeaked as a glimmer of color winked in and out of existence in the mouth of the hole.

"Toma," she hissed through gritted teeth.

A pebble rolled lazily from the hole.

"Toma!" Mouse nearly shouted, her hand straying to her pistol.

"Huh?" Toma finally answered, his dagger poised midair. "What's up?"

"QUIET," Mouse said, more loudly than she would have liked herself. She jerked her head toward the mine, her words coming in a punctuated whisper. "There - is - something - in- *there*."

"You can't be serious," Toma replied, but his protest fell silent. A flash of color moved within.

Mouse leveled her pistol at the hole and took a shaky breath. "Now?"

"Wait," Toma said quietly, withdrawing his own weapon. "Until you can see it. Get a clean shot."

But before Mouse could blink, something launched toward her from the dark.

18

Mouse would have discharged her pistol, she was sure of it, but the thing that came flying out of the mine had moved so fast that all she could do was stare stupidly as it came to rest at her feet. Toma, for his part, *had* pulled his trigger, but the shot had hopelessly missed its target. Instead, a jet of white light blasted directly into the middle of the hole, exploding in a spray of soft dirt and rock a few feet inside. Rotted timbers within collapsed with the rattling concussion, followed by a puff of dust. With an embarrassed "oof," Toma sheathed his pistol.

The attempt on the thing's life, however, had not seemed to bother it all. Instead, the creature rested calmly on its haunches, licking the ruddy, black-lined fur on its lithe, feline body.

"What... what is it?" Mouse asked.

"Well," Toma said, scratching his head. "It looks kind of like a cat. But uh... I'm pretty sure it's not."

Mouse knew what cats looked like. This was no cat. The padded paws, pointed ears, and pink nose with whiskers could have fooled her; the ridge of black and gold porcupine-like quills along its spine, flowing down to cover the tail that terminated in one sharp, scorpion-like stinger, could not. This tail arched up like a scorpion's would, hovering between the creature's shoulder blades and behind the nubs of two horns on its feline head. It turned its large sea-green eyes toward her, full of expression and intelligence Mouse could not readily recall in a normal cat, and yawned, exposing three rows of tiny, sharp teeth. Mouse squeaked again as it rubbed its head against her leg and purred.

"At least it's friendly," Toma chuckled.

Mouse shot a panicked look at Toma. "A little help?"

"Not a cat person, huh?"

"It's not a cat!" Mouse hissed.

With a grin, Toma pulled some dried meat from his pants pocket and kneeled down by the creature. A strange whispery cooing sound escaped his mouth as he extended the meat toward it.

"Here, kitty-thing. Sorry I tried to shoot you," he said. "How about a little snack, hm?"

The creature gave him a rueful glare but mewed hungrily. It snatched the meat deftly between its paws as Toma tossed it. With the creature's many teeth occupied, Toma bravely scratched it behind its ears. He beamed as it purred approvingly.

"This little guy reminds me of a cat we used to have when I was a kid," Toma said. "I called him Little Bear. He was supposed to catch rats, but all he did was sleep in the loft and get fat. Hey! We should name it!"

Mouse crinkled her nose. "Don't do that. You'll encourage it to stick around."

"C'mon, it likes you! Now let's see..." Toma screwed up his face in thought. "How about... um... Flash... or, uh... Fang? Ooh! Quill?"

The cat-like creature cocked its head and swayed its terrifying tail.

"Do you think that stinger thing is poisonous?" Mouse shuddered. "I don't like the idea of that."

"That's it!" Toma snapped his fingers. "Sting. That's his name. Perfect. Hey, look at you, Mouse. You're good at this!"

"Why isn't it touching *you?*" Mouse cringed as it circled her legs, quills snagging on her pants.

"Maybe not a cat, but it sure acts like one," Toma laughed. "They always go for the person who likes them least. Here, Sting–"

Mouse sighed with relief as Toma produced another piece of meat and tossed it some distance away. With a loud mew, Sting sprung forward and snapped it up in its little jaws. Mouse turned out her pockets in a hurry, throwing any rations she had on her in Sting's general direction before sidling cautiously behind Toma.

"Do you think it will follow us?" she whispered.

Sting sat up straight and gazed back at them lazily, a strip of meat dangling from its mouth. He cocked his head again, as if considering the question. With one final gulp, the strip disappeared, and Sting darted back into the mineshaft.

Toma shrugged. "Guess not. But I think you hurt his feelings."

Mouse rolled her eyes. "Or maybe something else scared it away. Look."

She pointed to the figure cresting the ridge into the clearing. "Is that Fraeda already?"

Both Toma and Mouse squinted toward the ridge. Mouse couldn't make out much except the flash of red hair. The figure looked in their direction and offered a vigorous wave.

"It's gotta be," Toma agreed. "Come on, she seems excited."

Mouse glowered toward the mine as she snatched up her things. "Don't have to say that twice."

They ran to meet Fraeda closer to the ridge. She hurried down the other side, panting and dabbing sweat off a face nearly as a red as her hair. Mouse picked up her pace. Fear that Fraeda brought bad news filled her, but as they drew nearer, she changed her mind. Fraeda may have looked a little worn from the journey into Ervandas and back, but the broad grin promised something extraordinary. Winded, Fraeda stopped short and hunched over, hands on her knees as she caught her breath. Still, she smiled as she watched them approach.

"You're back sooner than expected!" Toma said. "What's the news?"

Fraeda stood straight, smiling as she wiped her brow. "You aren't going to believe this. There's a circus in town. You can barely turn around in the market square."

Toma laughed. "A circus? Man, that's lucky!"

"Maybe not luck," Fraeda replied, a knowing smile on her lips as she nodded toward Mouse.

"What's a circus?" Mouse asked, exasperation creeping into her voice. "How does that help us?"

"It's like... a big carnival," Fraeda explained, her eyes lighting up. "A party that comes into town. There are performers, food like you wouldn't believe... and wondrous animals! They've come before, at least once, when Sister Raelin and I traveled to Ervandas for emergency medicinal supplies a few harvests ago. Of course, the sisters forbid participating in that sort of merriment, so..."

Fraeda traced the dirt with her toe as she mumbled sheepishly, "We left before I could really see anything."

"Party?" Mouse screwed up her face in confusion. "What's that?"

Toma placed a hand on her shoulder. "I think you'll just have to see it for yourself."

Mouse sighed. "So now that there's this 'circus', what's our plan?"

"There's a tent camp on the far side of town, by its northern gate. Mostly the performers and workers, I expect, but I'm sure the one inn in Ervandas won't be able to hold all the town's visitors," Fraeda said. "I think you two will blend right in. It might be safer to stay in the villages and out of woods when we can, anyway."

"What about Coats?" Toma asked. "See many of them?"

Fraeda shrugged. "A few. As always. But not a lot, and they've got their hands full."

"Why don't we head into the village at dusk and leave before full morning light?" Mouse suggested. "It's harder to look for fugitives in the dark."

Toma rubbed his chin and nodded. "That should work. We'd

probably look more suspicious just passing though. And the best part is we get to see the circus!"

"Alright, but I think I've had my fill of wondrous animals for the day," Mouse said, tossing a glance back at the mines.

Fraeda furrowed her brow. "What did you see?"

"Um..." Toma said slowly. "Just a weird cat, that's all."

"A weird cat!" Mouse scoffed. "With horns on his head! And a scorpion tail, and way too many teeth!"

"A manticore?" Fraeda replied, wide-eyed. "You saw a manticore? You know those things *eat* people, right?"

Toma rubbed the back of his neck with a nervous chuckle. "His name is Sting!"

19

Darkness crept down the Elmling mountain slopes and cast deepening shadows along the one barren road that led into Ervandas. A chill wind blew across it, unhindered by the stumps of felled trees and low boulders along either side. Mouse shivered, pulling her jacket tighter around her small frame. The sudden cold as night approached surprised her, given the suffocating warmth of the afternoon. She was no stranger to cool nights. The Summit had frosted over with snow and ice on winter nights before, but still, it seemed different here. *No soot and sulfur, for one thing*, she thought, and she took a deep, grateful breath.

Ahead, the path rolled upward, leading into an open gateway hemmed on either side by a massive wall. The outer perimeter of Ervandas, as Fraeda had told them to expect, stood as the town's only barrier against what might lurk beyond it in the night. Mouse took in its proportions: rolled boulders, roughly squared and mortared together, at about ten feet high. Fraeda had assured her that Mistwolves weren't common in this part of Elmnas; they preferred the low valleys and their creeping, thick mists. Nonetheless, Mouse looked about her and up at the wall with suspicion. She herself might have been able to climb it, given the right footholds; the creatures she knew and feared could probably clear it with a single bound.

Soon enough, they passed through the gate. Mouse adjusted her hood, pulling it low over her eyes as a lone traveler overtook them on horseback. Toma did the same, covertly glancing in her direction. The amber rings of his eyes shone out from beneath the hood's shadow, and as the rider passed, she detected the flash of white as his mouth spread into a toothy grin.

"See?" he said. "Nothing to worry about."

"Not yet," she grumbled under her breath.

"Look!" Fraeda exclaimed, pointing. "You can already see it from here!"

Mouse squinted, now able to see Ervandas. The rectangular silhouettes of squat shacks, long lodges, and other low buildings spread out in front of them. In comparison with Lilien, the only other city Mouse had passed through, Ervandas was little better than a trading post. The sad, leaning buildings spoke volumes of the fortunes of the Elmlings who still lived there, toiling under the thumb of their conquerors. But beyond, in stark relief, emanated the soft glow of multicolored lights, illuminating the sloping sides of shiny, bright tents and the assorted shapes and sizes of the colorful circus caravans. Even outside of Ervandas Mouse could hear the excited rumble of the milling crowds, the eerie tinkling of strange music, the boom of the performers' carrying voices. Her mouth dropped open.

"I've never seen anything like it," she whispered.

"Just wait until we get there!" Toma replied. "You're gonna love it!"

Groups of revelers joined the three as they wound up the main road, squeezing in on either side. Mouse peered at the faces, surprised to see people of all sorts pouring into Ervandas. Most Gormlaean, some Elmling, but a few of them neither.

"Who are all these people?" she mouthed to Fraeda.

Fraeda leaned in, her voice low in the growing commotion of the crowd. "Traders, hunters, and settlers. When the Coalition conquered Elmnas, they tried to give most of what we had left to their own. There aren't a lot of southern Gormlaeans here, though. Mostly what they call the last tribes of Old Gor, people who aren't quite Gormlaean but not friendly to Elmnas, either. Anyway, the Coalition lets the right sort of people in... just remember, they don't let any of the wrong ones out."

Mouse tugged her hood lower.

Soon they came to the town itself, its entrance marked only by a rotting post with "Ervandas" burned into its rudely cut sign. If she had thought Ervandas unimpressive at a distance, Mouse found it absolutely miserable now. Dim lamps lined the main street and cast a paltry, sick glow at the ground directly beneath them. The windows in the building were dark, but now and then, Mouse saw a dirty face peer out before ducking out of view.

She hopped around a few agitated chickens, narrowly avoiding trampling their scraggly bodies as they flapped underfoot. But still the people pressed in around her, surging toward the drawing lights without a second thought for her or the poor creatures beneath them. Mouse tried to spin, panicking. A familiar hand found her arm and squeezed.

"It's alright," Toma said. "I'm here."

Mouse turned to answer, finding him far closer than she expected. The crowd pressed them together, and Mouse bumped into his chest. Toma reached around her and steadied Mouse against him. She could feel his heart beating fast and hard, and her face reddening as she realized her rhythm kept pace. Mouse looked up, his face inches above hers. Their eyes met, and Mouse's gaze drifted to his mouth. *Why have I never noticed his lips before?* She thought. *They're... nice.*

"Uh," Toma said, pulling back. "Sorry."

Mouse attempted an answer and failed. Thankfully, a bump against her other side gave her an excuse to look away. There, Fraeda tugged on her shirtsleeve and smiled.

"Easy to get lost in this madness," Fraeda said, looping her arm into hers. "Stay close!"

Mouse nodded, grateful for the distraction. With Fraeda leading, they made their way into the market. Mouse gasped as they stepped within its bounds. The festivities sprawled from the market through the back of the village, infusing the meager square with a vibrancy far greater than Ervandas could ever hope to supply on its own. Garish booths of various amusements lined the square on all sides, the lights so bright and numerous that it might as well have been day.

In the center of the square stood a large, box-shaped podium. Colorful letters adorned each side, and Mouse squinted to read the flourishes of whimsical script. It read, "Needar's Wandering Circus" in the common tongue. On top of the box gesticulated a bombastic man, as wildly gaudy in appearance as the rest of the circus. Needar, Mouse could only presume. Even in his ridiculous suit, striped orange and red, with the ends of his curling, crimson-dyed mustache and beard jingling with tiny, silver bells, Needar made a striking figure. Passersby lingered to watch and listen to the attractive, charismatic ringmaster, and as he spoke, they stared up at him in awe. Needar held his tall, striped hat in one gloved hand and waved a black cane in the other, flashing a devilishly handsome grin as he worked the crowd.

"Welcome! Welcome to Needar's Wandering Circus! Step right up, step right up to this booth on my left for your tokens, and you will witness the wonders of the world! Drown in the elegance of Reidara's most beautiful and talented women. Look on in terror at this world's most fearsome beasts! Come! Get your tokens! Witness the most amazing feats of supernatural skill and strength. Laugh until you cry at our performers' unparalleled antics! And yes, yes, see the most scandalous oddities among man and creature alike! Only Needar's Wandering Circus boasts of the strangest, rarest, most one-of-kind assortment of curios, so be certain to visit the booths on my right. You'll never find a carnival's equal elsewhere, I promise you, dear travelers. Come, one and all, for the best show in the Four Dominions! Nay, the best show in Reidara!"

They siphoned the crowd toward the token booth, where an attendant stood to wait on the eager arrivals. As they drew closer, Fraeda nudged Mouse and leaned in furtively.

"Don't look now," she said, offering a subtle nod toward the side of the market. "But we have some company that weren't here before."

Of course, Mouse looked. She wished she hadn't. Two grim-faced Coalition guards eyed the crowd at the market's edge. Behind them, several more Coalition soldiers congregated at the door of a ramshackle barracks. Mouse could read the foreboding sign written in stern letters on the building's facade: COALITION LIAISON OFFICE.

"I thought you said it was clear!" Toma whispered urgently.

"It was!" Fraeda protested, panic in her voice. "They weren't here when I came earlier. A transport must've arrived just for the circus."

"You don't think..." Toma began. "They're not expecting us, are they?"

Mouse narrowed her eyes. "Maybe not particularly, but I wouldn't put it past them. Dane said news about the price on me has been circulating. You've said it before, Toma... that bounty hunter won't be the only one after us."

"And here I thought she was the worst thing they could throw our way," Toma grimaced.

"What do we do?" Mouse said.

"Let me handle the tokens," Fraeda said. "And then..."

She craned her neck to survey the booths.

"There," Fraeda said brightly, pointing. "That might work."

Opposite the Coalition Liaison Office, in a garish booth on the far side of the market, the empty eyeholes of wild masks gazed back at them.

"The quicker, the better," Mouse said, doing her best not to fidget as the eyes of one guard flitted toward them, and lingered.

Fraeda pulled a bulging coin purse from her pocket and hefted it into her other hand. As Toma and Mouse gawked, she dumped a few coins in her palm and lifted it to the attendant. "I'm certain this will do for the three of us. The rest is yours if you'd like."

The attendant grinned widely, pocketed half the coin, and handed Fraeda three tokens.

"Enjoy the show," he winked, and waved them along.

With a gentle smile and nod, she drove Toma and Mouse into the crowd.

"Fraeda!" Toma said, pointing at the coin purse. "Where did you get *that?*"

Fraeda shoved it inside her jacket hastily and shrugged. "The sisters insisted."

Sure to avoid the watching Coalition guards, they weaved toward the masks booth and shortly donned them. Toma charged ahead, anxious to both see the entertainment and get out of view himself. Mouse trailed behind, feeling safe beneath her disguise and feasting her eyes on every novelty they passed. She stared greedily at the various food booths strewn throughout the market and breathed in the delicious scents mingling in the air: the sticky-sweetness of glazed pastries, the savory seasoning of fried delectables, the smoky heat of roasting meat. Her stomach grumbled. Among the food booths were games of all sorts. People congregated beneath tents to throw darts at targets or rings onto glass bottles. She edged in to watch, but the wares close by caught her eye. There, the wayfarers manning the booths shouted out their stock.

"Moonstone, sundrops, and star-gems! Genuine relics of the ancient days that glow with their own light! Miss the sun? You won't when you wear this one! Get your astral rarities at a bargain!"

"Enchanting elixirs! Potent potions! Alchemical remedies for any ailment!"

"Miniatures! Live miniatures! We have goat, pig, and pony! Won't get no bigger than a puppy! Selling at an absolute steal!"

"Wooden swords for yer tykes! Finely crafted! An extra bronze piece and I'll engrave any name!"

Mouse stopped by the gem booth, entranced by their bright twinkling beneath the carnival lights. Each shimmering stone lay artfully inlaid into a variety of necklaces, bracelets, and circlets. One necklace even boasted of genuine Cardanthium. She peered expectantly at the stones, expecting the swirling of indwelling light in their little crystalline forms. Her face fell. The gems reflected their surroundings brilliantly, but even Mouse could see that no innate light flowed through them.

"You're right to be wary, you are."

Mouse snapped her gaze to the side of the booth, where the speaker stood in its shadow. She felt for her dagger, already emanating warmth beneath her hovering hand.

"Who's there?"

The speaker shuffled forward, revealing himself as an old Elmling man. He leaned on his staff, stroking his impressively long, silver beard as he squinted at her. The Elmling could not have been more than 5 feet tall. His short stature enabled Mouse to look directly into his emerald green eyes and become annoyed by the impressive glare bouncing off his bald head. Mouse relaxed, at least enough to lower her hand from the dagger hilt, and cocked her head.

"What did you say?"

"These little trifles," he finally said, waving a gnarled hand toward the gem booth. "They aren't what they purport to be. It's true. Pretty, but common. Just common stones. And we both know that it's not the common you're after."

"And how do you know that, sir?" Mouse asked suspiciously.

The man chuckled. "I'm just an old man, but I know a seeker when I see one. A seeker of the... uncommon, shall we say? No shiny baubles will do when one must find the truth. And such a truth it is! A truth to overturn the world itself."

Mouse said nothing, but her mind raced, sensing that somehow, she was exposed. She squirmed, forcing her twitching fingers to remain at her side and not to adjusting the mask. Not that seeing her face would have given him insight into what she was doing here, anyway. Despite herself, Mouse met his piercing gaze. Her words, meant to be a challenge, came out in a waver.

"You don't know anything about me."

"Maybe, maybe not," the man scratched his chin and smiled. "But it matters not what I know. *Isa* says you need this. And I do as *Isa* says."

A bewildered Mouse watched as the old man produced an old bronze key from beneath his beard. It dangled on the brown cord as he pulled it over his head. With a twinkle in his emerald eye, he tossed it.

Mouse reached out instinctively, but only managed to deflect it from hitting her in the face. It thudded to the ground, and she swooped down to pick it up.

"Now why in the world would you–"

Mouse straightened, rounding on the old man to chastise him. Her mouth hung open, now wordless. No one stood before her. Mouse turned, searching for the bald head and staff in the crowds, or behind the booth, or anywhere at all, but she saw nothing. He was gone.

Her gaze traveled to her fist, still clutching the key with the cord looped through the bow. She opened her palm, laying it on the flat of it to get a better look. A veneer of dirt dulled any shine, and its long stem bent slightly to the left. It was... just an ordinary key.

"Mouse!"

Startled, she looked up, finding the masked figures of Toma and Fraeda now standing in front of her. Toma had something edible on a stick, still steaming in the cooling night air. He pointed it at her accusingly.

"What are you doing?" he asked, vexed. "We thought something happened to you."

"Not exactly a good place to wander off, you know." Fraeda added in a low voice.

"I– nothing." Mouse closed her hand, stuffing the key in her pocket. "Nothing's wrong. So much to see. I got distracted, sorry."

"No wonder," Toma sighed. "And you haven't even seen any of the good stuff yet! Well, come on, anyway."

Mouse stepped beside them, keeping pace as Toma made a beeline for the big top. She elbowed him playfully and nodded toward the treat in his hand.

"Where'd you get that?"

"Here," Toma chuckled, handing it over. "There's more where that came from."

Behind the dilapidated shacks of Ervandas and beyond its market square reared up the main draw of Needar's Wandering Circus, the big top. The tent seemed to possess impossible proportions as it covered a distance of nearly the entire village itself and stood maybe twice as high. Bright red flags fluttered in the wind, the sound of their flapping drowned out by the roar of the crowds already within. She could see a Coalition guard or two milling around the outside, their stern eyes roving the crowd and long, black coats billowing behind them. The torrent of people hid any would-be offenders, including the masked trio creeping toward the big top's entrance. With Fraeda directing them, Toma and Mouse easily slipped their tokens into a bored attendant's hands and pushed inside.

The main acts of Needar's Wandering Circus seemed well underway as performers flurried around the arena. Mouse gazed in wonder at the woman dangling in the air by what appeared to be satin ribbon; an impossibly long ribbon that she twisted, swung, and rolled along in a series of graceful, dancelike movements. On the ground, horses and elephants paraded around the outer ring of the arena, men and women doing handstands on their backs. A bear danced on one side, bells jingling on his paws and head, while little foxes jumped through rings of fire on the other.

Mouse searched for somewhere to sit as the crowd roared their approval. Outside the arena, the circus had set up rows of makeshift benches, tiered to ensure everyone in the audience had a good view. Even with the deafening noise of the loud revelers' amusement, Mouse could almost hear the benches creaking and bouncing under their weight. She grimaced and covered her ears, noticing a sly smile quirk Fraeda's mouth.

What? Mouse mouthed.

Fraeda tapped her chest. *I can feel it,* Fraeda mouthed back. *Must be loud!*

Mouse nodded with a grin.

Toma did not even bother to utter anything, but instead motioned to a space left at the end of one of the rows. Mouse and Fraeda scooted into it. It wasn't as bouncy as Mouse imagined, but she tried to sit lightly.

Jaunty music played as Needar himself strutted into the ring, holding up his hands and waving in response to rounds of raucous applause. Parading animals and performers exited on the far side of the arena, leaving Needar alone in the great space. He hopped onto the small stage at its center, and the crowd settled. The ringmaster quieted them with another wave of his hands. Once again, Needar commanded everyone's attention as he spoke.

"Welcome, once more, welcome, one and all to Needar's Wandering Circus! I am Needar, and as you may know by now, your ringmaster and humble servant. And humbly I bring to you these many wonders of the world" –he smiled warmly, pausing for the next round of applause– "these many wonders I see you have enjoyed. And it is my great pleasure to share with you things even more wondrous, things that inspire awe and fear, hope and dread, joy and terror. Yes, my dear people, you will be moved, as I'm sure you already have been, especially at the ravishing sight of our exotic performing beauties."

Needar bared a rakish grin as laughter erupted.

"Still, what I offer to you next will be unlike anything you have ever witnessed before."

Needar's voice grew softer. The melody of the buoyant tune faded, transitioning into the rhythmic thud of drumming. It beat along to Needar's monologue, dramatically punctuating as he spoke. Mouse leaned forward to catch his every word.

"It has been called a creature of myth and legend, a whispered rumor of the ancients, a shadow haunting Reidara's lost history," Needar continued. "It has devoured men, women, and children alike, tribes and even nations in its insatiable hunger. Teeth of steel, claws of Cardanthium, barbs of death. The sting of its tail and horns have impaled many a victim, and its roar has shaken the resolve of the strongest warrior. Even the mighty Mistwolf slinks and cowers in its presence. It has no equal in this world. And believe me when I say it would swallow up every one of you tonight if I had not discovered the secret for mastering this frightful monster."

Needar waited, drinking in the silent tension, only breaking it when it became unbearable.

"What you are about to see is real, my friends. Stay, witness this beast in all its terrible glory, but I warn you, looking upon its visage is suitable only for the bravest of the brave. I implore you, exit now if you are of weak constitution, my friends. I give you the opportunity now."

Mouse peered around, as did everyone else, which was unfortunate for any would-be cowards. As Mouse could have expected, no one moved.

"Ah, a stalwart bunch indeed. I knew it when I looked upon your courageous faces. No danger is an obstacle to you, my friends. I see that now. Very well! You shall all receive your reward."

Needar stepped to the side, gesturing theatrically to the far side arena exit.

"Behold!" he shouted dramatically. "The terrible, the mighty, the man-eating manticore!"

A low growl ricocheted around the quiet arena. Mouse held her own breath as she stared at the inky opening. In the shadows, a pair of wicked yellow eyes glinted in the low light.

20

Not a soul dared to blink as the creature padded into the open arena. It stalked forward, body lowered, razor claws extended from its giant paws, and gaze burning at the ringmaster. The antelope-like horns protruding from its head were far longer than Mouse could have believed possible, twisting upward until they terminated into deadly points. Quills along its spine seemed to bristle in fury, glinting metallic shades of green and blue beneath the big top's many lights. Its tail followed, arched menacingly, with its scorpion stinger swaying above its head.

Another growl escaped its broadening mouth. It crescendoed into an ear-splitting roar, wild and enraged. Rows upon rows of teeth flashed yellow in the arena spotlight. It snapped its jaws shut, eyes now turned on the audience. The manticore thrashed its head from side to side and roared in agitation. It tried to rear on its hind paws, but the bevy of nondescript handlers, which Mouse now noticed, pulled the beast down. They heaved on the heavy chains attached to the manticore's iron collar.

Furious, the manticore whipped its tail forward, slamming the stinger into the dirt only feet from one handler. The crowd gasped.

Other handlers rushed in with long staves crackling with electricity, a fact that did not go unnoticed by the angry manticore. It roared again, but the threat of the painful prod cowed it. At least for now. They gave it slack in the chain, and the monster moved forward.

Mouse wondered how many more handlers must be standing by, just out of sight of the audience, ready to restrain it at any sign of trouble. *But would they really be able to?* She thought. Mouse recalled the speed of the little manticore cub, and she shivered. *Speaking of manticore cubs...*

Mouse leaned toward Toma and whispered. "What are the chances this manticore is some relation to Sting?"

His eyes widened. "Better than the odds of it *not* being related."

"His mother," she said.

As soon as she spoke it, Mouse knew it was true. She could see Sting in this manticore's red and black markings, the shape of her tail and in the patterning of her spiny barbs.

Are you looking for him? Mouse wondered. The thrashing, frantic wrath made all the more sense now, and suddenly Mouse felt sick to her stomach.

By now, Needar faced the manticore, eliciting hushed "oohs" from the crowd as he produced and played a wooden flute. The reedy tune stopped the beast in her tracks. She cocked her head, ears swiveling toward the ringmaster. He played on, causing her to lower to her haunches and sit calmly.

The ringmaster turned to the crowd once again, lowering the flute. "See how music calms even the most frightful monster? For a time, at least."

As if on cue, the manticore leaped to its feet and pounced, roaring. Someone in the crowd screamed. Needar smirked, watching the manticore strain and growl against the bonds that kept him just out of her reach. Fire flared in her powerless eyes. The tail flung forward, but that fell short, too.

"Settle down, kitty!" Needar said, and he piped again on the flute.

But this time, it wasn't working. The manticore roared again, swiping with its massive paws. A handler cursed as its backside caught him and flung him off his feet. Just as quickly, the staves closed in on all sides. The handlers buried them in her fur, and the manticore cried out piteously.

Needar kept playing, but nodded to the handlers. They dragged her back, the staves now coming around her front, forcing her to retreat.

"That was exciting, wasn't it?" The ringmaster laughed, lowering the flute. "How about a round of applause for the incredible tamers of the Wandering Circus, the finest and only team to subdue a living manticore!"

The audience erupted in applause, whistles, and shouts. Most of the people were already on their feet. Needar basked in it, bowing and smiling as the band whipped off into another playful melody. Mouse shot a glance at Toma. He clenched his jaw and glared straight ahead.

"Are people really entertained by this?" he whispered. "It doesn't seem all that fair to the animal, even if it *is* a man-eating monster."

Mouse moved to squeeze Toma's hand, but thought better of it. She grunted in acknowledgement instead and turned her attention back to the arena. By then, new performers entered the ring, beginning the next act so seamlessly that it seemed the audience had already forgotten about the manticore. Clapping and cheering went up intermittently with each new acrobatic feat. The crowd hushed as the next performer, a knife-thrower and a target, took the center of the arena.

Two things became apparent to Mouse as she peered down at him. One, he was the only Heibeiathan in a sea of Gormlaean or, as Fraeda called them, Old Gor, entertainers, and two, he could not have been much older or younger than Mouse herself. He scoured the audience with solemn brown eyes, a look that seemed both scornful and melancholic. With a stiff bow, he acknowledged them, and the audience applauded cautiously.

Now the performer held up his hands, and the tapering points of eight sharp blades glinted between his knuckles. After counting paces an impressive distance away from the target, he widened his stance, sized up his mark for only a moment, and loosed a flurry of blades. In an instant, one set struck home, followed by the other, grouping in a tight circle at the very center of the target. The crowd clapped louder. The knife-thrower bowed as another trouper, an attractive young woman, pulled the knives and brought them back. This time, however, she returned to the target. Her back against the board, she splayed her arms wide and stood still. The audience murmured as the knife-thrower counted paces and lined up his throw.

"He's not really gonna do it, is he?" Toma asked breathlessly.

Mouse did not answer as the performer slung the knives. The audience gasped as they thunked deep into the wood, inches from the woman's arms, head, and torso. She pulled away, a dazzling smile on her face as she revealed the knives' perfect outline of her form on the target. The audience erupted.

Another stiff bow, and the performer prepared for his next trick. The audience quieted, except for one voice close to the ring. There a man leaned over the side, cupping his hands around his mouth and hollering something. Mouse could not make it out, but judging by the look on the woman's face, it was unpleasantly crude. The knife-thrower continued to ignore him, but the man's voice rose loud enough for Mouse to hear.

"Commere, sweetheart," he slurred. "Lemme show you some tricks I'm sure your friend hasn't."

Mouse cringed. Both entertainers ignored the heckler as the woman pulled the knives, smiled, and offered a sweeping wave to the rest of the crowd. She returned his weapons. The performer took a few deep breaths and carefully repositioned his throwing knives, but the man continued to shout. It was unintelligible to Mouse, for the most part, but what she caught made her grimace.

His features drawn in intense concentration, the knife-thrower lined up his next throw. The heckler was far from finished. Before anyone could stop him, he leaped over the side of the ring. The man's face purpled with rage.

"How dare yeh ignore me, slave! Yeh *Sannat*! I'll teach you a lesson you won't forget soon!"

He stormed forward. The dark eyes of the knife-thrower flashed toward him, and his lip twisted in utter disgust. He lifted his knuckles, brandishing the knives between them with threatening dexterity. At that moment, several enormous men entered the ring. Mouse guessed they served a singular purpose: crowd control. Their muscular arms swayed as they strode to intercept the show's interrupter, and at the sight of them, the heckler's bravery withered. He sidled back toward the edge of the ring.

The performer glanced over his shoulder at the security force's approach and smirked. Mouse watched the woman jerk her head sharply and mouth, "Don't," but his gaze turned to the heckler backed against the wall of the ring. Their eyes locked, and the man's jaw went slack. A savage grin split the Heibeiathan's lips.

"Hold still," he said, as if it were a mere suggestion.

Knives sliced the air. The heckler screamed. He tried to lift his arm to cover his face, but it was too late. Blades bit deep into the wood, pinning the man to it by the fabric of his baggy shirt sleeves. He tugged at them furiously, only coming loose when his pulling ripped them apart. The man gaped at his sleeves, which now hung in useless, ragged shreds from his shoulders. At this, the audience laughed raucously and applauded.

The young performer grinned and bowed, his stern eyes lightening for a moment. His grin faded quickly; the heavy hand of one of the circus security force clasped his shoulder and guided him out of the arena, while the others roughly grabbed the heckler and dragged him out of the exit.

Other acts came into the arena at a run, impossible jumps and tumbles catching the audience's eye. The volume and tempo of the band increased sharply as they played with frantic abandon. But

Mouse watched the young Heibeiathan leaving the ring, an unmistakable mask of fear upon him as he disappeared behind the tent flap.

Mouse's pulse quickened. Sweat beaded on her forehead, and her tongue felt thick and woolly in her mouth. Every muscle tensed as her heart pounded painfully in her chest. She laid a hand on Toma's shoulder as her vision blurred.

"I need some air," she said, standing to push past him before waiting for a reply.

"Sure, just wait for me to– hey!"

Mouse made for the closest exit, or at least hoped she did. All she could see were the images, images flashing through her mind in rapid succession like lightning strikes. The woman's face, the flames, the bodies, the guns. *Go to sleep.* Screams. Horrifying, sanity shattering screams. The sizzle and flash of energy rifle blasts. Flying, flailing, falling. Bodies. The smell of burning flesh.

I knew them, she thought with terrifying ease. *I knew them all.*

No names, but faces. Warm, loving, safe faces, now bleeding or burning or staring upward with never closing eyes.

Mama? She cried in her head. *Where did you go?*

A hand slipped in hers and urgent voices hurried her on. She ran, the meaning of their speech as hazy as the burning smoke that filled the air. A familiar voice cut above the haze.

"Get her out– to the secret hollow! Go!"

Papa?

"What are you doing?" a voice shouted. "You won't make it!"

Mouse's eyes stung as she peered through the smoke. A shape rose beside her. A comforting shape. It squeezed her hand.

"I'm not leaving without Niiri."

Papa let go. Strong hands pulled and carried her on. He disappeared into ash, into nothingness, and Mouse tumbled forever into the dark. *Goodbye, Mama. Goodbye, Papa. Goodbye, Shomroh.*

"Mouse?"

Mouse blinked. The sounds of merriment returned in an instant, the world fading from black to blurry to the entrance of the big top. She looked down. A hand *was* in hers. Her gaze traveled up the arm and into the eyes of a distressed, unmasked Fraeda. Mouse looked languidly at her shoulder, where Toma's firm grip held her. He shook her gently.

"Mouse? There you are," Toma smiled in relief, pulling up his own mask as she turned to him. "What happened? Are you alright?"

Mouse shook her head, her expression pinched and tight. She could not speak, could not loosen her lips for fear of tears spilling out instead.

"Take your time," Fraeda said softly. "And if you don't want to, don't say anything at all."

Mouse nodded gratefully and took a cleansing breath.

"I remembered things," she managed. "But now's not the time. Let's walk."

Toma raised an eyebrow but said nothing. Fraeda bit her lip and nodded. They donned their masks again and guided Mouse outside. Emerging from the massive tent, they stepped once again in the midst of the outdoor festivities.

Why now? Mouse anguished. She looked around, the jovial atmosphere tainted by her black memories. What she had imagined she might discover now slammed her with startling clarity: finding the truth would come at an agonizing cost. Could she survive *that?* Reliving that brief horror had been enough to paralyze her. How could she continue on like this, unlocking doors in her past to reveal the monstrosities that lived within? Mouse hugged her arms to her body as they walked, aching inside and out. Exhaustion and vulnerability had stretched her to the point of splitting, and she didn't know what to do with it. She wanted to laugh, despite herself. After what she'd been through to come this far, she was shattering over a past she could not change.

Isn't this the reason I'm here in the first place? She thought. *Could I turn back even if I tried?*

No, she decided. She could not. It was only forward now, no

matter what that meant. Her thoughts refocused on the young man in the ring, and something bigger than herself blossomed inside her, renewing her resolve, grounding her in the present.

They walked on, melting into the foot traffic. On either side of them, booths and tents with side-shows and briefer amusements clamored for their attention. Mouse surveyed the scene with growing disgust. It was far more sinister now as she thought about it: all this frivolity invading a miserable, destitute village, its inhabitants hiding like rats from trampling, unconcerned pleasure seekers. She looked, really looked, into the faces of the men and women who belonged to Needar's Circus, convinced she read a similar misery there. A pit formed in her stomach. *Too much*, she thought. *It's too much to bear.*

"Mouse," Toma whispered with cool urgency.

His hard tug on her sleeve shook her from her thoughts, and Mouse saw the reason why. Ahead of them, fighting against the current of the heavy crowd, four Coalition guards moved toward them. She locked eyes with the guard from earlier. He sneered.

Mouse spun to face Fraeda. "We gotta go."

"On it," Fraeda veered into the shadows between booths, pulling Toma and Mouse with her as they broke into a run.

Shouts echoed behind them. Mouse held tight to both Toma and Fraeda, pumping her legs as they swerved this way and that. They stumbled into a maze of tents, crowded together beyond the main attractions of the circus. Fraeda kept running. The sounds of people faded, and their footfalls fell muffled in the close corridor. Fraeda swerved sharply again. Mouse hopped, narrowly missing a rope staked into the ground right in front of her, but the damage was done. Losing her balance, she toppled and dragged her friends with her.

They rolled beneath the tent flap, tumbling to a stop. It was dark, but a little light bled beneath the flap. Fraeda held her a finger to her mouth, her expression severe. She mouthed, "Don't make a sound."

Mouse held her breath as the familiar thump of footsteps pounded outside the tent. She could see the shadows of the Coalition guards, the silhouettes of their drawn weapons back lit against the bright circus lights. Mouse exhaled slowly as they sped on. In fact, they all did. They sat in silence, nothing but the sound of their hesitant breathing filling the closed space.

"Well," Toma ventured after a while. "What now?"

"We've got to get out of Ervandas as soon as we can," Mouse said. "Maybe we can make a break for the back of town?"

Fraeda shook her head. "The gates will be closed for the night. And now that they're looking for us..."

"Yeah, not good," Toma said. "I can't see a way out."

At that moment, someone loudly cleared his throat.

Mouse whirled around and blinked into the shadows. She could make out rows of gleaming bars on the other side of the surprisingly large tent.

Cages, she realized.

Shapes rested in various corners of each; some rising and falling slowly in sleep, others erect, with glowing eyes narrowed toward her. In a cage set apart from the rest, a slighter shape, a human shape, leaned against the back bars of the cage's frame.

Toma yanked his pistol from his coat. "Who's there? What do you want?"

Mouse pulled her dagger as well, its soft glow touching the bars of the cages as she held it out in front of her. A figure stepped out of the shadows, curling his fingers around the bars as he reached the front of the cage. His brown, sullen eyes swept the three with methodical precision. Even in the low blue-green light, Mouse recognized him. *The knife-thrower.*

"Forgive me," he said, his melodic voice pleasant. "I do not mean to pry, but you are having a problem, yes? Perhaps I can be of some use."

21

"You," Mouse said, lowering her dagger as she stepped closer. "You're the performer from the ring. I can guess how you ended up here."

The performer smirked. "Indeed, it is. Impressive, was it not?"

Mouse nodded. "I can't believe you didn't hit him!"

"To be honest," he replied, lowering his voice to a conspiratorial whisper. "Neither can I."

He flashed a smug grin at them, but his countenance fell into somber introspection again.

"But Needar does not suffer insubordination. I await punishment for my transgression, and I suspect he will not be merciful." The performer sighed before turning sharp eyes on the three. "That is enough about me. I sense there is much trouble to go around. Who are you, and why do the *tagh* chase you?"

"We don't make a habit of telling our business to strangers," Toma answered, eyeing the knife-thrower suspiciously.

"And what does this stranger have to gain from knowing that?" He replied, raising an eyebrow. "Even if I could give you up to the *tagh* tonight, my master will still beat me within an inch of my life tomorrow. The *tagh* will not help with that, but you might."

Mouse exchanged glances with Toma and Fraeda. It seemed to her he made a good point.

"I shall make it easy for you," the performer continued. "You seek a way out of Ervandas, yes? I know of one, a supply gate on the west side of town. Circus use only at the moment, no *tagh*."

"And what's the catch?" Toma asked.

"No catch," the performer said, raising his hands. "But your exit may be smoother with a friend to help you. A certain knife-thrower motivated to make an exit himself, perhaps?"

Toma nodded approvingly. "Can't argue with that."

"Good," Fraeda chimed in. "If it's alright with the both of you, I'd like to stop being strangers now."

Mouse and Toma shrugged their assent, and Fraeda reached through the bars to grasp the performer's hand. "I'm Fraeda Fierling, daughter of the Naphta tribe of Elmnas. Nice to meet you. This is Berr-Toma Breythorn of the Dell, and this is Mouse. She's, uh..."

"Former slave, current fugitive, so-called seer, but I have my doubts. My pleasure," Mouse quipped flatly.

"Such interesting company you keep, Fraeda of Elmnas," he replied, shaking her hand in return. "And I am Rhavin Ipshalok, of Heibeiath. There is more, but I shall prefer to tell it at another time, when I am not behind bars."

"And how *do* we get you out?" Fraeda wondered. "Do you know of a key?"

"Yes, on my master's keyring," Rhavin huffed. He nodded toward Mouse. "Your dagger. Real Cardanthium, is it not? Steel bars should yield easily to it."

"It'd be easier to just shoot the lock," Toma murmured.

Fraeda let out a snort. "Now I might not hear that, but surely everyone *else* would?"

"Eh, good point," Toma said sheepishly.

"We don't have time for any of it," Mouse whispered. "Do you hear that? Listen."

They looked at each other in nervous silence, the sound of hoarse shouting growing louder outside the tent.

"More than four of them now," Toma breathed. "That's not... great."

The three backed against Rhavin's cage. Once again, Coalition guards thumped around the tent. Mouse could see their boots in the light just beyond the bottom of the tent flap. They passed, but still she couldn't control her heavy breathing as she pressed herself against the bars. She winced when her hip smacked into one with a distinct *tink*.

Wait a minute, she thought, reaching into her pocket. Her fingers coiled around the slender end of a key. She held it up by the cord, examining it.

"What's that?" Toma whispered.

"The old man's key," she muttered.

"Sure, that clears it up," Toma replied, his expression one of befuddlement, terror, and annoyance.

"I wonder..."

Mouse faced the cage, holding her breath as she slipped it into the lock. Slowly she twisted it, her eyes widening as it continued revolving. The lock clicked open with a decisive clunk.

"No time," Mouse said, registering the shock on everyone else's faces. "I'm sure they'll be back. What do we do?"

"Find a distraction," Rhavin said, pushing open the door and stepping among them.

"Have anything in mind?" Toma whispered.

Rhavin gestured to the other cages. "Perhaps that key of yours works elsewhere."

Again Mouse peered into the shadows, examining the creatures within. Her skin prickled with the awareness that the eyes of all the occupants were already turned upon her. Waiting.

"Um," she shuffled apprehensively. "What exactly is in those cages?"

"The most exotic stock of Needar's traveling menagerie," Rhavin answered, his gaze following every shadow passing along the outside of the tent. "And some of the fiercest, too."

Mouse and Fraeda took a step away, but curiosity seemed to get the better of Toma. He walked along the row, muttering in amazement each time he looked inside a cell. Mouse could see the glowing animal eyes tracking Toma as he moved, their own interest seeming less ominous and more benignly inquisitive. Growing braver and rather curious herself, Mouse moved closer. She had few words to describe the beasts she saw. Something like a milky-white stag looked out from one, while another, a shaggy and magnificent golden horse, rubbed a spiraled horn against its hoof. Farther down, Mouse could make out more predatorial things; the hooked beak of a monstrous bird preening the feathers that melted into fur on its feline torso, a great, red fox waving its six bushy tails, and a winged, reptilian creature that she might have thought carved from stone, except for its shifting red eyes.

"They're so quiet," Toma said. "It's strange."

"Can't you see it on their faces? They're... broken," Fraeda added, closer now but still at a safe distance.

"They fear the whip, as do all of Needar's spectacles." Rhavin shook his head. His next words he spoke so softly that Mouse was sure he hadn't meant to say it aloud. "We are poor monsters, are we not?"

"Hey," Toma said in a low and urgent voice, beckoning emphatically. "Look."

Mouse, Fraeda, and Rhavin joined him, looking past his pointing finger to the final cage. It was larger than the rest, set back against the furthest end of the tent, with space between it and the stone creature's cage. A massive tarpaulin hung over its top, but whether by accident or by design, it had fallen back enough to reveal the front bars. From where they stood, Mouse could see the colossal, furry shape coiled inside. It lay with its back against the bars, black horns rubbing against one end of the cage, and though she couldn't see it, Mouse guessed the scorpion-like tail protruded from the other end. If she had any question about what lay within, the glistening sword-length barbs that quivered with each of the creature's ponderous breaths confirmed its identity.

"The manticore," Fraeda said.

"She's even bigger than I realized," Toma added softly.

Even Rhavin regarded the creature with awe as he observed her resting form. "They call her Eris. Needar purchased her. About a year ago, in the jungles somewhere along Gormlaen's southwestern boundary."

"He just 'purchased' her? How is that even possible?" Mouse asked.

Rhavin shrugged. "Only Needar knows for certain. I could speculate, however. With much silver and much blood. Or maybe pregnant manticores are more vulnerable. She had a cub not soon after he brought her in."

"A cub, you say?" Toma pried. "It didn't happen to go missing recently, did it?"

Rhavin nodded in surprise. "It did, indeed. A crafty little brute, he is."

"I knew it. It had to be Sting," Toma chuckled to himself.

"We came across a manticore cub before we got to Ervandas," Mouse explained to a confused Rhavin. "Of course, we didn't know it at the time."

Seeming to understand, Eris raised her head and stared at them. A low growl rumbled from her slightly open jaws, and the quills bristled and stood like spears along her back. She stood, towering over them even at a distance, and dragged a massive paw along the bottom of the cage door. The group took a step back.

"What now?" Toma asked.

Mouse took a shaky breath. "Which way to the side gate, Rhavin?"

"There," he gestured in the opposite direction of the manticore's cage.

"Okay," she said. "And what happens when I open these cages?"

"I cannot say," Rhavin admitted. "They are all very different. Perhaps they run, perhaps they attack. Perhaps they decide to stay in their cages. It is hard to say."

"We'll have to get out of the way, and quick. Maybe even pull up a tent flap for motivation," Toma said.

"I would suggest leaving Eris where she is," Rhavin began thoughtfully. "You saw her in the ring. I would not want to take my chances against her."

"You don't have to say that twice," Mouse nodded, although she thought she detected a hint of sadness on Toma's face.

"But then again..." He looked back at the terrifying beast. "What better distraction is there than a loose manticore?"

"It might give us a fighting chance," Fraeda agreed.

Mouse grimaced. "Yeah, but what's worse? The Coats or the manticore?"

"There is a bright side," Rhavin said. "Eris is quite efficient in dealing death blows. If she chooses to eat us, she will at least do it quickly."

"I'll do it," Toma said, his jaw set with determination. "I'll let her out. You all get clear, and get ready."

"Toma..." Mouse began. "You don't have to–"

"Sting and I got along, didn't we?" Toma grinned weakly. "I just need to turn up the charm for momma."

"If you're going to do it, make it quick." Fraeda whispered. "They're coming back. I can feel their footsteps."

"How can you–" Rhavin began, but Fraeda held a finger to her lips and pointed.

Sure enough, the silhouettes of Coalition guards rose and fell along the tent, the sound of stomping and barked orders quickly following. Everyone's faces went pale as they distinctly heard, "I don't care what that buffoon Needar says, start checking the tents! They're here somewhere!"

"The key!" Toma hissed.

There was no time to argue. Mouse handed it off, pausing only briefly to watch Toma run to the first cage. Fraeda and Rhavin hurried to the tent's side, hands positioned to raise the flap. She followed but kept her eyes on Toma, one hand to her dagger and the other to her pistol.

"It's now or never," Toma breathed as the shouts outside grew louder.

He stuffed the key in the first lock and turned. At the sound of the telltale thud, he yanked it free and jumped to the next. *Thud. Thud. Thud. Thud.* Each lock clicked open. Toma hopped back. The creatures blinked back at him from the corners of their cages. Mouse moved to pull up the tent flap, but Rhavin stayed her hand.

"Not yet," he mouthed, and jabbed a finger toward the slit in the opening.

Mouse looked through the gap, her eyes widening in fear. A whole squad of Coalition soldiers had amassed outside. A number of them had already broken off into groups to investigate the other large tents, and to the small band's good fortune, had taken some time to do so. But Mouse could see their luck was running out. Two men were just exiting the tent beside theirs, gun barrels flashing. Her heart thumped as they conferred with their fellows in hushed tones and pointed to their tent. Between them and Needar's deadly collection, it seemed to her they stood little chance.

Recalling the open cages at her back, Mouse snapped her attention to the tent's interior. Though the cage doors hung slightly ajar, the creatures made no indication they intended to go anywhere. Instead, their attention seemed turned to what was happening elsewhere: the manticore's cage.

Mouse held her breath as Toma approached Eris, his hands up in deference. The manticore threatened him with a rumbling growl. Her eyes flashed fire, and she whipped her tail menacingly.

"Easy," he said soothingly. "I'm not going to hurt you. I'll get you out of here, okay? We can help each other, right? Look–"

Toma pulled the remaining dried meat from his pocket, tossing them at the manticore's paws. Still eyeing him and snarling, she dipped her massive head and sniffed. The wad of rations, which could have easily filled both of Toma's hands, was hardly a morsel for Eris. Her spiky tongue swabbed the floor of her cage, and the entire offering was gone. All the while, Toma approached, speaking softly to her. He reached the cage, and his hand trembled as he raised the key to the lock. Mouse could hear it rattling in the hole. It occurred to Mouse that if Eris really wanted to, she could kill Toma even now. One flick of her scorpion tail, a swipe of one claw, or the sting of a quill – each of these weapons in her arsenal could easily fit through the bars. It could happen in a blink.

But it *hadn't*. Her cold, feline gaze impenetrable, Eris watched Toma turn the key. She tilted her head at the unlocking *thud*. If Mouse wasn't so focused on keeping her heart from jumping out of her ribcage, she might have thought the movement almost kitten-like.

Toma had barely cleared the door before Eris exploded from the cell, which slammed back so hard that its hinges shattered. She soared through the air, magnificent and terrible, landing with Toma just between her paws. Everyone gasped, but Mouse saw that this wasn't the worst. As Eris was loosed, four Coalition guards rushed through the tent flap. Mouse, Rhavin, and Fraeda were knocked aside in their entry, pitching to the ground and into each other.

The nightmarish scene played before Mouse's eyes in slow motion. Toma in the dirt, his face inches from three rows of pointed teeth. The four men, regarding the scene with first hardened, shocked, and then horrified expressions. And out of that still scene, a cacophonous lion-like roar, followed by a strident bird scream, and braying, grunting, chittering, and bellowing, sounds inconceivable to Mouse's ears.

She covered them at the sound, but the cries filled the tent and pounded in her brain. Their cage doors banged open, and the first five beasts burst forth. Mouse hunkered against Fraeda and Rhavin as the creatures angled toward the flung-open tent flap, bearing down on the terror-stricken guards. White light flashed around them as they discharged their weapons. She cowered lower as the blasts struck everywhere: pinging off cages, exploding boxes of circus cargo, searing gaping holes in the tent canvas. Mouse watched as one blow glanced off the shoulder of the stone-like creature, hitting its brittle flesh like a hammer to a rock. Black blood seeped through splintering cracks, but the wound did not slow it. The creature bellowed, spread its bat-like wings and razor claws, and mowed down a guard. Half-running, half-flying close behind came the bird beast, followed by the galloping stag and horned horse. The remaining guards scattered. Mouse squeezed her eyes shut, unwilling to watch the monsters stampede into them, screams drowned out by pounding hooves and wild animal cries.

Fearing for her own life, Mouse braved a glance. The fox darted through the mangled tent opening, its body low in the trampled grass. Outside, tent pegs, ropes, and support beams lay on the ground. If there had been guards waiting before, they were gone now, but not too far away echoed more screams, the blast of energy rifles, and the primal calls of strange creature voices. Dazed, Mouse stood, but a snarl froze her in her tracks.

Eris.

22

Mouse gulped and turned slowly. The manticore watched her with terrible scrutiny, one paw on Toma's back and the other resting in front of her. Mouse chanced a glance at Toma, consuming fear boiling up inside her as she imagined the horrible end her friend may have met. He faced her, his eyes wide and unblinking. Toma's lips twitched as his gaze met hers. *Still alive!* Mouse thought, and she breathed a shaky sigh of relief.

With an air of warning, Eris waved her stinging tail and straightened her bristles. *She could kill us all in an instant,* Mouse thought. *What is she waiting for?* Curiosity edged in alongside Mouse's abject terror, and she considered the possibilities. It occurred to her that maybe not all monsters were the same. Maybe some of them weren't truly monsters at all.

Moving slowly but deliberately, Mouse held her hands out and open, mimicking Toma in the moments before he had opened the manticore's cage. Eris, though still snarling, cocked her head in that kitten-like way again. *Was it working?* Mouse felt the blood rush between her ears as she inched toward Eris. She had no idea why she was doing *that*. It seemed right, though, and she heard herself cooing soft, reassuring words.

Out of the corner of her eye, she saw Rhavin and Fraeda, watching in anxious silence. The two of them had wisely remained on the ground, and their obeisance seemed to please Eris. She paid little attention to them but guttered a chiding growl as Mouse approached. Mouse stopped within a paw's reach. Her growl quieted into a deep rumble, and Eris seemed curious herself, almost pensive, as she studied Mouse. The great beast dipped her head and sniffed, her snout wrinkling as it brushed up against Mouse's clothes. Mouse stifled a scream, and for what seemed like an eternity, she stood there, letting Eris do it. And she did her best not shiver as she observed Eris in return: all several thousand pounds of her sleek, muscular form hulking around her, all three rows of teeth, each of which were longer than Mouse's arm, within a handbreadth of her defenseless limbs. But as Eris nosed against the leg of her pants, Mouse understood why.

"He's alright," Mouse said as loudly as she dared. "Your cub is out there, and he's okay."

Eris pulled back and cocked her head. With her unreadable gaze, she studied Mouse, as if weighing the truthfulness of Mouse's claim. At least, that's what it looked like to Mouse. And as Eris eased down and settled on her haunches, it seemed she had made her decision. Eris lowered her weaponized tail and lifted her paw. She peered down at Toma, who still lay prone in the dirt. Cautiously, Toma got on his hands and knees and crawled out from under the manticore's massive body. He made an odd squealing sound when she helped him on his way with a nudge from her large feline nose.

"You okay, Toma?" Mouse asked.

With Mouse's help, he pulled himself up and did his best to stand on wobbling legs.

"Never better," he said, his voice cracking.

Toma steadied against Mouse as both kept their eyes on the

creature. Eris, however, seemed to lose interest in them and began nosing through a storage bin at the back of the tent.

"Hi, uh, friends?" Fraeda whispered as Eris ambled away. "We can't stay here."

Mouse turned back to Fraeda, who pointed upward. Rhavin stared, eyes widening with unease. Mouse followed their gaze and froze. Fire licked along the tent's canvas ceiling and ignited the wooden beams holding the structure in place.

"Where'd that come from?" Mouse said in shock.

"The blasts from the Coats' rifles," Toma replied. "It's catching fast. What do we do?"

"Run!" Rhavin shouted.

Just then, an enormous crack and a growl from the back of the tent garnered their attention. Mouse looked again at Eris, who stood beside the storage bin, or rather what was left of it. The manticore had reduced it to splinters, but now held something large in her mouth. Another growl rumbled out of her.

"Is that a... saddle?" Toma asked.

"Indeed, it is," Rhavin answered. "Her training equipment."

"It's for *her*?" Mouse said, the pitch of her voice rising in disbelief.

Eris set the saddle down and laid beside it in reply. She nudged it and looked over at the four with her terrifying, large eyes.

"Incredible," Fraeda whispered. "She means for us to put it on."

Toma exhaled slowly and turned to Rhavin. "You think she'll actually let us saddle her?"

Rhavin shrugged.

Mouse grabbed her hair in distress. "Who in their right mind thought this was a good idea?"

"It is an appropriate question," Rhavin said. "But you do not know Needar."

"I think I'm glad I don't."

"Well," Toma said, rubbing his hands together. "Now or never. We don't have time to spare."

A loud crack above them and the growing cloud of smoke emphasized his point. The four approached Eris.

She snarled as Rhavin and Fraeda took steps forward. They halted in fear. Toma, however, continued toward her, drawing close enough to place a hand on her great, shaggy side. He whispered to her, the rumble in her chest desisting with his patient, calm words. When he finally grew brave enough to reach out, the rumble began again, but this time without threat. To Mouse's ears, it sounded something like a cat's purr. Swallowing her own fear, Mouse moved slowly to Toma's side and reached into the manticore's fur. It was softer than she had expected. She buried her fingers in the thick, mane-like part by Eris's neck, growing more hopeful with each passing moment of contact that the creature meant them no harm.

"Come on," Toma said, one hand still on Eris's side as he beckoned Rhavin and Fraeda with the other. "Slowly, but I think we can manage."

Rhavin and Fraeda exchanged looks, but they advanced with caution. Eris simply watched them now, but as they drew close enough to touch her, she looked away. Toma nodded. Together and moving quickly, the four pulled the saddle onto the manticore's back. Eris growled at the growing flames, but otherwise she waited with extraordinary patience. Finally, they cinched it tight around her chest. The construction of the saddle was such that the seat rested between her shoulder blades, just in front of where her quills began. Even so, a hard ridge that served as the saddle's seat back afforded any riders necessary protection. And judging by the size of the saddle, the number of riders could be anywhere from one to three people. Woven into the wide leather strap that held the saddle in place, metal rungs stuck out as footholds, presumably for both getting on and off, as well as providing handholds for ambitious stunts. Whatever circus escapade Needar had planned, Mouse could not quite guess, but if he had ever pulled it off, it certainly would have made Needar's Wandering Circus the greatest show on Reidara.

"Right," Toma said. "Out of the frying pan, into the fire."

With that, Toma scrabbled up first, offering a hand to Rhavin. Warily, and with an eye to Eris, he took it, his shoulders relaxing slightly as Eris licked her paw instead of biting him in two. The two boys helped up Fraeda next, with Mouse to follow. The three hoisted her small frame up with ease, and she scrunched in front of Toma and next to Fraeda.

"Not quite like that ride we took on Dane's ol' Sunshine, is it?" Toma whispered into her ear.

"You mean the running-for-our-lives ride to the river that tried to swallow us?" Mouse couldn't help but smile. "You're right, that was downright boring."

"Uhhh, guys?" Fraeda said, pointing to the rising smoke. "Time to go!"

"And how would we do that? Kick her on the sides like a horse?" Mouse asked.

"Yeah, I don't think that will work," Toma replied nervously. "Something tells me Needar never got this far."

Rhavin nodded, his face grave. "Hold on, my friends. I expect we are at her mercy."

Eris turned her great head toward them, the slit of one gold eye narrowing slyly. Her lion-like mouth parted, exposing rows of saliva-flecked teeth in an unsettling, macabre grin. Had Toma not wedged himself behind her, Mouse might have jumped off and taken her chances elsewhere.

But with that, Eris bounded forward. Mouse covered her face as Eris loped toward the tent flap. And not a moment too soon. Wooden supports now fully burst into flame. They cracked and collapsed behind them. Thick smoke stung her nostrils and eyes, but it rushed past, a blur of sooty black and smoldering red. Eris reached the tent flap with a bound, flattening her body to squeeze through an opening now ringed with flame. Eyes tearing, hands buried in fur, knees gripping the saddle, Mouse screamed. The other riders did the same, terror in everyone's voices as the searing heat whipped their faces. In an instant, they were through. Mouse watched burning beams, large enough to kill a person her size, fall on the manticore's hindquarters before bouncing off her quills. They scattered and snapped like matchsticks.

Unbelievable noise replaced the crackling of the conflagration behind them. Mouse raised her head as Eris zoomed away from the burning tents. Dumbfounded, she gawked at the passing chaos. There were screams of fear, confusion, and pain as they streaked by running crowds and shouting Coalition guards. Mouse glimpsed the work of the first wave of fantastic creatures, no doubt aided by mass hysteria: trampled tents, overturned booths, broken carnival games, and littered goods. Smoke and occasional flames rose from all directions, though circus workers scurried to put fires out. But at the sudden appearance of the colossal manticore, shrieks of frenzied panic started anew. People vaulted out of the beast's path, but Eris seemed not to notice any of them, nor any other obstacle. Even one still-standing tent, which, though sagging in the middle with tent pegs splayed on the ground, remained very much in front of them and in their way. All four riders protested as she barreled straight for it.

At the last second, Eris leaped, soaring over the top of the tent. Mouse's stomach flipped, and she braced herself for impact, but Eris landed with such soft grace and ease that for a moment Mouse forgot everything but awe. Toma's loud "Yee-haw!" shattered it, and the incomprehensible ludicrousness of their current actions hit Mouse like a mallet. *What am I DOING?*

Eris ran on swiftly, her eyes already to the open fields of outer Ervandas. The sounds of chaos faded as they left the frightened crowd behind them. Mouse looked back, gazing with a little guilt on the sad state of Needar's Wandering Circus. All its splendid sights, bright lights, and garish aura had collapsed in ash and disarray. Rhavin, Mouse noticed, looked too, a mean grin on his face and a satisfied glint in his eyes. And as she remembered what had just taken place there, she could not blame him.

"Hey!" Fraeda shouted over the rushing wind, nudging the others with her elbows. "What's that coming toward us?"

Mouse peered where Fraeda pointed behind Eris' left flank. Out of the now semi-darkness of Ervandas, four shafts of light approached them, growing brighter and bigger as they gained with alarming speed. Shapes of single riders and smooth, metallic frames resolved behind the headlights, the familiar whirring and glowing discs of blue light beneath each vessel now unmistakable. Coalition raiment fluttered behind each rider.

"Hovercrafts," Mouse shuddered. "Eris! Look out!"

Eris let loose a mighty roar as the crafts flew up beside them, but the riders edged in, angling to surround her. Though they kept their distance, keeping out of range of Eris' whipping stinger, claws, and teeth, Mouse could now see them clearly – Coalition men with determined concentration and ill intent as each one guided his craft closer. There were two on each side now, keeping with Eris' amazing speed but holding their box-like pattern. Mouse gasped as each hovercraft began extending electric staves. The electricity leaped between the prongs and inched closer to Eris' exposed flanks. She snapped at them, hopping and twisting and using every natural weapon in her arsenal to bat away the hovercrafts, but they were too fast. They moved aside just as quickly as she attacked, drawing tight once again around her.

It was all Mouse and the others could do to hold on. She grabbed fistfuls of fur and squeezed her knees tighter, grimacing at the death grip Toma had on her waist. Fraeda had abandoned her hold on Eris, opting to clutch the saddle horn with both hands, while Rhavin held her and the saddleback as tightly as he could. Mouse could barely see anything as they bounced, jostled, and knocked into one another, but she could see her fear mirrored in their wild expressions.

Sensing the futility of it, Eris stopped her offensive and instead increased speed. Her head no longer spinning, Mouse swiveled to note each hovercraft's position. To her chagrin, they had no trouble keeping alongside, and with dismay, she watched them dodge Eris' swinging tail. Eris bounded on, and Mouse checked their progress. The wall was still far away; *too* far away. Mouse arched her neck to figure out where they were headed.

"You see what they're doing, don't you?" Rhavin shouted. "We are being corralled!"

All looked as Rhavin pointed his chin out toward the wall, not daring to lose hold of Fraeda or Eris. Mouse could see now they were now running parallel to it, and she sensed the closeness of the sparking staves on their right and the leading of the crafts on their left.

"They are turning her back, somewhere they can get her to stop or be too tired to go on," Rhavin continued. "And then..."

Toma completed the thought grimly. "And then we're goners."

Mouse glanced again at the riders, catching their satisfied half-grins and glinting eyes. Whatever their plan was, it was succeeding.

"We gotta do something!" Mouse yelled.

Pressing against Eris' neck, Mouse lifted one hand from the fur and searched for her energy pistol. Understanding her intention, Toma held her tighter, steadying her as she tugged the pistol free. She looked up. Her gaze met that of one Coalition guard, one hand on the craft's controls, the other reaching for his own weapon. Mouse did not think. She took aim, pressed the trigger, and released.

White sparks exploded from her weapon, and her hand snapped back at the force of it. Both gun and hand hit her on the side of her face. She cried out from the impact, blinding light and starbursts of pain blurring her vision. Toma held on, keeping her upright, but let loose a volley from his own weapon. Eris roared in anger as one incoming blast hit her side, burning fur and stinging flesh but not penetrating her thick monster hide. She kicked out, claws tapping a craft's hull with a metallic ping. Her frenzied speed somehow grew faster, and Mouse felt another searing blast fly over them. Mouse shook her head; the starbursts faded and her eyes adjusted from sudden light to inky dark again. Both crafts on their flank were now gone. She looked back; the burning wreckage of two collided crafts lay mangled in the field behind them.

Now two hovercrafts remained, and they whirred around Eris with renewed urgency. One swerved to get back on Eris' left side, still working to guide her toward Ervandas. *Toward reinforcements*, Mouse realized in a panic. Though Eris had adjusted her course, once again facing the village's outer boundary, Mouse could sense her strength was waning. The musky smell of animal sweat rose around them, and the manticore panted, her tongue lolling and mouth frothing as she ran doggedly on. She roared at the closing staves, but her snaps and strikes were weaker now. And though they were wary, the last of the Coalition guards could see it, too. They pushed harder, forcing Eris on as they took aim at her riders.

Mouse frantically tried to work her pistol. It didn't respond.

"I'm jammed!" she cried. "Toma, do something!"

"I'm out!" Toma yelled in reply. "It's gotta charge or something!"

Rhavin elbowed them both and opened his jacket. His knives twinkled.

"My turn," he said.

Mouse could not see how he managed to do it, but in a flash Rhavin had four knives between his knuckles. He did not even seem to aim. Rhavin breathed in slowly, and with a quick exhale, the blades spiraled from his hand. Four thuds sounded, the first followed by a short cry of pain ended by its successors. On their right side, the third hovercraft listed away before wobbling and careening into the dirt.

"One left!" Toma shouted. "What do you got, Fraeda?"

Fraeda, of course, did not answer. She had her eyes shut tight, hands clenched on the pommel, and lips moving rapidly in silent prayer.

Eris slowed, eyeing the last craft with confidence as it whirred alongside her. It slowed too, keeping out of range of her tail. Mouse gauged the driver, wondering why he had not tried to shoot them down yet. He tried to get closer, and Mouse could see fear had replaced the pleased smirk that had been there. Still, he worked his way in, the electric stave sparking ominously and keeping Eris from acting. And a thought sprung into Mouse's mind.

"Toma, Rhavin! Hang onto me!"

They did the best they could as Mouse reached now for her dagger. It glowed blue-green as she exposed it to the night air, singing against the rushing wind. Just as the Coalition soldier made his move, forcing the prongs into Eris' shoulder, Mouse leaned out of the saddle and swung down on the stave. Eris jumped as the stave jabbed her hide, and Mouse toppled dangerously. She cried out as her foot, hooked into a rung on the cinching, twisted unnaturally as she slipped. For a moment she dangled there, bouncing hard against Eris' side and being knocked nearly senseless by it. But she saw the dagger had done its work. The prongs fell uselessly to the ground. She felt strong arms dragging her upright, and Mouse scrabbled back into place as best as she could, wincing at her sore ankle.

Eris howled with rage and turned on her last oppressor. With a powerful paw, she batted the nose of the craft down. She sprung back as it bit into the dirt, waiting for it to stop completely. Though stunned, the strapped-in guard shook his head clear and quickly began undoing his buckles with one hand and aiming his pistol with the other. But Eris was faster. In a flash, her scorpion stinger shot forward, impaling the man through the heart. She whipped it back, wrenching his body from the seat and flinging it into air. Her roar of victory reverberated in the barren vale. Chills ran down Mouse's spine as she covered her ears, terror and awe electrifying her entire being.

And then they were off again, padding quietly into the dark night. The wall of Ervandas rose high and foreboding before them, but Eris ran on. Mouse sensed her pace quicken, almost as if Eris could already taste the freedom beyond the village walls. The wall came alarmingly close. Eris coiled. She sprang. And once again, everyone screamed.

Up Eris went, her claws outstretched in front of her. They clattered against the wall. Mouse and Fraeda clung harder as they tipped backward, nearly dumped out of the saddle. They slid into the boys, who thankfully slid into the seatback and remained there. Eris dug into the wall, ripping chunks of old stone out as she scaled the side. Beyond Mouse's ability to comprehend it, Eris hauled herself and the riders easily onto the top. And just as quickly, she launched over the ledge and into open country on the other side.

23

They bounded onward. Mouse's heart thumped away in her chest; so loud it seemed now with just the whooshing of the wind and the soft thud of graceful paws on the ground. *Did that really just happen?* Mouse thought. She wanted to slap her cheeks, rub her eyes, and wake up from this frightful dream. But she felt the night air, the hard seat banging against her tailbone, the fur in her hands and the arms of Toma around her waist. They were alone, the village far behind, chill darkness enveloping them in the blanket of night. It was impossible for Mouse to say how long or how far they had gone on like that. No one spoke; perhaps, as Mouse thought, silenced by the odd dreaminess of their flight, or the weight of the question growing in her own mind: *What now?*

At the very least, Mouse had the presence of mind to watch where they headed. In the inky darkness, there was not much to see, but the path Eris took seemed to track north of Ervandas, over rolling hills and past shrubby land where the villagers had hewn the forest for the Coalition. The country soon became thick with hardy trees, and Eris' paws thudded on rocky ground. In time Eris slowed to a trot, then to a walk, and then stopped altogether.

"Here's where we get off, I think," Fraeda said breathlessly, and with that, began shimmying off the saddle.

The others followed, doing their best to get clear of the massive monster that had graciously not eaten them. At least not yet. The group huddled together and watched fearfully. Mouse unsheathed her dagger, bathing their close circle and the looming form of Eris in its glow. She looked into the illuminated faces of her friends, drawn in various expressions of worry, discomfort, and confusion. They gazed at one another, teeth chattering, and Mouse wondered if they all brimmed with questions of what to do next as she did. *What would Eris do now?*

But Eris, unconcerned with them in every way, set to sniffing the air between pants and staccato yowls. She lowered her nose to the ground and wandered around them in a circle.

"What's she doing?" Fraeda finally whispered, finding courage in her curiosity.

"It seems she is hunting for something," Rhavin answered, shrugging. "I cannot say. But it does not appear she is hunting for us. That is good."

"I'd feel better about that if she wasn't circling us," Mouse hissed.

Eris yowled again, and this time, a faint mew answered. Out of the darkness glowed a set of sea-green eyes.

"Sting?" Toma said.

The slight feline form of Sting clambered up to the stone shelf where they stood, his little quills shuddering as he hopped up to them. Sting mewed in a way that Mouse could only describe as pleased as Eris bounded to meet him. A deep, contented rumble came from within her chest as she nuzzled her cub. Sting purred like any happy kitten would, and Mouse smiled, forgetting her fear for just a moment.

Sting glanced toward them, his large eyes lighting on the group. Mouse squealed in fright as he dashed toward her, and then flinched as he rubbed himself once again on her pant leg, purring. Toma laughed and kneeled down.

"Hiya, bud," he said, stroking Sting's chest.

The little manticore greeted Toma in much the same way as Mouse before nosing into his pockets. He looked disappointed as Toma turned them out empty.

"So, this was the friend you made while I was gone," Fraeda said shakily. "Thank the Unseen. That worked out well. Oh!"

Fraeda shrank as Eris joined the reunion. She loomed over them, her mouth so close they could feel her hot breath. The four drew closer together. Eris stared at them, unblinking. Waiting.

"What do you want?" Toma breathed.

The manticore turned her great head, rubbing a horn on the strap of the saddle.

"One last favor, it would seem," Mouse said.

With her dagger in hand, she carefully approached Eris. She reached out with her free hand, patting the beast and feeling her coiled strength. Even now, a wrong move might cost Mouse her life. Mouse breathed sharply as she brought the dagger close to the strap. With a quick flick, she cut it loose and jumped back. The saddle fell to the ground with a loud thump. Eris arched her back in a great stretch, shaking out her quills so that they stood straight and proud. And as she stood before them, completely free of all the trappings of Needar's circus once and for all, Eris appeared all the more wild and terrible. But it was more than that, Mouse thought. More than anything, Eris became beautiful.

Sting sprinted around his mother, yipping gleefully. Eris let loose a triumphant roar, so loud and so powerful that it shook the trees and rang off the rocks of the mountainside. It was the second time Mouse heard it that night, and the awe and terror it inspired still rattled her to her core. The magnificent roar ended, and then they were gone. Eris and Sting ran back down the slope, blending into the shadows and leaving the four shivering in the autumn night's frosty chill.

"Well, now what?" Toma finally whispered, his voice seeming too loud in the forlorn wilderness.

Each looked at the other, all of them stupefied by their current situation. With no answers forthcoming, they occupied themselves by taking in their surroundings, rubbing their arms and bouncing on their heels as little protection against the cold wind now whistling through the trees.

"I don't know," Fraeda eventually replied. "But maybe we could think better if we could just get out of this cold?"

"I thought I saw something back there, before Eris took us up this slope," Rhavin said, pointing beyond the dagger's glow. "It is worth a look, perhaps?"

Mouse waved the dagger in the direction Rhavin indicated, still unable to make out anything useful. She shrugged. "Better than standing here, I guess."

Walking close together and guided by dagger light, they picked their way down the slope. It was higher and steeper than Mouse had first thought, and they struggled along slippery granite, loose gravel, and gnarled roots. Of course, Eris had made bounding over it all look so easy. *And where is she now?* Mouse wondered. Though Eris seemed content to leave them, the thought that she might return at any time still frightened the spirit out of Mouse. Even worse, though, was the possibility of what *else* might show up before she did.

As if hearing her thoughts, Toma spoke up cautiously. "I hate to be this guy, but uh... should we be worried about Mistwolves?"

"When are we not worried about Mistwolves?" Mouse muttered wearily, but she tapped on Fraeda's shoulder and mouthed Toma's concern.

"I can't say for sure," Fraeda said. "I don't know where we are. Eris moved so fast it was hard for me to keep up. But we did go up quite the mountain. Elevation is good. Mistwolves don't usually leave the mists, and they never come up this high. That's the best we can do, I think."

"What you are saying is that we are still in some danger," Rhavin said gloomily.

Mouse exhaled sharply. "What else is new? Welcome to the adventure, Rhavin."

With that, she stomped ahead. Raising practical concerns was one thing; adding worries to her already worry-crowded mind was another. *Obviously,* she didn't know where they were or if they were safe. How could any of them possibly know *that?* After charging into the wilderness of Elmnas on the back of one of Reidara's most fearsome beasts and barely escaping death or capture at the Coalition's hands, Mouse thought it laughable to consider anything else. And why bother, anyway? None of them could muster any more strength. Even now her body ached, and her ankle throbbed from the chaotic ride, and exhaustion fell heavy on her limbs and eyelids despite the growing chill determined to keep her awake. Mouse tried not to, but she kept thinking of that bath at the Priory. She snorted in annoyance and tromped on.

Fraeda, who had hurried to keep pace with Mouse, re-linked arms with her. She said nothing, but gave Mouse's arm a reassuring squeeze with hers, followed by a sympathetic smile. Mouse took a deep breath and managed at least a knowing look back, which helped her feel a little better. Though careful to stay within the sphere of light, the boys lagged behind, whispering among themselves. Mouse tried not to listen, but could not help hearing Rhavin.

"I sense I have frustrated your friend."

Toma offered a noncommittal grunt. "She's frustrated a lot."

Soon the group came to flatter ground. It broadened out, forming a wider, natural path striated with granite and strutted with boulders. Twisting, stunted trees grew up among the rocks where they could find dirt to lay roots, but otherwise the ground was barren of undergrowth. Mouse waved the dagger out ahead, cautiously exploring the boulder field. Mostly, she found the place broad and effectively sheltered from the wind. Leading the others, she continued to explore, discovering that the path tapered on one side to a ledge, from which the slope dropped off again below. Some feet below that, the slope ended in a barren valley at its bottom. At least, it looked barren in the dark.

"I believe this is the place," Rhavin said, pointing to a natural alcove between two boulders.

Toma dropped his pack and flopped down beside it. "Even if it's not, I'll take it."

"Ah ah, don't get comfortable just yet," Fraeda tsked. "How about some firewood? It'll go quicker if we all look."

Toma groaned, but pushed up to his feet. "Is that even a good idea?"

"I don't care," Mouse said. "I'm freezing."

"It'll be worth it," Fraeda added. She withdrew a delicate silk bag from her belongings. "Sister Raelin sent along her best teas. We'll all be feeling better in no time."

Though bone-tired, everyone did as Fraeda suggested. It was hard work in the dark, but the little trees by their chosen camp had dropped enough dead branches to make an acceptable fire. They gathered quickly and built as far back into the niche between boulders as possible. Protected from the wind and hidden by the alcove, the little flames crackled to life and brought enough warmth and light to cheer everyone, Mouse included. It eased the aggravating cold out of her bones and muscles, and her stiff ankle felt better resting on the ground than walking or riding. Despite his initial protests, Toma left the fire more than once to keep a steady supply of kindling upon it, and as promised, Fraeda shared Sister Raelin's tea, distributing it in small wooden cups she had thought to bring. Mouse rooted around in her bag for provisions and warmed them over the flames, sure to give Rhavin a little more than the others. They had left the Priory that day with their bellies full; Rhavin looked as if he hadn't had a proper meal in weeks.

"Alright, Rhavin," Toma said, easing back against his pack and placing his hands behind his head. "Let's hear it. Tell us about yourself."

Rhavin considered the request with an austere gaze as he sat cross-legged beside the fire. He took his time finishing the last of the meal Mouse gave him, eating with a reposed dignity that the current circumstances generally prevented. At least, Mouse couldn't imagine why someone would display such refinement, given his semi-starving state. She knew she wouldn't. She would have eaten her body weight in provisions and stuffed as much as she could carry in her pockets.

He sipped his tea, his grave, dusky eyes examining his new audience. By the light of the fire, she could see him clearly for really the first time that night; the chaos of their escape hadn't provided that opportunity, and there was only so much she could observe about him far off in the ring. But now, she could observe Rhavin, the performer they whisked away from Needar's Circus: dark, straight hair that tufted in a rakish way, the two sides of his head shaved close, strong nose and jaw, defined cheekbones and angular face. Indeed, there was a regality to him that made him unlike the friends she had made so far. He sat straight and tall, rigid and reserved in his mannerisms, and yet graceful in each of his movements. Mouse could understand, in his disciplined demeanor and almost dancer-like fluidity, how naturally his skillful knife-throwing must have come to him. And though so far he had been polite, exceedingly so, given their bizarre circumstances, Rhavin's sharp features gave him a severity that made her nervous. She recalled the incident in the ring and knew it was no small thing to be on the receiving end of his displeasure.

"Seeing I am a guest to this venture, certainly." Rhavin placed the cup in his lap. "You may well have recognized that I am Heibeiathan, and a stranger to these lands. The story of how I came to Needar, as you have seen, a slave, forced to entertain, and this being the only way to earn my meals and spare my back the rod, that is not all that uncommon in my home. These Old Gor Northmen, as it goes, are well-practiced in the taking, buying and selling of people, as are some of the nomadic peoples of Heibeiath who prowl the deserts and the mountains. You will find every Coalition city or town crawling with them. Slavery of non-Gormlaeans is permissible, of course, and as a young boy, I had seen the practice often. But never did I believe that I would..."

Rhavin paused and shook his head. "But I get ahead of myself. Let me take you to the beginning, to life before. I come from a grand and ancient city called Durai. It was a magnificent place, nestled in the green and lovely lands of southwestern Heibeiath, between the meeting of the great rivers, Jord and Kushan. That is where I was born, almost 18 years ago.

"My father ruled this city as the *Imyr*. I then, was a prince of sorts, the youngest of four brothers. I know what you are thinking. How can that be? Yes, I have seen how the Coalition rules in other lands, but it was not so in Heibeiath. Our cities are full of wealth, art, and beauty. Even these coarse Gormlaeans could appreciate that. So long as the *Imyrs* and the chieftains of the land pay them tribute; we lived at peace, and I thought nothing of the Coalition in my young years in Durai. I grew up in plenty, loved by my father, happy. And so loved I was by my father, it was his desire to raise me to be the next *Imyr*.

"This was no small thing. In Durai, it is our tradition that the oldest son is to become *Imyr*. I was foolish then, thinking only of the honor granted me. I know now this is where my troubles began.

"Three years ago, my oldest brother, Ranar, sent me on an errand for Father beyond the city gates, to the mouth of the Jord at the Ayadar Ocean. I was to oversee the building of our merchant fleet and return with a report on their progress. He insisted I go alone to ensure I did not find the workers idle."

Rhavin took a deep breath. "I never made it to the fleet. Lawless men attacked me. Before I could fight back or even cry out for help, they had bound me, thrown me over their horses, and rode away from Durai. And I would have thought it a plot from enemies beyond Durai or even simple misfortune had I not heard one captor say to another, 'these sons of the *Imyr* paid much for his blood, but are we not wise? Let us double our gold. It is a waste to kill a good slave.' Perhaps fate, in her cruel way, smiled at me then, for the others agreed."

Rhavin swallowed hard and stared into the fire. No one dared to speak or move. Mouse wondered if that was all Rhavin wished to say, but with a sip of his tea, he gathered himself and continued.

"My kidnappers took me north, winding through mountains and deserts for more days and nights than I could count. I wanted to escape, but I was hopelessly lost in that strange country. For a long time, I held hope that Father would discover my brothers' actions and come for me himself, but he never did. He still has not. I can only assume he believes me to be dead, as my brothers had hoped. We eventually came to Gormlaen, where Needar bought me in some dump of an Old Gor village. I have been with the circus since, as you have seen, performing my cheap knife tricks for loathsome peoples around the world. And maybe I would have been a slave forever, or else beaten to death for my impudence this night or died in some other way the next... had you not tripped into my prison."

He turned his intense gaze on each of them, the somberness of his face softening, if only a little. "You have my eternal thanks. And now, you have my story. What stories do you have to share, my friends?"

Mouse felt the eyes of all needling her, and she sighed. "Right, I'll start."

She told Rhavin all she could remember, from the moment she woke up at Misty Summit to their journey leading up to Ervandas today. Some details that she never intended to share with anyone flowed freely now, bidden by the warmth and welcoming privacy of their little circle of firelight. In that frozen quiet of the Elmnas wilderness, surrounded by people she wanted to call friends, she spoke of her losses, her survival, her hopes, and her fears; and finally, of their need to find the northern tribes before the Coalition destroyed them for good. As she spoke, Mouse herself realized the strangeness and even absurdity of her story. Coincidental meetings with just the right people had preserved her life, protected her from terrible fates, and given needed help and direction along the way. She spoke a little of her dreams, but skipped the details of her latest painful vision. Mouse still needed to process that, and Toma and Fraeda graciously did not press her. And when she finally got to one of the strangest parts of her tale – the old Elmling with the master key – everyone marveled as well.

After she had finished, Fraeda and Toma also told their stories in turn. Mouse learned more of Fraeda's difficult childhood, the wounds of her own prison experience, and the love of the Sisters who began to heal them. Toma shared a new perspective of his family's farm and perseverance under Coalition rule, and his admiration for the strength of his father and mother.

"In part," Toma continued. "I left for them. I knew the Coats would always see Maiendell as their footstool. Nothing would ever change for my family or for any of the Dell people if someone didn't try to do *something*. Mouse may not see it this way, but when she came, it gave me that chance."

Toma smiled at her fondly, and she did her best not to cringe. Mouse knew he had his reasons for joining her, but it did not lessen her nagging guilt. He would not have put himself or his family in danger if not for her. And if she were honest, Mouse had wanted him to do that. *She* wanted him to come, no matter the cost, and she knew it was the most selfish thing she had ever felt. And all his talk of family brought that fact to the forefront of her mind.

"Anyway," Mouse said awkwardly, turning her attention back to Rhavin. "Now you know our weird group and our even weirder story. I'm guessing now that you're free, you'll want to head back home, but I think I speak for everyone when I say you're welcome to continue with us as long as you'd like."

Fraeda and Toma nodded in affirmation. Mouse smirked as she continued.

"I can't promise any amount of traveling with us will be that great for you, though. We tend to attract the wrong kind of attention."

Rhavin raised his eyebrow, with something like a smirk of his own playing at his lips. "I would say it could be worse, but you do boast an impressive list of pursuers."

"And we're very proud of that," Toma added, chuckling.

"Perhaps your journey is perilous, but that is a small matter to me. For these many years, I have been little better than dead." Rhavin shook his head and smiled. "You have given life back to me, and now, a chance I never thought would come again: an opportunity to regain my honor and rightful dignity. I am in the most noble of debts. I must repay it in full and see your path through. You have my loyalty and friendship."

At this, Rhavin softened. He looked to each of the three friends across from him until his gaze rested on Mouse. It lingered, and he stared with intensity into her eyes. Mouse felt the color rise in her cheeks. She nodded and looked away.

"Well, welcome!" Toma reached over to Rhavin and held out his hand. "But keep your knives handy. I'm sure you'll need them."

24

Year 113
47th of Sun's Wane
Northern Wilds, Gormlaen

The dull light of daybreak filtered through the Swaying Forest, a cold fog wrapping around the trunks of the damp pines in the wake of the tempest of the night before. It was quiet and still as Blade and Fox labored along the steep pathways, and they shuddered beneath the steady dripping of the drying trees.

Fox shook off the stray drop of rain that had landed on the bridge of her nose and focused on the steep ravine as it dropped precipitously below. The beast hunter walked ahead of her with annoying ease, seemingly unperturbed by the wet, treacherous incline. Fox led her horse and cursed under her breath as the running mud squished and slipped beneath her feet.

"If my horse breaks her leg–" Fox paused, digging her heels into the mud to stop from careening into the small but fast-flowing stream at the bottom before them.

The horse was doing better than she was, but even the mare had to scramble to find purchase. Fox cursed, louder this time, as her boot slipped into the water. Blade hopped across the stream, landing gracefully and spinning to face her, even with his hands bound and a leading rope constraining him.

"You'll break one of mine," he said, smiling wanly. "Yes?"

"No, that would be stupid," Fox replied with a deadpan glare. "I was going to say, 'If my horse breaks her leg, I'll break your teeth.' That way, you can still walk, and I won't have to look at that idiotic smirk anymore."

Blade shrugged. "My apologies for assuming."

Fox leaped to the other bank, her horse splashing across behind her. "Apology accepted."

The Guardian offered only his hawkish stare as he waited for Fox to remount her horse and pull him along for the next leg of their journey. She did so swiftly, keeping her own eyes on him the entire time. Fox tugged at the lead rope.

"Come on then, we're burning daylight."

"Daylight," Blade said quietly. "Do you remember the light of day, bounty hunter?"

He's gathering intel, isn't he? Fox thought, smirking. She scanned the forest ahead of them, not committing to answering the question but considering it. If she answered truthfully, he would know something most did not: her true age. Or at least, an approximation of it. Which would still be around 95 years old, if she could remember what sunlight looked and felt like. Indeed, she was older even than that. Maybe not much younger than Blade himself. Judging by the cunning of the question, he already knew the answer.

There weren't many like them; those ancient legends of Reidara her people called the Ageless. Not immortal, but lives capable of thriving five to nine times longer than that of a normal human lifespan. This was a secret of Elmnas that Fox had learned long ago. Their Guardians, chosen for service to the Unseen, dedicated themselves to the Way; in turn, they received supernatural vitality.

Or so it was said. Fox had also heard legends from other lands much of the same, even from her own people. Unlike Elmnas, the means of accomplishing such vitality elsewhere usually arose from the powers of darkness, in dangerous knowledge not understood and deeply feared. In particular, Fox remembered one legend Gormlaeans used to tell – the one about an old woman and the volcano demon who offered her the power and agelessness of the earth in exchange for her fealty. As the story goes, she accepted, bound to him by the jade stone she wore around her neck. And also, as the story goes, it didn't end well. When she spurned his lordship, the stone consumed all the years she had stolen, and she melted into dust.

Fox almost laughed. Years ago, she would have dismissed the Ageless as a myth. But here she was, one hundred long years past the flower of youth and having only aged fifteen or so years in that time, and she was riding alongside another being who stepped right out of myth himself. And yet, she knew the secret behind the myth of the Ageless was now being unlocked through other avenues. How else could one explain the longevity of the Supreme Chancellor and his own house? Fox did not understand or know that story well, but it certainly had horrifying implications. And if they had accomplished *that*, what other natural laws had the Coalition defied? Elmnas had its secrets, but the Coalition had more. Fox suppressed a shiver. *Father, what have you done?*

She kicked the sides of her horse, spurring them forward. "I remember it, Guardian."

"There are few who do," he replied. "And even fewer who look like you."

"I can't decide if that was a compliment on how gracefully I've aged or an insult to my femininity and lineage," Fox said. "Well done."

"It is not your being female or foreign that I am concerned with," Blade answered. "The Way of the Twin Blades has called many of both to our ranks. But I am curious... You have never vowed to protect Elmnas and serve the Unseen, as those who learn the Way must.

What brought you on this path, Arctura Fox? Why have you been allowed to walk it?"

Fox blinked at the questions. *Why, indeed?* In all her long, solitary years, there had been no answers to them and the many other questions she had. None that satisfied, anyway. It was why she had rejected so much of the Way, taking from it only the mastery of its techniques that made killing an art. An aged face long forgotten swam into her memory, and she could almost hear his chiding voice:

Will the hungry be satisfied if they reject the hand that holds the bread?

She pushed away the words even as she remembered them. It was nonsense. Still, what had all her retribution and rage accomplished? Did it bring back the dead and the lost? Did it bring her any peace... even a little?

With a snort, Fox ungraciously yanked the rope and leveled at withering glare at Blade.

"You show your foolishness," she scoffed. "Believing that our paths are determined in any way. It is why your people have died in vain, and it is why you will follow them soon enough."

Blade held his silence. With a sly glance, Fox tried to gauge his reaction as they weaved through the forest path. There was only thoughtful repose on his features as he followed the horse, not the anger she expected. *This Guardian is quite the enigma*, Fox thought. *At least he will die well.*

She checked their position, ensuring they moved in the right direction. Their storm-sanctioned detour had caused them to lose ground and time, and Fox worried she would miss the rendezvous altogether. Fox did not dare confirm with Dervish while Blade was conscious; the last thing she wanted was the Guardian to know how desperate his situation truly was. There would be no escape once he was within Myergo's grasp. With her, he still had the opportunity to escape, if even only a slim and unlikely possibility. And for that reason, Fox did not sleep a wink. Blade seemed to hardly sleep at all, but when he finally *slept*, she made use of it. In her last brief interchange with Dervish, Fox had confirmed their checkpoint, finding that the contact had been delayed by the storm as well. If her sense of location was correct, they should meet him within the hour. *At least one thing has turned out right*, Fox thought.

But the serene forest and the thoughtful Guardian unsettled her more than anything now. Her neck prickled, as if at any moment all chaos should break loose. Fox's fingers twitched near her wristband, and she had pulled Blade beside her, where she could watch him without turning her head. He continued to do nothing; nothing but walk and glance at her with his knowing eyes. A nervous restlessness entered her extremities, and it was all she could do to keep from fidgeting, or cracking and cutting Blade down before he could crush the life out of her.

You're just anxious about getting this over with, and you're tired, she assured herself. *That's all. Keep it together.*

And yet, Fox could not shake the feeling that she was heading into a trap. To calm herself, she calculated all the likely scenarios and outcomes. Scenario one: The Guardian attacks. Well, that is a possibility she is prepared for. She would simply twist her band and render him unconscious. Delivery would proceed as normal. Scenario two: Myergo changes his mind and demands his pound of flesh from both her and the Guardian. She could release Blade from his bonds in an instant; they could fight their way out and she would deal with consequences of that later. Scenario three: The powers that be finally decide she no longer serves their purposes; the Coalition turns on her. That one was harder. But she was quick. She would survive. Fox always survived. Even when she miscalculated.

Is this what life would always be like? Will I always be trying to stay one step ahead of destruction?

Blade's questions rang in her mind. The path that brought her here... that senseless, winding, agonizing path. Many times she had wondered why she must walk it, and many times had concluded it was a pointless question. Though myriad forces conspired to destroy her on that path, nothing *guided* her. Nothing but herself. She walked it thanks to the folly of luck, the horrors of coincidence, the accident of birth.

And yet...

Arctura eyed the Guardian, unable to stop herself from revisiting the question once again.

25

Year 19 of Glorious New Era (Year 5 of the Honored Reign)
1st of Sun's Pale
Sutra, Northern Heibeiath

Arctura Vipsanius peered out of the self-propelled transport and gazed upon the great market square of Sutra. Its citizens pressed in around her vehicle and the rest of the caravan, conversing and shouting excitedly in their native tongue. Still trying to grasp the language, Arctura closed her eyes and listened. There was too much commotion to pick out anything helpful, but some words registered in her newly acquired vocabulary. Words like "royalty" and "riches", words that denoted mostly praises, but some that insinuated a curse. The people came as close as they dared while the motorized ground transports rolled slowly along the sandstone street. Arctura sighed. Already she was weary of the motorcade's ostentatious show of progress and strength, and this trip was nowhere near its end.

The civilized world praised Heibeiathan cities like Sutra as centers of human progress, especially in the arts and sciences. Still, they lagged on technological advances. They always would, Father insisted, and even though they were just as powerful as that wild country of Elmnas, the Heibeiathans knew wisdom that the Elmling barbarians did not. Vassalage to the Coalition would benefit them more than a drawn-out territorial war.

Yet it did not hurt to remind Heibeiath what devastation the Coalition could inflict upon them, and the comings and goings of Cardanthium-powered transports did just that. These advances that were quickly replacing beasts of burden in Gormlaen remained a novelty here in their neighboring country. Much of that could be attributed to its unfriendly terrain. Camels and horses could traverse the mountainous wastes and barren deserts far more effectively than a motorcade could. Still, as Gormlaen hammered out the details of Heibeiath's entry into the Coalition with its various *Imyrs* and chieftains, such technologies continued to bolster their case. And with the advances Arctura knew were to come, the Heibeiathans would soon learn just how wise their submission to rule would prove to be.

Curious onlookers gazed through the windows of the transport, bouncing on tippy-toes or climbing on the square's structures to get a better look at Arctura. She rearranged the veil that covered most of her face, conscious not to touch the scars that marred the left side. With the veil and the flowing raiment of her ambassadorial Coalition dress, she knew she must have appeared wonderfully mysterious. If the crowd hissed curses before, they only gave fawning awe now. Hating every second of their adoration, she waved demurely. The crowd clapped and sang their pleasure, and the caravan rolled on.

Arctura rolled her eyes in disgust. How pleased Mother would be to see she had finally become a prim and respectable lady, thanks to the necessity of her veil to cloak her in intrigue and hide the wages of her indiscretion. She thought more would know of that and treat her accordingly, but still rumors of Arctura's beauty had gone before her, making her all the more fascinating to the commoners of Heibeiath. And it turned her into the Lily's daughter; just another dazzling accessory that the Coalition put on the display of their power, wealth, and attraction. Arctura passed a hand over her forehead, unable to decide if this perdition was more bearable than the other she had lived.

The first days of public appearances after the attack had been the hardest. Father had shamelessly used her horrific wounding to his advantage. He paraded her about Gormlaen, using her mangled face as the prime example of what folly it was to entertain thoughts of life outside the safety of the Coalition. He demonstrated with impossible ease how the enemies of the state would use anything, even an innocent, pretty girl, to accomplish their nefarious purposes. That these enemies would try their hardest to destroy the Coalition from within if the people let them. That always moved the masses. How they rallied behind him! How they ate up every single word! And afterward, they would kneel before Father and reach up for blessing, trembling with reverent fear and bursting with joy at his approval. Then they would come to her, stare at her face, pat her slack hand.

Poor, stupid girl, they seemed to say. *How much hurt your rebellion has caused! And yet see how your father loves you! Why would you ever stray from his care?*

And just like that, Father united the provinces and annexed Maiendell. The Honored Reign of Supreme Chancellor Vipsanius could not have had a more auspicious beginning.

Now they looked forward to bigger things. Plans. Father always had plans. And in this particular plan, Father needed Arctura to present her best to the *Imyr* of Sutra. Not as a potential *Imyra,* for in that, the attack had rendered her infertile and useless. But if she could intrigue him with her hidden beauty, dazzle him with her wit and knowledge, demonstrate the strategic advantages of the proposal Father sent with her – then maybe, despite her imperfection, the *Imyr* would see fit to add her to his harem and forge the alliance Father craved.

There were worse things, Arctura knew. A life in the palace of the *Imyr,* despite however he made use of her, would still offer all the luxuries and conveniences to which she had grown accustomed. Even she, a foreigner to Heibeiath, had heard the stories of Sutra's cultural wealth and significance. Just one glance at the city confirmed that and more. Its glory certainly matched Pardaetha, if not outstripped it. And who knew? Maybe the Heibeiathan royalty would be kinder to her than her own family had been. Father expected complete deference to him as a servant, no longer an heir, and Mother had washed her hands of Arctura entirely. Even Turo, whom she thought loved her as she loved him, could not bring himself to speak with her for long. Especially now, as his marriage to Tyranna Malatesta drew near. Arctura either suffered in tortured solitude at Kyma or toured Gormlaen as Father's main campaign device. Could Sutra be any worse?

No, she decided. *Nothing was worse.* Arctura came to Sutra willingly, her broken spirit acquiescing to Father's plans. She was a pawn, and she always would be. She knew that. But what Father did not know is that just this once, his plans would serve *her*.

The transport stopped just outside the palace gate, swarms of Sutra's citizens following behind. Palace guards had already pushed them back and created a buffer between the people and the caravan. Arctura's Coalition escorts exited their transports and added another layer of separation between her vehicle and the commoners. She stepped out, glancing at the eager throng. They cheered for her attention. Another wave, another cry of adulation, and she made her way through the now open palace gates with her entourage. It clanged shut, and the noise of the city was left behind.

She entered the palace courtyard and gazed in appreciation at its appealing design. Glittering fountains and pools, magnificent flowering plants, and beautiful shady palms greeted her. The courtyard bustled with servant activity as the palace prepared to receive its guests. Arctura looked up to the palace itself, fascinated by its masterful Heibeiathan architecture so unlike anything she would see at home. Golden domes and lofty towers sparkled in the noonday sun. The Coalition and its ambassador may have come in their cavalcade of progress, but Sutra showed proudly the achievements of its ancient past. In a time in her own past, she would have studied these achievements and failings, and she would have found a way to use both to Father's advantage. She might have brought Sutra to its knees, not as a vassal and ally, but as easy plunder. A sad, rare smile graced her lips beneath the veil. Only a shell of that political ambition and prowess remained now, fragile and fracturing with the weight of her despair and pain. It had become terribly obvious she would never redeem herself in Father's eyes. Even as Arctura fought for every scrap of dignity she could grasp to reattach to her name, she knew no true reconciliation would come. And now, no longer tied to Father's power or graced by his gain, all those things done for "the good of Gormlaen" meant little. But one thing still mattered, one thing that she might yet control – one last hope for personal satisfaction. There was still the search.

"Ambassador? Ambassador Vipsanius?"

Arctura searched for the speaker. She found him waving and grinning as he emerged from beneath a palace colonnade. The small, rotund, and thickly bearded Heibeiathan hurried toward her, his rich palace robes glinting with precious gems and flecks of gold. Bejeweled rings on his hands and golden hoops in his ears glittered and jangled as he approached.

"We are honored to host you, Ambassador," he said in fluent Gormlaean, bowing so low his nose fell below Arctura's knee. "I hope your journey was pleasant, or as pleasant as it can be crossing those infernal sands."

"We fared well on our journey and arrived safely. A most fascinating experience, thank you." Arctura curtsied and dipped her head in acknowledgement. "You must be Sai'yn, the honorable *Imyr's* administrator, who has been so wonderfully accommodating in all our correspondence."

"One and the same. And it is my joy to be at your disposal today, Ambassador," Sai'yn replied, offering another sweeping bow that threatened to tip his turban from his head.

It slipped, revealing some of his bald pate. Sai'yn grabbed it hastily and straightened as he continued.

"His Excellency is currently occupied with matters of state, but looks forward to your presence at the evening feast. In the meantime, I would be most honored to give you a tour of the grounds and show you to your quarters." Sai'yn glanced around covertly and lowered his voice. "And thanks to your generous gift, I can show you even more than that. As I told you in our previous communications, it is not exactly the prize you seek, but still... it should be of great interest to you."

Arctura locked eyes with Sai'yn, remaining stolid even as her heart beat faster. Though it was rare her face ever betrayed her true thoughts, she still felt grateful for the veil that hid any twitch that might have escaped her control.

"I see," she said. "I trust you have been discreet?"

"Undoubtedly. Only a few most trusted souls have any knowledge of our dealings, and that vaguely."

"Excellent. I should like to get to our business as swiftly as possible." Arctura gave him a knowing look. "If it is as promising as you have made it sound, I am prepared to reward you handsomely."

Sai'yn ran his chubby fingers through his beard and smiled slyly. "You are most agreeable, Ambassador. But first, let us take care of niceties. To your accommodations, yes?"

Arctura inclined her head in agreement, and Sai'yn clapped and called out in Heibeiathan. Palace attendants quickly assembled to direct the Coalition entourage, gather her things, and usher them inside. Arctura glided gracefully along with them, her mind now turned to what would come next. Sai'yn babbled from the front of the group, pointing out a particular archway here and a certain piece of furniture there, but Arctura heard none of it. Anxiety and anticipation competed within her. She folded her hands in front of her to keep them from shaking.

The search! Is it finally over?

How many hours, how much effort, how much pain had she

spent on this interminable, infuriating search? In the days and months that followed the attack, when no satisfying answers came, when no trace of Reylas or his troupe could be found, when the Drake had vanished like vapor over the Mican Sea, Arctura took the search into her own hands. Secretly, of course, for Father had closed the matter with the execution of the Onestis and had forbidden her to dwell on it any longer. But even as Arctura knew her life was forfeit to Father and his will, in this grievance she could not surrender. There were too many incongruities to appease Arctura's anguished curiosity.

Up to this point, the search had yielded nothing. Her resources limited and her discretion of utmost importance to any success, Arctura ran into more dead ends than she could count. A torment atop her already daily suffering, Arctura could hardly bear it. As she toiled in futility, her obsession stole life from her in a way Father had not, could not, even if he tried. Yet even so, the search kept the despair from flattening her into nothingness. It kept her alive. And if all went as she had hoped; if fate or luck or whatever else had finally smiled upon her, the search for Reylas Fox would end today. She would finally get what she deserved. After all these years, after all this bitter affliction –

Retribution.

26

The cool dankness of the passage prickled Arctura's skin as she followed Sai'yn by flickering torchlight. It had come as a shock after the dry, sweltering heat of Sutra's sunbaked streets. Even the lovely cross-breeze that ruffled the gossamer curtains of her apartment had done little to lessen the sweat pouring off her brow, reminding her that Pardaetha still had something on Sutra.

At Sai'yn's recommendation, she had exchanged her dress for a palace girl's attire – a voluminous, colorful skirt with a tasseled sash at her waist, and a long but roomily sleeved tunic. A teal Hebeiathan-style veil covered her face now, and she could feel its golden tassels bouncing lightly against her nose as they walked. As lovely an outfit as it was, Arctura wondered if she could stomach it as her daily expected attire, spending the rest of her days as a consort to the *Imyr*. She pushed the thought away.

It seemed unlikely that such a simple disguise would allow Arctura and Sai'yn to move about the palace without anyone asking questions, but somehow it had. By virtue of his position or by his own clout with the palace staff, Sai'yn enjoyed the unobtrusiveness of virtually everyone. At least, no one paid any heed to the administrator and the strange palace girl with him as they trod the palace's halls, and no one saw when they ducked into a secret door to which Sai'yn alone had a key.

"We are far enough within," Sai'yn said, still in a whisper. "I can be freer with you now. I have entrusted this matter to only three others: the captain of the Sutra guard and two of his lieutenants. They are honorable men and have sworn secrecy. The Bidythine you sent will ensure that. I am pleased to present the prisoner to you shortly."

"Just one?" Arctura said sharply. "There should be a number more than that. You had more than enough information to identify them, and my sources tell me they were well within your grasp. What happened to the others?"

"Ah, that." Sai'yn stopped and turned, the torch glow creating grotesque shapes in shadow across his face. "The targets proved more prepared for trouble than my agents suspected. They came upon the five you named, as expected, capturing two and killing one in the assault. Two escaped, I'm afraid, and one later died from his wounds."

"This does not please me," Arctura hissed. "I expected your men to be more professional."

"Forgive us," Sai'yn replied with a dip of his head. "But this sort of thing can be unpredictable, and messy. And please remember the risk my guard and I are taking to keep your secrets. We did what we could."

The sly raise of his eyebrow told Arctura they had done the bare minimum, given the coin she spent to have it done. She withheld the curse itching on the tip of her tongue, eyes burning with anger and impotence. Her impetuous bribing of Sai'yn gave him all the power he would ever need to blackmail her later, whether she stayed in the court of the *Imyr* or not. He might come calling for his due at any moment from here on out, and until she could figure a way out of it, she would just have to hand it to him. But what else could she have done? Those she had hunted from afar for years had wandered unwittingly into her grasp, and she was desperate to close her fist and crush them. Arctura bit back her worst insults, but the glare she leveled at Sai'yn still made him recoil.

"It will have to do," Arctura said.

Sai'yn dipped his head politely, searching the ambassador with a wary eye before proceeding once again. Yes, Arctura was young, and she still had much to learn about how to best get what she wanted. Even so, Father had taught her well, whether intentionally or not, and Sai'yn seemed to understand that. Maybe Arctura could yet leverage her position through intimidation. She would have to try.

They turned down another interior corridor, deeper into the bowels of the palace. The air felt close and stale down here, the scent of decay and festering infection wafting toward Arctura from indistinguishable sources. Illuminated by the oily light of greasy wall sconces, the corridor widened into a room. Two rows of heavily barred cells lined the sides, while monstrous devices stained with blood and bile filled much of the space in between. A hanging cage creaked on a rusty chain from the ceiling, still holding the skeletal remains of its last victim. Arctura scowled at these, and the sounds of clinking manacles and faint moans coming from within the occupied cells. She hated prisons. Father had brought her to enough of them. Whether to display their effective pragmatism in his expanding empire or to intimidate her with the threat of harsher punishment, should she cross him again, she was never quite sure, but the effect now was that she disliked being in them the way she hated being in alleys stuffed with refuse and human filth. Both confronted her with the miserable existence of the degenerate poor, which never seemed to learn. Rather, they continued to reproduce instead, never doing the world the favor of dying off entirely.

But judging by the torture machines and the room's obvious secrecy, this prison held a greater purpose than discarding impoverished criminals. Places like these contained traitors, rebels, political enemies, and those who had offended the *Imyr*. Arctura could only speculate on how the captain of the guard carried out his duties here, but if the abominable conditions offered any insight, she suspected he relished the work with uncommon zeal.

"I can see now why one of my detainees succumbed to death," Arctura said, peering at the emaciated, ragged forms crouching or lying in the dark cells as they passed. "What is the state of the other?"

"You'll find the prisoner as you had requested. The captain was not so severe in his dealings." Sai'yn assured her, but a cruel smile split his mouth. "Well, not more severe than necessary."

Sai'yn paused at the farthest cell. He fumbled with the key ring hidden within his robes and placed one in the lock. It disengaged with a loud clank that echoed within the room, and the bars scraped noisily as Sai'yn heaved the door open. He gestured inside.

"The time is yours. I will wait out here until we must return."

Arctura nodded her understanding, and with a deep breath, stepped inside.

This is it.

The slight, female figure balled in the corner of the bare cell shuddered as Arctura approached, manacles on her wrists and ankles clinking faintly. She did not uncurl or acknowledge Arctura's presence, but the piteous whimper denoted the prisoner's fear of what came next. Long hair splayed in tangles over her face and on the floor, but Arctura recognized the once proud and luxurious locks. Ragged garments, though torn and dulled by the crust of dirt, blood, and waste, still reflected some of their former glory in the spots of bright color that remained. The soles of the prisoner's feet faced Arctura, one bare, the other with the shreds of a filthy slipper. One little bell clung by a thread to the slipper's side.

"Erhi," Arctura said icily. "What a pleasant surprise."

Erhi craned her neck and swept the cell with a bloodshot eye. With a groan, she pushed herself to a sitting position, and Arctura ground her teeth as the heavy chains dragged across the concrete floor with an intolerable scraping. Erhi was too weak to tug at them for long, though, and she gave up when she had turned enough to observe her visitor. She stared up at Arctura, swollen gashes and black bruises disfiguring the easy beauty Arctura remembered. It was all Arctura could do to not recoil as pity and grief welled inside her.

What have I done? she thought, but her anger surged once again. *Nothing that she didn't deserve. Don't forget that.*

Confusion furrowed Erhi's brow. She opened her cracked lips, revealing the teeth missing from her once delightful smile. "Who– who are you?"

Arctura stepped closer. "Don't you remember your pretty princess?"

Erhi's eyes widened as Arctura wrenched the veil from her face. She leaned close, her lips curved in a malicious grin.

"Not so pretty these days, am I, Erhi? And who do I have to thank for that?"

"I don't know," Erhi cringed and blinked back tears. "Oh, *tengri*, why am I here? Arctura, why?"

"You know why you're here!" Arctura yelled hysterically, pointing to her face. "You were *there*. With *him*. And after he betrayed me, you all fled. Tell me, Erhi, do innocent people run? Do they leave their tracks untraceable and hide like criminals? Do they do business with the Drake and smuggle conspirators out of the country? Do they?"

Arctura screamed. A tidal wave of rage washed over her, clouding all thoughts and dispelling any consternation she had felt in Erhi's wretched state. The raw emotion and anguish she had stuffed down for years cascaded from her now in a tirade of accusations.

"I have been searching for you and your band of traitors for so long now. You were so crafty... moving fast from little village to village. Never on the main roads, never in a city. My informants could give me an idea of where you were, but always too late for me to do anything about it. All I could do was wait. Wait for you to feel far enough from Pardaetha, from the Supreme Chancellor, to relax. To make a mistake. And you finally did, didn't you? You thought you could hide your deeds in Sutra, but you forgot who I am. I am Arctura Vipsanius, daughter of Lucan Vipsanius, child of the

Honored Reign. And for your crimes against me and my house, there will be justice."

Tears fell freely down the cowering Erhi's cheeks. Arctura buzzed with adrenaline, realizing that this felt... *good*. She felt better than she had in years. The troupe was paying for their part in the plot that stole Arctura's life, and soon, she would have the final piece of the puzzle. Finally, after all her suffering, she would find vindication. She would have her revenge.

Arctura kneeled beside Erhi, resisting the urge to wrinkle her nose at the smell of urine and infection that rose from her.

"But I might be able to free you from this," she whispered.

Erhi looked back at Arctura, a mixture of emotions contorting the unmarred features of her face. "What do you mean by that?"

"Tell me where he is," Arctura said. "This is all I ask. Tell me where he is, and you can go from here. You can rejoin the rest of the troupe, and I will pursue you no longer. I just want *him*."

"Reylas? You think I know..." Erhi trailed off.

Arctura cringed at hearing his name. "Don't be obtuse. I know you know. He left Pardaetha with you."

At this, Erhi began to sob. Arctura stepped back, uncertain.

"You are wrong, princess," she wailed. "So, so wrong. He is gone. Reylas is gone. And now so is Jonz... and Kershan..."

"Stop this," Arctura said sternly, but her uneasiness grew. "Explain yourself."

Erhi fought to catch her breath, silent sobs still wracking her body. She wiped a dirty sleeve over her eyes and looked up pleadingly.

"That night in Pardaetha... we were waiting at The Lonely Siren, just as you and Reylas had planned. Reylas had been anxious about it all night. Couldn't sit still for a minute. He decided he'd meet you halfway, something about... the love of his life wouldn't have to carry anything other than his baby if he could help it."

Despite herself, Erhi smiled. Arctura's stomach turned over, emotions she had thought long dead suddenly stirring.

"It started to get late. We were packing it in for the night when the innkeeper burst into our room. 'Don't want no trouble,' he kept saying, but he insisted we leave at once. Jonz pressed him. He finally told us that a man had come in after Reylas had left. A man... with a green claw for a hand. Looking for a group of Samrasine musicians. The innkeeper booted him, but it shook him all the same. We were shakin' too. Jonz agreed it was big trouble, said that there were mercenaries, and then there was the Drake. I never seen Jonz that worried about anything. And we'd been in some tight spots before.

"Jonz pulled some strings to get us out of Pardaetha before the gate opened. We left a note for you and Reylas with the innkeeper, to let you know where you could meet us. We waited for two days. And then..."

Erhi looked back at Arctura, her gaze falling on the red scars that lined Arctura's face. "We heard what happened, and my heart shattered. We assumed the worst about Reylas, and I wept... for both of you."

Arctura leveled a stony glare at Erhi. "And yet you continued to run."

"Of course we ran. Once all those Gormlaeans heard rumors that a Samrasine betrayed their beloved Supreme Chancellor's daughter, the lives of all of us were as good as gone. We were run out of towns everywhere, or worse, they'd start calling for our blood. We *had* to run, don't you see? All the way to Heibeiath, to here... it was the only way."

"Rumors, you say! There was a note," Arctura countered. "Written in Reylas's own hand. He betrayed me to that monster as part of a plot by my father's political rivals."

"Do you really think that Reylas could do that to you?" Erhi whispered in disbelief. "He loved you. More than anything in this world. How could you not know?"

"Explain the note!" Arctura fumed. "Explain his convenient disappearance!"

Weariness and sorrow filled Erhi's eyes. "I can't. I'm no

mastermind of anything. I just dance. If you knew me at all, if you ever called me your friend, you'd know that. And you'd know the person who really loved you, too."

Arctura reeled, the words like a blow to the face. All her reasons, her arguments, her evidence stuck tight in her throat as she was forced to consider the immeasurable refutation of love. Erhi was right, wasn't she? The Reylas she had known... had loved... could he *really* have been so cruel? Truth be told, he did not expect her to come back after she first ended their relationship. Reylas had never thought more than one step ahead. How could he have planned and executed so complicated a treason? And why would a note, in his own hand, be so conveniently found as evidence of his collusion? Could there be another explanation?

In her wild grief, in her obsession for vengeance, Arctura had not explored any other possibility than the lines others fed her. She never considered that she had only gathered details and coincidences, just barely scratching the surface of the truth. Could it be that her very suppositions were lies? Had she built a case against Reylas, thinking she would uncover all his deeds if she only got to him, never once recognizing that the search would exonerate him?

Arctura swallowed hard as the weight of her miscalculation hit her. All this time, instead of pursuing her friends, she should have been seeking justice for them. And Reylas... all her ferocity and anger should have gone to destroying his murderer: the green-clawed monster who had taken everything from the both of them.

She looked down at Erhi, who had sunk down to the ground and was resting her bruised face on the cool concrete. All the spirit and rhythm of life that had once been in her soles had bled out in Sutra's secret prison. Erhi had no strength or desire to muster even hatred and rage, which Arctura expected and, now realized, she deserved. She looked at a husk now. How could she bear to look? How could she live with what she had done?

"It is enough," Arctura finally said. "You will be released from this place, Erhi. I promise."

Erhi closed her eyes and nodded in acknowledgement, new tears puddling on the floor. Arctura replaced her veil and backed out of the cell. She turned to find Sai'yn, grim-faced behind her.

"It is time," he said, nodding toward the cell. "I trust you got what you needed."

"It would appear so," Arctura replied. "Though it was not what I wanted."

Sai'yn dipped his head. "It is often that way. Even so, you recall our agreement. My captain can fulfill my end when he returns from his duties in the city in the evening."

"No," Arctura said, her voice breaking. "Release her now. Please. She need not suffer any longer."

Sai'yn raised his eyebrow. "Now, Ambassador? Are you certain?"

"Yes," she answered resolutely. "Now."

Sai'yn shrugged and moved toward the cell. Arctura watched him tug something from his waistband before he entered. She turned away, her eyes fixed on the sputtering flames of their guiding torch as it hung in its resting place on the wall. It burned low, guttering into darkness just as a flash of light illuminated the slimy prison walls. The familiar hiss and crack of a discharged pistol resounded and receded.

She blinked away the rolling tears.

27

Y*ear 19 of Glorious New Era (Year 5 of the Honored Reign)*
2nd of Sun's Pale
Outskirts of Sutra, Northern Heibeiath

"This is unwise."

Sutra's chief of border patrol spoke in Heibeiathan as he crossed his arms and shifted against the back of the seat, looking at the flat, ecru landscape blur by the transport's window. His two brows, if one could call them two, frowned together in disapproval, and his sulking, dun eyes flitted over Arctura scrupulously before resting on Sai'yn. Though some words still took her time to process, one night of immersion among native speakers of Heibeiathan had been enough. Arctura picked up the language splendidly; at least she thought so. And since she spoke slowly and deliberately when using their tongue, some, like this officer, felt comfortable speaking their minds around her. *Their mistake*, she thought.

"The Ambassador does not need to see outside the walls of Sutra," he insisted, glancing with annoyance in her direction. "I've had enough headaches dealing with raiding parties on our merchants along the north road as it is. We invite trouble by being out alone, rolling along in this metal death trap."

"Captain Ahmar, how you worry!" Sai'yn laughed, also picking up the conversation in Heibeiathan. "This mechanical transport is... how do you say it in Gormlaean? *State-of-the art*. Don't be so quaint. Do you really think your problematic raiders could even catch up to us now? They would be choking on clouds of sand before coming close. Besides, as you surely recall, it is the will of the *Imyr* that the Ambassador assesses our borders. The Coalition is graciously offering to help with your headaches, Ahmar, not make more of them."

"Help, possibly." Ahmar said coolly, staring at Arctura as she held his gaze. "Graciously? That seems unlikely."

"Do you believe the Coalition has dealt unfairly with your grand city, Captain?" Arctura asked sweetly.

Ahmar's big brow shot up in embarrassment, but he recovered with a decisive answer. "Sutra gains nothing from allying with Gormlaen. Only a tribute-bought peace that smells of funny business."

Sai'yn opened his mouth to reprimand Ahmar, but Arctura held up her hand.

"I understand your concerns, but you speak from ignorance. Sutra gains much from the Coalition. Technology and progress that will put Sutra far ahead of the other cities of Heibeiath, for one thing. Like this very transport you are so enjoying– now the property of Sutra, as of last evening. It is just one of many gifts to come from the Supreme Chancellor. And as allies, your enemies are our enemies. These raiders, they are from a nomadic people that have been bothering you for some time, yes? The Coalition has a way of making problems like that disappear, which you shall see soon enough. I wonder, Captain, are there other peoples, other incursions that Sutra could do without?"

Ahmar dropped his gaze and grunted. Huffing, he resumed watching out the window. Arctura tried not to smile, knowing full well that Sutra's tenuous relationship with their neighboring city-state of Kytri had come to the forefront of his mind. Out of the corner of her eye, she caught Sai'yn grinning and rubbing his hands together, no doubt also thinking of Kytri, but more so of the vast wealth that the Coalition might help Sutra requisition if this treaty worked out.

"You see, Ahmar?" Sai'yn piped up, this time in Gormlaean. "It is as I said. The Ambassador speaks truly, and his Excellency agrees."

"Wine, among other things, tend to make men more agreeable in such matters," Ahmar grumbled back in Heibeiathan.

"Indeed, I'm certain the Ambassador has a certain *jins n'al* about her that aids her cause," Sai'yn said with a surreptitious glance at her figure.

Arctura was not familiar with the phrase, but she could guess at its meaning. She feigned ignorance altogether, but her insides boiled.

I might, you boor, she wanted to say. *But certain alchemical elixirs loosen tongues, pockets, and command with much less effort and far more efficiency. And you give your aged* Imyr *far too much credit.*

After their long night of feasting and drinking, Arctura was uncertain the *Imyr* would even make it back to his chamber. She accompanied him, of course, or rather, held him up as he stumbled along. Once there, she offered him a tonic to clear his head. To her surprise, the old man unwarily accepted. The mixture, a work of art by the Coalition's best chemists, had been a precautionary measure from Father, and Father could not have asked for better results. The *Imyr* not only signed the treaty that Father would have massacred whole tribes for, but the ruler also promised to give Arctura whatever she wanted. And before he fell into a stupor that would last well into the next morning, he did just that.

She had discovered much. The history of Sutra and its political strife and struggles, the weaknesses of its borders, the fading of its cultural prestige and the threat of economic collapse. Topped with the feeble *Imyr*'s waning ability to lead and the petty squabbles among his sons, and Sutra was proving ripe for the Coalition's picking. But Arctura aimed for other information, particularly that which would lead her to the truth behind the Drake's attack and Reylas' disappearance. A bit of the old Arctura awakened that night, relentless and ruthless in drawing it out, and she was rewarded for her efforts. For now, for the first time in all her years of fruitless searching, she knew how to contact and maybe even trap the mercenary who had destroyed everything.

As it turned out, the Drake was a reputable assassin among the well-connected. One only need to know how to reach him and have the coin to lure him out of whatever hole he slunk into during his leisure time. The *Imyr* had given Arctura that information, and even promised to provide some help in capturing him after she shared an altered version of her encounter with the Drake. She knew he wouldn't remember that part. In fact, the *Imyr* would probably only remember signing the treaty, but it was enough. Now, Arctura could move forward. If she just planned carefully enough, she could lay bare the truth entirely. And maybe the death of Erhi would not be totally meaningless, but serve a greater purpose in Arctura's pursuit of justice. She would make sure of it.

Now Arctura just needed to fulfill her current duties: do whatever would make the *Imyr* happy and bring the fruit of her long-suffering home to Father, even if that meant riding around the desert with these buffoons at their inconstant ruler's behest. *The sooner I can leave this wasteland, the better*, she thought. With more patience and kindness than she had ever possessed, Arctura nodded graciously to Sai'yn and Ahmar.

"We have traveled far," Arctura commented. "Are those mountains I see in the distance?"

"Indeed, Ambassador. That would be the Kamarian range. Technically, our border butts up against the mountains, but it is a desolate place and not even the savage Elmlings see fit to come down through there. Of course, there are still the nomads, and any help the Coalition could offer to secure the area would be very welcome. An outpost, perhaps, since your transport seems to make the trip so easily?" Sai'yn said with a grin.

Arctura nodded in acknowledgement. "That sounds like wise counsel, Sai'yn. Did you doubt the transport could come so far, so quickly?"

"It seemed prudent to test its capabilities. Ahmar, you must at least agree with this: your patrols would be far more effective this way than on horseback, eh?"

Sai'yn elbowed Ahmar, who responded to the prodding with a noncommittal grunt. The palace administrator shrugged.

"I find it well pleasing. Though I wonder how it would fare off the rocky ground and in the shifting sands. The transport will make it back to city limits, I hope?"

"You needn't worry about that. The driver is monitoring the power source and will let us know when we need to return." Arctura waved her hand dismissively. "As for terrain, the Coalition is already working on solutions to that problem. If I'm not mistaken, our engineers will have transports that can traverse any sort of ground you can think of, even mountains, within the next decade."

Ahmar raised his caterpillar brow with skeptical interest. Sai'yn rubbed his hands together excitedly.

Arctura might have rolled her eyes, but just then, something clanged and scraped against the undercarriage of the transport. She gripped the seat as the unknown obstacle seemed to latch onto the bottom with its claws, its scraping upon the metal emitting a deafening screech. The wheels exploded with four concussive pops, and the vehicle swerved and spun even as the driver tried to regain control. It slid to a crunching stop, sand and gravel pelting its side and entering the transport through the driver's open window. Arctura coughed forcefully as the dust settled, but Ahmar shoved Arctura and Sai'yn down to the transport's floor. He unholstered his weapon and peered out his own window.

"Raiders!" Ahmar hissed, sliding down to the floor with them.

Sai'yn cursed. "How can that be? I thought your patrol swept the area this morning!"

"They used a spike trap. They must have seen our dust cloud miles away." Ahmar glared at him. "I told you this was unwise."

Sai'yn stood to retort, but Ahmar pushed him down again. Motioning for them to be quiet, Ahmar pointed forcefully out the window. Arctura's heartbeat quickened as she heard the sound of hoofbeats and whooping calls approaching from outside.

"Driver! Get down!" Ahmar commanded.

The driver's eyes widened as he looked out his window. Tugging his own pistol out, he took aim outside and squeezed the trigger. It hissed and boomed, and a dying shriek of pain answered. Encouraged, the driver aimed again. Whistles and thuds filled the air, and he screamed and choked, slumping back against the opposite window. A grouping of arrows, burrowed into his body up to their poison yellow and black fletching, quivered with his dying shudders. Arctura looked in horror as blood dripped down the interior of the transport.

Sai'yn cursed again and drew his weapon. He looked impatiently at Arctura and then gestured toward the dead driver.

"Well, Ambassador, will you defend yourself, or do you wish to die empty handed?"

Arctura's eyes darted toward the pistol dangling from the driver's curled fingers. All these years of plotting revenge against those who had wronged her, and not once had she picked up her own weapons. She had only enacted violence through the hands of others.

I am a coward.

With a deep breath, she reached for the pistol and yanked it loose. It was heavier than she expected, and awkward in her elegant hands. She wrapped her fingers around the grip, squeezing so tightly her knuckles blanched.

Outside, the hooves continued to beat as they circled the disabled transport. Arctura tensed for another volley of arrows clanking off the vehicle's sides, but it did not come.

Why would it? she realized. *Why waste ammunition on hidden targets? All they need now is patience.*

Arctura gulped.

"How many, Ahmar?" Sai'yn asked.

Ahmar inched up toward the window. "Must be at least a dozen."

"What are they doing?"

"Approaching," Ahmar said. "Cautiously, but surely."

Sai'yn cursed.

"That is not all," Ahmar said. "Their leader has an energy rifle. And a Kytrian war sash."

"Outrageous!" Sai'yn sputtered. "Treason! A spy of Kytri must be in the palace! This is an act of war!"

"Your spy, I'm certain, does not expect to be discovered. We are not meant to survive," Ahmar replied darkly.

"What then?" Arctura whispered.

Ahmar's eyes hardened. "We take as many of them as we can. Sai'yn, the windows."

Still keeping his head low, Sai'yn leaned forward and stretched his hands toward the controls in the front of the transport. He fumbled with a few buttons before finding the ones that lowered the windows.

"Right. Ambassador, Sai'yn– you cover that side. I will take this one, their chief first. No time to lose."

Arctura crawled toward the opposite window. With the veil on, she could barely see anything. She whipped it off and threw it on the floor, catching Sai'yn and Ahmar with looks of surprise and some revulsion at her deep, puckered scars.

Good, she thought. *At least it's not pity.*

Arctura climbed carefully onto the backseat and curled up below the window. Whoops and war cries outside grew louder with the raiders' closing approach. She could hear the spray of sand, kicked up by their horses' hooves, beating against the transport. Sai'yn inched up beside her and tucked in his paunch to fit comfortably on the transport's floor. He removed his turban and set it carefully beside him, his bald head gleaming with sweat.

Ahmar looked at each of them, his jaw set and his pistol at the ready. He nodded.

"Now," he mouthed, and he sprung to the window.

Arctura sprung up beside Sai'yn, the sound of Ahmar's pistol already registering in her ears. No sooner had Sai'yn raised his head high enough to see out the window he was squeezing his trigger, and shouts of pain and surprise filled the air. The raiders had come close; only a few more strides and they would be close enough to reach out and touch the transport. Arctura could see the foam flecking the mouths of their horses and the glinting of the sunlight off the tips of their aimed arrows. But the raiders themselves appeared to her as dusty corpses, the cowls shrouding their heads and faces covered in sand, and their large, darkened goggles obscuring all human features. Terror gripped Arctura to the core. Her hands shook on her weapon.

"What are you doing?!" Sai'yn shouted. "Kill them!"

He loosed another blast, catching a raider just as he was drawing back his bowstring. The man fell to the sand in a puff of dust. Sai'yn ducked, narrowly avoiding the arrow that sailed into the window and thunked into the transport's interior. Arctura flattened against the seat as several more followed, some clanging against the vehicle's side. She breathed.

"They're falling back!" Ahmar shouted. "Regrouping! Hit them now!"

Arctura blinked. Fury and disgust at her inaction filled her, and she shook with both fear and rage. Would she always be the victim of circumstances, impotent and unprepared to face the violence that never ceased to find her?

No more. I will be a coward no more.

Arctura sprung back up toward the window, squeezing the trigger of her energy pistol as she did. Its blast hissed and screamed through the air, burning through the torso of one raider. The air reverberated with the sounds of hissing, screaming, and shouting as she loosed an unholy volley against her attackers. Men fell. Exhilaration raced through Arctura. The whooping outside the vehicle quieted, leaving Arctura with nothing but a soft yet persistent buzzing whine in her ears.

"There is your self-defense, Sai'yn of Sutra," Arctura said smugly.

But Sai'yn did not answer. Arctura looked down, breathing in sharply at his body crumpled beside her. A single arrow protruded from his throat, his hands resting just below it, as if reaching to stem the flow from the wound. Blood bubbled out of it and puddled beneath Sai'yn's head.

She twisted toward Ahmar, but the cry for help died on her lips. Sutra's chief of border patrol had collapsed against the side of the transport, the entry point of an energy rifle's blast still steaming above his monobrow. Arctura ducked below the windows, her breath hitching as she surveyed the transport's interiors. Arrows stuck into the seats and littered the vehicle, and blast points seemed to have left their singed pockmarks everywhere. How had they missed her? And was there anyone left?

Arctura smothered the sound of her frantic heartbeat against the seat and strained to listen for signs of life elsewhere. She only heard the idling of the transport's engine, the whinny of a horse, and the whistling of the desert wind. Cautiously, she peered out the window. She caught the tail-ends of some riderless horses as they galloped away, but that was it. Scrambling toward the other side while carefully avoiding Ahmar's body, she searched the outside in that direction. Nothing but the bodies of raiders, already partially mummified by the relentlessly whipping sands. The sparkle of a black barrel beside one of them confirmed that not even their leader had survived. Ahmar had gotten him somehow, and it cost him everything.

She moved to the center of the transport, hugged her legs to her chest, and squeezed her eyes shut. There was no plotting her next move now; there was only the dead, surrounding her on all sides and trapping her among them. Arctura could not look or go anywhere without being haunted by their presence. And soon, in this desert heat, they'd bloat and suffocate her with their stench. Arctura slammed herself against the transport door, fumbled it open, and fell onto the packed, gravelly sand. She wretched.

Wiping her mouth, Arctura stumbled away from the transport and searched her surroundings. Ahead, she found the Kamarian Mountains closer than she had thought when she first glimpsed them through the shimmering heat haze. They stretched from horizon to horizon. To her left, the endless undulating waves of beige met blue sky. Beyond that, she knew, would be the sea. To her right it was the same, but miles away, across these forsaken wastes and far out of reach, she imagined the greenery and forested lowlands of Gormlaen. Arctura looked south, and just above the line where the sky met sand, she caught the gold twinkle of Sutra's palace dome. Maybe she could make it back. But how?

Not far from her, one patched brown and white horse lingered. It stood by the raider leader, nosing in the feed bag that had fallen on the ground beside him. Arctura placed a thumb on her lips. She did not enjoy riding, mainly because Mother had only allowed her to ride side saddle. Her current attire would certainly inhibit a more efficient mode of riding, and she was not exactly keen on showing up in Sutra in a way that most Gormlaeans would find offensively immodest and coarse. Arctura moved on to survey the transport. She groaned softly at the state of its wheels. They had been mangled beyond even professional repair, let alone her own inexperience. She bent down to examine it more closely, finding the steel teeth of the trap wrapped around the wheel wells and also imbedded in the undercarriage. *Nothing I can do with that*, she thought.

She circled the vehicle, looking for anything else that might help, when a red, blinking light on its dashboard caught her attention. In the chaos, Arctura had forgotten about the communication function built into the transport's console. It flashed rapidly, transmitting a distress call that her driver must have managed to send out before losing his life. Of course, that far out in the desert, Ahmar and Sai'yn rightfully had not counted on reinforcements to aid their efforts. But maybe now, a rescue party might come. Arctura gazed back to where Sutra should have been, and her spirits lifted.

Coming from the south, slightly west of Sutra, clouds of dust rose off the ground. She shielded her eyes, now able to make out the shapes of horses and the silhouettes of riders as they approached. And by the size of the cloud, she could tell they were coming fast. Was it Ahmar's patrolling guard? Arctura ran to the back of the transport, raised her arms, and shouted.

They galloped faster, it seemed, veering toward her on a direct course. The attires of the riders became clearer as goggles reflected the sun on the otherwise shrouded figures. Bows and quivers bounced against their shoulders. Arctura frowned and lowered her arms slowly. Poison yellow and black fletching peeked out of them.

28

The raiders had spotted her. She could see it in the way they urged their horses on, closing in like lionesses on defenseless prey. Arctura raised her pistol at the approaching charge and depressed the trigger. An animal cry of pain met her ears as a horse stumbled and fell, tossing its hapless rider into the sand. She squeezed the trigger again, but this time, nothing happened. Arctura shook and banged on the grip. *Jammed.*

She looked back at the wave of raiders, some of which had already unsheathed their bows. Arctura knew little about warfare, but she did not need to know much to understand she'd be in their range soon enough. With a panicked cry, she threw the pistol down, turned on heel, and ran. Passing the transport, she skidded to a stop a few feet from the dead raider's horse.

The shouts and wild advance of the raiders had not bothered it at all, but Arctura's slow approach did. It knickered and swung its head toward her. Arctura paused as he examined her with his big brown eyes, more annoyed, it seemed, by the interruption to his meal than anything else. Arctura might have tried to win the beast over, but she had no time for that. She snatched up the feed bag and, with a nimble hop, hiked up her skirts and swung her leg over the saddle. The young stallion bucked. Arctura squeezed his sides and pulled on the reins. He reared once, dancing atop the sands, but gave up the fight after that. *So I have some skill after all,* she thought with relief, *even if I despise it.* The horse looked back at her, awaiting command. And not a moment too soon. Arctura gasped as an arrow thudded into the sand beside them.

She kicked her mount's sides hard, and he broke into a fast trot. Arctura bounced painfully in the saddle as they head north toward the Kamarian Mountains. She looked back. Sand flew up behind them, but even in their flight, she could see the raiding party was still closing the gap. *Not fast enough.* Arctura dug in, the horse finally relenting and pushing to a canter. She kicked the stubborn creature harder, shouting as an arrow whizzed by her head and clattered against the rocky ground. Her heart thumped in her throat. Arctura found the riding crop in the saddlebag and thwacked the horse as hard as she could. With a testy neigh, he responded and opened into a full gallop.

The mountain range drew closer. Arctura lowered her head against the horse's neck to shield herself from the kicked-up grit and stone. She chanced another glance backward, releasing a shuddering sigh and patting the horse's neck as the distance between her and the raiders grew. Still, the strong mount increased his speed. Arctura continued to watch as the band of raiders became smaller and smaller. They slowed, then stopped, finally giving up the chase altogether and circling back to transport's wreckage instead. *Enjoy your treasure now,* Arctura thought, anger coursing through her. *The Coalition will make you answer for it soon enough.*

Arctura slowed the horse back to a trot, the sound of his labored snorting loud in their solitude. His hoofbeats beneath her thudded with more force and substance, echoing in the vast expanse of wasteland. Arctura looked around, surprised to see them well in the shadow of the Kamarian range. The winds no longer ripped past her, and the arid, intense heat of Sutra's desert faded. Rocky ground inclined upward toward the mountains and echoed with their passage. Eroded boulders and piles of loose rock dotted their ascent. Arctura shivered, aware of the sudden chill in the air. The Kamarian range had siphoned off any warmth that had lingered from the desert off. It was, she knew, technically winter everywhere else, but that had been easy to forget within the walls of the ever-sweltering Sutra.

The path inclined even farther, slowing the horse to a strenuous walk. She looked back once again. Unbeknownst to her, their course had taken them beyond sight of the raiders or even much of the desert itself. The desert that she *could* see was already small and growing smaller far below. Her entire body shivered now, and with chattering teeth, she rooted around in the saddlebag. Arctura pulled out a dirty but warm-looking woven blanket and wrapped it around her shoulders. It smelled of horse sweat and a stranger's body odor, but she hardly cared about that. The rearing wall of the mountain, the dropping temperature, and the unsettling silence absorbed her senses, filling her with dread and fear.

There was a reason the nomads and the Sutrans alike kept out of the Kamarian Mountains, she thought with a shudder. *I shouldn't like to find out why.*

She considered turning around and making her way back into the desert. Maybe she could travel along the mountain range and head to Sutra along the shoreline. But there was no telling who or what she might run into in that direction. Wouldn't the nomads and their raiders prefer to move by the sea instead of the miles of nothingness between Heibeiath and Gormlaen in the east? Arctura wasn't willing to risk it, especially now that the malfunctioning of her pistol had left her entirely defenseless. It was possible she could return to the site of the raiders' trap and wait for Sutra's patrol to find her there, but again, she remained defenseless. That second wave of raiders surely would have stolen everything useful from the place, maybe even carting off the transport itself. And if they didn't take that, what was stopping them from stripping the transport and even figuring out a way to end its distress call? Arctura had no assurance that anyone – the Coalition or Sutra's patrol – would be able to respond to the signal... or if they did, they might have seen the carnage already and assumed the worst. Did they think she was still alive, maybe a prisoner of the nomads or wandering the desert alone? Or would anyone even be looking for her now? And what would Father do when he found out?

He'll find some way to use my tragedy for his gain, Arctura thought. *But he won't search for me, not now. Not with Sutra already in his hands. He wrung everything he needed out of me. What cause does he have to find me again?*

Her face contorted, loneliness and despair rolling over her. She pinched her lips and pushed the feelings away. Even alone, Arctura Vipsanius refused to allow weakness to spill out of her. And Arctura Vipsanius would neither die in the wastes nor fall victim to the territorial quarrels of Heibeiathan lords. She would rise. She would find a way out of this. Never would she allow death to exact its toll from her before she tasted vengeance. Arctura Vipsanius would survive.

She guided the horse farther into the Kamarian range and formulated a new plan: she would forge a path down the mountainside and cross back into Gormlaen, find an outpost or a village, and contact Kyma from there. Arctura had a blanket, and the horse had its feed bag; it would be a long few days, but they could make it back to safe boundaries. At least she had to try.

They plodded on that way for some time and wound up the mountainous path among its stony desolation. Not a friendly tree or welcoming flowering bush came into sight, and it occurred to Arctura the mountains would be bare from here all the way to Gormlaen. A cold, hollow wind replaced the hot blast of the desert air, penetrating her blanket and freezing her nose and fingers. The horse's hooves clattered noisily against the stony trail and echoed along the mountain rock corridor. That disturbed Arctura more than anything: their foreign presence in a hostile land, intruding on its solitude with their unseemly clamor, inviting misfortune with their ignorant presumption. But what else could she do?

The path narrowed as it spun to the left and farther up the mountain. Arctura looked down at her right. She wished she hadn't. Jagged rocks jutted out of the mountainside like hundreds of teeth in the mouth of a monster. She guided her mount closer to the interior rock face, hoping he wouldn't stumble. He kept his footing, but as he turned up the path, the stallion stopped short. Arctura raised her heel to spur him, but she paused as she watched his ears press flat against his head. His entire body tightened. Arctura could hear his breaths coming in shallow and fast snorts.

"What is it?" she asked the horse, patting his raised, stiff neck as soothingly as she could.

It didn't help either of them. The horse remained in his anxious position, and Arctura could not see what had spooked him, despite swinging all around to find it. No present danger revealed itself, but she gripped the reins, anyway.

"C-come on," Arctura said shakily, pressing a timid heel into her mount's side. "It's nothing. We'll be fine."

A slight shifting of rock from above and a low hissing caught her ear. Arctura looked up just ahead of them, confused at first by what she saw. The stone, it seemed, was moving very slowly toward them. It slid down the rock face in a sort of slithering, serpentine manner, deliberate and unnatural in its falling. She shrieked as the slithering stone separated itself from the mountain, and a large, lithe body lifted by four stout, clawed limbs skittered down from among the boulders and blocked the path before them.

It turned its reptilian head and watched them with emotionless, black eyes. A purple forked tongue darted out between its short, sharp teeth, tasting their terror. Twice as long as the stallion, it filled the narrow path, trapping them between its jaws and a treacherous descent. And in a flash, it sprung forward. Arctura froze, the clicking sound of its scrabbling three-toed claws paralyzing her, but the horse reared and kicked in primal dread. She scrambled to hang on. Her hands slipped from the reins and her legs lost any hold on the saddle. The horse's front hooves struck the mouth of the terrible lizard just as she tumbled off his back. He whinnied, the monster's talons raking his shoulder as it latched onto the horse's fetlock. But the horse was powerful. He kicked free, careening past Arctura as he fled down the path.

Meanwhile, Arctura fell. She rolled away from the main fray, bouncing down the rocky path with scraping, grinding smacks. Her descent came to a painful stop at the path's steep curve, where a boulder prevented her from rolling to the jagged rocks below. She groaned, the boulder pressing hard into her bruised back. Arctura looked for the horse, watching for only a moment as it hobbled away; her attention snapped back to the creature bearing down on her. It hissed, opening and shutting its wide, shovel-like jaws. Slate-gray scales scraped the ground as the monster slinked toward her. Arctura realized with immobilizing horror that there was nothing she could do. Running was pointless. If it could catch a powerful, fast stallion in its jaws, how could she possibly hope to escape it? And those claws... those terrible, familiar claws. Shivers of fear raced down her back. She cast about in the dirt, prying at embedded rocks for a small hope of defense, but the rocks were unforgiving. The monster approached. She screamed.

"*Smyga!*"

A commanding voice rang out and echoed along the mountain path. The creature froze, his open mouth only inches from Arctura's face. She could smell its putrid breath, see the bits of rotting flesh still clinging to its jagged teeth, and look down the length of its widening gullet. The voice cried out again, booming and rolling around the Kamarian range like thunder. The monster closed its jaws and scuttled backward. With its great, black eyes, it searched for the source, its head inclining toward an overhang ahead on their left.

A diminutive robed figure stepped to the edge of the overhang, leaning on a wooden staff for a support. The long trail of a silver beard hung outside the robe and ruffled in the wind. He pointed a bony finger at the creature, the power of his voice a surprise considering his feeble frame. The words that followed sounded like none Arctura had ever heard before. In fact, she was not entirely sure that he spoke a human language at all. They slid in and out of hard consonants and animal groans and hisses, weaving together in an unbroken string of sound. All while he seemed not to take a single breath. The creature listened calmly, almost reverently, if Arctura could call it that. It turned to face the strange man. But what happened next seemed impossible, for as soon as the man had finished, the thing *responded*. Her eyes widened with disbelief as it sibilated back. And if Arctura didn't know any better, the robed figure was listening. She heard a few grunts and sympathetic "mmhmms" as he nodded along. Finally, when it seemed the monster had spoken its piece, the man spoke again, and this time, replacing the rebuke and power with softness and understanding. At this, the creature dipped its head. Without a second glance at Arctura, it slunk between the rocks of the mountain and crawled out of sight.

"So," the figure said, lowering his hood. "Here at last, are we?"

Arctura peered up at him, considering the odd man. He was some sort of hermit, that was certain. His tattered robes flapped unsubstantially, his unkempt beard and skinny arms and legs a testament to an ascetic lifestyle. Liver spots dotted his pale, bald head, and the skin of his face crinkled like discarded parchment. But his eyes! Emerald green, sparkling and keen like a young man's, he gazed down at her with an intensity that made her squirm. Arctura stuttered as she tried to comprehend both the man's peculiarity and the question he posed to her.

"W-what– what in all of Reidara could you possibly mean by that?"

"That rock drake," he said instead, pointing down the mountain in the direction that the creature had taken. "It has been a long time since he had a proper meal. They are hard to come by in these lonely mountains. Though it was *Isa's* will, I have taken from him what he had rightly earned. You would have nourished him well for the hard winter months to come."

Arctura opened her mouth, shut it, then opened it again, only to find herself at a complete loss for words. The man simply stared at her, neither with malignant nor benign intent, but with those green eyes that she found incomprehensible. He shrugged dismissively.

"But *Isa* will provide. *Smyga* will find a mountain goat soon enough, and more likely than not that steed you had been riding. Innocent portions in your place. It must be so."

"*Smyga*." Arctura said flatly.

He nodded. "In the language of Elmnas, it means something like stealthy or cunning. It is a fitting name for the creature, wouldn't you say?"

She found her voice and wit again as she stared back at the ascetic with a scowl. All at once, it began to dawn on her that this was the most ridiculous conversation she had ever had.

"You named it? That's that thing's– that rock drake's– name? What, is it your pet that it should come when called and go when it is told?"

"Of course I named him." The old hermit chuckled. "I have named all things, for I know all by name. I know even you, little one. And indeed, the day is coming when all manner of the named, both with names men speak and those that shall never be mentioned, will come and go at the cry of the Phoenix, in *Isa's* time. For the Unseen sees and soon shall be seen. But come! Now *Isa* has brought you to me, and there is time enough for all that will be done."

"Such riddles," Arctura snorted. "Either you are a seer, or your mountain solitude has addled your old brain."

With more agility than even Arctura could have mustered at that moment, the wizened hermit launched himself from the rock face and landed gracefully on the path. Arctura's eyes nearly popped out of her head as she tried to maintain her composure. He proffered a spindly hand.

"You shall see soon enough, Arctura, once favored of the House Vipsanius. For now, allow this addled old man to show you some hospitality. We shall need to weather the approaching storm, after all."

All the snark left Arctura in an instant. She looked into his eyes, baffled and terrified, but now insatiably curious. What other mysteries did this old Elmling seer know? Curiosity outweighing all else, Arctura tentatively reached forward and took his hand. The hermit lifted her far too easily and released his strong grip. Turning, he beckoned for her to follow as he hobbled on his staff farther up the mountain. Arctura picked up her fallen blanket and wrapped it tightly around her shoulders, gazing up at the darkening sky with a shiver. She watched the ascetic as he labored up the path – and wondered.

"Seer!" she shouted after him, just as he was about to turn out of sight. "You have me at a disadvantage. What shall I call you?"

The old man halted, his staff raised. He brought it down with a clatter as he turned again to face her.

"There have been many names," he said. "In these expectant times, you may call me Hiraeth."

Thunder crashed. Large flakes of snow began to swirl in the air. She took a deep breath and followed.

Year 113
  47th of Sun's Wane
  Northern Wilds, Gormlaen

The incessant chill had finally begun to wear off as Fox guided her captive and mount out of the ravine and through the thinning forest.

She stared ahead, noting the abrupt break in the tree line as it gave way to open field. As they approached, Fox yanked on the reins, drawing the horse up short of the edge of the wood. Blade hopped aside as the mare nickered and danced at the sudden command. She snorted indignantly, but Fox ignored it. Fox sat stonily in the saddle, staring out at the ancient burial ground. It was a desolate place, littered with the broken remains of memorial stones and markers for the dead of a long-forgotten people. The circular cairn that rose out of its midst, however, had stood the test of time. Except for the erosion of its archaic inscriptions and the blanket of moss that covered most of its surface, it had remained intact. Even the iron-clad wooden door, though hanging off its hinges, showed some durability, though Fox guessed that grave robbers pilfered anything of value decades ago.

On the other side of the cairn, Myergo's men waited for them. The curling smoke of a cooking fire, visible as it puffed into the sky behind the cairn, indicated a human presence, and Fox knew no other souls who would even dare to frequent ancient resting places, let alone light fires in them. She watched it with narrowed eyes, her mouth hardening into a rigid, bitter line. In the periphery of her vision, she sensed other eyes watching her. Blade stood motionless beside the horse, bound hands lowered in front of him, hawk eyes probing.

"Answer me this, Guardian," Fox said, still gazing at the rising smoke. "What is the smallest weapon with which you could slay a Mistwolf?"

He raised his eyebrows in surprise, offering more expression than she had seen from him thus far.

"Be truthful. I'm not interested in braggadocio."

Blade considered the question. "It is difficult to say. The hide of a Mistwolf is so thick as to be almost armored, so that conventional weapons, great or small, can be useless against it unless one knows where to find its weaknesses. Even glancing blasts with a standard energy rifle do not penetrate, and sometimes direct hits do little damage. I have only ever destroyed Mistwolves with my ancient blades, but it could be possible with a Cardanthium dagger."

"What about this?" Fox said, pulling a miniature explosive from her weapons holster.

Blade looked askance at her. "That would be effective if placed well. But it would place the user at great risk also."

"The user would be facing down a Mistwolf," Fox said with a slight smile. "Great risk has already been incurred."

"Indeed." Blade nodded appreciatively, a curious expression on his face.

In one swift motion, Fox jumped from the mare's back and approached Blade. Though he stood tall, Fox matched him. They said nothing as they stood face to face, each looking at the other. Blade's storm-gray eyes sized her up. Calculating, it seemed to Fox. Always calculating. And she had to wonder which of them had calculated right this time.

Fox held up the explosive between them.

"Risk is the last hope of the desperate. It might spare you from at least one death this day, but I cannot promise it will save you from any other."

Blade narrowed his eyes, clenching his fists. "Why are you telling me this?"

"I truly don't know," Fox admitted. "Maybe that old fool Hiraeth is finally getting to me."

Blade's eyebrows jumped once again, and Fox almost found it amusing. Almost. She was certain he would rip out her throat if he knew where she was sending him. He *definitely* would if he knew what she was going to do next. Fox squeezed the sides of the obsidian device on her wrist between her thumb and forefinger. Blade jerked, a cry strangled in his throat as a stunning electrical impulse ran through his hands, feet, and neck. She stepped back as he flopped face first to the ground, twitching at Fox's feet in unconsciousness.

Fox prodded him with her foot. When he didn't move, she rolled him onto his back. She gripped the explosive, seeking a discreet place to stash it. Her hand wavered between his groin and his boot, grimacing as she wondered how thoroughly Myergo's men would search Blade.

"You will have to make do, Guardian," Fox said, and she tucked the explosive into his boot. "That, or die."

She re-secured Blade to the hoverboard, swung back onto her horse, and trotted out of the forest. They had an appointment to keep.

29

"Does she sleep, love?"

Mama fretted with her long, blonde curls as she peered past the sheer curtain that covered the small doorway to Mouse's room. Mouse peeked through slit eyes at her, trying her best to appear asleep so Mama wouldn't know she was listening. She sunk into the soft furs and woven blankets piled onto her little bed, her eyelids growing heavier by the moment. The warm, diffuse glow of their stone hearth wasn't helping matters, either. Mouse focused on Mama instead, who fidgeted with nervous energy. Her brows knitted together, and Mama chewed her bottom lip. The soft padding of fur-lined boots met Mouse's ears, and she squeezed her eyes shut as the curtain flap rustled. The floor creaked as the boots entered, and she could hear the familiar, deep, rumbly sigh of Papa. He probably had that thoughtful look on his face, the one he wore whenever Mama was anxious about something. Mouse chanced another peek to see his back toward her, his strong arms around her mother.

"She sleeps, Niiri. You needn't worry so."

Mama looked up at Papa with nothing but worry on her face. "But the Keeper, Brehn. You heard her oracle."

Papa sighed. "Hearing is one thing. Trusting it is another. Your people have not seen a living Guardian since the Coalition conquest. Why should this Alvilde truly be one of them?"

"She carries the ceremonial dagger of her order, possesses the wisdom of the Ageless, and she speaks with the authority of the Unseen. I know you may not understand or believe, but I do. And if her oracle is true…"

Mama gazed past the curtain, her eyes falling on Mouse.

"There are more than enough girls in the village the oracle could mean," Papa answered quietly. "It does not have to be ours."

Mama's brows drew together once again. "Yet Alvilde looked only to one. *Our* one. Then she said, 'this knowledge is a sign, a hope, but also an arrow to pierce the soul'– She turned to me… And… I-I just knew. Brehn, I *knew*. She was speaking to me."

Papa hugged Mama closer and stroked her hair. A tear slipped down Mama's cheek.

"I know that I should trust… I should believe the good that could come of it… but oh… my love, what of the evil? What of the suffering the harbinger must bear? What if… what if she has to bear it alone?"

Papa comforted Mama, kissing her on the forehead and cradling her head against his chest. Mouse could hardly bear it. She longed to jump out of the bed, to wrap herself around Mama and Papa's legs and tell them it wasn't true. It was going to be alright. Her eyes opened fully now; she peeled back the blankets hemming her in. But Papa saw her, his charcoal eyes locked on hers. She froze. With a knowing but comforting smile, he lifted his hand and gestured for her to stay. Mouse obeyed, pulling the blankets back up to her chin. Papa spoke.

"But she will never bear it alone," he whispered. "Even if we are taken from her, and Reidara turned upside down, it will not be so. You taught me that, Niiri. And if she remembers what we have taught her, it will be enough. She can be brave."

Mama nodded and sniffed. "We were so happy these short years. It was naïve to think I might put my past afflictions behind me. The

Unseen preserve me. You know I've done all that I could. For us. For her. I can't outrun this anymore, can I?"

"Maybe not. But you are not alone. Everyone tries to flee from fate, but fate is always finding us." Papa replied.

"I only wanted for her to be safe," Mama said softly.

"Now, now, don't you forget what you always say." He gazed lovingly at Mouse once more. "There is no place more dangerous, yet no place safer, than on the path the Unseen leads."

Year 113
47th of Sun's Wane
Elmnas

Mouse woke up beside the cold embers of the dead campfire, tears staining her cheeks. The frigid early morning air stung them, and Mouse could feel where the tears had rolled and crystallized when she worked her facial muscles. As much as she wanted to brush off the traces of her still vivid dream, she wanted much less to expose any more of her body to the elements outside her cozy bedroll. Drawing her head inside it, she cocooned herself and rubbed the back of her hand against her face. Sleepiness still clung to her, but even with the renewed warmth and darkness that warded off the chill and brightening gray of dawn, her mind churned in unrelenting wakefulness. When she first escaped Misty Summit, Mouse had no real reason to think her dreams would ever lead to anything. She had hoped for some direction, and even Toma had been optimistic that more of her past would come to her. But this? As much as her heart soared with these new revelations, with names and even *faces*, it still felt like more than she could possibly hope to process.

Niiri. Brehn. Mama and Papa.

Their brief dream visitation swirled in her memory, and there were pieces of other memories that she felt even now were rising to consciousness; like waterlogged corks, stirred from the murky depths that had held them captive for so long, suddenly on the cusp of breaking the water's surface. Its weight, its anticipation, its elation and heartrending sorrow – the dream overwhelmed her. Mouse wanted to hide in her bedroll cave forever and block out every implication, every painful truth, every emotion these new revelations would catalyze. She longed for dreamless, memory free sleep, and yet, she longed for sleep with nothing *but* those memories. What would it be like to see the kind, lovely, worried faces of her parents, hear their strangely familiar voices, feel their presence beside her again? How many joys, how many embraces, how many nights of sweet, safe bedtimes had she forgotten? And still... what else had she forgotten? Her mother spoke of dangers, of sorrows... of things perhaps better left unremembered. *My mother.* Mouse's head spun as she simultaneously craved and feared the past now awakening within her.

These dreams, she thought, wrapping her arms around her head. *How will I get any rest from them?*

She sat up with a groan, shuddering as the icy mountain air touched her neck. Mouse huffed and watched the breath curl and dissipate from her mouth. It was light enough now to see, and she surveyed the place they had made camp. Somehow, they had come to a good place amid the inhospitable wilderness, and not just as a suitable shelter from the elements. Their place there on the mountain also hid them from other dangers. No wild animals seemed to inhabit the area. The strange rock formations rose up and enclosed the light of their fire, and the mountain winds scattered its smoke. And throughout the night, they did not hear the cries of creatures or the voices of men, as they had all feared. Even the mighty roar of Eris, now indelibly marked on Mouse's memory, had not punctuated the late evening or pre-dawn silence. They were truly alone. All in all, their mountain shelter had been a lucky find. *Lucky*, Mouse snorted. *Lucky doesn't begin to describe anything that just happened to us.*

Mouse's eyes fell on her company, and despite the chilly air, she warmed as she remembered their presence. Fraeda's bedroll rose and fell rhythmically beside hers, a shock of orange poking out of the top of the bag. Toma lay on the other side of the firepit, stomach down, his face turned toward her and mouth wide open. A bit of drool dribbled from it. Mouse suppressed a chuckle and shook her head. Even Rhavin seemed still as he slept with his back against the rock wall, the group's extra blankets tucked around him and his chin dropped into his chest.

She watched Rhavin for a moment, her emotions tangled as she regarded him. Rhavin possessed an undeniable charm, an easy confidence and comfortability that made him even more magnetizing the longer the group spent getting to know each other around the campfire last evening. And yet, he was still a stranger to her. An interesting, attractive stranger, but a stranger nonetheless. Mouse had to wonder what other secrets he might harbor from his noble past. What might they discover if he truly opened up to them? The thought unsettled her. His cruel brothers sounded so much like the Coalition Party Representatives that Mouse had come to fear; ruling without justice or mercy. And with Rhavin being raised to rule... was he like that, too? She had seen a glimpse of it in the ring at the circus. But she also knew what captivity did to people. She knew too well what survival required of the soul.

And how could she blame him for any desire for revenge? The faces of Misty Summit's torturers swam into her memory: the healers, supervisors, Enforcement Squad, and above all, the barracks ward, Milgrim. Her anger burned. Mouse remembered every instance of cruelty, every moment of delight in the prisoners' collective suffering. She may have lost her memories before coming to the Summit, but she would never forget what they did to her there. And then there was everything after that – the despicable Coalition guards, the vicious criminals of the sewers, and that bounty hunter – that ruthless, murderous woman. Why should they walk free and unpunished? Mouse had told herself that all she really wanted was justice, just as Blade had wanted, but deep down, she knew she craved more. Those that had taken everything from her ought to feel the pain she endured. They deserved to suffer, and she *wanted* them to.

A little shame crept into her anger at this realization. Who was Mouse to judge Rhavin's motives when she held her own hatred so tightly? And then there was Fraeda. Fraeda, who had bared her soul to them and named the atrocities committed against her and was still somehow... whole. She had spoken candidly, but also without malice, without a thirst for vengeance, without the weight of the past imprisoning her spirit in turmoil. Fraeda, who had been robbed of hearing and of even her words for a time, walked in more freedom than Mouse could ever imagine. And Mouse was ashamed.

She tore her gaze away from the sleeping Rhavin and her mind off such dark thoughts. With a stretch, she shook herself free of her bedroll, rose, and tugged on the messy, pulled back bun of hair that Fraeda had helped her with the night before. *Now, what was that trick she did with the cord?* Mouse put her fingers in the loop she had made, which was now quite loose and allowing pieces of wild hair to escape on all sides. She tried to re-secure it, but gave up with a sigh after a few attempts.

She trudged away from their cold campfire. Jamming her hands into her pockets, Mouse looked out past the edge of their mountain. She knew that Eris had taken them far, but still awe filled her as she viewed the vast, untouched country all around. Their mountain rose up, a small, lone peak among undulating hills. Unbroken forest spread to the northern horizon and reached down to the east, where the forest seemed to end before a cold, glassy shimmer so far off that Mouse had to squint. *Water*, she realized. With the mountain in the way, Mouse could not get a good view of any other direction, but she peered down its edge to find a way down. Wisps of mist spread through the valley below, but already it was ebbing in the weak, burnished haze of morning light. *No Mistwolves there*, she thought with a sigh of relief. *Now, how do we get down?* She located the drop off, which was rather precipitous, but a small trail snaked around the edge and meandered to the western side of the slope.

"We have come far, and I suspect no closer to the place you seek."

Mouse jumped, whipping around to see Rhavin now standing behind her. He had crossed his arms over his chest and was staring out at the valley, his dark eyes scanning the horizon. Mouse placed a hand on her heart and sighed.

"I'm going to die of fright before this is all over," she grumbled.

Rhavin shrugged. "There are far less pleasant ways to die."

Mouse rolled her eyes, but a smile tugged at her lips. "I guess you're right."

"Hm," Rhavin replied, cocking his head and studying her. "From what you and your friends told me last night, you would know. You have come close enough to death many times."

This time, Mouse shrugged. "I've been trying to stay alive since the day I woke up at Misty Summit. It's what I know. Maybe it's what I do best."

"Perhaps you truly are blessed. Let us hope it is a gift you can share with the rest of us." With a smirk, Rhavin stepped up beside her.

Mouse scoffed. "Doesn't feel that way."

"Blessing, curse... it is one and the same. At home, they used to say the only difference between the two is the malevolence of the one who bestows it. Either way, something has a hand on your destiny. I've seen many strange things these long years. Of course, I was a part of circus known for its oddities and wonders, so perhaps that is not so uncommon for me. But never in my time had I witnessed anything like our marvelous journey last evening."

"It was... unbelievable," Mouse nodded in agreement. "I hate to say it, but I'm starting to think there is something to this 'seer' thing, after all."

Rhavin said nothing, and they watched the brightening horizon in silence. She sneaked a curious glance at her new companion, who remained stoic as he contemplated the morning. Even as his intense solemnity unsettled her, Mouse could not help but notice his other qualities, either. Rhavin had all the marks of a future ruler; handsome, noble features and all.

An obnoxious yawn garnered her attention, and Mouse turned toward the campfire to see Toma opening his eye along with his mouth. He focused on Mouse, and then Rhavin standing beside her. The eye narrowed slightly. With a leery clearing of his throat, Toma sat up.

"Didn't mean to sleep in," he said, still eyeing Rhavin. "Did I miss anything?"

Mouse began to answer, but Fraeda, lost in her own world, interrupted.

"Who wants tea?" She set the kettle on the restoked fire and gathered her teacups. "And maybe someone could go hunt for some warbler eggs? I'm sure there's got to be birds of some sort on this mountain. We could use a little variety in our provisions, don't you think?"

Mouse smiled brightly at Fraeda. "You didn't have to do that. I didn't even think you were awake! I had thought Blade was sneaky, but you and Rhavin both keep surprising me."

"Not sneaky," Fraeda giggled. "Well, at least as I speak for myself. I just thought I needn't bother anyone."

"I might be sneaky," Rhavin offered with some amusement.

The girls laughed, but Mouse thought she saw Toma roll his eyes.

"Anyway," Fraeda said. "Are you always up so early, Mouse? I had always been the first to wake at the Priory."

"Not always, and not by choice," Mouse replied. "It's usually something else that wakes me. I guess I ought to tell you all now. I had another dream. And this one..."

Mouse shook her head and exhaled sharply. "I now know I've been dreaming about my parents."

Everyone's attention snapped to her. Fraeda dropped the teacups with a clunk.

"Was that what you saw at the circus?" Toma asked.

Mouse nodded. "And more last night."

"I guess breakfast can wait," Fraeda said. "Go on—tell us what you saw."

The company crowded close to the fire. Mouse took a deep breath and relayed her dream.

"There's so much there," she said as she finished. "So much I didn't know. But I'm more confused than ever before. Why was my mother, an Elmling, not with her people? Who was my father and *his* people? And this Alvilde... what did she say? Why did her oracle upset them?"

"Alvilde... Alvilde..." Fraeda scrunched up her face as she continued to mouth the name. "A Keeper, you said, right? I know I've read that name somewhere..."

Fraeda dove into her bag and began sifting through scrolls. She looked up and smiled. "I have some more recent histories here. Maybe I can help."

Mouse looked on with incredulity. "Sister Alba let you take sacred writings with you?"

"They're not originals," Fraeda shrugged. "Just copies. Besides, she insisted I continue my studies. I hadn't gotten quite up to the present in modern history, and I still haven't worked through any ancient mystical literature yet. And don't even mention my general Reidara histories. I'm very far behind."

Mouse might have said more, but Fraeda had buried her nose in her manuscripts.

"So, your mom was from here," Toma said. "What about your dad? What did he look like?"

"Um..." Mouse searched her memory, but the faces in the dreams were already becoming less distinct in her mind. "He had dark hair. That's not really helpful, is it? What else... um... and these dark gray eyes... eyes that seemed to laugh when he smiled. I don't know. He looked like my father."

Toma scratched his head. "Yeah, that's... not much to go on."

Mouse gasped. "Wait a minute. I just remembered something. Something that one of the sisters said to me."

She tapped on Fraeda's shoulder. Fraeda's eyes came off the page hesitantly, a faraway look in them.

"Fraeda, the elderly sister who used to tend the garden. What's her name again?"

"Oh, uh, Sister Legathe. Why?"

"She said some strange things to me, things I didn't think about later since she sounded so confused. But now..." Mouse shook her head. "She called me Niiri. The name of the woman in my dream. My mother."

Toma and Rhavin exchanged glances as Fraeda's eyes widened. "What else did she say?"

"She said..." Mouse scrunched up her face, trying to remember the odd conversation from only the morning before. With everything that happened afterward, it had been easy to forget.

"She said I was a lost one, returned from the Succor of Samras. Does that mean anything to you?"

Fraeda held up a finger. "Succor... of... Samras. Yes. Here it is. In the scroll of modern histories. Give me a minute to translate... okay, I'll read it here:

"*...and the failure of the rebellions fractured Elmnas further, dividing the already scattered tribes along political lines. The larger Northern and Western tribes retreated to the far north to regroup, while the smaller Southern and Eastern tribes yielded fully to Coalition rule in exchange for peace. But some from among all tribes rejected both, decrying what they called faithlessness in their brothers and sisters. There rose a sharp and bitter conflict. With one last show of unity, the tribes convened in the year 95 of the New Era to judge the minority's position. And as had been done to the apostates of ancient times, the tribal council named the malcontents Cut Off, and exiled them from Elmnas. But many chose exile willingly, and they sought the descendants of their Cut Off ancient kin in the plains and lowlands.*

There was then found the Samrasine peoples, those who are called the
wanderers. And in the Succor of Samras, the Samrasines welcomed the
exiled Elmlings, and the malcontents settled among them."

"Cut off?" Toma questioned. "What does that mean?"

"Over four hundred years ago, there was a civil war in Elmnas," Fraeda explained. "Over a number of things that would take too long to explain. But when the war ended, the losing side was forced out of Elmnas. They were the original Cut Off. From what I understand, the Cut Off spread to different parts of Reidara, but some settled just outside of Elmnas, joining with exiles from Heibeiathan nomadic peoples and refugees of the Old Gor land wars. They became the Samrasines."

"So in this Succor of Samras, my mother, along with other Elmlings, lived among those people," Mouse said.

"That's what it seems like," Fraeda nodded. "And given your dream, it seems like your father was a Samrasine."

"But what of this prophecy?" Rhavin asked, rubbing his chin. "Can you speak yet into that?"

"Hold on," Fraeda said, unraveling another stack of parchment and leafing through the manuscript pages. "Alvilde is mentioned in the history right after the Succor of Samras, but only as speculation. There doesn't seem to be evidence that she existed outside the Golden Age of Elmnas at all. Oh, and if you're wondering–"

Fraeda glanced up and grinned. "The Golden Age would have been from around year 1000 of the Ancient Era to just before the civil war. That was when the Kin of Enesh, the first Guardians, drove out the Kr'Garian giants and established Elmnas."

"That sounds made up," Toma said.

"Perhaps there is some truth to it," Rhavin replied. "My people also have legends about the wilds of Kr'Gar, a realm of monsters and the man-like giants who ruled it."

Mouse waved her hand in annoyance. "Okay, another time for that. The prophecy. If it's not in the history, where are you looking for it now?"

Fraeda gestured to her stack of parchment. "The sacred writings, of course. Any oracles of the Keepers should be in here. She didn't record much, but I remember reading Alvilde's oracle before. Now I just have to find them..."

"I'm the only other person who can read our language," Mouse said. "Let me help."

"Alright, start... here." Fraeda thrust a handful of parchment at Mouse.

Mouse scanned through the pages while Rhavin and Toma watched. She wished she had time to process them, to know intimately her people through the sacred writings. What wealth of knowledge was right here in front of her eyes? But there was no time for that now. Mouse searched each page for Alvilde's name as quickly as she could, but having not really *read* her native language for who knew how long, she struggled to keep up with Fraeda's furious pace. Fraeda had flipped through five sheets before Mouse could get through one.

"Ah ha!" Fraeda shouted triumphantly, smacking the page with the back of her hand. "Here it is: *An oracle of Alvilde, in the days of captivity, and the last words given to the Eneshkin.*

The Unseen sees, the Unknowable knows
The evils that defile his people's inheritance
And spreads its corruption abroad.
You are great, O Mighty Lion,
Who put a leash on the Bear
Who lulled to sleep the Cobra
Who crushed the Bird in flight!
Yet your deeds are not forgotten—
The Unseen sees and knows,
He stirs up the heart of the harbinger
And stores up your reward.
In flames the Phoenix rises
He shall break the teeth of your mouth
And shatter every bone

With blood, He will conquer all.
This shall be a sign:
A mouse to drive a thorn
into the Mighty Lion's paw;
From the hand of the Samras maiden
shall your death knell sound."

The company sat in silence as Fraeda finished, even ignoring the hissing of the kettle now boiling over the fire.

"I'm sorry," Toma finally said. "Did that clear things up for anyone else? I have no idea what you just said."

Rhavin offered only a vague shrug.

"The harbinger," Mouse said, frowning with intense concentration. "I've heard that before. Blade said... the people of Elmnas believed the harbinger would prepare the way for the Phoenix, right?"

Fraeda nodded. "In the sacred writings, the harbinger is a sign of the Phoenix's return. And the Phoenix is supposed to reclaim Elmnas, rule in victory, and usher in a forever peace."

"My parents..." Mouse whispered. "They thought *I* was the harbinger."

Toma's eyes grew round as Rhavin thoughtfully pursed his lips.

"And that did not bring them joy, but fear," Rhavin observed. "Why?"

"The sacred writings don't paint a nice picture of the harbinger's 'stirring'," Fraeda supplied. "It's almost always paired with times of great trial, darkness, and suffering."

"Alvilde gave her oracle in my village," Mouse said breathlessly. "My village... Shomroh. It was called Shomroh, and it burned to the ground. I remember. I remembered last night, during the show. My mother... she... she was carrying me. My dream, always the same dream. Her face, the fire. And then, my father... What happened after that, Fraeda? What happened to my family? What happened to my home?"

Fraeda quickly flipped through the histories before raising her hands helplessly. "I don't know. It's not here."

Mouse pressed her hands against the sides of her face and rocked on her heels, forcing back the tears.

"I'm so sorry, Mouse." Fraeda put her arm around her shoulders and squeezed gently. "I wish I could tell you."

Her eyes stung as Mouse shut them fiercely, unable to keep the emotion from spilling out of them. Grief, confusion, and fear overwhelmed her as competing threads of thought whirled through her mind. She felt utterly lost. *Am I really the harbinger?* she thought. *Is it because of this that my village had burned and my family was lost? What am I supposed to do now? And how can I bear the weight of it all?*

She felt a strong hand on her shoulder, and then another. Mouse looked up, the concerned faces of her friends around her, grieving with her, not allowing her to face it alone.

"What can we do to help?" Toma asked gently. "Ask anything, and we'll do it."

Mouse wiped her sleeve across her nose. With shaking legs, she stood and turned to look out at the valley below the mountain.

What else is there to do but follow?

"All I ask is that we go on," Mouse said. Resolve replaced the quaver in her voice. "We go on. We find Titans' Rest. We find the last of Red's rebellion. We stop the Coalition from doing what they did to Shomroh to anyone else, ever again."

30

Year 113
      47th of Sun's Wane
Northern Wilds, Gormlaen

The mare navigated the forest pathways at a brisk trot. Unburdened by a bounty and finding the muddy trails now dry, the horse ran with ease, the falling of her hooves surer than when they came that way before. Fox breathed a sigh of relief. *To the outpost, and then after the girl.*

Even with their quick southeasterly progress, Fox spurred the horse on. Time had been wasted. It would not do to lose any more of it. At least, that is what she told herself. Fox gripped the reins tightly and rode closer to the horse's neck. Her thoughts drifted back to the Guardian, to what she had done; Fox took a deep, cleansing breath and pushed the horse to go on even faster. *Distance*, she thought. *Let's just get some distance, and it'll be alright. It always is. Stop being such a coward.*

They splashed through the ravine's stream, smaller now and

moving along with a lazy burble instead of the agitated, swollen current they had crossed earlier. Fox dismounted, leading the mare up the steep side of the gully. As they reached the top, she looked back the way she had come, the peaceful trickling of the stream at the bottom at odds with the restless unease ballooning inside her.

Fox had been foolish. Incredibly, unforgivably foolish. What in all of Reidara could have possessed her to extend any measure of leniency to that beast hunter? She could explain away the action for any typical person: a little mercy, a little pity, for one destined to die a horrible death at Myergo's hand. But Fox was not merciful. She never pitied her quarry. For all the groveling, bargaining, threatening, and cursing directed her way, Fox never bowed, never showed fear, could never conjure even a single tear. She was, as even the other hunters said, the Iron Huntress, a heart of ice and two ears of stone. And why should she be anything else? Her bounties always deserved what they got, persuasive explanations and moving pleas notwithstanding. Fox's only concern was to complete her contract. Complete it, and then get paid. And if this were any other contract, she would be on her way to celebrate her newfound riches at the closest tavern.

Celebration flew far from her mind now. Only one refrain replayed over and over:

What have I done?

The variety of consequences her uncharacteristic mercy could now have mushroomed in her imagination. Myergo's men could find the explosive and come after her, suspecting her in league with the Guardian. That would not surprise her. They had been furious when she refused to give them Blade's swords as a gift of goodwill for their master. What reason more would they need to follow her and try to take them by force?

Or Myergo himself might find the detonator. The thought of his rage made her stomach clench and a shudder run down her spine. Not even the Coalition would be as ruthless in tracking her down and making her pay as she knew the crime lord would be.

And now the last possibility came to mind. What if her actions *saved* the Guardian?

Not many could figure out how to battle a Mistwolf with a bomb and survive, but the beast hunter had to be one of them. She had given him enough time and warning to figure it out. Perhaps he had already awakened from being stunned and was plotting his next move. Perhaps he had used it to escape his current captors, and he was on his way after her even now. *That* was a thought she did not relish.

At any rate, if the Guardian survived, and if he escaped, he would come for her. He had made that promise plain. All her hubris would be put to the test then, and this time, unlike almost any other, Fox had no confidence she would emerge the victor.

What have I done?

Fox returned to the moment she gave Blade the explosive, dissecting her rashness with surgical precision. No doubt the Guardian had impressed her. There had been no groveling or bargaining, and while there were some threats, she knew they were not empty. His unsettling ability to make her feel hunted even as she was the hunter earned her respect. Indeed, he had been unlike anyone she had ever hunted before. It had been decades since she could admit that a person had so affected her. And decades longer still since anything brought such strong memories of her past to the forefront of her mind. The things the Guardian had said had enraged her, but also... they moved her. He moved her to remember the path. Her endless, wretched, dissatisfying path. The one that Hiraeth had so many years ago told her would be inevitable if she continued forging her own way.

Hiraeth. Fox raced along the forest paths, thoughts of her time in the Kamarian Mountains racing along with her.

Year 19 of the Glorious New Era

The wind howled past the opening of Hiraeth's mountain hovel, causing the goatskin flap that hung from its entryway to smack against the makeshift doorposts with loud, intermittent thwacks. Arctura shivered and inched closer to the ramshackle fireplace. She examined the stovepipe hearth, built up in the middle of the hovel out of what looked like junked metal slapped onto salvaged piping. The wonky column of pipe climbed up and clung to an aluminum-plated hole in the roof, where it rattled with the winter winds. How it had remained there was beyond Arctura's comprehension. It was a wonder the configuration had not collapsed or burned the entire hut down.

Arctura's gaze swept the rest of Hiraeth's abode. She did not know what she had expected when they climbed the mountain pass to his dwelling, but she was certain she could have never imagined this. Except for a few cooking implements, a rude chair and table, a bundle of firewood, and one small bed of straw, the home contained hardly anything at all. Hastily placed nails held the rough wooden frame and planks of the walls together. Moss, straw, mud, and who knew what else filled the gaps between the boards, but light filtered in spaces as the wintry air seeped in with little impediment. The entire structure leaned against the mountain, a wall of stone forming the dwelling's backside.

At least one wall of this accident waiting to happen will remain standing, Arctura thought.

Hiraeth passed her a wooden bowl and cup, their warm contents steaming. Arctura took both eagerly and barely blew on the hot liquid before tipping it to her lips. The spicy tea singed her mouth and burned down her throat, but she did not care. She welcomed the delicious feeling of heat in her belly that spread to her numb limbs. Setting the cup down, she brought a spoonful of stew to her mouth next, which she ate far quicker than the etiquette of her noble upbringing would tolerate. The events of that day had left her famished; a fact she only realized when she entered the hermit's home and breathed in the rich aroma of slow-cooked mountain herbs and mutton.

"I thank you for your kindness to me," Arctura said. "And in no small part, that you have extended it, knowing full well who I am."

"Ah," Hiraeth said with a knowing smile. "You speak truly. It seems rather foolish for me, the Guardian of my people, to give hospitality to the heir of one who will set out to conquer and destroy all of Elmnas within five years' time."

Arctura did her best to mask her shock. *No one* outside of Father's inner circle knew his plans for Elmnas. In fact, she was not entirely sure she was even supposed to know. It was a secret among secrets. How could this strange old man, living in abject seclusion, know anything about it at all?

"I was speaking of our two nations' complicated political history," she replied, recovering.

"It is, indeed, complicated," Hiraeth said. "And will only become more so, hmm?"

"That will be up to you Elmlings and my father." Arctura took another sip of her tea. "And since you seem to know so much, you know that my part is nothing."

Hiraeth took up his own bowl of stew and slurped it. "We shall see."

She looked away, pretending to be distracted by the storm. Snow fell in a curtain of white just outside the hovel's doorway. It swirled and began to pile in the entrance. She strained to find anything of the rocky slopes that they took to get here, but she could see nothing through the blinding veil.

"I've never witnessed anything like this," Arctura said. "It does not snow in Pardaetha."

"This blizzard is the first of many, closing the mountain passes until the spring thaw," Hiraeth said. "Let us hope the novelty does not wear off for you too soon, since you must winter here."

Arctura set down her vessels with a clunk. "You mean to say I am marooned here?"

Hiraeth raised his wiry eyebrow in acknowledgement as he sipped his tea.

"Surely you can't be serious! Why, we'll starve, or be eaten by whatever else lives in this horrible place, provided we don't freeze to death in this breezy cottage of yours first!"

The old hermit set down his meal and took up his staff. He hobbled over to the mountain wall. Lifting the staff, he tapped three times against the stone. Hiraeth spoke. Words of an ancient tongue issued forth, their power and beauty rendering Arctura silent. Intricate inscriptions of brilliant green spread across the wall's surface. The rock split with a crunch, a portion of it depressing into the shape of a door. Hiraeth laid a wrinkled hand atop the pulsing light of the runes. The rock slid back into an opening.

"Come," he said, the tap of his staff echoing into the voluminous darkness.

"You certainly are full of surprises," Arctura muttered.

She stepped into the mountain after him. Once inside, Hiraeth's voice echoed off the cavernous walls in that same runic language, and the mountain wall slid closed behind her. She blinked in the sudden dark. Slowly, luminous hues of green and blue brightened and spread out along rough stone corridors. And now, Arctura could hear, see, and feel nothing of the storm. The modest but lovely light of the strange fungal blooms bathed her and the passage in a soft glow. Warmth rising from somewhere deep within the mountain roots took the chill out of her bones. Only one sound reached her ears – the soft tap tapping of Hiraeth's staff, echoing ahead of her as he tread farther down and further in.

Arctura followed at a distance, an uneasy curiosity burgeoning within her.

Am I really to be trapped here all winter? What does this old hermit truly want with me?

A mixture of frustration and fear roiled in her chest. Just when she was so close to finding more answers, to having the Drake within her grasp, it had all been taken away. Surely it would be harder, if not impossible, to find the shadowy mercenary after the time it would take her to escape the frozen Kamarians. She would have to start her search all over again. From nothing. Moreover, Arctura could not fathom spending months out of civilization, and in a mountain, no less, alone with this puzzling but unnaturally powerful Hiraeth. A man she could not size up and dissect with ease, despite her rather easy aptitude for doing so. Instead, the seer had cut to the core of her in the first words of their meeting. Frighteningly, she found herself in the position she usually occupied. Arctura loathed it.

And yet, Hiraeth continued to intrigue her. Why had he rescued her? How could he talk to creatures? Who was he? All the legends Arctura had long ago heard about the strange Elmlings and their mysterious Guardians rolled around her mind. The tri-fold ruling class, governing a fierce and reclusive people at the alleged behest of an all-powerful, invisible deity. And in return, their so-called god gifted them powers beyond the reach of normal men, transforming them into those called the Ageless.

Before today, Arctura would have never believed such drivel. What controlled any people was the illusion of limitless power. Whether the Guardians actually held it was another matter. And surely, when Father's plan finally went to effect, he would test and probe and discover the supernatural greatly exaggerated. The power of the Elmlings' Unseen would crumble, trampled underfoot by the Glorious New Era's relentless march of progress, just like the animal spirits of Maiendell, the elemental powers of Heibeiath, and the old gods of Gormlaen. Father's voice echoed in her mind: *All fall at the feet of truth; either be crushed beneath or take hold of her heels.*

But Hiraeth challenged what she knew. He was a walking

paradox. Old and feeble to any discerning eye, yet capable of moving like a warrior and commanding monsters. A knower of things he should not know. A speaker of languages she wasn't positive even existed. An enigma. A problem. Whether she liked being stuck here or not, Arctura would have to get to the bottom of it.

"Hiraeth," she called.

Her voice echoed with a mournful timbre along the empty tunnel. It seemed to go on forever, carried deeper and farther than Arctura could conceive, as if all words spoken within the ancient Kamarians carried the weight and finality of eternity. Arctura shook off the chill that proceeded from that thought. The hermit stopped and turned, waiting for her to catch up.

"Ask, and it shall be given to you," he said.

Arctura cocked her head. "Earlier, you said you were *the* Guardian of Elmnas. But I have studied your people. You have three ruling classes of Guardians. Master, Warrior, and Keeper. Why not say *a* Guardian? I know for a fact there are more of your kind out there, living in your Silver Sea Sanctum past these horrid mountains."

Hiraeth laid both hands on the head of his staff and gave a crooked smile.

"Are you not simply a Keeper?" Arctura continued. "I called you seer, and you did not dispute it."

"Indeed, I did not."

"So I was right?"

"You were right," Hiraeth smiled slyly. "And yet, you were not. You shall see. Come along, little one. Are you not anxious to behold your destiny?"

Arctura snorted. "And what destiny is that? Where I come from, destiny is something we make, *outside*, in the world. Do you strange solitary Guardians hang it on racks in ancient caverns so you can dust it off and hand it out to the first decent conversation that comes your way?"

"You suppose destiny is only for the great to grasp. And yet, *Isa* holds the destiny of all, little and great, evil and righteous. Just as the tiger tracks the gazelle in the thicket, destiny hunts you. Why should it not be here, waiting? And what makes you believe you can harness it? Will a dragon be led on a leash, or will the serpent of the sea be brought in on a hook?"

Arctura scoffed. "And your *Isa*– I suppose he controls destiny? If so, he isn't doing such a wonderful job of it."

"Do you deserve better, Arctura Vipsanius, murderer of friends?"

She opened her mouth, but there was no quip to counter this pronouncement of truth. Arctura's lips tightened, and she swallowed hard. Anger, fear, and shame roiled inside her.

How could he know?

Hiraeth's eyes pierced her, ablaze like an emerald fire, dancing and dangerous. Arctura shrank. Biting her lip, she looked at the cavern floor, silent and brooding.

"Come now," he said, gently this time. "There is much to learn and unlearn."

Hiraeth hobbled forward. Arctura trailed him at a distance, her steps heavy with guilt. If Hiraeth knew *that*, what else could he know? What other hidden truths would he reveal? Her pulse quickened. She felt like a rat trapped in a rattlesnake's den. Despite herself, Arctura brushed her hand against the moss and lichen on the tunnel wall and scoffed.

An apt metaphor, she thought as she observed the burrow-like passage. *But then, why did the snake save me?*

The seer disappeared around a bend. While his disturbing ability to see into the very depths of her encouraged Arctura to linger behind, curiosity at what lay ahead and a distaste for getting lost and wandering until she starved proved the stronger impetus. She picked up her pace and rounded the same corner, only to stop short in awe.

Before her, the mountain tunnel broadened into a cavern so large that all of Pardaetha could fit inside it. The mountain walls rose up and up as the cavern floor sloped down and down. Phosphorescent plants twinkled like stars at twilight as they climbed up the massive walls and flowered among dripping stalactites. Tunnels the size of small mountains themselves broke off from the main cavern. Through one, Arctura could make out the shimmer of steam and the hint of a red glow; through another, a beam of far off, cold light revealed the silent spread of an ancient forest dusted lightly with snow. Except for the gaping shafts that let in the sky above, the mountain otherwise enveloped the biome. Arctura looked out at the unspoiled beauty, wondering if any living person other than Hiraeth or her had ever set eyes upon it.

"What is this place?" she whispered.

"It is called *Edenii*, in the tongue of Elmnas. A lost, ancient stronghold of the Guardians."

Hiraeth stood a little below her on a wide shelf of hewn stone, which glowed green with the same strange runes of the mountain's secret entrance. The words flared and ebbed like coals of a fire blown back to life with a steady breath. Arctura followed the runestone path with her gaze, seeing that it wound down into the floor of the cavern and broke into several roads that led to the wide tunnels themselves.

He gestured to the path. "It was here, long ago, that the Trivium was truly born. In this sanctuary, the Guardians grew and thrived. Many generations were in this sacred mountain brought up in the Way. But that time is ended. The Trivium abandoned *Edenii,* and *Isa* gave it to the creatures of the air and the crawling things of the dirt. What you see before you now is only a shadow of the old *Edenii*. But one day, its glory will be reborn. Come."

The sound of Hiraeth's staff tapping against the runic path echoed throughout the massive chamber as he walked deeper within. Arctura hopped down from the ledge and fell in beside him. She gazed down at the small man, realizing now that his head came to just below her chest.

"It is magnificent as it is! Never have I witnessed its like. I cannot fathom what it had been. Why would they leave here?"

"The Guardians failed to uphold law and truth from within

Edenii, and so the brothers and sisters of the Elmling tribes fought against each other," Hiraeth answered. "The Guardians were meant to go out into the world, but often chose to hide from it here. The people needed their guidance, but they did not give it. And there was war. An evil time it was. Even Guardians turned upon Guardians. So *Isa's* wrath burned against them. He emptied *Edenii* with fire from Reidara's depths. The way to the sanctuary was blocked to all. When the Trivium could not return, they made peace among the tribes and moved to the Silver Sea Sanctum, where all Elmlings can now approach. That is the way of these stubborn people. Only when all other paths are closed or destroyed do they walk in the right direction."

"You speak of it as if you were there," Arctura mused. "And how have *you* returned if the way had been closed? What sort of Guardian are you?"

"In time," Hiraeth answered. "You shall see."

They reached the bottom of the cavern. Paths split out before them, the glow of green runes shimmering toward the tunnels. The rest of the cavern floor remained shrouded in darkness, except for the small patches of blue bioluminescent fungi. Their dim lights glowed like lanterns burned down to the wick; enough to be seen but not enough to see by. Arctura could also make out the distinct sounds of dripping, trickling, and pooling water, and heat coming from the glowing red tunnel mixed with the damp air in a steamy, humid haze. Somewhere far off, more water whispered down the mountain wall and flowed with might deep beneath their feet. It was not clear how far down the underground river went, but Arctura could feel it rushing in her soles. She looked eagerly to the vast caverns adjoining this one, wondering what worlds each might hold. But Hiraeth continued on the path that ran along the outer edge of the cave, his eyes trained on the mountain rock beside him.

Arctura narrowed her eyes and glanced at Hiraeth. "I have read of your civil war. A brutish affair over religion, if I recall. Father always said that such things weakened the strength of a nation."

His lip quirked up slightly.

"You trust the wisdom of the Supreme Chancellor then?"

"Yes," Arctura admitted. "Father is the most brilliant man I know. He championed Gormlaen's movement to abandon our old ways and squabbles, and we stand stronger and more united than ever before. How can I dispute fact?"

"Fact, eh?" Hiraeth chuckled. "How many years have you seen, little one? In the span of a man's lifetime, nations rise and fall. Everything in Reidara has its time. Yet the word of *Isa* stands forever."

"So you say," she muttered.

Hiraeth paused and leaned on the head of his staff. "So I do. But it is enough. Now, little one, see what has been prepared for you."

Hiraeth spoke once again in the strange language, and runes raced along the bedrock beside them. With a sharp thwack, he slammed the butt of his rod against it, and the rock rolled back into a wide opening. Darkness greeted them from within, and despite herself, Arctura shivered. His voice echoed from inside as he disappeared into it.

"You seek someone," he said. "A man of death and misery."

"Yes," Arctura answered tightly.

The tap of Hiraeth's staff on the cavern floor echoed back to her, hollow and ethereal like the dark room itself. It sounded different than what she had grown used to in the interior of the mountain. Arctura ventured in enough to feel out the ground with the toe of her shoe. It was as straight and smooth as carved marble. With a deep breath, she stepped forward and fell into shadow.

"I suppose I need not ask what else you know about my endeavors, or of this man I am after. Is that why you brought me here, hermit?"

As she spoke, Arctura could sense the vastness of this new room. She looked around for the dim glow of subterranean fungi or the flash of ancient runes. It remained utterly black. Arctura gasped as the door slid closed behind her.

"My purposes are my own."

Hiraeth's voice reverberated around her, and a chill raced down her spine.

"All will be revealed, at its proper time."

Light flooded the room. Arctura tensed and shielded her eyes. The peculiar scent of a fragrant burning oil reached her, and she lowered her hand to observe the room. It was as enormous as it sounded. Still, she could not have imagined its magnificence. Rows of braziers lining the walls burned brightly, revealing a marvelous amphitheater. She stood on the arena floor and looked up into rows of stadium seating carved into the mountain bedrock. Intricate and expertly fashioned carvings covered virtually every other surface: murals of grand battles, incredible beasts, and spectacular beings sprawled around the great cavern and disappeared into the darkness above. Shards of green crystal embedded into the mountain itself, glittered in the flickering firelight. Arctura turned her attention to the center of the arena, where, on a wide, raised platform of smooth, black stone, sat Hiraeth; cross-legged, his staff laid across his lap.

"The Drake. That is what he calls himself, it is not?" The lines on Hiraeth's face deepened as he frowned. "It is well earned. A hunter beyond parallel, just like his namesake. But unlike *Smyga's* kind, this one mangles and destroys not for survival, but for his own pleasure. Such evil is an affront to all good. The Drake has had his time, but rest assured, every weed is pulled up by its roots and cast into fire."

Arctura's jaw clenched at the mention of his name. *The Drake.* She raised a hand to her cheek, the scar burning as if his wicked claw had just torn through it. Hiraeth cocked his head. Arctura managed a terse nod.

"I know what you desire, little one," Hiraeth said softly. "It is engraved on your heart. All thoughts are laid bare before *Isa.*"

Terror and anticipation tied a knot in her stomach. She stepped closer.

Hiraeth's green eyes seemed to pierce her soul. "Tell me– if you receive the desires of your heart, will it make you whole?"

Arctura cleared her throat. "I don't know, Hiraeth. Will it?"

The old man smiled even as an infinite sadness filled his eyes. "All will be revealed at its proper time."

31

Year 20 of The Glorious New Era
   31_{st} of Sun's Rise
Edenii

"Acceptable, *nemii*, but mind your foot."

With the crook of his staff, Hiraeth hooked Arctura's ankle and tugged it a few inches forward, widening her offensive stance. Arctura held her weighted training swords in position, pressing one against the throat of the sparring dummy, the other at its thigh. Hiraeth held up a finger, indicating that she continue to hold. He drew his white, wiry eyebrows into a frown as he considered the rest of her. Finally, with a grunt of approval, he pulled back and leaned on his staff.

"It will do. Continue."

Arctura sucked in an exasperated breath. "Yes, Teacher."

Hiraeth chuckled as she worked through the remaining stances and movements. "Yes, the Way of the Twin Blades is wearying, and I am more wearying still, but I haven't taught you all this time for you to be bested over poor foot placement. Now, *nemii*, finish the set strong. Evasive maneuvers next."

Arctura held her tongue and worked through the attack stances. She knew he was probably right, but that fact did not help her feel any less annoyed. Hiraeth had been more than generous to her over the last few months, but his rigid insistence on precision in her training put her former tutors at Pardaetha to shame. He was a zealot when it came to the Way of the Twin Blades, and anything less than perfection merited correction. In some ways, even Father had not demanded as much; but then again, Father had punished her mercilessly when she failed. Her missteps in *Edenii* led to correction, and with Hiraeth's help, success. That did not mean it was not hard. Not even life at Kyma had prepared her for the mental and physical rigors of her current studies, but discipline of the body and mind at the hand of Hiraeth had brought more reward than anything else had. She pushed her frustration aside, at least for the moment.

With one final flourish, Arctura finished, both swords at the throat of the training dummy. She stared into its empty face but watched Hiraeth out of the corner of her eye. He nodded and "hm-hmmed" – his way of approving a break. Stepping away from the target, Arctura wiped away sweat with her forearm and set down her weapons. She took in her surroundings as she ambled out of the arena. Not long after their arrival in *Edenii*, Hiraeth restored this massive room, the training arena, to some of its former functionality. Obstacles, dummies, targets, and other athletic equipment filled the stadium's center, and it was here Arctura had spent her waking hours beneath the Kamarian Mountains. Hiraeth explained that long ago, all *nemii*, or Guardian apprentices, would spend their first years here to train, Master, Keeper, and Warrior alike. They learned the First Way together, since this encapsulated the basic disciplines and tenets of the Guardians' beliefs. All trained in combat, law, and oracles to some extent. Only when the First Way had been mastered would each class move on to its specialization. Like many before her, Arctura was learning the Way of the Twin Blades. Unlike them, she had bypassed the First Way altogether. Hiraeth had agreed to this, but even now Arctura wondered why. She had been clear about her intentions for her training. Once completed, she would confront and kill the Drake, as well as any other enemies in her path. Hiraeth did not dissuade this, and when she asked about it, he remained infuriatingly cryptic. He'd tell her something about his *Isa* instead. Arctura learned to stop asking.

She made it to the edge of the arena, where natural springs flowed in man-made troughs beneath the carved edge of the stadium. Looking up, she imagined the rows of seating full of apprentices and other Guardian hopefuls observing practical demonstrations, or maybe full-fledged Guardians gathered in solemn assembly to perform some ancient ritual or hold secret counsel. What had that congregation been like during the events of the Elmling Civil War? What had they done when magma bubbled up through *Edenii's* cavern floor, the Kamarians spitting them out with its overflow of ash and molten rock?

The steady, clear stream whooshing by her shook Arctura from her thoughts. It was an ingenious design; a water source from within the mountain had been tapped and directed into a slanted, spiraling trough that ran all around the arena. It terminated in a tasteful drain in the floor, where presumably the water joined the river running beneath them. Arctura dipped her hands in the flow and let the cold water run over them. Her raw blisters had become callouses by now, but extended sessions like today's always left her palms sore. She flexed her fingers beneath the rush. No more the delicate hands of a pampered princess or the professional repose of a respected diplomat. These hands had bled, healed, and toughened. Arctura hardly recognized them. And in the bouncing reflection she caught in the obsidian basin's bottom, she hardly recognized herself. She looked harder as she drank from her cupped palms. Who was she now? She shared a sardonic smirk with herself as Hiraeth's favorite words came to mind: *All will be revealed in time.*

Arctura ran wet hands through her tied-back hair, taming the wild frizzing that never seemed to go away in *Edenii*'s humid caverns. There was not much to complain about amidst the grandeur of this ancient stronghold, but that was definitely one problem. Still, as much as she missed the luxuries of the high society life from where she had come, she was beginning to rather enjoy the simple comforts offered here. She had food and fresh water aplenty; the rushing springs and the strange, mountain-sheltered forest Hiraeth called *Isanatre* ensured that. Even the plain and practical training garb left behind by the host of evacuated Guardian apprentices suited her far better than the beautiful but inappropriate ambassadorial finery she had come wearing. It pleased her. In *Edenii*, no one despised or dishonored her due to her womanhood. Hiraeth had once said that though all be different, all came equal to the Way. There was nowhere in Gormlaen where such a statement as that were true. But here there was something new, something simple, something she did not know how to describe. A place where productive work, training, and discipline had given her some reprieve from the tormenting despair that her life had thus far brought her. Arctura had purpose here, and sometimes, she dared to hope some happy thing might come of it. Even Hiraeth, in his own peculiar way, had become dear to her as a teacher. *Yes*, she thought, *I like it, but it will never be my home.*

Home. Why not? It was not as if she had any place she could call home now. Kyma would never feel that way, not after the betrayal. Arctura bristled at the idea of returning to Sutra or any other place Father needed to acquire. She had nothing, and this place... it had given her something. And yet, at the same time, Arctura knew *Edenii* was not for her. Not really. By not embracing The Way, she remained an intruder here, a foreigner unwilling to bow to backward beliefs that, frankly, she found abhorrent. The stark differences between her and Hiraeth hung between them like a heavy veil, blocking Arctura from the mystical communion with the sanctuary he seemed to so easily imbibe. And for all the tranquility *Edenii* promised to offer, it could not overcome her pain. As soon as she lingered on what she had suffered on the surface of the Kamarians and beyond, all sense of peace crumbled into nothing. Indeed, the stillness and solitude which Hiraeth so deeply loved had never befriended her. It consumed her. In the dark and quiet, there was no peace. A fire burned in her chest, and she remembered why. Hope of happiness came only through vengeance.

A shadow fell across her shoulders. Arctura jumped and rolled sideways, wheeling around to see Hiraeth's staff hit the edge of the stone basin. The arena reverberated with the sharp crack. With a crooked smile, Hiraeth pulled in the staff and spun it deftly in his wizened hands.

"You've gotten quicker."

Arctura raced toward her own weapons, leaping, twisting, and rolling as Hiraeth had taught her. She vaulted obstacles and slid beneath them with the grace and strength of an acrobat. Even her breath, which not long before would have been blistering in her lungs as she tried to catch it, remained measured and steady. Somehow, Hiraeth kept pace alongside, gliding like a specter to the center of the arena. She snatched up the practice swords and bared her teeth in a grin.

"I could say the same about you. You would have rendered me senseless had you made contact."

"Then it is good you have gotten quicker."

As soon as Arctura readied her weapons, Hiraeth began. In this sequence, Hiraeth attacked in every way possible, always in random patterns. And Arctura's role was to respond with the evasive maneuvers she had learned. It was easier said than done. Hiraeth moved like a manticore, flitting around her at impossible speeds and striking with the force of a man many decades younger. Their first time squaring off in the training arena had left her with more bruises than she could count.

Now she blocked, spun, pushed, rolled, and danced out of the path of the swinging staff. Her body tensed for action at every small movement of his eyes, hands, and feet, automatically calculating each permutation and her necessary reaction to avoid being struck. Hiraeth continued his unyielding flurry of attacks, jabbing and sweeping the staff to probe for weakness. Arctura dodged and leaped, avoiding a crook around her calf as well as the butt of the staff in her stomach. She parried a blow aimed at her head, but her knuckles screamed as they made contact with something hard. Biting back the pain, she rolled away and threw off another stroke. Arctura twisted to avoid yet another blow, but Hiraeth was faster. In the blink of an eye, she wound up on the arena floor, the end of his stick at her neck. Panting, she held up her weapons in resignation. Hiraeth withdrew his own and reached his hand toward her.

"Almost, *nemii*. One day, when you grow old enough, you will be as swift as the diving falcon."

Old enough? Arctura tried to untangle the old man's strange aphorism, but the pain in her hand made it impossible to focus on anything else. Not that if she thought long on it, it would make much more sense, anyway. She shook out her fingers and hissed through gritted teeth. Once her knuckles stopped tingling, she accepted Hiraeth's proffered hand and pulled herself up. At her full height, she towered over Hiraeth, and she imagined they looked a comical pair in these ancient, empty halls. Even so, Arctura eyed her teacher with respect.

"I will never understand how you can move like that."

The old Guardian smiled. "All will be–"

"Revealed in its proper time, yes, of course," Arctura interrupted, waving off his words.

Hiraeth's eyes twinkled. "I see I have indeed wearied you much today."

"Other things weary me far more," Arctura sighed.

Hiraeth hmmed and nodded, his gaze extending past her to the cavern ceiling above. "You have learned much, and yet, there is still so much to unlearn. But it is enough for now. The spring thaw is upon the Kamarian slopes, and the world above is waking. And you, dear child, are to be prepared for what comes next."

Arctura raised an eyebrow as Hiraeth shuffled past and toward the door, his staff finding purchase on the uneven stone beyond the main arena. She knew better than to ask any questions; Hiraeth wrapped everything he said in enigma. But if she followed, he did not fail to show her. Arctura caught up to him as he exited, curiosity brimming. Hiraeth turned onto the rune-etched path, which had retained its effervescence during Arctura's entire stay at *Edenii*. She had these paths and their unique designs nearly memorized by now; daily walks on them with Hiraeth as he spoke about the techniques and philosophies of the Way of the Twin Blades, nightly heading up to retire in her private quarters, and weekly following the road to where it ended in *Isanatre* to hunt for food. Their training routines had made the paths as familiar as her own two feet. But now Hiraeth hobbled along one path she had not yet taken. Arctura's gaze traveled ahead, to where low red fires burned deep within the mountain and all of *Edenii* gathered its warmth.

The path sloped downward, and sulfuric heat streamed past them like the exhalation of a monstrous breath. Arctura rolled up the sleeves of her tunic, and with the sweat accumulating on her forehead, smoothed back her frizzing hair. As the mouth of the tunnel drew nearer, she could see its smoke-blackened ceiling and its sides glittering with the crystalline fragments of various precious stones and metals. She lowered her eyes to the unfamiliar runic patterns and tried to maintain a semblance of patient interest, but excitement got the better of her the closer they came to the red tunnel.

"Teacher, are we now going to the forge?"

Hiraeth craned his neck to meet her eye and nodded.

"It is time, little one."

Arctura took a deep breath as awe, anticipation, and anxiety swirled inside her. Nonetheless she followed. Hiraeth entered the great crimson mouth, striking his staff against the volcanic rock that swallowed and crusted over the runic path like a frozen, black river. Here the path began to descend steeply. Arctura would have wondered how the lava had flown in this direction, but she remembered that the mini-eruptions of magma that eventually emptied the sanctuary had taken place all throughout the caverns. She could see that the source of this flow had come from somewhere closer to the mouth of the tunnel, for here the volcanic river had stopped. But down at the bottom of the tunnel, gouts of flame and writhing, thin veins of orange and red proved the rivers of lava were still very much alive.

Now the Guardians' decision to leave appears all the wiser, Arctura thought, swallowing back fear. *This place could blow at any moment.*

Even so, and despite the searing draughts rising up through the tunnel, shivers ran down Arctura's spine. They approached the final stage of the Guardian journey, the time when initiates completed their training by hand-crafting their own swords in the fires of the volcanic forge. From the moment Hiraeth had spoken of this, Arctura had longed for her training's fruition with an ardor only rivaled by her oath of vengeance on the Drake. Here, she would truly be united with the Way of the Twin Blades. In the fires of the forge, her power would be made manifest, her anger be given teeth, her life be made worthy. Arctura's concerns of the forge's instability paled beside the reality of its potential. And it did not seem to bother Hiraeth, either. He hobbled down the slope and into the forge below.

She stepped gingerly into the furnace room, its every feature filling her with amazement. Another large cavern stretched before her, its heat and fumes tolerable thanks to its size and natural venting that sucked out the worst of it. Cracks in the cavern floor revealed little rivers of fire, but the forge itself provided the greatest source of heat as magma boiled perpetually in the middle of the cave. An elevated path led to the forge, and a fortifying wall of stone surrounded the pit. Beside it sat the rack of all the blacksmithing instruments Arctura would need to complete the task at hand. Beyond the forge and the concerning but small flashes of flame, the cavern walls stood firm. Glints of ethereal green emanated from points in them, and as Arctura gazed past the forge to a tunnel at the end of the cavern, she could see it glowed more intensely.

She stepped down toward Hiraeth, her hands trembling as she folded them behind her back. Hiraeth swept his staff over the room and spoke.

"Welcome, *nemii* Arctura, to the Guardian Forge of *Edenii*. There are other forges hidden in the mountains of Elmnas, but none as extraordinary as what you find here. It was discovered and built during the golden age of Elmnas, when the Kin of Enesh established order and peace in these wild lands. Volcanic forges are rare enough, but those that have stood for hundreds of years are rarer still. All others have been swallowed by their mountain's lifeblood, but by the grace of *Isa*, this one has remained. This very day, you will awaken its might. May the Unseen guide you."

"I am honored, Teacher." Arctura swallowed back tears, a frenzy of emotion overcoming her. Terror, pride, guilt, hunger, and excitement welled within. *Does he know I should not be here?*

"This work I will oversee, so that all may be done rightly." Hiraeth pointed to the far side of the cavern. "Now, go into the Cardanthium mine, take up the pickaxe you shall find there, and be chosen."

Arctura wrinkled her brow in confusion. "Teacher, do you not mean, 'go and choose'? I understand I will have to dig out the Cardanthium myself."

Hiraeth's face remained inscrutable. "I have said what I have said."

When Hiraeth offered no other explanation, Arctura shrugged and made her way to the Cardanthium mine, careful to avoid the searing cracks in the earth spitting magma bubbles up at her. She ducked into the mine's entrance. It was cool inside, much cooler than the blasting heat of the rest of the cavern. When she looked back, she saw Hiraeth silhouetted behind the burning forge, waiting. She ventured farther in. This time, when she searched for Hiraeth in the room beyond, she saw nothing.

Inside the mine, however, everything seemed to glow with an eerie, green light. Crystalline Cardanthium coated the walls, jutting into the tunnel all around like the circular rows of teeth in the mouth of a leech. Dirt and sheets of solid rock made up the tunnel. Arctura found the pickaxe as Hiraeth had predicted, and she pulled it from its place on the wall. She held the shaft in two hands like a club, unable to shake the feeling that the teeth hanging from the tunnel mouth might clamp down on her at any moment. Even so, she continued on, driven to seek the Cardanthium ore that would become her own two blades.

Leaving the crystals behind as Hiraeth had before instructed, Arctura sought the ore imbedded in rock. Though the crystalline Cardanthium had powerful properties, properties that she had seen Father trying to unravel back in Pardaetha, the ore deepest in the mountains provided the fabled, renowned weapons of the Guardians. The crystals seemed to retract into the walls the deeper she went, leaving them glittering with soft metallic hues. Arctura moved closer to the rock, searching for Cardanthium. She whistled at the abundance of everything else – gold, silver, palladium, bidnythine, malachite, platinum, and others she could not identify.

I might have made every Coalition city wealthier than Sutra had I known about this place, Arctura thought. The irony was not lost on her. Every care she once had about the prosperity of the Coalition had died with her heart that fateful night near The Lonely Siren. In fact, it made her grin, in spite of herself, that the Elmlings might have far more resources and secrets than Father realized.

She passed the precious metals and went farther still. The tunnel sloped down, and Arctura forgot the boiling heat of the forge room. Cold air seeped up from somewhere below. She paused, now bathed in soft, undulating hues of blue and green light. Arctura looked around, finding an alcove off the main tunnel. The recess glowed with Cardanthium ore. For a moment, Arctura stood transfixed, watching the walls ripple with something she could only describe as life. And it seemed to call to her, too; a high, quiet thrum vibrated almost beyond her range of hearing.

Arctura stepped into the alcove, hefting her pick.

Any spot seems as good as any other, she thought. But as she raised the pick over her head, the thrumming shifted suddenly into a persistent, painful whine. She dropped the axe to cover her ears. And just as abrupt as the shift into the squeal that nearly deafened her, the sound returned to its peaceful thrum.

"I believe I understand you now, old man," Arctura grumbled as she dug a finger in her ear and shook her head. "If that is the way it is done... then so be it. Choose me."

Arctura raised her palms and reached toward the patches of Cardanthium. She trembled as energy from the ore reached out to her and licked at her skin like microscopic bolts of lightning. Arctura flinched, finding the sensation more painful the longer she was subjected to it. As she moved along the wall, Arctura began to feel something else. Was that judgment? A testing? As if the Cardanthium itself were deciding if it would take to her or not. Her stomach clenched as its rejecting whine continued. What if it found her wanting and refused her entirely? How could she return to Hiraeth empty-handed?

And then the Cardanthium changed. The whine stopped. A richer tone reverberated through her as her palms passed over a section of the wall. She paused and hovered over it, feeling warmth instead of tingling shock. The thrum vibrated in her chest now, and the Cardanthium ore beneath her fingers brightened.

This is it.

Arctura retrieved the pickaxe, her fingers almost numb with the ore's strange behavior. She hesitated as she raised it, but nothing stopped her this time. As she swung the pick into the rock, the thrum of acceptance grew, a wordless, unutterable song swelling inside and flowing through every part of her being. Tears rolled down her cheeks as she chipped with all her strength. The Cardanthium glowed all the brighter.

32

The long, gray shadows falling across Fox's shoulders did not disappear when she finally exited the Swaying Forest farther east. They deepened beneath the cold, dark watch of the Jagged Jaw Mountains, now staring down at her from her left as her horse panted across the tree-lined ridge. Fox grimaced. She had wanted to make the Coalition outpost crossing by nightfall. That wasn't going to happen. Not only was the mare spent, but exhaustion overwhelmed Fox herself. Her back ached from the long hours of hard riding, and her limbs were worn beyond usefulness. Fox's head pounded with lack of sleep. Hunger and thirst also exacted their demands upon her, groaning for a real meal and cool water. She had to stop, and soon.

Fox cursed. At the moment, stopping for any amount of time seemed more foolish than ignoring the limits of her physical ability. While no one had pursued her through the forest, Fox had not survived this long by believing for one moment she was safe. Nothing was safe. Especially not these wilds, where any one of her many enemies could be lurking. She looked down at her sagging mare and watched flecks of greenish, frothing spittle fly from the bit in her open, ragged mouth. Fox sighed and slowed the mare to a walk. She scanned the darkening wilderness. Ahead, just beyond where the vale rose and disappeared, Fox caught a familiar sight: the North Road signpost.

The North Road cut through Gormlaen and led to an old bridge that spanned Thunder Run's tamer counterpart, Elmgor River. There Fox would find the Coalition outpost, where, with the jingle of her heavy purse, she might obtain a private speeder into Elmnas. Finding the girl and her friend would be a matter of days then; she had no reason to believe they had gotten far. Still, though Fox was no true enemy of the Coalition, she was no friend, either. Fox disliked the idea of approaching the outpost at night, let alone in her currently compromised state.

Another night, Fox huffed. *Another wasted night.*

It was no use griping any more about it. She would have to find somewhere to recover until morning. She searched along the crevices of the mountains as well as the edge of the pinewood. Not much lay between the far-off sign post and her, but a grouping of angular boulders just within the forest's edge caught her attention. Fox steered her weary mount toward it.

The last, weak rays of light reflecting off the red clouds finally dipped below the horizon behind her as Fox arrived at the rock formation. She hopped off the mare and left her to graze as she explored it. It was a loose, semi-circular arrangement; not of boulders, as she had thought, but of sunken slabs of hewn stone. Green-gray moss slicked the sides of what once stood as some sort of building, and pines grew in the cracks between crumbling walls. Fox wandered cautiously inside, finding the remains of its flooring littered with rotting wood and ancient debris. One wall still stood between her and the Swaying Forest, and in front of it, a raised dais with a lone statuette. Broken and dilapidated, it hardly had any discernible form to it, but hints of ample feminine curves remained visible in the pitted stone. She could not say what goddess the shape represented. The superstitious worship of stone and iron-bound deities had long since passed from Gormlaen's collective memory, but Fox knew she stood in the remnants of a forgotten shrine to whatever it once was. She observed the rest of the altar. Water burbled from somewhere and pooled around the dais. Fox reached into the flow and cupped it in her hands. Seeing its source from a fresh spring, she drank greedily.

"I suppose this is as good of a place as any," she said aloud. "It will suffice."

Her voice sounded strange as it fell dead on the long-fallen shrine's walls. Fox took another look around, chasing away the watched feeling that crept over her. She was not superstitious, but her mind was not as closed as it once had been.

Still, she was not a child, either. Fox brought her horse inside – if it could be called inside – watered her, and unpacked the saddlebag. Muscling down some hardtack and dried meat, she settled against the most comfortable part of the wall that faced toward the North Road. Through a crack in the ancient slab, Fox located the signpost, a little blot of white now fading into the falling darkness. She reached into her pack for flint and stone, but withdrew her hands and grasped the hilts of her blades instead. There would be no fire tonight, and no easy way to locate her in the forlorn wilds. Fox pulled out the blades and laid them by her side. Their Cardanthium glow illuminated the small space of the collapsed shrine, comforting her far more than any fire would.

Her swords. Her mysterious, fearsome, perfect swords. All Fox's strength could be as dried up as an air-bleached bone, but still, she would have all she needed as long as she had them in her hands. The Way of the Twin Blades, however impurely and irreverently she had followed it, still blessed her through them, the blades' power always at her disposal. It was enough for every enemy she had faced until now; it would be enough for tonight, too. Fox traced the elegant engravings on each sword as the pall of night covered the vale and forest, her eyelids fluttering with the heaviness of her fatigue.

I've taken so much from you. She thought, feeling their warmth and life beneath her fingertips. *What do you want from me?*

No answer came, of course, as she drifted into sleep.

Year 20 of The Glorious New Era
    Sun's Rise
    Edenii, Elmnas

"They are yours. You must name them."

Hiraeth leaned over the twin blades cooling beside the blistering forge.

Arctura drew an arm across her eyes and forehead, failing to remove the sweat that poured from every inch of her. She hardly recognized the discomfort. She recognized little of anything else now. For days she knew only the steady, guiding hands of Hiraeth, the heat of the Guardian Forge, and the glow of the Cardanthium. It occurred to her then how peculiar that was. The long hours of tedious, backbreaking work should have crushed her, but it hadn't. Instead, she had been absorbed, hardly sleeping, barely eating, moving through the tasks of each day in an almost trance-like state. From the time she had touched the Cardanthium until now, Arctura felt its call to use it, to mold it into the blades she would wield. The vague, harmonic hum still rumbled in her chest, and it had pushed her on, bleeding enough vigor and vitality for each day into her work-worn limbs.

And now, the work was nearly done. She gazed down at the two new Cardanthium swords, crafted by her hands and with Hiraeth's master expertise, waiting for her to take hold of them forever. Even in the red heat, they pulsed like a heartbeat with their own pale light. Arctura clutched her chest. They glowed in rhythm with hers.

"Name them," she repeated slowly. "In keeping with the Way of the Twin Blades?"

Hiraeth nodded. "The naming officiates the bond between the Guardian and the Cardanthium that has chosen her. When you name your swords, I will inscribe the words in the sacred and ancient runes of the Eneshkin. Then the blades will be yours alone, and the power you have touched here in the Guardian Forge will be given over to you completely. Choose the names wisely, *nemii*, for it shall be a reminder and light to you always."

"And as I recall, the names are quite personal?"

"Many in the Way have chosen to never disclose their blades' names to any but the forge master who guided them. It is considered a secret; a thing of mystery," Hiraeth said. "And yet, secrets have often been shared with the ones we love most dearly."

Arctura smirked. "So, it would be rather impertinent to ask you? I suppose I'll never see your swords, but I assume you must have them. Your mastery gives you away."

Hiraeth chuckled. "Do I need to say it?"

"All shall be revealed," Arctura rolled her eyes. "I should be content to know I will learn their names someday."

"In its proper time." Hiraeth poised over the swords, an ancient chisel in one hand and a hammer in the other. "But today, you must give names to your own. When you are ready."

Arctura exhaled and shut her eyes. She could not see the pulsing light, but she could feel it ebbing and flowing like each breath she drew and released. Hiraeth had explained that it would be like this during the bonding, but it did not make the sensation any less surreal. She recoiled at the strange and growing intensity, desiring and yet loathing the connection to the blades. A foreign essence seemed to touch her own. A claustrophobic panic reared up inside her, but Arctura forced it down. She concentrated on the pulse and splayed her fingers out over the twin swords.

What shall I call you?

Images swept through Arctura's mind. The flash of Reylas' charming smile and his loving eyes ripped away with the cruel blow that mutilated her face forever. Mother's disdainful glare, Father's cold, inscrutable gaze as they looked down upon her. The wicked glow of the Drake's claw, illuminating his horrible grin. A leering Sai'yn, the mutilated Erhi, an anguished Turo, the scornful Drake. The eyes of all passed through her mind, probing her with their pity, terror, contempt, and despair. She focused on the last, the evil, dark eyes of the Drake, and she saw them widening with fear and pain before finally going dim. Arctura held the image in her mind, enlarging it, reveling in it, coveting it more than anything else in the world.

She opened her eyes.

"They shall be Wrath," Arctura said. "They shall be Vengeance."

She glared at Hiraeth, ready to defy his objections. But Hiraeth said nothing. His face held no reply one way or the other. She searched his enigmatic gaze and found only silence. It was almost worse than if he had rebuked her.

He bent down and struck the first blade with the chisel. Hiraeth worked quickly, but the intricate designs flowing from his aged hands onto the Cardanthium canvas bespoke the unmatched skill of a master craftsman. Arctura watched the work in amazement, awed, as he swept the tool across the blade like ink strokes on parchment. Runic symbols she remembered seeing along the cavern paths wove into the engraved tapestry. These too glowed in their own right, sparkling like the facets of diamond or blazing suddenly like embers catching flame. The light within light was too dazzling to watch for long, but Arctura could not look away. She blinked and rubbed her eyes as Hiraeth moved on to the second sword.

New but similar designs flowered onto the next blade. Hiraeth worked far faster than any artisan should, let alone a gnarled old hermit whose best years were clearly behind him. At an earlier point in her training, the obvious paradox would have merited one of

Arctura's sharp-tongued remarks, but nothing came to her now. All she could do was watch in reverent silence.

Hiraeth tapped one last flourish onto the blade and straightened. He set down his tools, and grasping the swords by their hilts, held them up, the rune-etched sides facing her.

"Wrath and Vengeance. So it shall be." Hiraeth whispered. "*H'rot.*"

The left blade buzzed as its glow intensified.

"*Ysgrat,*" he intoned, and the blade's twin pulsed with recognition.

With a deft twist, Hiraeth flipped the swords and extended the pommel first to Arctura.

"They answer to the names and purpose you have given them. Use their true names well; though all Reidara forget the first language, these words of power will not pass away."

"Teacher," Arctura bowed her head with respect, and then reached forward.

Her fingers shook as they laced around the grip of each sword. Electrifying jolts ran through her hands. The pulsing, pale light of the Cardanthium became a solid, bright green, intense and hot in her grasp. Arctura stared in wonder, watching the runes flash and darken with a trail of strange light that raced up and down each blade. She swung them in graceful arcs, each moving as an extension of herself. No, it was more than that. It was as if the blades had always been a part of her. Their essence mingled with her own, so indistinguishable that she found separation from them as abhorrent as losing an arm.

"Well then, *nemii,* what do you think? Are they satisfactory?"

Arctura twirled, jumped, and twisted, her blades a blur of green light as she wielded them with expert ease.

"Satisfactory?" She laughed. "They're perfection, Teacher. I... I do not know what to say."

Arctura's smile faded as she turned her attention back to Hiraeth. By now, he had regained his staff. He leaned over it, shoulders slumping as he watched her test the swords. His brow fell low over his eyes, wrinkled with sorrow.

"It is enough," he said with heaviness. "And now it is time."

"Teacher?" Arctura questioned, lowering the swords.

"There is an island chain in the south, not far from the shore of the Heibeiathan stronghold of Mecanja. They call it the Mautardu Islands. Do you know of it?"

"I do."

"On the largest, you will find the one you came seeking," Hiraeth said.

Arctura's breath caught in her chest.

"The Drake?" she whispered. "That is where he is hiding?"

Hiraeth nodded slightly.

"Then it is time," Arctura said, clenching her jaw.

"Do what you will," Hiraeth said. "But remember all I have spoken. Your path diverges ahead of you, *nemii*. Choose wisely which you shall tread."

"I have already chosen," Arctura replied, pulling the sheaths onto her shoulders and depositing her new weapons inside. "There is no other way."

Hiraeth gazed long at Arctura before he answered.

"Little one, there is always another way."

The slaver ship rounding the southernmost part of the Mautardu Islands stunk of urine and human misery. Even topside, far away from the shut-up hold where its unlucky cargo stewed in filth, the smell permeated everything. Arctura grimaced in disgust as she pulled the hood of her cloak down until it touched the bridge of her nose. She had been on the dirty old tanker for hours, and despite the captain's assurances, it hadn't gotten any better. Not that he would know the difference, anyway. It had become clear the captain's sense of smell was as numb as his sense of morality. Arctura shot a side-long glance in his direction and glowered.

Still, she had no choice. Weeks spent gathering intel on Troll's Head, the Mautardu chain's largest isle, revealed that not one respectable ship did business in the lawless islands. Since Arctura did not have the time or the desire to waste resources on a private expedition, she was down to two options: a slave ship headed to Junker Cove with its supply of disposable miners, or any number of other vessels that carried raider or mercenary bands staking their claims to the islands' abundant hideouts and riches alike. Arctura did not know what sort of loyalty existed among such people and deemed it best to avoid them altogether. Certainly, a young woman traveling alone in such places would attract unwelcome scrutiny, and she did not need word of her arrival on Troll's Head circulating where the Drake might hear. She needed surprise on her side. That, her training, and the power coursing through *H'rot* and *Ysgrat*.

To the slaver captain's credit, he exhibited no such scruples about her personal motivations. In the waters of the west, where the hand of the Coalition had not yet grasped, treasure alone ruled all. Arctura could speak that language well enough. A couple of *Edenii*'s uncut gems buttoned him up and allowed her unquestioned passage on the barge. A handful more in other places gave her all the information she could possibly want on the Drake himself. It was only a matter of time before she would find him now.

Arctura tried to focus on the task ahead, pushing *Edenii* and the accompanying thoughts of guilt aside. They bubbled up anyway. *But Hiraeth had to have known, did he not? He made his knowledge of hidden things plain enough. If he had really cared about my motives, or my use of him and of Edenii's riches to pursue my revenge, he would have stopped me. Right?*

Biting her lip, she gazed out to sea.

A shout rang out, cutting into Arctura's thoughts.

"Land! Junker Cove ahead!"

Junker Cove. Arctura clenched the rail with white knuckles as the island chain's busiest port came into view. A few other ships anchored there already, bouncing on the sparkling turquoise water. Bathed in the fading but brilliant light of sunset, the waves glimmered orange as they rolled gently to shore and foamed against its white sands. Beyond the sands, tangles of jungle vines and knots of lush green trees sprouted up and covered the whole of the island's mountainous terrain. Colorful birds rose and wheeled from within the steamy jungle, their exotic calls strange and new to Arctura's ears. In any other circumstance, Troll's Head Island might have been a paradise. But evidence of its defilement shattered that illusion. Scarred, brown tracks of downed trees snaked throughout the landscape, the acrid smell of smoke hung in the air, and the clanking of iron and stone rang faintly around the island. Down on shore, she could make out the shapes of people as they picked through the scraps and ship wreckage that currents brought to accumulate on the island's beaches, and for which the cove was named. The slaver ship angled into the cove and dropped anchor among the others.

"Ready, miss?" the captain called, waving a hand toward the side of the ship. "Your dinghy awaits! Unless you wanna hold yer nose and get on the next wit' the merchandise."

Arctura scowled but strode toward him quickly. She looked over the side, where two of his crew had already readied the rowboat to head inland. They glanced at her covertly, trying to hide their greedy interest in her stuffed haversack. Arctura readjusted the swords on her back with a dangerous smile. The men got back to work, even as the unflappable captain eyed it curiously.

"Looks heavy," he grinned. "Got things to barter on Troll's Head, eh?"

"It has what I need."

Arctura hefted the bag and tossed it into one of the crewman's arms. With breathless surprise and an ungraceful stagger, he fell into the bottom of the rowboat, clutching it. The captain turned toward Arctura, a mixture of astonishment and suspicion on his raised brow.

"I see the young miss plans to survive for a time." he said. "Perhaps she'll be needin' return passage to the mainland, then?"

Arctura hopped over the boat's side, landing with cat-like softness and grace in the dinghy. "Plan on it."

The captain let out a bark of a laugh. "Well, come find me wit' another fistful of your shinies, and you'll have it. They're always needin' warm bodies to throw inta the mines. I'll be called back for a fresh supply within the month. You can count on that!"

Arctura said nothing as they lowered the rowboat into the sea. Her eyes searched the shore, past the scavengers and into the jungle, up toward the mountain pinnacle that marked her way. If anyone spoke to her, she did not hear. She saw only the path to the Drake, and to her one enduring thought.

Retribution.

33

Arctura wiped the perspiration off her face and looked up at the moon.

Just after midnight, she guessed. *And still as hot as the Guardian Forge.*

For hours Arctura had wound her way uphill and over twisted, unfamiliar jungle paths. A more direct route to her destination might have existed, but out of caution, she avoided the travel-worn roads of the mining slaves and their taskmasters. Her caution had been well-warranted. More than once she saw groups of unsavory characters upon them, doing who knew what in these forsaken wilds. But dodging unwanted attention on the arduous, sweat-drenched hike up the mountain had not been in vain. It had led her safely here, to the pinnacle; beyond that, she hoped, she would find the hideout of the Drake himself.

By now she had stripped her cloak, but Arctura readjusted the light cuirass and checked the various weaponry she had picked up on her way to Troll's Head Island – explosives, one pistol, a bone-handle dagger with a steel blade, and of course, *H'rot* and *Ysgrat*. She pulled the first Cardanthium sword from its sheath along with a damp, folded parchment from her pocket. Crouching and unfolding the parchment across her knees, she studied it by the light of the blade. Arctura traced the path from the pinnacle to the next landmark: the big rubber tree with three gouges running across its trunk. From there, north of the tree, she should see the mouth of a cave in the mountainside. The current illustrious home of the mighty Drake. At least, according to her sources, that's where he had been holing himself up these days.

With a deep breath, Arctura carefully folded up the map and put it back in its place. She slid her haversack off her side and gazed into it, scrutinizing the provisions, packed tent, and the rest of the arsenal she had lugged along. She rubbed her shoulder as she wondered if she really needed it. *Are there really that many bootlickers here with him, doing his bidding, protecting him?*

Arctura recalled the cruel faces passing by her as she hid among the trees. *It must be so,* she thought grimly. *Much blood will roll down this mountain tonight. May it not be my own.*

She clenched her teeth, imagining what it might feel like to die, either on the sword or axe of one of the Drake's men, or by the horrid Cardanthium claw itself.

That monstrosity, Arctura shuddered. *How did he come to possess it?* No one outside *Edenii* knew, and Hiraeth answered only vaguely. She knew only that in the claw's making; the Drake had profaned the ore by doing what ought not be done. A blasphemy, Hiraeth said, against his Unseen, one that required the death of the perpetrator.

Of course, Hiraeth had qualified that statement with a warning. Being a chosen instrument of the Unseen did not absolve one of his or her own crimes. Arctura's sins passed through her mind. Maybe death was waiting for her after all. *A two-for-one deal,* Arctura thought with a morbid smirk. Either way, she had long ago decided her course. Cardanthium claw or not, she would confront the destroyer of her happiness. And if he did not die by her hand, he would at least suffer great loss. And she would start with whoever happened to be in her way.

Arctura gathered her things and continued past the pinnacle, eyes searching the darkness for the rubber tree. Moonlight bathed the exposed mountainside as the trees grew thinner among the sporadic mounds of rock. She slinked along in shadow. Ahead, a thick trunk rose out of the darkness. She nearly rushed toward it when a soft sound reached her ears. Arctura pressed herself against the closest tree and waited.

Her measured breaths seemed obnoxious in the otherwise still night. She slowed it even further, combing through the sounds of the jungle for the unnatural. Insects whined in her ears. The lonely cry of a night bird echoed in the distance. Nothing else seemed to move. Even so, Arctura crouched and edged closer to the tree, careful not to expose herself. She heard that soft sound again and paused.

This time, her caution was rewarded. A silhouette shifted against the tree ahead, its only evidence of actually being there a shimmer of movement before it melted back into shadow. Arctura stared hard at the tree. With effort, she could discern the outline of a man; armored, arms across his chest, a pistol dangling from his hand. He faced her, his back rested against the trunk, but he made no sign that he had suspected any danger.

As quietly as she could, Arctura put down her bag. She reached inside, grasping the handle of a crossbow, followed by a bolt. *Don't make a sound*, she thought, gritting her teeth and standing with her own back against a tree. Arctura chanced a glance back at the silhouette as the crossbow loaded with a click. She held in a curse as he tensed, his arms now up instead of over his chest.

Too late.

Arctura leaned out from behind the tree and raised the bow. She aimed and fired. A thump and gurgling groan answered the twang of the release as she moved back into cover. Arctura reloaded. With a few calming breaths, she ventured a look toward the rubber tree.

The figure lay crumpled at its roots. She pointed the crossbow at the body, a shaky exhale leaving her lips. Arctura searched the area around him, certain that at any moment another like him would be waiting with a bolt for her. The jungle remained undisturbed. With another calming breath, she grabbed her supplies and approached the first of the Drake's forces to fall.

She pulled her dagger and kneeled down beside him, just long enough to confirm no life remained. Arctura did not revel in the kill, but it had not sickened her, either. She felt... nothing. *And what should I feel?* Arctura stepped back and wiped the blood-soaked toes of her boots in the grass. *Should I not pity him, or feel guilt for what I have done?*

The thoughts quickly fled from Arctura's mind as her attention turned to the tree itself. Three parallel lines ran diagonally across the trunk. A white ooze had dripped down from the wounds and ran to the base of the tree where it had coagulated. She brushed her fingers lightly over the marks before bringing her hand to her face. The scars felt as raw as the still-healing gouges in the tree. Her cheeks burned hot with rage. A thirst unlike any other dried her throat and sent fire into her stomach. There was only one way to allay it. She would drain the cup of vengeance to the last drop.

Arctura emptied her pack of every weapon she could carry before tossing it into the undergrowth. Ahead, the mountain rose, a face of rock that blotted out the jungle and sky behind it. She searched for the black hole of the cave mouth, instead finding the dim light of a little lantern against the mountain stone. Arctura approached. The emptiness of a hidden cavern beside it resolved in the darkness. No one stood guard outside, but from within she could hear the soft echoes of voices and the glint of firelight. As silent as a shade, she slipped inside.

A narrow passage sloped down from the cave entrance. At the bottom, light blazed and flickered as shadows passed in front of it. The voices became clearer. Arctura pressed herself against the passage wall. She moved closer, listening.

"I already told you, he ain't coming out," a woman said. "We're to *lie low*. Besides, he got enough mutton and grog to last 'im a week. Give it a rest, will yah?"

A man answered in protest. "But, Dex, that job in Cretash–"

"Can wait. Don't worry, it ain't going nowhere, Skur. No one but us can get it done. That's why they asked for the Drake *personally*. We'll go out and get our pay, you'll see. Just as soon as he hears the coast is clear."

Skur scoffed. "What's he so worried about? You know how junkers are– can't trust a word that comes outta their mouths."

"You don't live to be Reidara's best mercenary for two decades without some healthy paranoia," Dex sighed. "Besides, I heard 'em say it was one of those warriors from the north comin' off the slaver ship. You know, with the glowing swords and all. Saw 'em burnin' green on her back in their sheaths, they said."

"Shiny dirks or not, there's only one of 'er and six of us, countin' Bryl," Skur muttered disdainfully. "I should think we'd do alright."

Dex laughed. "You don't know anything, Skur. Ever seen those devils fight? They say one can strike down a dozen–"

She snapped her fingers. "Just like that."

This time, Skur laughed. "Sounds like you been listenin' to old junker nonsense, too."

"You shut that stupid mouth of yours and you might live longer," Dex replied shortly. "Now hand me that grog."

"Ah ah– not too much," Skur said. "Can't have you seein' double on lookout, can we?"

"Shut. It."

Arctura chanced a glance down into the cavern, where the two squatted beside a roaring fire. They faced the passage opening, but by Arctura's good fortune, busied themselves with food and drink. She gauged the layout of the room before leaning back into cover. Only the speakers seemed present in the cavern, but she thought she saw the bodies of two sleepers not too far from the light of the fire.

That's four, she thought. *And if Bryl was the sentry, five. That just leaves the Drake. Now... what to do?*

Arctura reached for her explosives. A cruel smile split her mouth. She had no time for showing off her newfound prowess with protracted battle, and with this, at least there would be some element of surprise on her side. These few obstacles here meant nothing; not when her greatest enemy lay close at hand.

She activated the first and with a grunt, lobbed it in the direction of the fire.

"What the—" Arctura heard, followed by the sucking sound of a surprised gasp as she jumped back into the passage. The scream that followed was cut short. Arctura felt the detonation before she heard it. The cavern exploded. Rocks plummeted from the ceiling as flames licked into the passage. Plumes of hot dust and smoke shot out after it. Arctura covered her mouth as she waited it for it to settle; but not too long. When the heat dissipated and the pillar of smoke dispersed, she ran in, swords lighting the way.

A sinister haze curled in the air and crawled along the cave's fragile ceiling. Small shafts of moonlight touched its rubble-covered floor. Among the wreckage, Arctura found what was left of the Drake's little band of mercenaries. She moved on, sweeping the cave for the room he was hiding. A door in the corner drew her attention. Arctura gripped the sword hilts harder, her jaw clenched so tightly that her back teeth began to ache. She came closer. Each beat of her heart thumped in her throat.

The rough door fit snugly in the stone entryway it was made to fill, and its heavy iron deadbolt might have deterred a less eager hunter. But ever since the crafting of *H'rot* and *Ysgrat* and her binding to them, a strange power had taken hold of Arctura. Some new strength coursed in her veins, a strength that not even Hiraeth's rigorous training should have been able to give her. Had she found the Drake's lair on her own a year before, this final obstacle would have been infuriatingly insurmountable. But now...

Her boot plunged into the soft wood with a splintering crack. The lock hung uselessly on the hinge, and the door buckled inward. Arctura kicked through again, entering in a clatter of broken boards and dust. She scanned the interior, her eyes adjusting to the gloom.

A room opened up before her, peculiarly large and plunged in darkness except for the smoldering embers of a firepit in its deserted corner. She took in the details quickly: a stack of furs on a small bed, an open chest gleaming with overflowing precious stones and gold, a rude table. Upon the table, something glowed. Arctura's eyes narrowed. *The hand of the monster.*

A black chain attached the pulsating claw to the silhouetted figure behind it. Arctura could just see the slovenly, grizzled hairs on his chin and the blackened teeth exposed as they clamped down on the end of a cigar. He puffed, the dull red flare of light revealing the two eyes Arctura could never forget. Her scars burned with the flood of horrific memories, and Arctura could not be certain they hadn't burst and wept in his presence. She resisted the urge to check. A wolfish grin spread his thin lips.

"You?" His voice grated like steel on stone. "They said a Guardian. Wasn't expecting *you.*"

Blood rushed between Arctura's ears and thrummed with the fiery pulsing light of her blades. Could he hear it like she did? Could he feel the raw energy and rage that passed in and out of her through her swords? Arctura lifted *Ysgrat* and pointed.

"You took everything from me," she said through gritted teeth. "And before I cleave your cursed soul from your body, I shall know why."

The Drake's ugly grin widened. He set down the flagon in his intact hand and leaned back in his chair.

"Ain't the first time I've heard that, girl. Won't be the last."

A chill ran down Arctura's spine, but she reached deeper into the anger that had sustained her these long years. It flared like a furnace in her chest.

"I learned my lesson," Arctura replied. "It is high time you have learned yours."

She jumped forward, swords blazing and angled toward the Drake's throat. His cold, harsh laugh rang in her ears as he upended the table into her. Arctura sprang over it, growling, but the Drake was gone. Flagons, dishes, and coins clattered to the floor. Another sound registered in her ears. Clicking. Arctura raised *H'rot* just as the hurtling Cardanthium claw reached her. It slammed into her sword in a shower of sparks. Arctura staggered against its impact. A jolt of pain shot up her left arm. A laugh, and the hiss of an energy pistol. *Not good.*

Arctura rolled. White heat tore by her, exploding in a rain of earth against the cave wall. Blast after blast followed the first. Arctura's breath came in ragged gasps as she deflected and dodged, the unending barrage and hail of rubble and dirt marring her vision. She parried one final searing blow before diving over the now flaming table. Arctura hit the ground gracelessly, rolling to put out the fire eating at her clothes.

"It's always the same," the Drake laughed cruelly, throwing the spent weapon on the floor with a thud. "They never learn the first time."

He bounded across the room and launched the claw as he bore down. Arctura made it to a crouch. The claw hit her crossed blades. She tottered backward, but the Drake yanked on the chain. Arctura struggled to keep hold of her swords as the claw grabbed and dragged them in. She flung with all her might, succeeding as the claw fell and bit into the dirt.

"Ha–" she shouted triumphantly, but all the air left her lungs as a boot landed squarely on her chest.

Arctura flew through the busted door. Wood and rubble splintered into her skin as she tumbled into the main cavern. Pain shot through her ribcage with every shallow breath, but she forced herself to stand. *Perhaps I'll die*, she thought with despair. *But I'll do it on my feet.*

The caustic smell and taste of smoke hung thick in the air, creating a layer of haze that burned Arctura's eyes as she stared through it. A spectral glow emanated from the broken doorway. The Drake emerged. Arctura could now glimpse the feared mercenary in all his terrible glory.

The claw, still coiling back into place as the Drake entered the cavern, hung by a chain from a metal gauntlet attached to the stump of his arm. It clinked as it pulled the claw in, which snapped into place on its own. Arctura might have found the contraption ingenious if wasn't also so sinister; the Drake flexed his arm and rolled his wrist so that the claw twisted and turned as his own natural limb. With the other hand, the Drake plucked the still-dangling cigar from his black-leaf stained mouth and tossed it to the side.

He was smaller than she remembered, but no less frightening as his barrel-chested frame filled the door. The Drake swaggered, no sign of exertion at their struggle present upon him. Instead, he grinned dangerously and extended his fingers toward his waist, where an array of weapons glinted a warning in the moonlight. Arctura's hope plummeted. The shame of her childish foolishness washed over her. Whatever lesson she was meant to learn at their first hellish meeting, she had not. And the Drake would slaughter her for it.

Is this what Hiraeth foresaw?

Arctura fought to harden herself against that fear as it threatened to unravel her at any moment. With a deep breath, she looked the Drake in his dark, cold eyes. Unblinking, reptile-like, he stared back.

"My, my," he rasped. "How you've grown. You might've been quite an asset to daddy dearest, had you not come here to die."

Arctura took a cleansing breath and narrowed her eyes. "Yet you were the one sheltered in a cave behind a wall of hired muscle... all at the merest rumor of a worthy warrior. You are correct, I have grown. Enough to know what I am, and what you are."

The Drake's lip curled. "Yeah, and what's that, little girlie?"

"I know the odds are against me," Arctura said. "Still, here I am. Perhaps I am a hot-blooded fool, but I know what I am not. I am not the one who hides in the shadow. I am not the one who beats down the weak, who murders the helpless. I am no coward."

He pulled another pistol from his holster and grinned. "Wanna bet?"

Arctura cried out as he loosed another flurry of blasts. White heat ricocheted off her raised swords. She could smell her clothes and hair burning, felt the searing pain as a blast grazed past her arm. *This is it,* she thought. *This is how I die.*

The Drake's laugh rose above the scream of the barrage. Arctura registered the distinct clicking sound of the launching claw. Through the flashing light and haze, it flew at her face. It hit her blades with a ringing clang. Arctura grappled with it, knowing every half-second of entanglement spelled her doom. Another blast. She twisted, and the blow bounced off the claw. The claw's chain clicked and pulled. She stumbled, still warding off the Drake's well-aimed pistol.

Teacher... you were right.

The claw slipped, losing its grasp on the edges of her sword. She swung them free, knocking the retracting claw to the side. A new sound reverberated within the cacophony; a sound that hummed from *H'rot* and *Ysgrat* themselves. *Was that... singing?*

All at once, Arctura felt it anew – the surge of alien strength, the wave of unidentified emotion, the thrum of living stone. Fear, pain, and even rage melted into something else. Something other. Time slowed. One beat of her heart passed. She took a breath. Her blades danced in the haze of blinding light.

A final flash, heat, and smoke. Arctura sprinted forward, bellowing and bearing down on the steaming pistol. *H'rot* cleaved it in two, taking half of the Drake's hand with it. He roared, not only with pain, but with naked, wild rage. The Cardanthium claw clicked into place, poised to launch. It clinked into firing position. *Ysgrat* was faster.

The Drake grunted and looked down at the place his arm should have been. Arctura's eyes met his. No pain, no surprise; just two pinpoints of the black void. She plunged both blades into the Drake's chest. He groaned and sunk to the floor as she withdrew them. With an almost gentle push of her foot, he toppled backward. Dark stains seeped into the rubble beneath him.

Arctura knelt and placed *Ysgrat* across his throat. She stared into his eyes, those eyes that had haunted her for years, and watched as, even now, the sharp blackness of his pupils began to fade to gray.

In its increasing glassiness, a reflection stared back at her, a merciless, scarred face, spattered in blood, gloating, gold-rimmed eyes, and the hardened line of beautiful, cruel lips.

"Your time has finally come, monster," she said coldly, breathing hard. "Now, reach back in your memory. Recall the streets of Pardaetha and the atrocities you committed against me. Who sent you? And what became of my Reylas?"

The Drake worked his mouth, struggling to focus his scattered gaze on Arctura. With painful effort, he choked out a laugh.

"Ask..." But no words followed. His eyelids fluttered shut as his head lolled to the side. A long, faint breath escaped his still-grinning mouth.

34

Year 20 of the Glorious New Era
59th of Sun's Reign
Pardaetha, Gormlaen

The gates of Kyma reared up before Arctura, barred and unwelcoming, as she approached. *Has it always looked that way?* She wondered, and she quickly realized she had never seen them closed upon her return to the palace. No fanfare, entourage, or giddy crowds greeted her this day, although a few passersby squinted at her with curious and vague expressions. She did not expect anyone to recognize her for who she was. For one, with her dusty traveling clothes, obscuring cowl, and impressive weaponry, she bore little similarity to her previously known identity, and for another, it appeared everyone believed her dead. Newly installed image-reflecting holograstones, yet another ingenious innovation of the rapidly progressing Coalition, lined the illustrious street leading up to Kyma. She marveled to see they bore her younger, unmarred face in each stone.

"Arctura Vipsanius, the delight of Kyma," she mumbled to herself. "May she live forever in our hearts."

Arctura scoffed.

She weaved through the thickening crowd, which seemed to only get thicker as she moved past the city square. Arctura glanced toward it, regarding the amassing army forming ranks there. The black Coalition standard, emblazoned with crimson twin lions, reared up and roaring as their paws met, stood tall and proud among them. Weaponry winked in the fading sunlight.

"For the glory of Gormlaen!" Citizens of Pardaetha shouted in support as they gathered at the fringes of the square.

A raised platform in their midst caught Arctura's attention, and the memory of the three axe strokes that silenced Onesti house forever echoed in her mind. *They were innocent*, she realized. An involuntary chill crept down Arctura's back as time ran backward from that moment. Every terrible crime perpetrated here, against Arctura and many others, had one common source; the source she had come to Kyma's gates to confront and expose. The chill in her spine spread to her limbs and seared like ice in her veins.

Arctura readjusted the heavy bundle on her shoulder before placing a hand in her cloak. Her fingers brushed across crinkled parchment. She tugged on it, eyes focused on the blood-red wax seal in its corner containing one lock of thick, soft, black hair. Boiling rage washed over her and melted away the icy grip of fear. She turned away from the rejoicing crowd, setting her hard gaze and feet toward Kyma. Her pace quickened.

A single guard stood at the gate's entrance, leaning lazily against the wall as he watched the lively procession in the square below. His gaze flicked toward Arctura as she approached, his slack jaw tightening into a scowl. The scowl deepened as she smirked, undeterred.

"Halt! Get back!" The guard growled, brandishing his gun. "What do you think you're doing?"

"You would not ask if you knew to whom you speak," Arctura snarled.

She pulled back her hood and eyed him with contempt.

"M-miss Vipsanius?" The guard quaked and stuttered as his eyes darted to her scar, and then to her gleaming swords. "You– you are... alive?"

"Obviously, fool," she spat. "I seek an audience with the Supreme Chancellor. You will take me to him."

"My deepest apologies, Miss. Uh– uh, yes, of course, I'll take you right away. The Supreme Chancellor and his advisors are in the Great Room. This way."

Arctura brushed past the guard into Kyma, hardly noticing him tripping over himself to keep up. She flung open the doors of the palace. Startled servants paused in their duties to observe the strange visitor, only to gasp as they recognized their lost princess. They shrank from her presence as she strode through the voluminous halls, and whispers followed her all the way to the Great Room.

Arctura threw open the room's wide double doors. They groaned at the force of her entry and slammed loudly into the walls. Her eyes swept the room, and Arctura studied each face seated around the table. All looked back in stunned silence: Father, Mother, Arcturo, Tyranna, several Coalition senators she recognized and others she didn't, and Pardaetha's highest ranking security official. *A war council.* She stared at each with wild, defiant eyes. Turo stared down at the table.

"Can it be?" Father said with surprise. "My daughter, believed lost to ravagers in Sutra, still lives?"

"That she does," Arctura answered coolly. "Though I have seen my death has benefited you far more. Congratulations on your complete control of that region."

"Don't you dare speak to the Supreme Chancellor in that presumptuous tone," Mother snapped.

At this, Tyranna openly smirked.

Father raised a hand. "Peace, Eufemia. Would we not welcome

our lost child back into our arms? And no longer a child, I see. She has returned a woman and a warrior. Come now, this is an occasion for joy. We ought to be celebrating."

Nothing in Father's tone or in the hard stares or blanching faces around the table confirmed his suggestion. Arctura sneered.

"Allow me to begin the festivities."

She tossed her bundle to the table with a thunk. It slipped open, revealing its contents: a Cardanthium claw, still attached to the arm *Ysgrat* had sheared off at the shoulder. Mother and a few of the senators covered their mouths.

"I'd have brought you his head, but this seemed a far more fitting present."

Father's eyes narrowed. He turned to the Coalition senators.

"Gentlemen, there is a family matter I must attend to. Please enjoy a brief recess and refresh yourselves on the palace grounds. Our council will continue within the hour."

The men quickly left the table, anxious glances lingering on the severed limb before the door shut behind them. Arctura stared defiantly at the remaining figures: Father, Mother, Turo, and Tyranna.

"Impressive," Father said. "You bested the Drake."

Arctura wanted to laugh. *That was almost a compliment.* She smiled ominously instead.

"Oh, but Father, there is more."

Arctura slammed the sheet of parchment onto the table with one hand, and with a swift motion, pulled *H'rot* from its sheath and drove it through the middle. It lodged into the stone with an echoing crack. Father said nothing, but stared at the graceful, flowing script on the page written unmistakably in his own hand.

"After I slew the Drake, I couldn't help but peruse his personal effects," Arctura continued. "As you have said yourself, Father, 'To the victor goes the spoils.' Well, other than being filthy rich, the Drake was quite the record keeper. Hundreds of contracts I found, all completed, all sealed with one lock of hair from some unlucky soul. But I was looking for just one. One little contract from the Year 14."

Her burning gaze fell on the parchment, blurring with anger as she read its words once again, words that commissioned the murder of Reylas and her own mutilation. *Do not kill her*, she saw. *Only the Samrasine vagrant and their wretched offspring. However, teach her a lesson in any way you see fit.*

She jabbed a finger toward the elegant signature, one she had seen Father sign many times before.

"I might have saved myself the trouble, had I known you had its duplicate."

Arctura looked for shock or surprise around the table and found none. Turo's eyes remained glued to its dark surface, misery twisting his face. Tyranna leaned back in her chair, her arm draped arrogantly over his shoulder and her eyes twinkling with gloating triumph. Mother stared past Arctura with an upturned nose. *They knew*, she thought. *They all knew.* She balled her fist and brought it down hard upon the table, causing the others to jump as she focused on Father.

"You did this," she said, her rage barely restrained. "You murdered Reylas and my innocent child."

Father's eyes grew cold. "What would you have me do, Arctura? Let you run off with that mongrel and live in squalid ignominy? Allow you to sully your noble blood birthing half-human brats? Shame all of Pardaetha and spit at the purity of Gormlaen with your base lusts? No. I would not stomach your disgusting choices. In the best interests of you and our noble house, I took action."

"In *your* best interests alone!" she shrieked. "You destroyed me."

A small smile formed on Father's lips. "No, daughter. I *re-created* you. See what you have become? You have redeemed yourself through the shedding of blood and by learning the secrets of those northern barbarians. How do you not see it? You have been forged for such a time as this. Behold how much more useful now than you were, had I not punished you."

Father swept his hands across the room and toward the open

319

balcony. "Think of it, Arctura. We are on the cusp of the invasion of Elmnas. Lead my forces against them. Win undying glory and honor and make yourself worthy again to be called by the name Vipsanius. Stand by my side, and you will forget the hardships you have suffered for your folly."

"How did you know?" she whispered. "How did you discover my plans?"

Father said nothing, but all eyes turned to her brother.

"Turo?" Arctura asked in anguish. "You betrayed me?"

"It wasn't like that!" He burst out, tears in his eyes. "I... I was trying to help. I wanted to keep you from making a mistake. I never thought... I couldn't fathom... I never intended for you to get hurt. You have to believe me, Rah. Please. I'm so sorry."

"You did the right thing, my love," Tyranna said, massaging his neck. Turo flinched.

Arctura swallowed back the cry threatening to tear out of her throat, shaking her head in disbelief.

"It is done, Arctura. You can change nothing about the past," Father said. "But you may still yet reclaim your future. Choose the path I have placed before you. Join me for the glory of Gormlaen and the redemption of your name!"

Arctura looked at the faces before her, people she had once known and trusted. Her insides grew cold and numb, even to the anger that drove her back to Kyma in the first place. *What is left for me?* she wondered. *How many times can a soul die?*

She pulled *H'rot* slowly from the table. Father's eyes betrayed his excitement, his hunger for another acquisition in the Coalition's great conquest. Her gaze hardened upon his, and *H'rot* flamed in her grasp.

"No."

"No?" Father laughed mirthlessly. "My dear, what other option do you have?"

Arctura stood tall, ferocity burning in her eyes as she addressed the room. "I can renounce the name Vipsanius forever. I'd rather die free of this wretched house than walk a moment longer carrying its burdens."

Mother stood suddenly and stabbed her manicured finger toward Arctura. "Then die you shall! Have her executed, Lucan."

Arctura raised her swords, tensing for battle. They flamed in her grasp. Time stopped. In the moments between breaths, she saw everything. Tyranna raised a pistol and aimed it toward her. The guard beyond the door nosed in, creaking it open ever so slightly as tensions rose. But she could take them. Arctura could take them all.

"No!" Turo shouted.

Father and Mother both looked at him in surprise. Tyranna twisted her lip in disdain, her weapon still leveled in Arctura's direction.

"Please, Father," he said, more timidly this time. "This will not do. Exile her from Pardaetha if you must, but do not harm her. You have heard it with your own ears. She alone killed the world's most fearsome man. Can you not see that this ends poorly for us all? That she will be of more use alive than dead?"

Mother and Tyranna opened their mouths to protest, but Father silenced all with a wave of us his hand. He paced toward the balcony, a finger on his chin as he considered the troops congregating in the courtyard. Father's voice was low when he spoke.

"I have led the Coalition to glory and greatness beyond the lot of any empire in Reidara. And we shall be greater still. Do you know how I have done that?"

Father turned, focusing on Arctura. The room remained silent.

"Go on, Arctura, you should recall this lesson," he said. "How have I prospered?"

"Fear," Arctura replied softly. "For in fear, even the enemies of Lucan Vipsanius are his allies."

Father smiled. "Yes. And if they do not fear?"

"They die."

Father moved toward the table and reached for the Drake's claw. He hefted it by the arm stump, placing the wicked curves against

Turo's throat. Turo stared at the far wall, frozen in terror. At this, even Tyranna shuddered. Father smiled.

"Leave if you wish. Keep your miserable life for now." Father pressed the sharpened points into Turo's neck. Turo did not move, even as three pricks of red swelled and rolled down his neck.

"Cross me in any way, and it is not just your life I will require. You know better than most. My eyes and ears are everywhere." Father's eyes gleamed. "Remember well."

Arctura did not answer. There was no need to answer. She turned and walked. Far beyond the resounding thud of Kyma's closing door, away from the clang of palace gates, the marching boots, the city noise. She walked, leaving the silence forever behind her.

She walks on. On, on, always on. To the north, cold eyes on the horizon. Machines of war and the eternal stream of soldiers pass her on the right and the left. She walks on. Up rises the smoke of desolation, the smell of fire on the wind, the red cloud that blooms across the sky and blots out the sun. She walks on to the Kamarian Mountains, even as she sees they are burning. Ash blankets her hair like snow. A cauldron of fire boils out of Edenii and spills into desolate, Heibeiathan sands. Nothing left. Not here, not anywhere.

She walks on. Days, nights, seasons, and years soar by, melting one into the other in the relentless march of time. It loses all meaning beneath the purgatorial haze of the sunless sky. She walks on, never weakening, never aging, never resting, never still. She walks on, now knowing the gift of the Ageless is a curse.

On, on, always on. Always killing, always fighting, always surviving. She, the hired sword, the final retribution. It is what she does. It is the only thing to live for. Pardaetha forgets her, but she remains. She walks on, a specter, a myth, a nightmare.

And wherever she walks, a shadow falls, and the sword follows after.

Fox woke with a start. Swords up and ready, she crouched in a defensive stance before she even felt fully awake. Shadows fled from the green arc of light and bounced off the crumbling walls of the shrine. The limbless goddess seemed to be the only human-like form there, looking especially misshapen as it bathed in the ghost glow. Fox did not believe her surroundings for a second.

"I do not have to see you to know you're there," she said as she scanned the space. "And I would sooner kill you than suffer your silence. Don't be a fool."

The soft trickling of water and annoyed stamping of her mare were the only reply. Fox crept away from the wall where she had rested, her swords sweeping gracefully out before her. The light revealed nothing. She sighed, her gaze traveling toward the night sky above. Amorphous, dark clouds rolled across it, swirling, separating, and combining like eddies in the unsearchable depths of a tempestuous sea. Fox hated that sky. She still could not say with confidence what had caused the persistent cover that, in the first years, had caused weather changes, crop failure, famine, death, and despair world-wide. The eruption of *Edenii* provided the most natural explanation, which she might have believed had the effects diminished over the long years of her life. But Hiraeth's death and the loss of the Guardian stronghold were all too convenient. And as the Coalition swooped in with its progress and technology, alleviating swiftly the worst of the roiling, red sky's pall of destruction, she knew something even more terrible had taken place. Something Father had his fingerprints all over.

And so it goes, she thought.

"You've suffered far worse than my silence, little one."

Fox spun in the voice's direction, jabbing violently at the darkness. A hooded figure stood beside her horse, a shadow obscuring his face. His wrinkled hand reached out from his earth-colored robe, producing what looked like a sugar cube in his palm. The subdued mare knickered contentedly as she found it. He gently patted her forehead. From the hole of the black hood, two green eyes flashed toward Fox.

"How did you come here?" Fox demanded. "What do you want? Why should I not strike you down where you stand?"

The man chuckled.

"I invite you to try." He pointed to his shoulder, where a ghostly glow emanated from the sword sheaths strapped there. "Besides, *nemii*, is that any way to address an old man?"

Fox froze. Her eyes darted to the runic blades, shining with a green so pale it was almost white. In the shadow of the man's hood, she detected a familiar, wizened smile.

"You perished years ago," she said with conviction, but even so, her swords lowered to the ground. "Nothing within ten miles of *Edenii* could have survived. Despite that, I still searched for you, listened for word about the Guardian hermit of the mountains. I had been told the Coalition had tracked you, cornered you in your stronghold, before it finally erupted. That for all your secret arts, skill, and wisdom, you died there."

Hiraeth shook his head and patted the mare's neck thoughtfully. "Always so certain, little one."

He picked over the rubble of the shrine, and finding a suitable slab of rock, perched upon it. Fox still could not see his face, but every movement of his was as familiar and alive as if she had only left *Edenii* yesterday. He placed his elbows on his knees and steepled his aged fingers in front of his hood.

"This is a dream," she scoffed, dropping her swords and slumping back against the wall. "This old ruin is affecting my rational senses, and I am too weary to combat its nonsense."

"Spooked by a pile of ancient stones?" Hiraeth clicked his tongue. "Has the fearless child grown fearful in these last haunted days?"

"That is not what I said," Fox replied shortly. "It is only that these old things fill my mind with the past, and that is a place far more haunted than what remains between these walls."

She crossed her arms and huffed. "Not that I owe any explanation to you. You are not real. I need not indulge in unprofitable talk or thoughts."

"Is that so?" A hint of a smile played in Hiraeth's voice. "Is it unprofitable? Does not even the wolf retrace his steps when the scent is lost?"

Fox raised an eyebrow. "That sounds like one of your riddles, but not one I recall ever hearing. This is a most peculiar apparition."

"Indeed," Hiraeth answered. "So why not speak with me? It can do no harm, unless you fear to look behind you for even a moment."

"I do not fear," Fox glared. "All things fear me."

"It may be so," he replied. "And still, the most fearsome beasts have been killed, conquered, or tamed."

Fox laughed. "Is that a threat?"

"An observation."

"Yes, of course," Fox sighed. "My ever-observant hermit, even in my imagination. It seems you will not disappear, no matter how I shake my head or pinch my skin. Fine, Teacher, I relent. I will indulge this fantasy. What else have you observed?"

"The devouring lion looks to the north," Hiraeth said in a low voice. "He gathers his children for battle. But he does not see the winds change, that even he is a leaf upon it. The breath of the Unseen blows across this dying world, and all within it is stirred for their destiny. I know you have felt it yourself. But to where shall you be carried?"

"I am carried nowhere. I fly to wherever I please."

Hiraeth shook his head. "So says one drop of rain in the flood."

"If I have no choice, then why bother me at all?" Fox said angrily. "You have always wearied me with your double speech. Have the courage to speak plainly!"

"Would you have listened to me otherwise?" Hiraeth asked gently.

Fox scowled, but as her eyes met his, she looked away. Her expression softened.

"No, not then," she admitted. "And I am not so sure I would now."

"And yet, all will be revealed at its proper time."

Fox looked up. "Teacher?"

"I once told you your path diverged ahead. I have seen the one you have taken. *Isa* sees and knows."

Hiraeth's gaze bore into her. Despite herself, Fox closed her eyes, her scar and cheeks burning.

"You believe you forge your own path, and you have walked it long. Grievously long. But I tell you, the road of destruction is deceivingly broad, and it holds the paths of many." Hiraeth waved his hand toward the world outside the shrine. "And yet, any who have not walked it to its utter end may yet still turn."

Fox huffed. "I can only assume you speak of my contract. For the girl."

Hiraeth said nothing but reached down and traced his finger in the dirt collecting on the shrine's floor.

"Why did you show mercy to Falkir Eneshkin, my wandering one, *nemii*?"

Fox raised her eyebrow.

"Is that who he is?" She crossed her arms and let out a joyless laugh. "Only your *Isa* knows. I certainly don't."

Hiraeth leaned forward and whispered. "Walk with me a moment more, and you shall know."

"It is not so easy." Fox dropped her head into her hands. "You do not understand. I cannot forsake this path. That girl... in all my years, I have never seen the Supreme Chancellor so desperate to call upon me. I fail in this, and my life will be as nothing, and he will still have what he desires, anyway. Do you not see? I must. There is no other way."

"Little one," he said gently. "There is always another way."

Hiraeth stood and placed a hand on Fox's head. She started at the touch, fear jolting through her at the realization it held true human warmth and presence.

"You live? You are here?"

"I am."

Hiraeth stepped back and drew his swords. Their light shone with such intensity that Fox had to shield her eyes. She gazed at them as long as she could stand, catching the dark, green script of runes running the length of each with dazzling artistry.

"Hear me, and remember the names which I speak." Hiraeth lowered the swords slowly, pointing the ends down to the ground. "*Kirja* and *Kutsum,* Covenant and Calling! The time comes when all will be revealed."

In their light, Fox could finally see his face, glowing like the sun she once remembered and appearing far younger and more vibrant than the Hiraeth she had recalled. Shame washed over her, and she wanted to look away, but in that moment, the tips of the swords caught fire. The flames licked up the blades, first white, then blue, then orange as they spread. Fox gasped and pressed herself against the wall as they engulfed Hiraeth, but he stood perfectly still. He wore the fire like a cloak.

No, she thought, wide-eyed. *Not a cloak. Like wings.*

It was obvious now. Great fiery wings shimmered from what was once the tips of Hiraeth's swords, and it seemed the man himself was now a bird, flowing up and out of the shrine's open roof in a shower of celestial sparks. In the face of the bird, there was another face, so familiar and all at once something she did not know. Fox stared up in awe. And in a rush of wind, the sweeping of wings, a flash of flame, it was gone.

She blinked away the white spots floating in her field of vision. The lingering chill and damp of the night set in once again as everything returned to darkness. Fox rubbed her arms to ward off the sudden cold. She would have sworn she had just awakened from sleep, except she still felt the heat of the feathered flame searing her fingertips. With a shiver, she paced the length of the shrine and looked outside its crumbling enclosure.

Though still quite dark, a sliver of gray touched the eastern horizon. Fox was already making out more than just the shape of the landscape, and she could just about distinguish the signpost from its bleak surroundings. Fox glanced toward her bundle of supplies, where the muted glow of Blade's swords emanated through the sack. Her gaze lingered before traveling back toward the road. A mixture of dread, anger, and confusion came over her. At any other time, she would have thrown out a colorful curse and buried the emotion altogether, but for once, Fox lacked both the will and the words to do so. She looked to the east and clenched her jaw.

What now?

35

Year 113 of the Glorious New Era
47th of Sun's Wane
Elmnas

Tall blades of scraggly grass snagged at Mouse's ankles as she put one foot ahead of the other. The uneven ground of the valley had not been unpassable, but the matted undergrowth hid the abandoned burrows digging creatures had left behind. Mouse had already nearly turned an ankle in a few of them. That was the last thing she or anyone else in the group needed. She trod on in silence, too hot and too tired to speak. It seemed her friends felt the same way, for no one had spoken since the late morning. There was only the sound of the grass, their breathing, and the few insects that had survived the frost of the night before buzzing listlessly beneath their feet. All of them watched the ground and continued plodding at their slowing but steady pace. Mouse's back ached under the strain of her belongings. It felt heavier with every step, but she knew she'd miss her bundle sorely at nightfall if she was so foolish as to drop it. Mouse sighed, focusing on the ground.

"We've been walking forever." Toma re-shouldered his heavy pack as he broke the silence. "Where *are* we?"

Mouse shielded her eyes against the red glare of high noon as she looked behind them. The mountain peaks reared up in the west, black against the dull haze of the clouded sky. Now they seemed impossibly tall, and it was hard to believe she and the others had come down from one of them some hours before. That might have lifted her spirits, but as Mouse looked to the east, they fell again. In the vale they had entered, the mountain range that started along the southern ridge of Elmnas hemmed them in on the left and had no end in sight. To the north, the forest rose out of the valley on hills that stretched on and on and disappeared over the horizon.

"Not far enough," Mouse answered. "Or... we're not going the right way."

"We're going the right way, it's just taking longer than I thought," Fraeda sighed, and buried her face in the map. "It looks like we just need to keep walking until we see the break in the mountain range. That will be south, to our right, here."

Fraeda paused and pointed to the map. Mouse, Rhavin, and Toma crowded around to peer down at the crinkled parchment.

"If I'm right, we're well north of the Jagged Jaw mountains and now walking alongside what people call the Saddle. It's a pretty small range, and we should come to the end of it here. From that point, we can orient ourselves by the Kr'Gorian range. It should point us northeast all the way to Titans' Rest." Fraeda continued, "Looks like a lot of forest and hills, if this map is any good. It will probably be tough going. But see the symbols here? That's for Mistwolf territory, which we get into if we continue on in the valley. Now, the only other way would be to turn north as soon as we can and get to the road. But that means outposts and settlements."

"In other words, Coalition," Mouse said grimly.

Fraeda nodded. "The closer we get to free Elmnas, the more of them we ought to expect."

"They will have a blockade," Rhavin said sagely. "No one in, no one out. That is no good."

"But listen, how far are we from that gap now?" Toma asked. "This valley... I get a bad feeling about it. I definitely don't want to be caught out in the open here when the light starts to go."

"If we keep up the pace, we should be able to get to the gap before nightfall. We might be able to even get up the Saddle a little way, and that would offer better shelter than the forest that comes down and narrows the valley," Fraeda suggested.

"Yeah, but what's stopping the Mistwolves from leaving their territory and sniffing us out after dark?" Toma asked.

"I've lived here in Elmnas all my life, and in the Priory, we were right against the Wolf Barrens," Fraeda said. "Mistwolves stay in the mists. And thankfully so. I wouldn't have ever made it to the Ameliorites otherwise."

"That might be changing," Toma said, catching Mouse's eye. "I'm not so sure that we can count on that anymore. I think we should head to the road. We'll be safer there."

Rhavin waved his hand dismissively. "Animals are one thing. People are another. A beast acts on instinct. One can predict instinct. But people are fickle, cruel, relentless. The Coalition most of all. Or do you forget our last adventures already? Those men took on a legendary monster to get to us, and I did not get the sense they cared for taking prisoners. A strategist knows to avoid his enemy, not venture right into their grasp because he is afraid of the dark."

"Not afraid of the dark, huh?" Toma's jaw tightened as he stared daggers at Rhavin. "Well, you should be. The wild doesn't care if you're a brilliant *strategist* or prince or whatever you want to call yourself. I've seen enough carcasses after the Mistwolves are through with it to know what's waiting for us in the dark. Not even your fancy knife-throwing would stand a chance against them."

Rhavin pushed forward, eyes flashing as he drew himself up taller than Toma. He jabbed a finger out toward Toma's chest as the two locked angry gazes. "I have seen more of the wild and the world than you could ever dream, farmhand. I can survive a night out of doors. I do not underestimate my enemies. What about you, hm? The Coats are ruthless and resourceful, and the closer we are to them, the easier you make their work. In fact, I am rather surprised we haven't been picked up by a scout craft yet, given how often they seem to find you two as it is."

"That's rich, coming from a guy who hasn't had much luck escaping anything until we showed up," Toma spat.

Both boys began shouting at once. Mouse hopped back as they raised fists to shove each other, but Fraeda stepped between them, her hands lifted to separate the two even more.

"Whooooah okay, how about this?" Fraeda said. "Both routes have their risks, right? We just have to make the best decision we can. Why not put it to a vote?"

Mouse rolled her eyes as the boys glowered at each other. Rhavin crossed his arms and broke the tense silence.

"I am reasonable." He puffed out his chest. "I vote we press through the valley. We shall have higher ground and no Coalition outposts. Both suit me well."

"Fine," Toma scowled. "I vote we go to the road. We can always hide in the woods alongside it to avoid patrols. The Mistwolves won't be a problem where the Coats could be. We'll work our way to Titans' Rest under the cover of trees. People don't hunt with their noses, after all. We're sitting ducks down here."

"Now," Rhavin said coolly, turning to the girls. "What are the thoughts of our fairer counterparts?"

Fraeda looked thoughtfully from Rhavin and Toma, to the map, and finally to the two directions they could take. "I think... we ought to press on. I'm not sure we'd even get quite close to the road before dusk, and then we'd have to worry about Mistwolves *and* Coalition patrols." Fraeda grimaced sheepishly at Toma. "Sorry."

Toma shrugged, also crossing his arms. All eyes turned to Mouse.

"I don't know," she said helplessly. "I'd rather not vote at all."

"You're the reason we're here," Fraeda said, her tone apologetic. "We need to know what you think."

Both Toma and Rhavin nodded their assent.

"Okay," Mouse sighed. "Fraeda, do you really think we can make the gap before it gets dark?"

"I think it's our best chance," she replied.

Mouse pursed her lips as she looked at her friends. Fraeda smiled her encouragement, and Toma watched her expectantly as Rhavin gazed out over the vale with a brooding expression.

He thinks I'll side with him, Mouse thought as she avoided Toma's gaze. *Maybe I should.*

The memory of the Mistwolves padding toward her out of the mist, saliva and blood frothing from their open jaws, sent shivers down her spine. She never wanted to experience that desperate terror again.

And yet, she realized, *I already have.*

As Mouse recalled every close encounter with the Coalition in their journey so far, the same intense fear returned. Rhavin had a good point. Their deaths would be quick between the teeth and claws of the Mistwolves; Mouse had no assurance of that with the Coalition. They knew she carried vital information north, information that could turn the tide of the coming war. And worst of all, after their latest escape, the Coalition knew she was close.

They're out looking for me right now, she realized with prickling horror. *And after we were responsible for those Coats' deaths last night, what will they do when they find us?*

"I don't like it at all," Mouse said slowly. "But I think Rhavin is right. We need to stay as far from the Coats as possible. Let's just get to the gap before night, and maybe we'll have a fighting chance."

Toma made no reply, his face as impassive as stone. He turned on his heel and marched on in the vale, his pace quickly distancing him from the group.

"Thank you." Rhavin dipped his head. "I knew you would understand and make the wisest choice."

Mouse scoffed. "You say that like the matter's settled. You better hope Toma is wrong. If he's right, we won't make it through the afternoon, let alone the night."

Not waiting for Rhavin's reaction, Mouse stomped off alone. She heard Fraeda sigh behind her.

"Before we make any more decisions, we ought to eat first," she murmured. "Everyone's nicer after lunch."

36

The afternoon wore on, and the four travelers walked. Gradually but surely, they had left the low, flat valley and trekked into difficult hill country. The ground rose and fell before them, blocking their view of what lay ahead. Mouse found each step laborious, but she could only imagine how Fraeda felt. Work at the Priory, though intensive at times, could not have prepared her for the journey. Rhavin managed, and Toma and Mouse pressed on as they had when with Blade.

If only he were with us now, Mouse thought, but she pushed the regret and grief away. Feeling sorry for him and herself wouldn't help anyone now, especially not Fraeda.

Mouse looped her arm through Fraeda's as they came to the next slope. By now, their pace had slowed considerably, even with Toma and Rhavin splitting the weight of Fraeda's belongings between them. Mouse's own weariness began to set in, and she watched her feet as they carefully navigated the incline.

How much longer can we go on like this? she worried, casting a suspicious glance at the tree line on her right.

The forest, which had been creeping steadily toward them, had narrowed the channel they took beside the Saddle. Amid the trunks of the trees it was already dark, and Mouse thought she had seen the flash of eyes or a flurry of movement among them. A hazy mist also began to slither along the forest floor and snake out toward them. Whether it was the sort that brought trouble or not, Mouse could not know yet, but she surely did not want to stick around to find out.

Finally, and with effort, they crested the hill, and all grumbled as they reached the top.

"Wait," Fraeda said, red-faced and breathing hard. She paused to scan the map before pointing. "There."

Mouse peered into the distance. A craggy gray line cut across the horizon before sloping down to the earth. There was a gap, as the map promised, and a hill thick and dark with dense conifers undulated away from it and into the north. Mouse looked up to the sky, jamming her hands in her pockets as daylight began to fade behind the gray line of the far-off mountains.

"That's too far." Mouse shook her head. "We're not going to make it before the light's gone."

Toma hung his head and groaned. Mouse shot him an angry glare, a chiding remark on her tongue. She bit it back, thinking better of it. *It's my fault, after all*, Mouse thought, kicking at the grass.

"Well, we can't stay here," Toma sighed. "Let's go on."

Toma looked dolefully toward the others but froze as his gaze landed on Rhavin. Mouse turned to Rhavin, his intense, fixed expression freezing her as well.

"Get down into the ditch," Rhavin whispered, tugging on Fraeda's sleeve as he slid down into the next dip.

Without a word, the other three did the same. They huddled together, looking around and at each other with trepidation. Rhavin held a finger to his lips. He crept forward, cautiously working his way up the next small hill. Flattening himself against the hillside, Rhavin beckoned to them. Heart racing, Mouse climbed up next and peeked over the ridge.

She saw nothing much at first. The hills began to smooth out ahead, opening a far more leisurely path toward their destination. Trees breaking from the thick tree line spilled into the open country, and something like a ditch zigzagged among them. The low, thin mist coming from the forest settled in the deepest parts of the gully and swirled lazily in the infrequent breeze. Then she spotted it. A sliver of black metal projected from out of the gully.

"Is that what I think it is?" Mouse asked, squinting.

"Hovercraft," Toma said.

Rhavin nodded. "I knew I saw something that did not belong out here."

"What do you think happened?" Fraeda wondered.

The craft was nose down in the ditch, its stern tilted at an upward angle. Muddy furrows in the earth behind it told of a rough landing, and the churned chunks of grass indicated it had not happened long before. Even so, the craft showed no signs of life. The discs on the craft's underside had been powered down, and the engine did not even steam.

"Hard to say," Mouse said. "But I think it's abandoned. I want to take a closer look."

"Is that a good idea?" Rhavin asked. "What if they come back?"

"No one's coming back," Toma said softly as he pointed. "Not Coats, anyway."

Mouse looked. Something slumped against a tree, and beyond the craft, several more objects dotted the field ahead. She did not have to linger on them to recognize the red and black of Coalition apparel, torn and blood-stained as it was, hanging off white spokes of broken bone.

Fraeda covered her eyes, her lips moving wordlessly, as Mouse gulped.

"This does not bode well," Rhavin said in a low voice as he scanned the rest of the area. "And I am loathe to say it... but was that fog there before?"

Mouse and Toma gazed out past the downed hovercraft to where Rhavin was staring. Far off and out of the east, a wall of white mist poured toward them. Mouse's pulse quickened. She wheeled sharply, searching for somewhere to flee. But in the valley behind them, another curtain of white rolled like waves out of the trees and over the ground. Already it was cutting off the too far route to the mountains in the south. Even if the four could get there, Mouse saw now it would be too steep to climb.

"Come on, to the hovercraft," Mouse said, tapping on Fraeda's arm. "It's the only shot we have."

Without waiting for a response, she vaulted the small hill and maneuvered down it at a run. She heard the others pounding close behind, reaching her as she skidded to a halt in front of the craft. Mouse jumped down into the ditch beside it, one hand on its smooth, metallic side.

"What do you want me to do?" Rhavin asked, standing above her.

"Door should be over there." Mouse indicated the starboard side of the vessel. "See if you can get in."

"I'll help," Toma said. "If it's locked or busted, we're going to have to force it."

Rhavin nodded, and Mouse walked slowly around the craft. Fraeda jumped down beside her as Mouse examined the hull more closely.

"What are you doing?" Fraeda asked.

"Checking for structural damage." Mouse rapped lightly on the hull. "It took a beating when it went down, but these light transports were built to do that. This one actually looks fine. I wonder why it went down in the first place. Must have been... a malfunction, or something."

Mouse bent down and scrutinized the underside, mumbling to herself. She traced her fingers over the claw marks along the dented bottom, revealing silver scars in the peeled paint. *When did that happen?* she wondered with a shudder.

"So you've seen these kinds before," Fraeda said.

"Not as often as the heavy transports, but the lighter crafts did touch down on Misty Summit occasionally," Mouse explained. "The heavys brought parts and raw material to the Summit, but these ones brought people."

"More prisoners?" Fraeda asked softly.

Mouse nodded thoughtfully as she continued her examination. "Probably, but we never saw them brought in. If people walked off, it was usually Enforcement Squad. One brought a Party Rep right before I escaped."

"They didn't bring us in on hovercrafts where I ended up," Fraeda said. "No need for that, and there were too many of us, anyway. They chained us together in the cargo hold of a rolling transport for days. No food, very little water. Some of us didn't even make it to the prison."

Mouse stopped and straightened, peering back at Fraeda. She stared at the ground, her eyes distant and wet. Fraeda lifted her gaze to meet Mouse's as she took a deep, shuddering breath.

"Is it better to not remember?" Fraeda asked.

Mouse was quiet for a long time.

"No," she finally said. "Not if it meant never remembering any of the good that came before."

Fraeda sniffled and managed a weak smile. "It *is* something to hold on to. Even if it hurts."

Mouse nodded stiffly and went back to examining the transport. She hopped back as it lurched and groaned, and from the port side she heard a few heated words.

"Hey guys?" she said, peering around the front. "Any luck over here?"

Rhavin had stepped back, his arms crossed over his chest as he stared sulkily at the vehicle. Toma had his fingers jammed in the seams of the door and one foot against the side. He grunted in frustration and exertion as his face turned a strange shade of red. With one last effort, he let go, but not before an unnecessary kick to the craft's side.

"Apparently not," Mouse sighed. "Guess the release didn't work, huh?"

Toma threw his hands up in exasperation. "What release? There isn't a single entry point on this door."

Mouse stifled a smirk as she and Fraeda joined the boys. After feeling around the door, Mouse put her hand in a small depression at the bottom. Something inside disengaged, and with a hiss, the door unsealed.

"Sure, make it look easy," Toma mumbled as he lifted it open.

Mouse chuckled. "Let's check it out."

"Maybe just one of us should go in," Toma said, peering inside. "Make sure it's really safe."

Rhavin pushed between them, knives flashing. "With pleasure."

"Be my guest," Toma shrugged, rolling his eyes.

"And be quick, if you can!" Fraeda said after him as she looked around nervously. "It's getting misty out here."

Rhavin stole inside. The others waited in silence, but Mouse scrambled out of the ditch again and scanned the wilderness. Fraeda was right. All around, the mist rolled closer. She could no longer see the gap ahead or beyond the hills behind them. Mouse shivered and slid back into the ditch just as Rhavin poked his head out.

"All is well," he said. "And the emergency lights work."

Toma hopped up, lending a hand to Fraeda as she climbed in next. Despite the desperation of their current circumstances, elation bubbled inside Mouse. She clambered into the craft, staring in awe at the flickering red interior and taking in the luxurious details. To her surprise, the main cabin was rather homey. Plush seating ran along the far side, beneath and above a number of finely crafted cabinets. A kitchenette occupied part of the stern, and through a narrow, sliding door beyond that, Mouse saw a latrine and a private bedroom. In the space fore of the central cabin, a pull-out table and a dark holograstone remained fixed in place despite the angle of the craft. A partition separated the cockpit from the rest of the interior. Mouse's eyes widened at the console full of dials and switches. The tinted window offered a full view of the muddy earth where the bow crash-landed. Even so, other than one crystal glass shattered across the floor, nothing else had shifted. Toma let out a low whistle.

"I am no expert, but this does not look like a simple troop transport to me," Rhavin said, tossing his pack to the floor. "Far too clean and comfortable."

"You're probably right, but no time to think about that now," Mouse said. "You've been in one of these before, Rhavin? Have any idea how to operate the controls?"

Rhavin shrugged. "My father had a speeder, which he insisted on piloting. I used to go with him."

"Congratulations, you're now the captain." Toma clapped a hand on Rhavin's shoulder. "Let's get this thing out of the dirt and far from here."

With another noncommittal shrug, Rhavin slid into the captain's chair and rested his fingers on the controls. Everyone crowded behind him as he surveyed the console. Tentatively, he pushed a large, red button. Nothing happened. Rhavin sighed.

"I do not know what I am doing."

"No, I think that's right." Mouse squeezed in beside and searched the console. "That's definitely the ignition, but it's not firing. Something's wrong."

Deep in thought, Mouse rested her chin on her palm.

"I bet the problem isn't up here," she said with a snap of her fingers. "I'll have to check it out. Toma, there should be a manual under the console somewhere. Help Rhavin figure the controls out."

"Wait, where are you going?" Toma asked as she pushed out of the cockpit.

"Gotta lift the hood," Mouse replied with a grin. "I'm going outside."

"Then I should come with you!" Toma exclaimed. "That mist is closing in fast. You're not safe."

"None of us are until this thing flies," Mouse said. "I need someone inside who I can shout up to. If Rhavin is operating, it has to be you relaying what's going on."

Toma looked at Fraeda, who nodded in agreement. "She's right, I'd be useless there. But I can help her outside. That fog makes us all deaf and blind, but if anything's coming, I'll be the first to feel it."

"You said something like that before, back at the circus." Mouse tapped her finger against her lips. "Can you really sense movement? *Even* from the Mistwolves?"

"By their vibrations, yes." Fraeda smiled and tugged her ear. "Not so magical as your gift, Mouse, but you learn a few tricks when you're one sense down."

Rhavin nodded in appreciation. "It sounds like magic to me."

"It's better than I could have hoped for," Mouse said. "Let's get out there."

Mouse dropped her things, but not before retrieving Red's pillowcase out of the bag. She jumped down from the open hatch, Fraeda following. The damp ground squished beneath her feet, and she walked cautiously toward the front of the craft, trying to ignore the other claw marks carved into its side. Mist slid into the bottom of the gully and swirled around her ankles, heralding the wall of it that was now only about a hundred yards away. Mouse swallowed. She removed a familiar creased square of paper from her pocket and carefully unfolded it.

"What's that?" Fraeda asked.

"Hovercraft schematics. I diagrammed them myself at the Summit." Mouse chuckled as she pored over the drawings. "You know, I used to dream about getting close enough to a hovercraft to look inside. Never in a million years did I think I'd get to pull one apart and put it back together again. It was the happiest thing I could imagine. Funny how it doesn't feel like that now."

Mouse pressed her hands against the craft's nose, prying open the panel that housed the engine. She smiled wanly. "Let's hope I made good observations. Hold this."

Mouse handed Fraeda the pillowcase and leaned in for a closer look. A mass of wires, cylinders, and other complicated contraptions filled the inside. Mouse sorted through the chaos, following the lines to their various connections. Most terminated at a central power core, which held a pulsing crystal. She frowned.

"Power source isn't damaged." Mouse tested the core, and it sparked as energy jolted through the adjoining wires. "Wires are hot. Toma! Did that do anything?"

"Not really," came a faint reply. "You better hurry!"

Mouse glanced over her shoulder. The mist crept toward her, now only feet away. *Think*, she thought. *What's the real problem here? What's out of place?*

Her eyes traveled along the conduits, catching on one connection in particular. It was a thin, gold wire, easily lost in the chaotic tangle of various connections. The wire rested loosely in the midst of it, and as Mouse pulled on the strand, it fell, unconnected to anything, into her hands.

"That's got to be it!" She slapped a hand across her knee. "Somehow this got knocked free, cutting main power. It should be attached... here."

Mouse wrangled with the wiring and frowned again, looking back at Fraeda. "The connector's missing. How could that have gotten loose?"

Fraeda shrugged. "These things shake a lot. It seems to me that stuff would fall out of place all the time. Maybe these Coats just missed their last tune-up."

"I don't think so... it's not designed that way. See? That's a crucial piece, and there's even residual adhesive here for where it should be." Mouse's eyes narrowed. "I don't think it was an accident."

Fraeda raised an eyebrow. "It's been tampered with?"

"That's my guess." Mouse groaned, placing her hands on her head. "Now what do I do?"

"I don't know," Fraeda said, her eyes widening. "But do it quick."

Mouse looked behind her just as the mist rolled over them. She shuddered and coughed; the sulfurous stench thick as the air clung to her. Silence fell. Mouse felt as if a bag had been wrapped around her head. She could barely see her hand in front of her face, let alone the engine.

"Fraeda?" Mouse groped toward her, finding Fraeda's clammy hand.

Her face swam out of the fog, eyes frozen wide with terror.

"I couldn't see you," Fraeda whispered, gripping Mouse's fingers tightly. "I couldn't find you."

"It's alright," Mouse said, squeezing back gently. "Just stay close, okay? Let's go find the door."

"N-not yet, we can't," Fraeda replied. She took a shaky breath, but her voice hardened with resolve. "The engine, you have to fix it."

"With what?" Mouse asked in exasperation.

Fraeda looked down at her other hand, which still held Red's belongings. It made a muffled clinking as she gave it a gentle shake. "Worth a try."

Mouse sighed but grabbed the pillowcase. Searching the contents, Mouse laughed as she caught a fastener and a metal nut between her thumb and her forefinger.

"Fraeda," Mouse grinned. "You're a genius."

"Hey, ladies?" Toma called nervously. He sounded miles away, but no echo of his voice followed in the deadening fog. "You okay out there?"

"We're alright," Mouse shouted. "I found the problem. Fixing it now!"

"Hurry!"

Mouse turned back to the panel, working the parts back into place as best as she could. It was deathly quiet, except for the sound of her heartbeat thumping in her throat. She jumped as Fraeda clapped a hand on her shoulder.

"Mouse," she barely breathed. "They're coming."

Mouse turned to the paling Fraeda, feeling her own blood draining from her face.

"Get inside," she urged. "I'll be done in a minute. Don't wait for me. Tell them to start the ignition as soon as they can."

"But–"

"No time! Go!"

Fraeda scurried into the fog. A clanging and soft, frantic voices floated and died in the air. The scent of sulfur grew stronger. Mouse's fingers trembled as she worked.

"Mouse!" Toma shouted. "Get in here!"

"Not yet!" She plunged her hand into Red's belongings for anything else that might help fasten the parts in place.

"I'm coming out!"

"Don't you dare!"

The pungent odor of rotting meat permeated everything. Mouse stifled a gag. Tears fell down her cheek as she threaded the delicate wire. She could hear them now. Growling.

"Now!" she cried out.

The engine sputtered. Like a flame, the crystal glowed to life. Whirring drowned out the growling. Mouse slapped the panel closed. She looked back just as two shapes loomed out of the mist. More shapes followed. Mouse sprinted.

Howls pierced the air. She screamed. Though it tore her fingers, she kept a hand on the craft as she ran. Even now it was rising, righting itself as it withdrew from the ditch. Mouse screamed again as the blast of an energy pistol seared past her shoulder. Only paces behind her, an unearthly voice yowled in pain. Another blast, and then another.

The hovercraft lurched, pulling away from her fingers. Mouse cried out, but strong hands grasped her arms. She jumped, and the ground fell away as gravity would have pulled her down. For a moment, she was dangling. Sudden, unbelievable pain shot through her leg and stole the breath from her lungs. She gasped. Screams, her own and others, rose above the craft's whirring. And she could still hear the feverish barks right behind. The craft lurched again, this time swinging up hard. Mouse bounced into the cabin, rolling over Toma and crashing into the sofa. Disoriented, she lifted her head to peer out the transport door. At first, she could not translate what she saw. Toma jumped back on his feet, shouting something, but her ears rang and nothing made sense. Anchored by the door, Fraeda squeezed the trigger of an aimed pistol. Blood and claw marks streaked the floor. A monstrous face full of teeth snapped into view. Huge, Mistwolf paws slammed against the floor, tilting the craft precariously. Another blast from Toma, and the creature fell back. Mouse banged her head as the transport rocked the other way. Dazed, she rubbed her forehead. The hand came away wet with blood.

"The door! Shut the door!" Fraeda yelled.

Toma stumbled forward, grabbing the hatch. He slammed it down, but not before something heavy hit the other side of transport and nearly knocked him right out the opening. Another bump against the sealed door staggered him in the opposite direction.

"Get us out of here Rhavin!"

"I am trying!" Rhavin shouted back. "There are trees! And monster dog-bears!"

Toma righted himself and bounded into the cockpit. "Up and out! That way!"

Mouse rolled to her stomach and tried to stand. She collapsed, her leg screaming with pain. Gingerly this time, she pushed up on her arms and the other leg. Another crash against the hull sent her sprawling yet again. She stayed down as the hovercraft rocketed forward.

"Don't get up yet!" Fraeda rushed over. "You're hurt. Let me help you."

With Fraeda's assistance, Mouse flipped into a sitting position. She looked down. Shreds of trousers hung around her right leg. Dark red droplets seeped up into the scraps of fabric, streaked down her calf, and pattered on the floor.

"Don't look," Fraeda instructed.

Mouse turned away as Fraeda lifted the fabric from the wound.

"Well," she sighed, pulling strips of cloth from her pack and wrapping it around Mouse's leg. "It's not as bad as it could be. I'll say that."

"That's not promising," Mouse hissed through gritted teeth.

Fraeda looked her in the eyes. "You're alive. If you had taken one moment more down there, you wouldn't be."

Mouse offered a thin smile, her voice shaking. "That's a happy coincidence. Or does it mean this 'seer' thing is working out for me?"

Fraeda gave her a look but allowed a little smirk. "I guess so."

Cheering from the cockpit garnered Mouse's attention. She craned her neck to see Rhavin and Toma high-fiving. Rhavin whooped again as Toma unstrapped himself from the co-pilot's chair and ran toward them.

"We made it!" Toma said breathlessly. "Did you know this thing can fly above the mist for a while if it has to? And wow, does it move! We'll be across Elmnas in no time" –Toma cupped his hands over his mouth and shouted theatrically– "thanks to our very own Captain Rhavin!"

Rhavin hooted in triumph.

Toma looked down at the girls, and the elation vanished.

"Mouse," he said softly, kneeling beside her. "You're hurt."

She nodded to Fraeda knowingly. "But alive."

"What can I do?" Toma asked.

"Let's get her onto the couch," Fraeda said. "And then see if you can find a medical kit somewhere."

Mouse balanced on one leg as her two friends lifted her to the couch. Fraeda pulled a blanket from her bag and gently arranged the wounded leg on top of it. With a squeeze of Mouse's shoulder, Toma disappeared into the transport's back room.

Fraeda searched the icebox next to the couch, retrieving a frozen pack of Coalition-issued military rations. "While he's looking, I'm going to help Rhavin navigate. In the meantime, you should relax. Put this on your head."

"Yeah, that seems like a good idea."

With a sigh, Mouse stretched out on the couch and closed her eyes. Her leg and head ached, but the cold package soothed at least some of the throbbing. She focused on the whirring of the hovercraft, allowing its smooth hum to fill her and displace the terror she had just endured. But just before Mouse drifted off to sleep, a thump and a piercing shriek jolted her awake. Mouse sat up and gasped.

"Um, didn't find the med-kit," Toma said. "But... I found something else."

He stood with his gun pressed into the back of a young woman in rumpled but fine red and black robes. She raised her hands in surrender, but not before pushing the straight, raven hair that flowed down her back out of her attractively featured face. Rhavin and Fraeda emerged from the cockpit, and the girl's defiant, nutbrown eyes swept over them.

"Even without the scars," Mouse breathed. "You look just like her."

37

Blade took a deep breath, keeping his eyes closed as the rest of his senses awakened. Moisture trickled down the wall against his back. Sewage, most likely, judging by the fetid smell. He lowered his roughly bound wrists to the ground between his knees and scraped his fingers against the slimy, moss-covered earth he found there. *It is just as well*, he thought. *I would as soon die here as anywhere else.*

He opened his eyes. Total darkness and a hangover-like headache greeted him, which he expected. It only took a moment for him to adjust, and the close, dirty walls of a subterranean prison cell resolved around him. Blade knew exactly where he was. Myergo, the slumlord of Lilien, had finally gotten what he wanted for years: the King of the Shadows in his vengeful clutches.

Not that I had made it easy, Blade smiled wanly to himself. Despite the bounty hunter's clean exchange, Myergo's hirelings almost failed to bring him to their master. He had awakened mid-transit, much sooner than any of the thugs had accounted for. Blade had waited quietly, almost with amusement, as he heard one of them say, "Fox could not have made it any easier if she had gift-wrapped 'em." But thugs were not professional hunters. Though Blade did not prevail against the eight armed mercenaries sent to recover him, they learned their lesson when he killed two with his hands alone. They took no chances after that, and sleeper's poison was his reward.

I've made a bad habit of being rendered unconscious, he thought wryly. *I'm certain young Toma would have something amusing to say about that.*

With a heavy sigh, Blade hung his head. The fears and questions that had plagued him these past few days hit him with renewed ferocity. Had Mouse and Toma survived Thunder Run? Where were they now? Who would find them first, the Coats or the bounty hunter? What horrors would the Coalition inflict upon them? Frequently, he had tried not to let his mind wander there, but he had been powerless in that regard. Blade knew what the Coalition did to its enemies. For all their strength and resolve, Mouse and Toma were but lambs headed to slaughter on their own. And now he could do nothing about it.

Blade shut his eyes and mind against the terrible possibilities. He focused instead on the journey that had brought them to him, and memories, good memories, replaced the darkest imagined outcomes. Again, he saw Mouse as he first encountered her at Pilgrim's Pass, terrified, clueless, and yet determined; as well as Toma's brave stupidity and tender concern for her, reminiscent of something he once felt long ago. He recalled their unrestrained, pure joy as they learned sword craft and found a way to embrace fun in the midst of a perilous adventure. Blade had forgotten that about young people: their resilience, their levity, their passion, their hope. And in their presence – especially Mouse's – Blade began to wonder if there could be hope after all.

She puzzled him. By all appearances, Mouse had no chance in Reidara of seeing her journey through. Certainly, she was resourceful, perceptive, and adaptable, but at the end of the day, Mouse was still just a teenaged girl, traumatized, oppressed, and hunted by a world power that had eyes, ears, and fingers everywhere.

What could one insignificant child do to the Supreme Chancellor and his regime? And yet at every crossroads, every life-or-death situation, every encounter with forces that ought to have swallowed her whole, Mouse simply... survived.

Could it be? He wondered. *Is she indeed the Harbinger?*

Blade raised his chin and stared into the black above him. He did not wish to dwell on a thought so full of hope and anticipation. Such a thought led only to despair. Hope would be crushed, anticipation disappointed, faith shattered. It was for such a thought as this that Blade abandoned the Way and wandered Reidara in raging sorrow. If the oracles held true, if the Unseen truly had power to mend Elmnas, to preserve her people and overthrow its enemies, why had He left them to perish? Why had He deserted them? Why had He betrayed *him?*

For one hundred years, Blade stalked the wilds with no answer to those questions. There was no answer, he decided, because everything he believed in was a lie. In the end, profane enemies slaughtered his beloved, his very heart, along with so many others he was sworn to protect. He lived on, compliments of sheer luck and his own cowardice. And for one hundred years, he lived on only to atone for innocent Elmling blood and his own failures, for as long as his cursed longevity allowed or until the day he finally fell to his enemies.

And now that day of reckoning has come.

Today brought the culmination of his chosen path. Blade had accepted that without fear or self-pity. Even so, the bizarre coincidence of his first encounter with Mouse and everything that followed left him doubting the surety of what was to come. Who was he – Blade, the Ageless vigilante, or Falkir Eneshkin, Guardian Warrior of Elmnas? For the first time in decades, he didn't know. Mouse, her visions, and the urgent news she carried to the Elmling remnant had changed all that. But how could he dare to hope? And how could he dare not?

Blade released a long sigh. He still didn't know what to think. But perhaps that no longer mattered. Perhaps he did not matter after all. But Mouse did. He closed his eyes and whispered.

"If you see, if you know... keep them safe. Fly with them."

He took a deep breath.

"Now," he murmured. "Do I wait for death or do I greet it with vigor?"

Blade felt along the walls and the ground, considering his options. As far as he could tell, the prison was bare as bone. Nothing would help him here. He sighed, longing to hold his twin swords once more. *What am I,* he wondered, *without* Av'tal *and* Ub'rytal? Emptiness as keen as the loss of a lover ached within him. *Av'tal* and *Ub'rytal*. Bound and Unbroken. Ever since their forging at Oranaheim, the Guardian sanctuary that had replaced Edenii, he and his ancient blades had never been parted. Only two others had been present at the forging ceremony: the forge master and Theana. Losing his swords felt like losing her all over again. In a way, it was worse. He had more time with *Av'tal* and *Ub'rytal* than he ever did with Theana. They had become an extension of his very soul. Perhaps he was just imagining it, but without them, he thought he sensed his strength slowly bleeding away.

It is just as well. At least I have one last recourse.

With another sigh, Blade stretched forward and reached into his boot. He pulled out the device lodged there. An explosive, compliments of Arctura Fox, the ruthless Coalition bounty hunter.

How am I to make sense of this? He mused, rolling the device over in his hands.

If anything were more puzzling than the conundrum he faced with Mouse, it was this. Why would the bounty hunter *help* him? Surely, she knew that if he ever escaped, it would be his sworn duty to seek and destroy her. He could not stomach her kind, let alone those who would hunt down children at the bidding of the loathsome Coalition. And in the few short days he spent as her hostage, Arctura Fox had proven merciless, vicious, and hateful. And yet... she handed him this opportunity, this olive branch. What did it mean? What had changed?

And he had no clue what to do with her passing comment about Hiraeth before she electrocuted him. Hiraeth was a legend of Elmnas, and if he had ever existed, a true ancient as well. He had been there, at the Scourge of the Scattering, long before the Eneshkin conquered Elmnas and brought about the Golden Age. Then he had also been known as Melek Tzedek; a Guardian of sorts, but perhaps something more, for only he was known to carry all three Guardian gifts of Master, Keeper, Warrior. Blade recalled how the Trivium used to hold debates about the references to Melek Tzedek or Hiraeth in the sacred writings and what it could possibly mean. Of course, he saw it all as little more than an intellectual exercise. All history between the Scourge and the founding of Elmnas had been lost.

Perhaps the bounty hunter had some familiarity with the sacred writings, he considered. *She fabricated it, to throw me and entertain herself.*

But how could Blade explain her mastery of the Way of the Twin Blades? And what loyal Guardian of Elmnas in their right mind would train someone so unworthy of it?

But he had no more time to dwell on it now. Out of the darkness beyond his prison, faint torchlight bobbed toward him. Blade tucked the explosive back into his boot and retreated into the shadows behind the cell door. Presently, the torch blazed right in front of the bars, and the oafish face and wide, deranged eyes of its bearer now appeared beside it. Light reached into the shallow cell, exposing Blade and allowing no opportunity for a surprise assault. The thug flashed a sadistic grin.

"That's right, no shadows for the King O' Shadows to hide in. Nowhere for you to go now. They says you a beast hunter now, eh? How you kill 'em without your shiny swords?"

Blade did not answer. The goon laughed.

"Time to find out," he continued with sinister glee. He unlocked the door, but not before waving his energy pistol. "No funny business now, eh? I'd just as soon be doing my duty shooting you than taking you to 'im."

Again, Blade said nothing, but he raised his bound hands to show he understood and believed him. The thug waved him out and jammed the pistol against his back.

"Alright, Sir King, move."

Blade walked along the low, twisting passage, weighing the risk of attacking his captor against its potential benefit. But Myergo's man, for as dimwitted as he appeared, had enough comprehension to handle a warrior like Blade. The weapon remained firmly in place. One threatening move, and Blade would have his torso blown to pieces.

Light flooded the passage as it turned once again. Blade squinted into what looked like a staging area. More of Myergo's mercenaries hustled about, moving crates and attending to cages. Cages, he noticed, filled with all manner of half-starved, yowling creatures. Bears, lions, wolves, boars, and more watched him pass through with wild, hungry eyes. The thug pushed Blade.

"Oi! No dawdlin'!"

They passed on through another winding tunnel of Myergo's subterranean labyrinth. Blade, who could find his way almost anywhere, found himself rather disoriented here. Many unfortunates had perished in Myergo's tunnels, and Blade had known some of the lost ones from his days with the Jackal Syndicate. Anger boiled inside him. Myergo only dreamed up torturous deaths for those who crossed him, and Blade could only imagine the cruelties they endured. Undoubtedly, Myergo had such a death reserved for him, but Blade would ensure he spoiled any enjoyment Myergo tried to squeeze from it.

The tunnel terminated at a heavy door, which muffled an indistinct but uproarious sound. Myergo's man pushed it open, and the clamor of an enthusiastic crowd filled his ears. Blade had to shield his eyes as the man roughly pushed him through it, and he stumbled into a wide, bright arena. The roar of the stadium stilled as the door slammed shut behind him. In the sudden hush, Blade blinked and gazed out into the sea of spectators.

"Welcome," a raspy voice echoed. "Welcome, my honored guest."

Blade peered toward the direction of the sound, which came from a raised dais at the end of the arena. Upon it, Myergo sat enthroned, lounging in a massive chair decorated with the horns, claws, and skulls of exotic trophies. Blade almost laughed at the sizeable Cardanthium crystal entwined in the circlet adorning Myergo's bald crown. Myergo folded his large hands in front of him and sneered, exposing sharpened teeth.

"It has been quite some time... yes?"

Blade betrayed no emotion as he answered. "Not long enough."

At this, Myergo laughed, and the crowd joined him. The lord of Lilien's underground silenced them with a curt wave of his hand and stood.

"Friends, this is the moment you have all been waiting for. Before you stands the one responsible for the deaths of your comrades, the loss of your profits, and the frustrations of your various enterprises. I present to you the highly sought-after Guardian, the silent swordsman, the so-called 'King of the Shadows.'"

The stadium erupted in boos and jeers. Myergo grinned as he gestured again for quiet.

"They say he hunts monsters now, and he seems to be quite good at it. But I, for one, am not so easily convinced." Myergo looked down at Blade, his dark eyes glistening with wicked intent. "What do you say, friend? Why not give us a little demonstration of your skill?"

At this, the crowd thundered their raucous approval. Blade glanced covertly around the arena, all too aware of the torn bodies that had been lying there when he entered. He looked down at his wrists, still bound, before eyeing the remains closest to him. A blood-spattered blade poked through the victim's back. Blade angled himself toward it.

Myergo held up his hands until the arena became deathly still. "Let the lights be dimmed. Hold your applause until the utter end."

The brightness faded away, leaving only the blue, bioluminescent glow of the fungi that grew deep beneath the ground. The floor of the arena pulsed with pale light, just enough for the spectators to see what was going on below. No one breathed a word. A gate on the far end clanked open. Something darted out.

Blade sprinted toward the body and rubbed the taut rope on his wrists along the rusted blade edge. Already he could smell the rancid musk of the Mistwolf. He could hear the rumbling growl in its chest and the thud of its huge paws. Blade worked his arms faster, cutting through the first strands of rope.

A hungry howl resounded. With a grunt, Blade pulled his arms apart, snapping the remaining strands. An instant later, he rolled to the side; only a breath between him and the enormous shape lunging past. Blade found his feet and turned. A grotesque, shaggy form shook dirt off itself and faced him.

The Mistwolf, though still formidable, took ginger steps toward him. A milky, unfocused look in its eye gave Blade the impression the creature had suffered sight loss in Myergo's care, among other things. Even in the dim light, Blade could see festering sores within missing patches of fur, the stark outline of each rib, and a crazed, ravenous foam dripping from its jaws. Captivity had weakened the creature, but it had also made it desperate. To Blade, that seemed far worse. He retrieved the explosive from his boot and set a finger on the detonator.

With an erratic swing of its head, the Mistwolf oriented itself. Its snubbed snout wrinkled, sorting Blade's unique scent from that of the watching crowd and the scattered dead. The cloudy, cold eyes landed on him. With a guttural snarl, it drew back its lips from rows of fangs, opened its mouth wide, and charged.

In one fluid motion, Blade detonated the device and tossed it into the open gullet. He rolled, but not quick enough. The shoulder of the beast drove into him, sending him flying. Blade's world darkened as he hit the dirt, his breath torn from his body. Excruciating pain ripped through his chest, and Blade was sure he had broken another rib. He willed himself to remain conscious. Black spots filled his vision as he searched for the Mistwolf. It had continued on after their collision, disoriented as it stumbled to the ground past him. The creature turned, eager for another onslaught. Blade stared it in the eyes one last time as it made ready to pounce.

The Mistwolf crouched. It howled in triumph. Then its throat exploded.

Blade lifted an arm against the shower of fur, blood, and gristle. A heavy hush fell over the arena as he forced himself to his feet, and, while holding his ribs, kicked at the carcass. Nothing more came from the beast but a spreading pool of red. Blade looked up at the dais, meeting Myergo's cold gaze with his own hawkish eyes.

"You are full of surprises, yes?" Myergo said with unnerving calm. "Surprise me again. I am certain you will not."

Myergo turned to address the crowd. "An admirable performance deserves a rousing encore, does it not? Let us release my other pets!"

Blade bowed his head as the crowd roared its approval. *It is just as well.*

But the roar changed. Confusion, and then panic, took hold of the voices. Blade snapped his gaze up to the stands and marveled at what he saw. Flashes of energy blasts arced over the arena. Some spectators picked up arms to fight, but a flood of dark clad figures overwhelmed them. Most of the crowd fled, ducking into the tunnel exit leading to Myergo's main cavern territory. But more than enough of Myergo's forces remained, and Myergo bellowed in fury as he picked up his own weapons and jumped off the dais.

"Cowards! It is only the Jackal Syndicate! Kill the fools where they stand!"

With the clang of swords and axes and the heat of rifle blasts, battle broke out everywhere. Blade hustled into the thick of it as it spilled out onto the arena floor. He kicked a thug in the back as he raised a blade against a young Syndicate member, ramming the brute into the thief's sword.

"Woldyff, there he is!" The man shouted. "Saved me life!"

A figure sprinted toward Blade, bowling over two mercenaries on his way. Blade smiled, despite himself, at the dramatic approach of his friend. They clasped hands briefly before Woldyff shot off a few warning blasts at any would-be attackers. He pushed Blade behind their lines.

Woldyff grinned. "Time to go, don't you think?"

"You have terrible timing," Blade said.

Woldyff emptied his clip and re-holstered his pistol, pulling another off his belt. "I've been worse."

"How did you find me?"

"Heh, um, about that." Woldyff pointed ahead, where the fighting had grown especially thick.

Blade's eyes widened as he saw, in the midst of them, the elegant, perfectly timed arcs of two glowing blades. The wielder struck her foes to the ground and met his gaze. With ruthless calm, Arctura Fox deflected a stray energy blast before striding toward him. Blade stood speechless, seeing she held his own *Av'tal* and *Ub'rytal* in her hands. Her blades remained crossed on her back.

"These are quite decent," she said, tossing his swords to him. "But they do not suit me."

Blade caught them, his energy and battle hunger returning as their weight became his once again. He slung them with elation, although no one watching would have been able to distinguish joy in his sober features. His eyes met Fox's once more.

"I do not understand."

Fox sighed as she unsheathed her swords. "Neither do I, and yet, here I am. We must move quickly. Word will spread and more will come. This ragged band of thieves is no match for Myergo's complete forces. If we fight our way out, we may yet get to the secret tunnels that brought us to this hell-hole in the first place."

Blade nodded, but his eyes hardened.

"You cannot expect me to trust you."

"I do not." Fox gave him an amused smirk. "But do you trust the old Way, Falkir Eneshkin?"

Without waiting for an answer, Fox pirouetted back into the fray, laughing. Blade and Woldyff watched. For a moment, Woldyff was at a loss for words.

"I like your scary lady, Blade," Woldyff finally said with appreciation. "Can I keep her?"

Blade allowed a sly smile. "My friend, if you value your life and limbs, you would do well not to suggest she could be kept."

"Alright," Woldyff sniffed, readjusting his holster. "Falkir? Is that really your name?"

Epilogue

Doctor Endiatus walked briskly through the ward, ignoring the sweat dripping down his neck and the agape glances of the scientists and staff he passed. The terrified stares were not for him; not this time, anyway, though he had gained quite a reputation for himself here at the Coalition's most secret research facility. This time, his colleagues looked past him, bowing, cowering, or something in between before the two figures who followed behind. Doctor Endiatus kept moving, clutching hard at the electronic tablet tucked beneath his arm. He took a deep breath as their destination came into view: a steel-fortified door at the end of the hall that only a handful of researchers had the clearances necessary to enter. The renowned doctor was one of them. He paused in front of the door, its high-tech lock blinking red. With trembling fingers, he reached into his pocket and lifted his badge to the scanner.

It blinked green and clicked, unsealing the door with a hiss and whoosh. Doctor Endiatus stepped inside, triggering its gratingly bright overhead lighting. On any other day, the doctor would have groaned and shielded his weak eyes as the lights whirred to life, but today he squinted into them and smoothed his white coat. He stifled a nervous cough as he felt hard glares boring through his back.

"Right this way," Doctor Endiatus said, daring only to look at the floor as he invited his guests inside.

They entered behind him, and without a word the figures swept to observation chairs placed conveniently on the far side of the room.

I'll have to thank Dyanat for that, Doctor Endiatus thought. *Though it serves him just as well. One more mistake and he'll be sent down to treat prisoners again.*

Doctor Endiatus shivered. He had hated his own time at Misty Summit. Sulfur. Everything smelled and tasted like it, even in the healing wards. The doctor thought he'd never enjoy eating again. But far worse than that was the grotesque, foul population of inmates he had been forced to deal with, though admittedly his interactions with the masses were limited. Even shaved and de-loused, the prisoners brought their contamination into the clean ward, and inevitably, it got on him. He felt like a pig herder, who, no matter how much he scrubbed and washed, would always carry the fecal stench of swine. When Doctor Endiatus finally got his break and left the Summit behind, he had to wonder if he still stank of them just the same.

But the sterility of this facility, and this room in particular, moored the doctor. No matter how messy the experiments became, Doctor Endiatus remained unscathed. He had orderlies now, a staff to take care of the business peripheral to his grand endeavors. No more did he have to mingle with the population or deal with their pitiful cries for mercy. The subjects that came to him these days were as docile and as witless as lambs. And to be frank, Doctor Endiatus never minded the blood or accompanying shrieks of pain, as long as his coat stayed clean.

He gazed toward the glass-encased chamber and its attached monitors that stood in the center of the otherwise empty room. He took a deep, cleansing breath, feeling his sense of purpose, his confidence, and his pride in his work thus far returning. The doctor assumed his usual demeanor as he became absorbed in what had been his daily tasks for the past few months. Pushing back his black spectacles to the bridge of his nose, Doctor Endiatus peered into the chamber. With a satisfied nod, he mumbled something unintelligible as he produced a stylus and scribbled away on the tablet screen. He pushed up the sleeves of his white coat, his excitement growing as he surveyed the data on the monitors.

"The subject is stable," Doctor Endiatus said. "Augmentations have been successful, and the healing process is nearly complete."

"You are certain, Doctor? I am growing weary of failure."

Doctor Endiatus swallowed as he turned to face the speaker. "Y-yes, Supreme Chancellor. We were able to ensure the best outcome based on the data we collected from the previous subjects. Even with your parameters, we were able to do some rather extraordinary things, things that have implications for many of the other subjects we've been–"

"I am not interested in the other subjects at the moment. That will come." Supreme Chancellor Vipsanius stood, clasping his hands behind his back as he approached the chamber. "The experiment appears successful, but appearances are not everything."

Doctor Endiatus looked sidelong at the Supreme Chancellor, both fascinated and terrified by the man beside him. He had never been this close to him before. Some of the other scientists here had, and the stories they told about Supreme Chancellor Vipsanius produced awe and fear among the staff. Doctor Endiatus never trusted second-hand information. He needed to experience it himself. Yet as he stood in the Supreme Chancellor's presence, forcing himself to remain composed before his impassive, calculating leader, he had all the data he needed to confirm their impressions.

"Your eyes do not deceive you, Sir. The de-aging process is both external and internal. We've brought the subject back to the prime of his physical prowess."

"Well done," the Supreme Chancellor acknowledged. "The technology has progressed considerably since my own House's augmentations."

The doctor looked curiously at the Supreme Chancellor. *Yes*, he wondered to himself. *And what sort of augmentations were those?*

He had a basic knowledge, obviously, since this was his field of study, but the details of the experiments that had halted the aging of Vipsanius House for nearly one hundred years were still classified far above his own clearances. The original scientists who had performed them had long since died, their secrets dying with them. But there were rumors. Strange rumors of the near-extinct Cardanthium and its bizarre properties that blurred the line between the scientific and the mystical. It brought to mind old myths, stories of the Ageless that still circulated among the common Gormlaeans. Doctor Endiatus did not believe that nonsense. He believed results. But whatever had happened at the dawning of the Glorious New Era, magical, innovative, or somewhere in between, the doctor's own work was building upon it. And he was producing the unbelievable because of it.

"Thank you, Sir. Much progress has been made," Doctor Endiatus said. He added shrewdly, "But of course, the effects of de-aging remain to be seen. We expect it will be quite temporary. The subject will begin to break down within two years, five years at most."

"That will be enough time for the purposes this prototype serves," the Supreme Chancellor replied, rubbing his chin. "Yes. What do you think, Ambassador? Do you find the subject satisfactory?"

Doctor Endiatus turned his attention to the other figure, who re-crossed her legs and arranged her elegant dress over them. The light fabric clung salaciously to her defined, slim figure, and the doctor adjusted his glasses as he pretended not to stare. She tilted her head in thought, her long, straight hair shimmering a glossy black. The Ambassador's beautiful, red lips curved in a knowing smirk.

"He will suffice," the Ambassador answered. "A year is the most we will need to give those northern curs a taste of what is to come. And if the subject breaks down, it is no matter. Just the sight of him will melt every heart in despair and terror. My main concern is that he will be controlled."

"Ah, of course." The doctor raised a timid finger. "I can speak to that, Ambassador."

He beckoned the Supreme Chancellor and the Ambassador to the monitors. They watched quietly over his shoulder as he tapped out several commands on the console. The doctor pointed to the data that came on the screen.

"Our earliest devices were effective but lacked nuance. See the results here of repeated testing. We had total control, yes, but subjects were rendered incapable of doing anything beyond basic functions. On top of that, each device requires its own guidance system, and for the scale you had envisioned..."

"Impractical," the Supreme Chancellor supplied. "It would fail utterly. But you must have a solution."

Doctor Endiatus stifled a shiver, the Supreme Chancellor's tone indicating the threat of dire consequences if he did not. "Y-yes, Sir."

The doctor produced a vial from his coat and swirled the viscous, red liquid within it. It glinted with flecks of luminous green beneath the harsh lighting. "I will not bore you with the mechanics and how we arrived here, although you are welcome to read the report I have prepared. But to keep it brief: the first devices could control thought processes, but they deadened impulse. Impulses are what keep humans alive; they make them eat, fight, breed. Emotions and instincts, you see, are what truly control the animal. They control even the thoughts. So, we began to wonder, what if we could control impulses? What if we could direct a creature's passions so that it acted as we orchestrated, all the while believing with every fiber of its being that it ought to do so? What you see in this tube is the result of those questions. The Praepotentia Serum. First iteration."

Supreme Chancellor Vipsanius reached out and took the vial, holding it up to the light. He narrowed his eyes, but the smallest hint of a smile quirked the corner of his mouth. "An injection."

"Once in the system, it behaves the same way a virus might;

multiplying, spreading, replacing certain cells, concentrating in key areas... and the like," Doctor Endiatus explained. "According to our initial tests on our prototype here, it is astoundingly effective. The greatest advantage is that all infected subjects can be controlled with one device, and that number of subjects can be virtually infinite. However, we are working on separate iterations and corresponding devices so that you may divide your forces as you see fit."

The Supreme Chancellor handed the vial back to Doctor Endiatus with great care. He faced the glass chamber and once more clasped his hands behind his back. "I am pleased, Doctor. You can expect this facility to be rewarded handsomely."

Doctor Endiatus opened his mouth to express his effusive thanks, but the Supreme Chancellor held up his hand. "But there is a condition. If the serum is not ready for mass production within six months, there will be consequences."

"Sir, I am not certain that–"

"I will not hear excuses," The Supreme Chancellor said curtly.

Doctor Endiatus shrank. "O-of course, Supreme Chancellor. It will be done."

"That was the right answer," he replied. "Go on and attend to your duties, Doctor. The Ambassador and I want to admire your handiwork."

Cautiously, Doctor Endiatus performed a Coalition salute and turned back to the console. He mopped his brow with the sleeve, eyeing his table with little comprehension. The Supreme Chancellor leaned close to the Ambassador, his voice low. Unable to curb his curiosity, Doctor Endiatus strained to listen.

"Our contact in Lilien gave me interesting news this morning," the Supreme Chancellor whispered. "It's come to my attention that our hired hand has finally defected."

The Ambassador scoffed. "It was only a matter of time. Arctura has had treason in her heart since the very beginning."

"There is more. The Guardian lives, and yet again, the girl has escaped. It falls to House Vipsanius to rectify these matters. I trust you will not fail, Tyranna."

She smiled cruelly. "I have not yet, Lucan."

"How many men for your proposed campaign?"

"A dozen shall do." The Ambassador stepped closer to the glass chamber, crossed her arms, and chuckled. "Easily done, especially with meat tank, here. What do you say, Grigus? Shall we pay a visit to your kinsmen?"

The hulking form suspended in fluid behind the glass breathed steadily through the respirator, green eyes wide and sightless as they stared past the figures before him. His shock of red hair swayed in the constant rolling bubbles. Despite himself, Doctor Endiatus shuddered.

About the Author

Kaylena Radcliff is a magazine editor, pastor's wife, mother, and indefatigable world builder. As such, she subsists almost entirely on coffee and prayer. A voracious reader and prolific writer from an early age, Kaylena was deeply influenced by the likes of C.S. Lewis, J.R.R. Tolkien, and Flannery O'Connor. She dabbles in many genres, but most loves writing and reading speculative and fantasy fiction. Aside from writing, Kaylena loves discussing history, theology, and all things nerdy. You might also find her unsuccessfully attempting to relive the glory days as a collegiate athlete on the community soccer eld. Despite extended trips abroad and the passport to prove it, she never did manage to escape her Pennsylvanian hometown. In true hobbit fashion, she happily resides there with her husband and two young children.

www.ingramcontent.com/pod-product-compliance
Lightning Source LLC
Chambersburg PA
CBHW070839260626
47170CB00007B/2429